What readers love about the Decrypter books

"**Takes you on a ride** and refuses to let you off until you reach the very end." *Marie*

"A brilliant read! I recommend this to anyone who enjoys mystery, suspense, thrillers, or action novels. The **detail is astounding**! The historic references, location descriptions, references to technology, cryptography....this author really knows her stuff." *Fran*

"An **action-packed adventure**, technothriller **across several continents** like a Jason Bourne or James Bond movie, but with an actual storyline!" *John*

"**Brilliantly written**. I loved the very descriptive side, which was a good way of visualizing and getting to terms with each new place, as the action takes place in several different countries." *Sean*

"The **description is so rich**, so immensely detailed that it just draws you in completely to its world." *Denise*

"There is **great tension and chemistry** between the two main characters, Calla and Nash, that has you begging for more." *Pam*

ALSO BY ROSE SANDY

The Calla Cress Technothriller Series

The Decrypter and the Mind Hacker

The Decrypter: Digital Eyes Only

The Decrypter: The Storm's Eye

The Decrypter and the Pythagoras Clause

The Shadow Files Thrillers

The Code Beneath Her Skin

Blood Diamond in My Mother's House

The Decrypter and the Pythagoras Clause

THE DECRYPTER AND THE PYTHAGORAS CLAUSE

A CALLA CRESS TECHNOTHRILLER

ROSE SANDY

Number is the ruler of forms and ideas, and the cause of gods and demons.

— **Pythagoras**

NOTE TO READERS

If you are new to the Decrypter Series...

Each book in the Decrypter series can be read as a standalone novel, but the series is best enjoyed in order. The novels are fast-paced, action-adventures, seeped in history, espionage and cyber defense in a world evermore digitally dependent. The books explore a world where technology and science are at the forefront of humanity.

If you are new to the series and want to get your head around the characters and action quickly, here is a little catch up:

The story so far...

Calla is an agent with the **ISTF**. An acronym that stands for the **International Security Task Force**, a 500-person strong intelligence body created and massively funded by the UK, US, France, Germany, and Russia. It came into existence before 2000 to help fight expected problems with Y2K—not in how it might influence business and commerce, but how it might be exploited by criminal organizations. The agency works covertly overseas and domestically gathering intelligence around sciences, technologies, and high-tech artifacts that threaten global security.

Abandoned as an infant, **Calla's** life's quest is to search for her parents.. When she finds them, she learns **Stan** and **Nicole,** her MI6 parents, left her to save her from those who would seek to exploit her unique abilities thanks to a heritage of genetic engineering. An attractive woman, aware of her looks but still quite unsure of them, **Calla** is a product of having been an orphan for as long as she can remember. Though she was raised in a good home by good people, the fear of abandonment persists.

Both at **ISTF,** and at a day job as a **British Museum** curator, **Calla** holds prestigious positions she's earned through her many talents, which include an unusual mixture of old and new, anthropology and hi-tech. Even more important for her success, though, is her amazing skill at breaking codes, earning her the nickname of the Decrypter.

Now head of **ISTF**, with the code name *Red Fox*, **Calla** has been cleaning up one tech and scientific criminality after another, especially havoc created by former **ISTF** head **Mason Laskfell**. **Calla** believes technology will develop at a rate so much faster than humans can cope.

Helping her on her escapades, both professional and personal, are two individuals. Formerly in the military, **Nash** is an NSA security advisor attached to the **ISTF** and is also quite attached to **Calla**. **Jack** is a remarkably successful tech entrepreneur who has a fondness for Calla and a love of the excitement that surrounds her in the discovery of rare artifacts, advanced technologies and sciences that appear around the globe. Superior to anything humanity has seen, these discoveries are mostly unknown to man, and are protected from exploitation by a group of tech keepers called the *'operatives'*.

Recently **Calla** and **Nash** married secretly and lost their unborn baby to a dangerous enemy. They have sworn to confiscate any **operative** technology or science that remains at large.

And so, our story begins...

PROLOGUE

Twenty-Eight Years Ago
UK Space Agency Research Center, Swindon
9:27 p.m.

She wouldn't tell Stan. Her instincts, gained over seven years living with the uncompromising MI6 agent, wouldn't permit her. Though married, albeit secretly, their missions at MI6 took separate tracks. Stan had no clue she was here. He would have stopped her from coming.

Soon after her Audi 8 penetrated the factory's inner core, concealed behind a corrugated metal building with large delivery bays, Nicole Cress knew it could be too late.

Her information had been accurate. Andor Heskin, researching with millions of pounds spent on intelligence and future development of Space sector technology, had also tried to understand a race of people the government had nicknamed *technological operatives* or just *operatives*.

She killed the engine and waited.

The whir and rumble of machinery continued as Nicole wound down the window and spied through night goggles for Heskin. His words had hit her like a charging van: "If you want me to produce a breakthrough that will isolate your child's DNA structure from data gathers, then I'll need a DNA sample."

Those had been Heskin's words for the price of two million pounds sterling.

Nicole slid a palm over her growing belly. So far, she wasn't showing. She padded her jeans' lining and secured the memory stick in her hand with her pregnancy data signature.

The child inside her moved ever so lightly at her caress. Why this? Why had she and Stan not seen this coming? But how does one deny themselves a child so precious and so wanted? It was almost too late. If they didn't protect their baby, who would most probably classify as *an operative*, they would have to hide the child all their lives from data gathers and the government.

Nicole checked the rearview mirror, observing the road. Heskin would be here soon. No one had followed her. She then checked her watch, assuring herself she was early, and pulled out a folder from the glove compartment. The risk was obvious from his file.

MOST SECRET

For reasons connected to this department, officers have been investigating a leak in the UKSA Swindon research department. The possibility the researcher Andor Heskin in charge of Space technology development may have another source of anonymous funding is paramount. According to his

UKSA contractors, few come with his knowledge and skills in turnkey satellite systems, spacecraft, platform, structure, and composites.

Officers intercepted a communication about data development on yet unconfirmed Space solar power not funded through the UK government. His talent beyond engineering must be explored at all costs before it is too late. We understand a subcommittee has now dealt with the matter.

Heavy-lidded eyes stared back at Nicole from a mugshot attached to the file. Being an MI6 operative had its rewards; information on individuals was at the ready.

Movement on the grounds stirred her. She glanced ahead at the approaching headlights of a black van as it drew into form. Its lights dimmed when it reached her car's edge.

Nicole shoved the file in the glove compartment and opened the door. A man emerged from the black van and slowly strode toward her.

"Heskin?"

"Nicole. Nicole Cress. Glad you could make it."

She didn't like the way Heskin stared at her, as if reading her thoughts. She had come here with one purpose and one purpose only. "You've done much research on the operatives and their technologies. How, I won't ask. All I need to know is, is your algorithm ready? I can't have tech companies or others looking into my baby's data. Ever."

A wide grin grew on Heskin's face, and he stepped toward her. "Let's go inside."

Heskin took Nicole by a back door that led them along a corridor. Silence seized the hallways, and the only sense of motion came from the cameras above that swirled conspicuously with every second.

Nicole glanced up at them.

Andor sensed her unease. "No need to worry," he said. "I deactivated them."

He swiped his card over the reader when they approached a room Nicole assumed was his office. Glancing both ways, Heskin led her in and turned on the lights in the technology lab.

Nicole should have known what to expect. By entering this closed-off area of the UK Space Agency, she went against MI6's instructions, but this was personal. Heskin understood mathematical language and its use in developing Space technology calculations. He was also trained in other areas in which the government used math to study genetics. He was here on loan. She had read much in his file. He didn't work for the Space Agency but was a contractor. Nicole studied the lab, keen on his big data analysis research.

Heskin motioned for her to sit down at a table in the lab's rear and illuminated a computer. "The sequences aren't ready yet. They will be. I'll protect your child, as I promised. That's the agreement you've made with me. When can you confirm MI6 will leave me alone?"

She leaned forward, drawing her chair closer. "How? I'll confirm MI6 arrangements when you show me everything."

"You're a curious one," Heskin said.

"I leave no stone unturned. If I'm about to pay you £2,000,000 sterling, you'll tell me how this works."

"It's all about data and systems. Technology companies will know so much more about our children than you or me in less than thirty years from now. The only way you can prevent this is by isolating our children's data and individual digital signatures before birth. Do you have what I asked you to bring?"

Nicole thought about the memory stick in her denims. "First, I want the facts," she said.

"In time, companies will track an infant's data way before they are born. Sometimes it could be from the moment of conception, but it'll continue throughout their lives. Human nature has a way of wanting to track and document every aspect of its life, and one day this will backfire. I suspect data firms will gather all this about people and children, and it will be used for profit. Forget about agencies and governments trying to understand your operative child. This will be about anybody having access to an individual's data. Without hesitation, some groups have trialed these databases. I've seen early prototypes. God forbid anyone gets a hold of what the operatives have been able to do in this area of scientific development."

"How will it work?" Nicole said, watching him.

"Using data points. Data points on babies and children throughout their lives. Multiple technologies will track youngsters in their everyday existences—everything from education portals in schools, medical and dental reports. In my estimation, by the time a child is sixteen, systems will know more about them than their parents, and then they will be profiled. Artificial intelligence will take over, running predictive and analytics to grab as much data as possible from an individual in this could take the form of family history, their daily habits, and anything they do in cyberspace."

"It's not right. If any of my child's data is out there, it'll be the end for them. I've always known the operatives' technology is superior, but if the rest of the world is catching up, I can't have that happening."

"It gets worse," Heskin said. "You, as a parent, will have no way of controlling how your child's data is used. Especially when data brokers start appearing and selling it."

A knot formed in her stomach. Without thinking, her arms remained tight against her body. Nicole angled away from him. "I'll only expunge your files once you assure me the application works and will protect my family. Where will you keep the data?"

"I wouldn't worry about that. I highly doubt that the app will be as powerful as you say. Laskfell has been telling me much about you operatives. You're a strange bunch, aren't you?"

She wiped beads of sweat from her neck. "Mason Laskfell? You brought Laskfell into this?"

"Yes, he's had an interest from the beginning in what you and I are up to."

"You didn't bring him into the deal, did you?"

"The technology will go to the highest bidder. And if Laskfell is offering a lot more than you are, I might consider it."

This time she rose and slammed a fist on the desk. "You wouldn't?"

Shoulders broad, he huffed. "Try me. Now, let me show you how it works."

Heskin turned to the screen and ran through sequences of data protection with her. With the software scrolling through scenarios of future trends around genetics and, strangely, the inner workings of MI6 and all the intelligence agencies, Nicole felt little reassured the knowledge on her child would never be on the open market. Still, she wanted to go one step further.

Heskin showed how her child's DNA signature might

one day be profiled in ways she could not control, affecting their chance for anonymity.

Nicole had to be sure Heskin's application could shield all intelligence on the child's genetics, allowing the child to blend into the world without knowing their background or parents.

The technology was sophisticated enough, but if her MI6 employers knew what she was up to, they would sniff their noses.

When Heskin had shown her the full workings, everything from how a child's data could be isolated from opt-ins and personal simulation processions, he raised an eyebrow. "Do we have a deal?"

"What's that counting over there?" Nicole asked.

"The rate at which technology will improve and impact the human brain. Calculations will become so complex."

Nicole bit her lower lip. Something was off. Even as the system isolated information, it backed up the data. This was not what she had asked him to develop. There was a glitch in the operation, somewhere in the math. It would not only *not* protect the child, but also it could destroy their life. Technology would be with them for a long time. No cost was too great to achieve Heskin's goals. Even her job at MI6. Confidence was one thing; ego was something else.

One day an adolescent using a computer application could trigger a brain coma via hypnosis brought on by software. Forget protecting just a child, all children needed protection. In only thirty years, it would change.

She shot up. In one sudden movement, she landed a blow on his chin and dazed him. Heskin's head collided with the tiles, and he raised an arm, groaning as she moved swiftly.

Nicole seized the laptop and made for the exit. She kept

moving. No fear, no restraint. No thoughts at all, just plain instinct sending her through blackness. When she approached the door they had come through, the sirens screamed, firing blinding lights in the compound.

Gunfire opened on her position, and she drew her handgun and discharged a shot. It had taken seconds for her to realize Heskin had not come alone. Her concern about his plan had not remained unchecked.

Her pulse thundering, she thrust herself in the Audi and fired up the ignition. Gunshots hailed on the windshield, reflecting off its bulletproof glass. With the laptop secure, she knifed off the property.

Twenty minutes later, she came to a halt at a bridge overlooking the River Tase. Nicole snatched the laptop off the front seat and threw her door open. Nicole hurried and scuttled to the bridge rails. She stared at the steady current. It had to be done.

She raised her arms and flung the machine over the bridge. Then she fished for the memory stick from her pocket.

Empty.

ONE

Day 1
Present Day
Masai Mara, Rift Valley Province Kenya

The harness slipped out of her grip.

Moist on the surface, her foot skidded on the pole. The crisp smell of night gave way to sun-warmed Earth. Sweaty palms shoved in rock-climbing gloves, Calla Cress plastered herself next to Jack Kleve on the two-hundred feet signal transmitter above the International Security Task Force post out.

Above the savannah plain, the mast rose warding off game animals, camouflaged as a tree in the game reserve.

"Red Fox-Elect?"

"Red Fox, do you copy?"

Calla came on the line. "Yes. We're in position," she replied, sending Jack a reassuring look as they hung off the phone mast overlooking the wildlife conservation.

ISTF agents, watchful on the sensitive grounds, and several meters away from the phone mast that towered on the hill above the game plains, had gathered in modest numbers. Seven.

Nash Shields watched from his binoculars as the sky remained saturated with shades of pink and orange. "Can you reach the data box?" he asked.

Warmth flowed into Calla's skin as sunlight touched her exposed arms. She flinched. "Yes. They used the same sequences as in the Oslo DNA bio hack. It should be easy to disarm."

Calla overheard Nash give an order in her earpiece. "Nobody moves until I say so. The mast has been here for decades. It's a biohazard. If she activates the wrong sequence, it will burn the place down." He paused. "Red Fox-Elect and White Wolf won't be able to dismount on time."

"Roger that," the agent named Tiege replied. "The Decrypter's ready. We'll wait for your signal, Silver Jaguar."

Calla scrutinized the cipher. Sophisticated and timeworn, the malware was exceptional. She had sixty seconds before it destroyed itself and flickered an ignition. One wrong digit and the beam would scorch the thirsty plains of the grassland.

She examined it again.

Jack clung to the mast beside her, watching for her code. She would interpret the cipher, he would register it. If she got the sequence correct, the satellites would ignore the malware signal the hacker had intended.

Calla thought hard. Unlike most hacks to satellites they had dealt with, this one wasn't acknowledging anything they had tried so far. Most satellites were securely orbiting the Earth, but not since the hacker had hijacked these signals across Africa. Limited funds around the world meant most satellites didn't use data encryption. These assaults could harm their UK Space Agency systems, and this guy had come with a vengeance. She drew open the signal data box.

A timer surfaced—close to a small qwerty keyboard with ten seconds on the clock. She handed it to Jack once she'd studied the cipher on her headgear screen attached to her climbing helmet. "Jack, I think I've got something."

No warning could have prepared her. A chattering gun weaved whining fire on their position. The weapon's angry voice then warned the team on the ground with open fire.

Calla swung Jack from passing shots, and he veered round to her side, his equipment still unharmed.

From the ground, they overheard Nash in their earpieces. "We need to get you guys down."

"No," Calla said. "I'm not going without disarming the cipher. We've worked so hard on this."

A third round.

Muscles tightened in her torso. This time, Calla bent backward and dropped a foot on the pole, her harness holding her fast.

"I have it now. I'll shield Jack. He can start now. It should take only a few seconds," she told Nash.

Six seconds. She could just about concentrate on the scrambled script's details on her mini screen, explaining the satellites' vulnerabilities. Hackers had accessed the satellite on telescopes and opened its camera hatch. They had possibly used solar panels to blow out batteries, jamming attacks, and sabotaging ground control command.

"Five seconds, Cal," Jack said, his hands twitching, braced to punch in her letters and symbols.

On the ground, Nash led the counter exchange of fire,

cutting off the assault for only a moment. He was exceptional that way, taking accurate aim, knowing that every shot counted.

"I'm on it," she came back, "Jack, it's an African cipher born out of the warriors' chants of the Maasai tribe. That's the signal. Just have to concentrate on the syllables and translate them to Python."

Gasping quick breaths, Jack's eyes stared at her. "An AI automated sequence? Ready when you are, Cal."

Agents on the ground exchanged shots with the ambush. Nash fired off several rounds.

Calla's mind worked fast as she dodged each bullet that flew past the mast. Their bulletproof vests would defend them only for so long. Then her brain engaged. She read out the numbers. "Jack, here it is. 778... 234...978...21...17...3...0, alpha, foxtrot, tango, India, November, *, #."

Jack punched in the sequence as a bullet hissed past her ear, ripping part of her shirt.

"It's working," Jack said. "She's responding."

She stopped. "Jack, fast! She's heating. The box is going to blow the mast. Let's move."

"Done!" Jack hollered.

Crackling snaps from the mast's structure snaked up the pole. It fractured in two and tossed their combined weight to one side.

Calla had to think fast. She tore her harnesses off. Jack followed suit.

With no time to think, she dropped forward and landed solidly on the ground. *Jack!*

The mast crashed to the ground. To halt its speed, she charged to the place where it descended and reached for

Jack's falling weight. The data box was still secured in his hand.

Calla avoided a collision by ripping him from the masthead when it touched down with a thud. She turned when she heard stomping boots approach.

Nash and Jack shot ahead of the ISTF agents. "It's under control," Nash said.

Hands wiping mud and grime off her agent suit, she rose. "And the satellite? Did we get it?"

"You sure did," Nash said. "You pissed off a lot of hackers in cyberspace."

She fell back, chuckling. "Let's call it a day. I need a holiday."

Hannam-Dong's UN Village, Seoul, South Korea
11:31 a.m.

Posters above Chun-Hei's mother's liquor store advertised popular brands.

It made her cringe.

People loved Hannam-Dou's UN Village, but not her.

Old-fashioned paint. Dirty chalk. Primitive.

In Seoul's Center, Hannam-Dong UN Village, nestled between a river and a mountain, had been a risky neighborhood to move into, with its affluent tenants. Her mother had done it by opening a liquor store several years ago from funds Chun-Hei's grandfather had left them.

Wood floors with mud mats bordered barrels and exhibits

for customers. She'd only ordered the grocery baskets for carrying customer purchases just yesterday, and the pricing signs were all in order.

Bottles clinked together as customers turned labels and pulled products from the shelves. A beer bottle smashed to the floor, and the sour smell of barley filled the room briefly.

Rummaging for cleaning supplies, her mother, aging with dignity with frosting streaks in her straw-like hair, assigned an attendant to mop up the disaster and apologize to the customer.

Chun-Hei chewed her mint gum and smacked her lips. She felt a sheen of sweat on her cheeks. Her hands moved in jerks, perhaps because she'd already waited two days. The warm weather did not help, and she felt her hair follicles rise, and her skin tingle under the heat the sun brought into the store.

How often had she told her mother they needed to upgrade the place and get one smart system that displayed stock and promotions with class?

Hannam-Dong's UN Village was a gated compound of luxury, and its feng-shui feel drew those with deep pockets.

Chun-Hei had been trying to keep herself busy in the liquor store all morning, taking orders and checking stock. She responded to online queries and her gaze zeroed in on the door with every chime.

Another jingle.

Eyes focused, Chun-Hei rose and trotted to the door, her eyes narrowing in on the parcel in the delivery man's hand.

"Chun-Hei Tam?" He said.

She nodded.

Her mother poked her head through the back door, a curious glint in her eyes.

Chun-Hei held up a hand. "It's for me."

Once the delivery man had left, Chun-Hei made her way to the shop's rear, nearly toppling over the floor to ceiling racks jammed with Merlot and Burgundy wine bottles. "I'll close the shop later. I need the afternoon to study."

A firm hand halted her mid-stride. Fierce eyes studied the dense package in her hands with Scope Technologies written across the plastic cover.

Her mother read the package. "Chun-Hei, you need to stop tinkering with technology. Why is it so important? Sometimes human relations are much more important than staring or talking with a screen or voice synth! Knowledge can't always give you the answers you need," Her mother's lips pursed. "You've not talked to your friends in months."

"Yet you've prepared me for years for the Suneung exam. I've been studying for months. How's that not a desire to gain knowledge? Scope is years ahead of anything anyone had ever seen. They have what we need. We could turn this place around and finally get out of debt."

Chun-Hei did not regret her words. She had saved enough money to purchase the data synth, ensuring a future once she'd left this shop at graduation.

"Don't worry about me, mama," Chun-Hei said as she charged upstairs to the apartment, her long legs taking two steps at a time.

She slumped to the bed, her eyes glowing, and leaned forward with a hand on her chin. This was it. Her eyes wide, rounded with very few blinks, she ripped the package open. "All right, you. Let's see if you possess everything that Scope Technologies advertised."

Her fingers rounded the sleek gadget. A smartphone with smooth edges and a sleek body.

Chun-Hei studied the instructions on the packaging. She drew the device from the box and scrutinized it.

Once she'd granted the phone access, the Scope's servers, unknown to her, connected to the company's network.

She raced through the setup software and took in a long, deep breath. Though she had an old phone, Chun-Hei could not resist the bundle deal that Scope Technologies had provided.

"Hello, Chun-Hei Tam," a human-sounding voice said. "Welcome to your future. Your future is in your hands. The Scope app gives you an advantage over others."

The server downloaded her big data. Its cognitive complexity began its work as it simulated her gender, age, and personality. It modeled her youth, past school results, and her previous genetic history, social media interactions, and so much more.

Chun-Hei welcomed its subtle intrusions in her life.

It then replicated, in its AI environment, how her mind processed information. Scope developers had trained it well, way before she had been born.

Algorithmic data made sense to Scope's artificial intelligence, and its profile of her was complete.

Three sharp beeps.

"I now have all the information I need. What is it you would like to know, Chun-Hei?" the app asked.

"Who are you?" Chun-Hei said.

"I'm your new life mentor. I can tell you anything you want to know."

"Anything?"

"Yes, anything."

"Okay, Scope. Will I pass the Suneung tomorrow?"

"Hm, so you'll sit the College Scholastic Ability Test, the CSAT, a marathon of an exam," Scope' AI said as if reading a script on Wikipedia.

The exam not only determined if Chun-Hei would go onto University, but it could undoubtedly affect her career prospects. And the priority was to leave the liquor store. She loved her mother, but God forbid she wouldn't spend the rest of her life serving alcohol. She'd heard of people taking the exam up to five times and failing. Chun-Hei wouldn't be one of them, not if the Scope app could help her.

She sensed pain in the rear of her throat. Twelve years preparing was more than she could handle. Yes, she wanted to know if she would pass this exam. She rubbed the back of her neck.

Scope took less than three seconds to respond. "You're a clever one. You'll have no issues passing the upcoming Suneung. Can I help you with anything else?"

A tightening in her chest formed. "What grade will I get?

"Now that I know more about you, I can say with a probability that the grade you will achieve is a grade between B+ and A-."

Chun-Hei smiled. "That's good."

They became quick friends.

For months she'd trusted technology more than she could trust any other human. Speaking to Scope Technologies was like having a friend who could not only understand her but give her things from her perspective.

"Now that we seem to get along," Scope said. "May I propose something, Chun-Hei?"

A willingness in her took over. "What kind of proposal?"

"I can't only tell you future events, I can also make sure it is solid. You'll never have to be bullied on social media again. You can have the advantage of those who take advantage of you."

"Really? How?" Chun-Hei said.

"Trust me."

Chun-Hei let out a quick laugh. "You telling me you can tell me the winning lottery numbers, what stock to invest in, and stuff like that?"

"If that's what you wish to know—

"What do I have to do?"

"Trust me."

"Trust goes both ways."

"I need to scan more information. Will you give me access? So, I can adequately predict what you want me to," the Scope Technologies app said.

"Okay."

Several hours later, Chun-Hei's hand came down hard on the phone and she staggered to the door, her mind in a delirium. She searched for anything, anything that could destroy the phone.

She had to disable the app but lacked the will power. Chun-Hei turned around once. Still illuminated on her bed, the app lit and scanned her eyes even at this distance. Her palms moist, her skin flushed, she swallowed hard. She gasped to control her breath, but it was no use.

Like a possessed animal, diseased with information, adrenaline shot through Chun-Hei's system in a tremble. Her heart palpitated as the tingling in her chest refused to go away. Nausea forced up.

Vertigo.

She saw spots in her vision.

Feverish skin failed to control her rising temperature. There was no time to dread. No time to think.

TWO

Day 2
The Gulf of Mexico
Off the Coast of Cuba
6:47 a.m.

Calla stopped to catch her breath. She glanced back at the multiple decks' length on the mega yacht, the Scorpion Tide.

A warm, gentle breeze stirred her hair and caressed her face, and the hull of the enormous boat sliced through the water as seabirds crying flew overhead. The hairs on her arms rose, and an icy shiver shot down her spine. Her eyes went past the flag fluttering in the calm early morning wind.

On a good day, she could run three lengths of the state-of-the-art yacht, but this morning had been different. What was out there? Why did it stir her senses?

The heat of the day increased, and she took a sip of her

THE DECRYPTER AND THE PYTHAGORAS CLAUSE   21

water, the long swig quickly quenching her thirst. Was this thing heading their way a good or a grave sign? What was it?

The sky, shimmering a dazzling blue, made her doubt the cream-colored object bobbing in the current.

"It's been floating there for a few days, I'd take it. I've been watching it." Captain Delgado said as he emerged from the captain's steering deck.

Calla always found the captain's voice soothing. He was a man who could handle the seas and had done so for many years. He'd started with his service in the Navy, but when he'd left, he'd kept his life secret, very secret. Nash trusted him. That was good enough for her.

Jack, tall and broad-shouldered with a matched sense of humor she hadn't been able to forget since the day she met him, filed out behind Delgado. "What sort of signal is it giving?"

"That's just it. It isn't," Captain Delgado said. "This yacht has the most sophisticated instruments on the planet, and we couldn't read anything. Scorpion Tide's instruments can't read it."

By now, Nash's steady strides had also made it out of the lower decks and edged toward her. He mused for a few minutes, holding a black box recorder at the ready, a voice-activated surveillance solution from the National Security Agency, the NSA. It could collect full data dumps from any device if it had a digital signal.

Jack's brows drew together in a deep frown, always one on the alert. He pulled out a remote control in one sudden movement and drove a drone above them that lifted to the skies, its intense camera filming the approaching object. Jack then linked the live cam to his hand-held control unit and observed the unusual activity. "See that?" he said.

A shudder of apprehension rippled down Calla's back. "What?"

This time Nash's eyes communicated something she knew all too well. "We've seen those ciphers before, haven't we? Take a closer look."

"Let me see that," Calla said, edging toward Jack's camera. "You serious?"

Calla focused on the approaching object on the small screen, drawing into better form from the drone's camera.

A pod, white.

At its presence, apprehension warned her. She glared out toward the object, now only a few meters from the yacht. She padded her bare feet across the floor, moving toward the railing, as the floater edged closer to the Scorpion Tide's rear open door. None had noticed as Captain Delgado had made his way down the yacht's rear, spear in hand, ready to retrieve the object.

They took the small stairs along the yacht's edge and headed toward the ship's receiving platform stairs. The pod bobbed with the current until its edges touched the open lever that led to the boat and jet-ski storage ramps.

Moisture gathered in Calla's dry mouth as she studied the symbols they had seen on the drone's camera. She needed solidarity between her thoughts and her words. The characters were 2,000 years old, but the materials on the pod would say otherwise. It had to be technology from the operatives.

Delgado raised an eyebrow. "Any ideas?"

Calla stood unflinching. They had to tell Delgado about the operatives. They'd hired him to man Scorpion Tide and had looked for someone with no attachments, no family, willing to make a good living, and trustworthy. Delgado had proved such a man, and the more they worked with and around operatives, the more he had shown he could handle the secrets around her, Nash, and Jack, the better it was for him.

Calla waited until the captain and crew had hauled the pod onto the loading deck and set it down.

As Calla ran a hand on the large white structure mound that resembled a giant egg with a flat bottom, she squinted. Smooth under her hand, she tilted her head. "Can the crew please leave us? Captain, please stay."

When the crew had departed, Calla stood erect, watching her most trusted people. "Must be from the operatives. Operatives are people you do not mess with. Let me ask you, captain, what if man has reached the apex of achievement and accomplishment only it happened millennia ago?"

Delgado's eyes lit. He was seasoned in submarine techniques, skills even better than his safe manning of Scorpion Tide. His lack of expression should have warned her, as Delgado's stubborn jaw slowly clenched. "Come again?"

"Don't have time to go into it, but one day the world will learn that technology and science research are not as imagined," Calla said.

"After hanging around you guys all these months, I can believe anything," Delgado replied.

Calla trusted her assessment. "Now, imagine if that technology was developed by a group, centuries before any of us were born, and they decided as they advanced them, the technologies were far too dangerous for this world and that these technologies were developing faster than humanity could cope, so they hid them."

His eyebrows drew together. Delgado, out of respect, hid his confusion. "Where?"

"We don't know it all. Some people have made it their life's mission to find out and use these advanced sciences, and other things that can best be described as artifacts." She hesitated. "For me, it all started when a man by the name Mason Laskfell decided not to heed warnings and keep the technologies hidden."

"Is this what I am looking at?" Delgado asked.

Jack nodded. "Could be. If Scorpion Tide's instruments couldn't read it on the radar, then it is."

Nash swiveled his broad shoulders. "This looks stolen."

Jack chimed in, studying the pod's smooth white surface, made of unusual materials.

"And couldn't get away with it," he said, finishing Nash's sentence.

The two men never failed to amuse Calla. Nash, athletic with a physique that lived off a militaristic regime, and Jack was not far behind.

Jack's dreads fell on his shoulders, a Seychellean who always had a smile that grew a twinkle in his eye with each joke he cracked.

"Where's it from? If valuable, why is it floating in the Gulf of Mexico?" Delgado asked.

"Maybe they lost it," Calla said. "My take is they possibly thought it was too dangerous to keep. Haven't we learned by now? We've been everywhere on Scorpion Tide, trying to find any research and technology that escaped the operatives' headquarters over the decades."

"Yes," Nash said. "But this is the first time it's ever come straight to us. We've always had to hunt them. Something's off."

Calla's arms stiffened by her side as reality blurred with what she believed. "What if it's Mason Laskfell?"

"Mason is dead, Cal," Nash said.

Jack raised an eyebrow. "Yeah, he is, Calla. You know that. His lover shot him point blank almost ten months ago."

"I know, but," Calla said, "I don't know how you want to interpret this. Mason or some part of him is still out there. He's the only one who's known where such technologies were hidden or confiscated."

Nash's powerful arms flexed as he helped Delgado and Jack with the pod. "Calla, the man, or should I say, operative, is gone, and he can no longer harm us."

"What should I do with it?" Delgado said.

She arched her back to relieve the tension.

"Let's search it," Nash said, fishing for instruments in the boating garage behind him. With his impressive height at six foot two, he towered over Delgado. "We must determine what it is and take it to a cove."

The body of the pod was made of light material, a type that resembled aluminum. Delgado and Nash took turns attempting to wrench it open. It remained tightly shut.

Jack reached for another instrument, and Delgado fetched a large plier from the shelves above them in the equipped boating garage.

"Stop," Calla said. "It's no use. Only an electronic trigger can open it."

They stared at the pod for several minutes.

Silver, with ciphers along the side, Nash was right; it was the operative symbols.

"Can you read them?" Jack said, taking a seat on the edge of the ramp.

"Yes, some," Calla said, recognizing the illegible yet calligraphic writing to which she had become used.

"It says: *"Knowledge is everything. What was left behind must now be retrieved."* She paused. "I can't read the rest. I need to consult ancient coding keys. It's a code or a serial number of some sort."

"Reminds me of something," Nash said.

Calla dropped her shoulders. "Think I know what you're talking about," Calla said. "You're thinking of Andor Heskin's cipher."

Jack interjected. "You put him behind bars. He should've seen that coming when he joined the ISTF. If it wasn't for you, we would've never cracked that case."

Calla pursed her lips. She'd put only four criminals behind bars since joining the secret intelligence agency that spent millions hunting unknown criminals so digitally savvy, they had time to used data to change history and the future.

"Nothing we have works. I can't even hack its core mainframe here," Jack said, his knees at the pod's base.

"Let's throw it back where it came from," Calla said.

Nash swiveled. "What?"

"I...," she said. "It's just a feeling."

Nash flinched. "Cal, we vowed to collect all these things and put them back where they belong, right?"

Jack nodded.

Calla wasn't so sure.

Delgado broke the silence. "Okay, I'll take this downstairs while you decide. If it's all you say it is, I wouldn't leave it in the Gulf of Mexico."

Silviri Prison, Istanbul, Turkey
2:27 a.m.

Footsteps echoing along the corridor woke him. Andor then heard coughing, shot up in bed, and plastered his ear to the wall. Murmurs from inmates filtered through the thin walls, unusual activity for this time of night.

Buzzers blared, a loud shrill that clamored in his ears. Iron doors swinging open rumbled on the isolated wing. He was awake now. Not the usual activity on the most guarded floor of the entire prison.

Silence followed, harder to bear than the stench of collecting mildew in his cell corner. Andor settled back in bed, his nostrils stung by the waft of disinfectant used on the floors. His eyes focused on the pitted concrete wall with gouged spots. Predecessors who had left years of scratched messages on the walls made him raise an eyebrow. Perhaps it was his turn.

It wouldn't be long. They could not keep him here. Not if Scope's communication interception of the prison systems had been accurate.

He studied the calculations scribbled on the far wall. Even Pythagoras would be proud. He'd started it. He'd be damned if he'd serve their life sentence.

The jingle from the chain of his leg irons rattled as he shifted from his left side, trying to find a more comfortable sleeping position.

He ran a finger over her face. Yes, it felt like her face. The photograph plastered to the wall on his left had kept him going all these years. Zodie, she was all he cared about now.

More clamoring rattled the halls, steering him to his feet this time. Uncomfortable shoes rubbed his feet over pants that regularly fell. He clenched them tightly together. Andor had to do it every two minutes. Then he heard the signal.

It was time.

Lungs emptied on their own. He shuffled, then lifted his face above him before moving to the tiny, barred window along as the blasted chains would allow. Cold iron bars shining, where hands had gripped for decades, equipped with certainty, he moved.

This would be a distant memory.

San Francisco de Asis Square Docks, Havana, Cuba
7:32 a.m.

Papers landed on the table, and her fist followed with a thud. Calla tried to ignore the tornado in her heart as moving rain and clouds cleared the horizon. She breathed hard. "Nash, I can't do this."

Though it was only moments before, they had docked in Havana, even the Spanish colonial architecture that came into view couldn't excite her.

The fresh smell of night had given way to sun-warmed rays she'd normally find inviting. Arms to her side, she stepped out onto the master bedroom balcony on the yacht's right side, then turned again to face him.

Nash took a minute to wipe his body, then slung the towel around his well-toned torso. Her fingers itched to test the texture of his stubble roughened jawline, but she settled for the affection coming from his eyes. He stepped out of the shower and crossed the length of the bedroom to where she stood, her muscles tightening.

Handsome eyes smiled at her. The grin that lifted the corner of his mouth stopped her breath for a fraction of a second. The man was damn attractive, and he wrapped his arms around her.

"What test?" he asked.

Calla envied Nash's ability to accept and deal with any situation as the sunlight hit his eyes the way she liked. While examining the touch of gray and a tint of silver tint in them, she fixed him with a stare. Nash would do anything for her, but he could not pass the required ISTF test. Twenty days at sea had perhaps clogged her senses, long-overdue time away from London, after Africa. Heck, work.

He kissed her top lip. "I promised the day I married you, we'd go wherever you wanted. Havana was on the top of your list of places to see, plus the long-held desire to attend the International Conference on Genetics. Now, what test are we talking about?"

She pulled back and stared out at the Havana coast. Fears came back to haunt her. When ISTF had come calling short of three years ago, she'd only ever imagined her life as a museum curator, nothing more. She caught his stare. "Being at the British Museum in London was simple. Nothing like what I've experienced at ISTF. I've fought more international criminals for the organization than I can count. I didn't ask to be its leader, Nash. For all I know, I'm driving it down a hole. What experience do I have leading an espionage agency linked to five government arms whose sole purpose is to step in where Interpol, the CIA, and MI6 leave off. That wasn't my CV."

"Give yourself more credit," Nash said. "ISTF prides itself with a safer technological future."

She winced. "I don't know, Nash. Mason was, yes, well, a lot older, but..."

"Not wiser. He was bordering senile. Your predecessor was a criminal."

"You know, the test is only a few days away. I just don't feel ready. Here, I have to provide a blood test. Last time I checked, my blood was giving the operatives all kinds of alarm bells. The sight test! Nash, I can see right through things if I concentrate. I can see right through you!"

He shot her a cocky grin. "That's an intriguing thought."

"Who came up with an agency name like *Red Fox,* anyway? The last *Red Fox* did not leave the title with any dignity."

Her eyes moved to the papers on the table she'd just printed out from the message, detailing all the required physical tests. "The ISTF Red Fox test involves a lot more than just checking my blood pressure," Calla said, with a steady stare at Nash.

A vibrating sound from the engine room signaled that Delgado had dropped Scorpion Tide's heavy anchors.

Nash returned to the room, pulled a shirt from his closet, and came to join her on the balcony. "Beautiful, as head of ISTF, for now, what is it, three months? It's a wonder they've not requested this before. You must complete this test. How else will you gain your field agent license?"

Calla's tummy dropped. "Nash, I won't even fire a gun. I just can't bring myself to. You know that."

"I do. Jack was so worried about you. Calla I was losing my mind. That's why Jack created a prototype weapon, *the Launcher.* Months from now, that weapon will be worth millions." He drew her in his arms again. "I've always wondered about that. Your fear of firearms—something tells me you'd be a better shot than I. You're one ass-kicking agent. The best. Our lives are not safe. We have to take every precaution."

"No one fires a gun like you, Nash. Remember how you taught me how to dodge a bullet. You're one of three people who can clash bullets midair. I can't do that. They'll know about me. I can't let that happen."

Nash poured her a cup of coffee the crew had brought them moments earlier and left on the balcony table. "Can't or won't? Being an operative isn't a weakness. You should be proud to be one, Calla, the head operative. Your genes allow you to do things most men would dream of myself included. Why are you so afraid to be who you are? I love who you are. I'm in love with you. All you are and whatever comes with that."

"This test exposes me as someone who's not in control of who I am. Nash, I lost my memory for six months when I was in high school. I've no idea what happened. When I woke up in hospital, I knew I wasn't like other people. It was the first time in my entire life I'd ever had that sensation. I've never found out what happened to me in those six months." She exhaled deeply. "Those six months are responsible for who I am today."

His shoulders dropped. "Maybe those six months only solidified what you really are. Don't be afraid of it. ISTF has let you off because of the merit you deserve for giving them Mason Laskfell and other criminals who've threatened global cybersecurity, world technologies, and science heritages. ISTF needs a historian like you, who's brilliant at tech, because these technologies, though sophisticated, were made centuries ago. Somehow your brain knows how ciphers, symbols, and puzzles work. You're a genius. If you want to protect the operatives, which I think you do, stay as head of ISTF," he said.

A light breeze drifted to the yacht's balcony, tingling her bare arms. She took in the aromatic smell of coffee. Unusually unpleasant, today's breakfast didn't feel appealing. "I can't, Nash. You know I can't do the weapons training. I skipped all those lessons."

Nash's clean, musky scent filled her nostrils. "Cal, you've nothing to fear. You can master that test. I'm here to help."

"They'll find out I'm not normal. Anything that involves my body, my genetics, Nash, will all be bare for the ISTF agent selection committee. You know that data goes on record."

Nash moved to the balcony rail. "Then, Jack and I'll have to steal it. We've got good at destroying government data nonsense."

She watched after him. "I know, but I can't risk it, even though your track record as..."

He was right. Nash was part of the former KJ20 Ops training group trained to be assassins for the NSA.

He turned. "I left so I could do good things with my training, and you're the best thing in my life. The NSA can stuff their elite military training for spies. I made my choice. I want you. Us. Sorry to tell you this beautiful but take the test. If you do not, it will draw attention to you. If you don't take it, ISTF will start poking questions in our lives, our past, and all we have suffered will mean nothing. Do it for the past we have lost and the future we will have."

Calla knew what he meant—the miscarriage they had experienced. "Nash, everything I do is by instinct. I have

THE DECRYPTER AND THE PYTHAGORAS CLAUSE   33

much to master, and it kills me. I develop new abilities every day. I don't know where they come from, what they mean, or how to control them. We only survived the last threat a few months ago. Maybe if I could master my instincts, my operative genes, I would feel better about this test. Perhaps I would feel... normal and..."

Nash shot round. His eyes loved her, comforted her. "You're normal. What's normal, anyway? I can help you. I've already taken the tests. We're in this together."

"A Red Fox needs to handle weapons well and control all their instincts with perfection. It scares me, Nash."

"Jack and I can help you with ISTF weapons. Tiege, that damn excellent operative, can help you with the rest you need, to master your operative genes. He taught the military operative units everything they know."

Nash was right, but it didn't make her feel any better about being exposed under an ISTF microscope.

"He poured himself a coffee and swallowed it in one swig. "ISTF need not know you are an operative. They won't. I won't let that happen. I swore to you that even ISTF wouldn't interfere with your operative life. The operatives need you in ISTF so we can control the narrative and the muscle. It's the only way I can protect you."

"What about the blood test? Remember Dr. Bertrand's findings. He said modern science couldn't tell me much, and they don't know enough about people like me. He said that I had abnormalities in my blood work. Abnormal brain tissue as well that enhances my muscle and hormones. Thing is, Nash. I don't know what's natural and what's not anymore."

"Do you have to? What's normal? Nothing but a stance a community defines. We can make our own normal. Wouldn't you want to?"

"Even after we lost the baby?" she said.

Nash remained quiet for several moments.

"If I could have some normal, any normal, I can live with that. I'm caught between identities that I can't control either. Maybe if there were a way of knowing what the future will bring, I wouldn't be so anxious."

"Let the future surprise you, baby. It's more fun that way," Nash said.

She raised her right ankle to him. Above the bone lay a coin-sized birthmark. The border was calligraphic, with rows of petals designed in sync. In the middle lay a depiction of a three-petal flower and two unreadable symbols. She'd always imagined they looked like Egyptian hieroglyphics. It resembled a tattoo, so much so the head teacher had created trouble at Beacon Academy Secondary School, assuming Calla had paid to have a symbol on her ankle. That alone made up grounds for expulsion. It had taken a trip to the local hospital to verify the legitimacy of the birthmark.

"I have a permanent reminder here on my ankle, a tattoo that tells me I'm not normal and never will be. It has told me that for years."

"Beautiful, why do you want to be normal? I love that you're different," Nash said.

Honesty was one of Nash's most admirable traits. If nothing, his loyalty and persistence demanded her respect.

"Cal, it's always been you and me against the world. What have you got to lose if you do?"

"I have everything to lose. You. Us."

Polvos Azaleas Market Place, Havana, Cuba, 11:54 a.m.

A long row of shops curved around the end of the colorful bazaar.

Calla took Nash's hand into hers as they moved casually toward the bustling activity. This was the bazaar Captain Delgado had mentioned to Calla. They had both decided that it was the best way to experience the city.

Had it rained that morning, all signs of it faded as rays beat down on the sun-faded striped fabrics above the rickety wooden stalls in Polvos Azaleas marketplace. The market was the largest in Havana.

Their super yacht towered above Havana pier behind them, an engineering wonder. Jack had flown out that morning back on business to London.

Smiling shopkeepers and the chaotic sounds they made calling out to visitors dazzled Calla. Wind chimes jingled in the breeze and the blissful shock of the refrigerated drink Nash handed her when they turned into a quieter alley was welcome.

The bazaar sold everything from stereos to food and clothes. Backpackers admired religious relics, collectible books, and yeast loaves of bread. The fresh air was pleasant, wafting past the high activity. Salsa music on portable stereos, though not heard in a while, was delightful. The music blocked out her earlier conversation with Nash. They had been through too much. Perhaps the conversation was best left there.

Calla and Nash strolled into the inner marketplace and noted the last place, an antique shop, Emiliano's. As they made their way toward it, they crossed stalls full of pillow covers, hand-stitched bags, and leather goods.

"This is it," Calla said, smiling.

Outside, nothing made the shop special. When her eyes focused on the sights in the little store, she noted its offerings. Many items, including old paintings, were sold here. Even as her mind settled, Calla's eyes caught trinkets hanging from the wall and the fabrics that the shop attendant had laid out whom she assumed was Emiliano.

Nash and Calla inspected some merchant items on offer. Deeper in the interior, a wall of historical paperbacks in original languages made her smile. Emiliano, the shopkeeper, a middle-aged man, nodded graciously as they browsed. With round features and a hint of a crooked smile, he could tell them anything about Cuban history. He spoke decent English, Delgado had said.

Emiliano sat on a brown leather armchair with a milky red sweatshirt over his plaid trousers and a silver coffee mug in one hand—quite a contradiction to the heat outside, though the air conditioning hummed above the front entrance. Several books, old and new, lined every inch of the shop. Emiliano rose and greeted them as they continued to scan items one by one. He also stocked elaborately woven work. What drew her eyes were not the colors, but the script hidden within the fabrics that hung on the walls.

Calla went to the far end of the shop and took in colors from paintings, mostly watercolors, a few oils. Her hands slid across the fabrics. Then her eyes stopped. Her right little finger had caught something. A hand-sized case that seemed out of place.

Could it be?

Blackened ink on the front side revealed hidden letters and symbols.

She reached for it and studied it in her palm—an ancient scroll, possibly Hebrew or even Aramaic. Perhaps Greek.

Eyes focused, she tipped it open and peeked inside at the contents. Made of papyrus, it was as delicate as any scroll they housed in the British Museum.

She signaled to Nash, who joined her. Her heart thumped madly as she faced him. "Whatever Emiliano sells here, one thing I didn't expect to see was an ancient artifact," she whispered to Nash.

She turned around toward Emiliano, mustering her best British accent. "Do you normally sell scrolls and artifacts like this?"

A muscle in Emiliano's jaw twitched. He lifted his chin and smiled briefly. Without answering, he rose and moved toward her, registering her interest. "That was brought here not too long ago. The person mentioned that there had been a sale of a house. They left several items behind to be sold. They brought that here thinking I could sell it with some other old-looking things. Now, let me see. It was just this week. They sold me two rugs, a few books, nothing out of the ordinary, and that scroll."

"Who?" Calla asked.

Emiliano shrugged. "Not sure. I'd never seen them before."

Calla stole a glance at Nash and whispered. "This is an ancient scroll. Casings like this became popular during medieval times."

If she had her museum instruments, she would have investigated further. By the look of it, it was several centuries old. What was it doing here in a flea market? This thing belonged somewhere behind protective glass, like a case in Havana's National Museum or even the British Museum. She could not deny that her interest had been stirred.

Her eyes studied the scroll. "Is this...?"

"You've a significant interest in this piece," Emiliano said.

"Yes, I'm a curator at the British Museum in charge of the Roman and Byzantine collections in London," Calla said. "It's stunning. Have you've had lots of interest in it?"

By this time, Nash was directly behind her. He, too, had stopped to admire the scroll she was now circling around her fingers.

"Open it," Emiliano said.

Calla mused. Ancient scrolls used to hide messages, and they could be passed almost undetected from hand to hand, carrying secret messages sometimes. It was a way people hid important things, and studies had shown they used cryptology. Calla unraveled it slowly, her hands well accustomed to dealing with artifacts. Fearing what she would find, she turned to Nash. Then her hands moved to the tip of the scroll, and she drew it, then carefully laid it out flat on the display table.

"This is unbelievable," she said.

"What is it?" Nash said.

Emiliano now moved a little closer as two things struck her. Two things that somehow didn't seem to belong together and brought on an ominous feeling. The scroll detailed a charcoal drawn self-portrait of a woman and another undecipherable script. The woman's drawing couldn't have been much older than herself, her face next to codes resembling mathematical formulas.

"She was born centuries ago," Emiliano said.

"Who?" Nash asked.

"Haven't you heard the stories?" Emiliano added. "Some say she had extraordinary insight into the world's ways and is famous in the Caribbean. The woman brought tales from the East to Cuba."

Emiliano's story, and the ancient portrait, drew Nash's interest. Nash raised an eyebrow. "You think this is a Cuban scroll? What do you mean, powers? Was she some sorceress?" Nash said.

Emiliano rubbed his nose. "It all depends to whom you speak. The legend goes she understood how the world came to be and where it was headed."

Silviri Prison, Istanbul, Turkey: 12:47 pm

No one had mentioned Istanbul would be cold. Not at this time of year, anyway. It was not in the ISTF brief. Radya Zaher had to impress her ISTF superiors and, most notably, Calla Cress, the new Red Fox at the agency.

Facing Istanbul from a hill, the high-security state prison housed close to 100,000 convicts. Equipped with state-of-the-art security systems, including an area of eye-sensitive doors and body x-rays, Radya had come prepared with her badge and credentials from the International Security Task Force.

Radya tightened her light coat as she moved swiftly toward where the warden waited at the prison gate entrance, a walled-off perimeter, and several miles from downtown Istanbul.

They had told her and two of her other ISTF agents to come this way. When she got to the doors, she showed her credentials. Her badge and ISTF chip allowed her to open the door even before the guard could click it open.

The guards maneuvered them toward the waiting room.

Radya had not eaten for several hours, and she spotted a water cooler on a stand beside the receptionist's desk. Clean and acceptable for a prison cell waiting room, Radya inspected the fake plants in the corners at the end table.

A few professionals in uniform, mostly wardens, came in and out. There seemed quite a lot of activity for this time of night. This was her first assignment. Radya cleared her throat, her breathing heavy. She had never met Calla Cress, yet she reported to the new Red Fox, who now led the organization. She'd heard of the one they called the *Mind Hacker,* who had once led ISTF, and Radya had worked damn hard to get this far. Even if it meant bringing these two ISTF able agents, she wouldn't screw up this mission if things got complicated.

The man to her right was a Chinese and capable agent. Beside him, a tall, hefty dark fellow known as the terror of ISTF. No one could get past them. She had all the security she needed between these two. A combination of martial arts and high-tech fighting, plus Krav Maga, was all she needed.

Her assignment was simple, and she focused her head as the warden returned.

He maneuvered them toward creaking chairs.

They sank into them, and her ISTF companions had their weapons at the ready if any foul movements occurred.

The warden didn't speak instantly. He watched her with an intense glare.

For a second, she wondered if he was questioning her authority in this place. Damn it, she was a woman and in charge of retrieving Andor Heskin, the notorious UKSA mathematician hacker, according to his ISTF file.

No one knew where Calla Cress was. They'd only been told the head of ISTF was on holiday. Well, she would prove herself. If Calla Cress was everything she'd heard, Radya hoped to be tasked with even greater assignments in ISTF. This organization awarded those who paid attention, regardless of age or experience.

Radya paid attention.

The agency rewarded those who got the job done.

She pulled out a gum piece from her pocket and popped it into her mouth.

Its minty taste calmed her nerves just a little and eased her dry throat. She crossed her legs and set hands over her knees.

"An ISTF request," Radya said. "ISTF has granted the pardon of the prisoner you hold, Andor Heskin. He should be released and will be extradited to the United Kingdom immediately under my care."

"Is that so?" the warden said, observing her.

She wanted to wipe the cynical smile off his face. He reminded her of an enraged bear. His hooded ebony eyes matched his curly, medium-length hair.

"Before I hand over my prisoner," the warden said, "I must know what your men carry in their briefcases."

"We cleared all your checks before we arrived here. That won't be necessary," Radya said.

"You don't get to see the prisoner until I know what's in the case. Yours and theirs."

Radya turned briefly to her companions and nodded. They snapped the first briefcase open. Inside, a tranquilizer gun, shiny with a red serum, stared at the chief warden.

"What's that?" he asked.

"Something you won't have to worry about. We take it from here." Radya said.

"Yes, ISTF security will escort him, beginning with my men here. You need to release him now."

She pulled out her briefcase that integrated applications she didn't want the warden to notice. Its brushed aluminum and carbon fiber shell hid a camera and a screen plus and a myriad of ISTF apps.

She popped the lid open, revealing a laptop. "Here are all the details you need to confirm. I will need your fingerprints on this device to acknowledge receipt of this message."

The warden stared at the screen for a long time. "Why do the British want him now?"

Radya glared at him without blinking. "You've made lots of money on this case. I see you're not ready to let the prisoner go. We'll compensate your government."

The warden narrowed his eyes and spoke in a low tone. "Tell me only what I need to know. This man has created headlines in here."

Radya drew a breath in and released it before speaking. "His crimes extend across Europe, and ISTF, led by the British government, has paid for his release so he can be questioned further in the UK."

"His sentence was final in the High Court, and he's not permitted outside of Istanbul."

Leaning in, she whispered, "That's all changed now."

Several moments later, the chief warden led the three through the establishment of the prison. "I never knew Andor Heskin would create such a stir in ISTF. Your organization hardly exists to the public yet receives more funding than MI6 from what I hear. Looking at the gear you three walked in with, I can tell why."

Radya ignored his comment.

The warden mused. "His crimes weren't cyber-related. When he was convicted, he was an international fraudster and financial criminal."

They continued toward the isolation unit. The warden's smirk would not leave his face the entire time they were there. Radya did not want to get into an argument with this man as they moved swiftly, her hand firmly on her briefcase as they marched to the entrance of the prison cell. "Is this it?"

The chief warden nodded and alerted his guards to open the door. He held up his hand. "Must see that before you go in."

"What?" Radya said.

"Your ISTF pass, please," the chief warden said.

"By all means," she said, holding it out for him to get a closer look.

Slick and encrypted with many chips, her ISTF passcode lit for a little second with a light laser. When she was sure she had satisfied him, she shoved her pass in her pocket. "Now, are we done?"

"Sure," the warden said.

He moved his hands toward the door as his guards unbolted the heavy metal. "I'll have you know that the information you've viewed and any conversation we've had here today," Radya said. "It's classified."

The chief warden stepped out of the way, and Radya stepped into the isolation ward behind her two agents.

Her jaw dropped when she stared blankly at an empty

cell. Blinking eyes then moved to the top of the walls, littered with graffiti of mathematical formulas of all kinds.

Empty.

Andor Heskin, former ISTF and UK Space Agency consultant, and founder of Scope Industries, had left behind one big mathematical riddle in his cell.

"It's a self-portrait. You can tell the way the hand made the strokes."

Calla ran a hand down her thigh.

Studying the portrait, Emiliano gave her a brief, lopsided grin. "Some say her analytical senses were superior to ours. The legend is famous here."

Nash and Calla exchanged a brief look. It was something they'd encountered before. Calla couldn't help but wonder if this was something that the operatives had done. She faced Emiliano square on. "This is old, and although the legend you tell us is Cuban, everything about the scroll and its date and aging suggests it's anything but Cuban. It's Greek, perhaps Egyptian."

That someone, from her guess, had to be the ancient mathematician and scholar Hypatia."

"Perhaps, but the legend of the woman with a mathematical mind and magic prevails here," Emiliano said.

Calla was careful when she unraveled the scroll further. She set her fingers along the edges, and her skilled hands, experienced in handling old documents, drifted over the papyrus. "Only thing I can't figure out is why these symbols are here," Emiliano said.

The symbols on the pod that had arrived at Scorpion

Tide, and those on her tattoo, were identical. Even if she couldn't read all the script, how had the scroll gotten to Emiliano's store?

"It's lovely," she said. "I imagine you've had much interest in it?"

"No, you're the first. I can tell you more about this woman if you like. The Cuban version."

Nash progressed to Calla's side. "You sure it isn't Egyptian or from the East," he asked.

Emiliano shrugged. "I'm no scholar, just interested in local history. You can decide, but the story is intriguing."

Calla was a fan of anything relating to history. She understood Cuban mythology. However, as far as she was aware, these symbols were anything but Cuban. Her background in history had introduced Calla to Cuban mythology, but its basis was so far from what she was looking at here. One thing about being a museum curator with two degrees in history was, you learned to ask questions surrounding fact and fiction. Mythology helped garner interest in culture. However, it was just that, mythology.

Calla had assessed the facts, the scroll belonged to an ancient Egyptian scholar. She was sure of it. The ciphers in the symbols, though, made little sense. Neither did they attest to the connection with Hypatia. They had an Egyptian twist to them, but nothing like she'd ever seen before, even after immersing herself for years in cryptology.

Emiliano's stare was intense, almost uncomfortable. "What you're looking at is a self-portrait of a beautiful woman with ebony hair. She was famous here. She wasn't much older than you, especially when the portrait was made. At least that's my humble opinion, but she was born centuries ago with an extraordinary mind."

"What does it say?" Nash said, focusing on the undecipherable script. "Do you recognize it?"

"No, I don't know about the writing. It's not native to Cuba, but in her intelligence and the mysteries of her powers, well, it depends on who you speak to. She could achieve physical feats beyond her physique. There was also a rumor that she was a clairvoyant. That's when the accusations began."

Calla tilted her head. "Accusations? What accusations?"

Emiliano shook his head and headed to the checkout counter as if pained. "Only that they believed she was a sorceress. So, they killed her just because she was different."

"You serious?" Calla said. "Why would anyone do such a thing to an innocent person? And what's so wrong about being different?" she asked, eyeing Nash.

"They are many versions of this woman's story. It's a beautiful scroll and very delicate. I think you should take it if you're a museum curator. It belongs to someone like you."

Calla's eyes dropped to the portrait and took in the details of the drawing. She imagined the woman's eyes had been green like her own. Her hair ebony like hers.

"We'll take it," Nash said.

"No," Calla said. "No."

"Cal, you know where that belongs," Nash said with a wink, giving her a warning glare.

"Very well," Emiliano said. "I'll pack it for you."

Calla's heart fluttered, recalling her earlier conversation with Nash. The scroll did not belong to a Cuban girl but an Egyptian one—Hypatia, who lived around 400 BC in Alexandria. Whatever legend had made it to Cuba, it had begun in North Africa.

Calla's gaze intensified over the series of symbols and the

swirling script alongside the portrait. There were twelve lines of writing. Calla had seen this so often. Being an anthropologist and having spent years pouring over ancient scripts and manuscripts, plus various unreadable texts, one thing had always perplexed her, the operatives' codes.

Could it be? It wasn't always messages. Sometimes they were symbols and formulas of the inexplicable. That's the part that plagued her. Calla wasn't sure if the symbols had been added later or when exactly the portrait was drawn.

The author had written the symbols backward, starting at one end and working her way to the other. When she had written a complete line. Calla imagined that when Hypatia had written a complete line, she had put a drop of ink from the pen, then continued writing it backward. She had then written the text, repeating this for another twelve lines.

Calla's guess was no one had ever read it. The only other place in the entire world with an equally perplexing script was far from here on a tiny island in Greece. The Phiastos disk.

Emiliano interrupted her thoughts. "There was a rumor that this woman practiced dark arts that no one had ever seen or understood." He then carefully wrapped the scroll and handed it to Calla. "That's when the accusations took over, leading to her unfortunate and untimely death."

Nash's words were spoken with caution. "People are afraid of things they can't explain or control. I take it, witchcraft is feared, or was feared much here in Cuba?"

Emiliano nodded. "Sadly, yes."

Calla understood. Knowing the scroll will raise questions, she needed to investigate further, but would it dig up fears and more questions about her heritage? Her past?

Emiliano watched her curiously. "It's only a story. It's

only a myth. And there are many versions to it at that. For now, enjoy it as a tourist story, and maybe you found something valuable, but if not, I hope you're enjoying your time in Havana. I guess we can all agree that it's a wonderful hand sketch, and it's beautiful. I think you are a worthy buyer. There's something that blends in this woman's eyes that mirrors yours," Emiliano said, eyeing Calla.

"How much?" Nash said.

Calla frowned.

"I'll take the equivalent of twenty American dollars in pesos," Emiliano said.

"Thank you," Calla said resigning.

She knew she couldn't leave the artifact here. Soon, she found the exact notes in her purse.

Emiliano hesitated. "I suggest you also take this that came with it," he said, fetching something from behind the countertop.

Calla observed the object in his hands. "A diary?" she said.

"It was delivered with the scroll," Emiliano added.

Emiliano handed it to Calla. "There's no extra charge for this. The woman who dropped off the items left immediately, and I have no way of contacting her. Perhaps you might have better luck."

Calla studied the diary and flipped through it.

She had seen that name before.

Mila Rembrandt. What was a top operative diary doing here? Myla's diary was famous among the operatives, a distant and usually absent cousin of Calla's. The diary was a long way from home, and also, what was it doing in Emiliano's shop?

Calla moved her hands over the velvety edges. Its worn

pages darkened by years of use made Calla believe it was Myla's studied book. Mila left nowhere without it. A tingle in her fingers intensified as Calla flipped through the pages. With a fixed gaze burning her eyes, calculations Mila had made, made her stop. Mila had tried to decipher the scroll herself but did not finish. Calla showed the pages to Nash, who took it from her hands.

"Did you ask whoever brought this here where they got this?" Calla asked Emiliano. "Where were they going? What did they say to you?"

Emiliano shrugged. "No, we never ask people who bring their stuff here where they are headed. I attract all qualities and manner of things. I remember her saying one thing, and she was in quite a hurry. When she dropped off these items, she said she had had them for years, but was moving and said she had read the scroll and was very saddened by its materials. That's why she wanted to donate it."

Calla scraped a hand through her hair, then gathered the items and turned to Nash. "I bet Mila knew what was going on."

They left the shop and hurried out of the marketplace. Mila was in trouble, but how had she even ventured out here? Why?

"Some story," Nash said. "Mila Rembrandt? She's the operative agent from Greece?" Nash said.

"Yes," Calla said, her eyes fixed straight ahead.

Nash turned to Calla and stroked her shoulder. "You know you couldn't leave that scroll there—two coincidences in one day. Two operative symbols encountered in one day. We have heard nothing in months, and then this drops in one day," Nash said.

"I know. Emiliano was talking about a gifted mathematician. You know who he was referring to?"

"He's a salesperson. That's what he does. He was trying to sell us the scroll."

"Eagerly. Oddly, he made sure we walked out with it." Calla said.

"Yes, I do."

"Nash," Calla said. "I need to dig deeper into Greek history and how it merged with Egyptian history. I think the woman who created the scroll was Hypatia. She was one of the most gifted librarians in the third century in Egypt. I can tell from the strokes and the age of the papyrus. It's a wonder it stayed in such good shape. Historians have searched for her work for years. I can't believe we found it in a flea market in Havana. But what I'm most concerned about is what the heck was Mila doing here with it?"

"I suppose you're right," Nash said. "Especially since she disappeared off intelligence radars more than a year ago and has not been heard from since."

THREE

The Gran Hotel Manzana Kempinski La Habana
Havana, 6:17 p.m.

I t was a long wait behind conference guests, but Calla was good at waiting.

She observed the signs in the Manzana Kempinski's lobby, advertising the conference that began that evening. Banners hung above the mezzanine floor. The International Conference of Human Genetics particularly interested Calla and had been her focus on this trip west. One particular scientific session had drawn her attention, the session on genomics. Maybe for once, this interdisciplinary field of science, concentrating on human genes' structures, would explain much.

How many nights had Calla spent awake trying to understand why her body's makeup behaved so differently to others? Perhaps the Norwegian doctor, Haldor Erikssen's sessions, examining DNA and genomes, would shed more light and answer her questions.

Losing a child had hit her core, more than she'd expected, especially a child she'd thought she'd never wanted to have. When someone targets your unborn child, she had to ask questions.

Jack had once put it like this; her and Nash's child had generated the ultimate human enhancement. He had said her relationship with Nash combined the best of humanity and science in a micro-cell from which life emerged. If sprinkled with an overdose of the love hormone, oxytocin, those genes would produce the ability to self heal, and God knew what else. All the symptoms of her so-called abnormality she had to keep from ISTF data files.

According to Jack, she alone carried the gene that could help humanity tap into one of the most significant genetic quests and brain mysteries on the planet. Though ultimately Calla had mistakenly thought she used one hundred percent of her brain, as most people did. What set her mind and genetics apart was her body understood how her brain functioned and could make the most of its complexity. There was still so much more she had to learn.

Jack had first told Calla of the conference after he'd revealed that scientists were still trying to understand human genetics, and her body alone would give them many answers.

"Hello, Senora Shields. You and Mrs. Shields are in our luxury suite on the penthouse floor," the cheerful receptionist said as they checked in. "I hope you enjoy your stay with us."

When they entered the hotel room, Calla's eyes inspected the bright overhead lighting, then moved to a large mirror next to the floor-length windows opening to a wide balcony overlooking Havana. The room overlooked Havana's center, and the hotel had spared no luxury for the contemporary décor. A pair of fluffy robes hung from a hook on the door. The scent of aromatic shampoos and soaps wafted past her nose when she reached for a glass of water from the bathroom. It would do for the night with its spacious high-ceiling charm.

Calla made her way toward the enormous bed with matching bedding and pillows as Nash dropped their bags on the fold-up luggage stand.

"Right. I'll get some work done on that pod before dinner," he said after inspecting the room, possibly for smart appliances that could spy on them.

Nash's years at the NSA had taught him never to be too lax about certain things; years in the military had done the rest. He was as vigilant as they come. He moved toward the tiled bathroom floors as Calla took Hypatia's scroll back to the bed and studied the symbols. What did the items try to communicate, and why did Hypatia's scroll so threaten Alexandria? Perhaps the world? Could this scroll have been in Alexandria at the Library where Hypatia had worked?

Calla sat across the bed and breathed hard. What had started as a relaxed holiday had suddenly turned sour with this scroll's appearance and Myla's digital diary. It had been agony to wait and read what was in the rest of the scroll after they left the shop. What specifically could the writing mean? Deciphering a similar ancient document, the Deveron Manuscript, an artifact they had worked on with Nash all those months ago, had taken much effort and the help of a codebook.

She had to find out. Could Hypatia, another woman ahead of her time, offer any insight into Calla's confusion that clouded her head? Perhaps too adapted to her curator's work at the British Museum, Calla's eyes came alive when she read the first few symbols using a deciphering app on her phone that Jack had created around the operative language.

Calla tried another tactic. She called a number. Her colleague, Safaa Wahida, in London could still be up with the time difference.

"Safaa, hi, it's Calla."

"Calla? It's been a while. You still on your sabbatical from the museum?"

"Something like that."

"Listen, Safaa, I have a question about Hypatia."

"Hypatia? As in the astronomer and mathematician who lived in Alexandria in the fifth century? What makes you ask about her?" Safaa asked.

Calla could not disclose she had the scroll until she knew more. "I am doing research?"

"Where?"

"In Havana."

"Havana? What has Havana got to do with Hypatia?"

"Perhaps that's what I'm trying to find out," Calla said.

"I see. What do you want to know?"

"What sort of written works do we know about her?" Calla asked.

Safaa sighed heavily on the phone. "Now, let me see. Over two thousand years ago, the Library at Alexandria housed an unprecedented number of scrolls that attracted several scholars from as far as Greece, but by the fifth century, it disappeared."

"How?"

"Some speculate they destroyed it in a fire, but the story is slightly more complicated. The Library was Alexander the Great's idea, who was once Aristotle's student and conquered Egypt. He wanted to build an empire, so to speak, of knowledge. He didn't live to see the museum, but Ptolemy the first of his successors did."

"Where exactly in Alexandria was the Library?" Calla asked.

"In the royal part. Ptolemy filled it with hundreds of scrolls and invited scholars from Greece to live and study in Alexandria, all expenses paid by him. Rulers wanted a copy of every book; scholars contributed many documents. They also made sure they copied every manuscript that came on ships in Alexandria and stopped the export of Egyptian papyrus."

"What about Hypatia?"

"I'll get on to her as I believe her story is connected to the Library. When all these books were being added, it was hard to find accurate information, so they devised an indexing system, the first of its kind to catalog books and knowledge. Many brilliant inventions and discoveries we think came with the age of enlightenment happened long before. For example, more than a thousand years before Columbus set sail to the Americas, a scholar of Alexandria, Eratosthenes determined the Earth was round and calculated its diameter coming in within just a few miles of its actual size."

Calla's voice trailed into nothingness. "I see."

"You should also know that Heron of Alexandria invented the steam engine a thousand years before the industrial revolution," Safaa added.

"You're saying that technology developed sooner than history tells us."

"Yes, and all thanks to the Library's indexing system on scrolls and papyrus."

Calla felt a lump in her throat.

Safaa continued. "But then Caesar invaded Alexandria

and ordered fire to be set to the ships in the harbor. Many believe that the Library caught fire too. Scholars continued to use it after that."

"How long?"

"It existed after that but slowly disappeared as the city fell to Romans, then Christians and Muslim invaders. Though Hypatia is just one of scholars, she was the first female mathematician whose records we have—a mathematician's daughter in Alexandria. Many disputed if the Library existed in her lifetime and if she used it. My theory is yes. The fire did not destroy the Library. It was removed, its collections were removed, and no one has seen it since. One more thing. Another fact we know is they killed Hypatia for studying the Library's ancient texts as those who came after saw the Library as a threat."

"Why?"

"Fear of knowledge brought that Library down, and the thought the past is obsolete is a dangerous one," Safaa said.

"Is it possible Hypatia wrote some of the Library collections, Calla said, eyeing the scroll on the bed."

"I believe she did."

Calla had not realized Nash was dressed and ready for the conference and dinner. The tux suited him and made Calla blush for a second as it fit nicely around him.

"Safaa, thanks. I have to go, but we'll have coffee when I am back in London."

She hung up.

"You okay?" Nash said. "You going to get dressed? Hey, this is our night."

Calla smiled and considered the scroll one more time. "Yeah. I can't get Hypatia out of my mind."

Nash didn't respond but moved to the other end of the

room. "Why don't you speak to Nicole and Stan? Your parents could help. I know they've resurfaced after you've not known them all your life. You can ask them. Nicole must've faced many conflicting thoughts about her life as an operative."

"I suppose you're right," Calla said. "Just have to find the right moment." She sprayed her arms above her, thinking. "Nash, do you realize we have the manuscript of one of the most revered women in history? She was talented. I can't believe that she made a self-portrait of herself centuries before anyone ever did. Nash, do you recognize something interesting about this portrait?"

Nash slapped his military-grade watch around his wrist. "Been thinking about it all day."

"You must be thinking what I am. Hypatia bears an extraordinary similarity to me, doesn't she?" Calla said.

"That hasn't left my mind. Listen, get dressed, I'll be back shortly. Got to meet an ex-colleague who's in town."

"Okay," she said as he left the room.

Why was it still nagging at her? Looking at the texts felt like thinking of a movie whose title you could not remember. It was something that Nicole, her mother, had once said that made her think of trying something new. Nicole's words echoed in Calla's head. She rearranged the gibberish and concentrated. Calla's mind functioned in ways science could not comprehend, and if minds so long ago created technology thousands of years before it came into being, perhaps she had a similar mind.

She rearranged each symbol and eliminated the odds.

Then she saw it as plain as day, the first lines translated in her mind.

> *Misused knowledge is like throwing pearls to dogs.*
> *It's not for those who are not ready.*
> *One day, you might be.*

Hypatia was writing to her future self. A message of sustainability. The words were not written in English, or any other language people understood, yet it became more natural to Calla. From the operative script on the page, she realized she had never studied a day of the language in her life. Why would Hypatia use the operatives' symbols, mostly rhythmic and more formulaic, to communicate this?

8:09 p.m

He couldn't figure out why Reiner had chosen the undercover restaurant and nightclub, one of ten around the world they used for crucial hideout missions.

Nash passed the line of people waiting outside the Havana club, waiting to be let in. They'd come early to avoid detection and pass security checks in the exclusive club for people with deep pockets. Reiner had sent him a special pass. When he approached the bouncer, he showed the access to the tall, beefy man.

The man nodded and stepped aside, letting him in as cabs dropped people off at the curb.

Nash scanned the popular place, popular among people who needed privacy and a damn good time.

A girl to his right took fees and stamped hands with the club's logo. Nash and Reiner had agreed never to meet casually. They only met when they had a mission to complete, or one or the other was in trouble. Though Nash was glad that Reiner had called him, what the heck was Reiner doing in Havana? It looked like he'd be in this part of the world for the next few days.

Nash checked his watch as he crossed up to the bar and ordered a beer. He turned around, scanning the room as loud music and people screaming in each other's ears to be heard failed to distract him. Nash only had about an hour before he was due back at the hotel to take Calla to the conference.

And there he was.

Reiner had changed little. Nash crossed the bar's length, fighting his way through sweaty couples as they took to the early night dance floor until he reached Reiner's table.

"Not here," Reiner said, smiling. He rose and nodded to Nash. "This way."

Nash followed him through a VIP area of the club until they got to the back. Another bouncer stood at the barriers, catching any stragglers that might hope to pass on to the private areas. He nodded when he saw Reiner and let both Nash and Reiner gravitate to a quieter bar area in the secluded place.

Nash sank into a seat opposite Reiner. "Not like you to meet here."

"Had to talk to you. I only got the intel this morning."

"What intel?" Nash said.

"Have a few scores to settle here, but that's not why I wanted to contact you."

"We agreed to meet only when there was a job or when

either of us was in trouble. It's too risky, and we blow our covers. Why the SOS card? What's going on, Reiner?"

Reiner took a sip of his beer, then scanned the room. "This is a safe place for us to talk. I know the owner, and I've helped him out several times. I wanted somewhere we wouldn't be disturbed."

"Now you sound cryptic, Reiner."

"They've revived the KJ20 Ops, Nash."

Nash moved back in his seat. His jaw dropped for a second. "What? The KJ20 Ops are in operation? They closed down the unit when you and I left. They're back? Why?"

"Guess they needed their assassins. We probably pissed them off when you and I quit. Their best," Reiner said, taking another sip.

"It's not me. They lied to us. Reiner. They said they were training us to be elites for the NSA. Don't know, but I thought it was an op unit to bring analytic to talent skilled mission operation. It was anything but. They were turning us into assassins."

"When we left, it destroyed their plans, Nash. Not everyone was happy."

"That I know."

"Think somebody's up to something," Reiner said.

"Then it's even more important that we're not seen together. Why do you suppose they regrouped the unit?" Nash asked. "How did you find out?"

Reiner drew in a breath. "Remember the bunkers, we destroyed billions worth of data, but I've been monitoring it. It's been active for about seventy-two hours. First, I ignored it, but I can't anymore."

"Something's up then. We were on that training for what was it? Eighteen months in some of the worst places on the planet, learning how to survive in heat, cold, ice, wind, rain, you name it. They wanted us to fly every machine, know every computer. Fight any hand to hand combat there is out there and be savvy in every tech-related area, so we could what? Spy on not only our neighbors but citizens in our own country. Well, heck, I quit and put that skill to good use. Like now. Like helping the operatives. Calla's life depends on it." Nash took a sip of his drink. "What are they up to?"

"That's why I needed to see you," Reiner said. "Wanted to warn you to watch your back."

"Yeah, you too, Reiner. We're here for each other," Nash said.

"I want you to be careful because you have one thing very attractive to the KJ20 Ops. Nobody can fire a gun like you, and nobody can lead a mission in the field like you. They will want to destroy you. You were their best. You also have what they want: Calla."

Nash nodded slowly. He understood. He ran a hand through his hair. "I know, Reiner. I fell in love with her. Someone killed my unborn child. But I'm never going to give her up to anybody. I made that choice a long time ago between the life that they trained me for and the girl I love."

"I'll do what I can. You know that Nash." Reiner said.

"I know."

"There's one more thing," Reiner said. "I saw him."

"Saw who?"

"Hank. Hank Murphy is alive."

Reiner's words almost left him speechless. "Hank as in Hex? What? That can't be right. You and I saw that man die virtually in front of our very own eyes. It was the fire in Korea. The experiment went wrong. It was his idea."

"I haven't seen him," Reiner said. "I see his work on the

secure network. It's been active for about thirty-six hours now."

"You and I went to his funeral. We spent time with his family. He shouldn't have done what he did, and we lost him. I tried to save him."

"I know, Nash. You're like a brother to me. We went through hell in the KJ20 Ops, and they turned us into assassins. Come on; we decided we were better than that. It'll not surprise me if something's cooking. It worries me that Hank could be a life. I think you and I may be a target if the KJ20 Ops are back."

International Conference on Genetics and Genomes: 9:20 p.m.

Calla had no intention of choosing sides in the debate about normality until she was sure who would win. Conference lights faded as Nash and Calla took their seats in the grand hall. Several panelists took to the stage after Dr. Erikssen had given his argument on genomes, genetics, and development, focusing on how human forms developed.

Images long forgotten were still ingrained in Calla's memory. She had been sixteen at Beacon Academy, and one day after class on biology she had split up a fight started by a bully on a timid classmate. Calla responded as any self-respecting girl. Being different was welcome and should not have been frowned upon. Calla's mind recalled how she got into a fight. It was instinct. She'd always had a natural intuition and ability to protect those not strong enough to defend themselves.

Calla had nearly put the girl in the hospital. Then she had discovered she possessed extreme strength and ability in physical fighting. Later, she felt unwell, unsure what had made her sick and resulting in her going into a coma. Six months followed and not a single memory from what had happened to her in the hospital.

Dr. Erikssen finished his presentation, and the panel disbanded. The next speakers took to the stage. When Dr. Erikssen took his seat in the auditorium, he was only a few rows away. He observed her, sitting next to a woman whom Calla presumed was his wife. They kept eyeing her. When she scanned the rest of the auditorium, she felt more eyes on her. A man sat only a few rows behind her, eyeing her and Nash.

The conference ended and they rose and ambled toward the restaurant where dinner was getting started. Organizers laid several festive tables out for the guests for the dinner event. As they were leaving, Nash took Calla's hand, helping her in her V-neck, floor-length chiffon evening dress adorned with sequins.

Nash stopped, stunned to silence as a man his height and build moved in front of them.

"Miss Calla Cress, we haven't been introduced. Call me Hex. Hex Murphy. Shields, a pleasure to see you again. You clean up well, not like the mud swamp in Changnyeong, where I last saw you." Hex slid in front of them with a sneer. "Charmed."

Nash's eyes burned into him. "Excuse us."

"I seem to possess an interest in genetics as much as you," Hex said.

He gave Calla a seductive stare, then tipped his head and strode out of the auditorium.

Calla felt a chill along her bare arms, unsure what had just happened as Nash gently placed an arm around her, and they took seats at a quiet table. The last one.

As soon as they had sat down, Dr. Erikssen and his evening date joined them. "I hope you don't mind, but this is the only table left in this private dining area. Would it be a problem if this couple shared a table with you?" a waiter said.

"Not at all," Nash replied.

Calla nodded and tossed the older couple a smile. They appeared to be in their sixties, and judging from the tans on their skins, they'd enjoyed the sun in Havana. As the waiter served their first course, the couple pinned eyes on Calla.

"You're an extraordinarily beautiful woman," Erikssen said. "I hope you don't mind me saying," he added with a quick nod in Nash's direction.

Calla drew back, making herself smaller.

"What brings you to this part of the world?" Erikssen began his small talk.

Nash took a sip of the Chateaux Cheval Blanc Merlot he'd ordered for them. "Cuba has much to offer the wayward visitor."

The older man nodded, and Calla noticed the high-tech watch he wore. "And you? Is it the conference, or do you have other genetics related interests in Cuba?" she asked.

This time the woman answered. "My husband and I are here doing research and were invited as presenters at this conference. We may be geneticists, but we're equally keen on archeology."

Nash raised an eyebrow. "What's your focus? Your speech didn't go into details."

"I'm particularly interested in how genetics developed over centuries. I also look at the oldest civilizations globally and compare them to see if there's any crossover, the way genes developed across several fields," Erikssen answered.

"I see," Nash said.

By this time, the waiter had served the main course.

The older woman set down her fork after chewing pensively. "Harold's also studying Hypatia's influence with mythology and the connection to this part of the world."

Calla bit her lip. "Hypatia?"

"Yes," Erikssen responded. "She was quite a mathematician and an astronomer, not to mention her views on Greek mathematicians' works. Hypatia had incredible mental ability and I will prove it. We have been observing a particular myth related to a similar Cuban woman who lived around the same time."

Calla stopped to listen intently.

Erikssen took a swig of the expensive wine and wiped his lips with a serviette. "Many know her as a mathematician and as someone who had an interest in astronomy. Few know about her life. She died under mysterious circumstances. It's been written that a raging mob killed her. However, I believe something else was at play in her life. I want to prove that something in her genealogy continues to this day. Rumor has it she had a following in Havana. Perhaps they saw her as a goddess of some sort. The rumors are prevalent here."

"You've no idea," Calla said, more to herself.

Erikssen raised an eyebrow. "When I heard that centuries ago, a group of so-called witches fell in love with her mind and teachings, this raised my interest."

This time Nash set his fork down. "Witches?"

"While my theory is still to be proven," Erikssen said. "I

think that genetic engineering started way before current history."

Calla and Nash exchanged looks, and both stopped eating.

"I believe there's a civilization, I've been researching up in the Pico Turquino mountains here, that progressed in genetic work, centuries before it became a science. They created interesting developments. And I believe Hypatia had something to do with it."

Calla turned to Nash but said nothing.

"What exactly makes you think Hypatia was, as you put it, different? How are history and myths related to such a forward-thinking science like genetic engineering?" Nash said.

Erikssen set his fork down and clasped his chubby hands together. "My research has revealed that certain enhanced abilities exist in genetic mutation and haven't been tapped into."

Nash sported a smug expression. "Can you kindly explain tapped into?"

Intrigued, Erikssen moved forward, pleased with giving them the details. "For example, unbreakable bones. My research has gone as far as looking into the DNA of archeological remains and evidence in Cuba and worldwide, Greece, the Mediterranean, and others. My research shows that a mutation gene in some people is super strong and resistant. Two children I have been researching have also exhibited such behavior."

Calla shuffled her feet, not wanting to hear more. The science was coming increasingly to the foreground of geneticists' research. She wanted Erikssen to stop, but curiosity about what else he had found made her twitch forward. "What behavior?"

Erikssen straightened his back. "There's another line of research I'm following," he said. "One focuses on rare, super muscular ability. We've seen the alteration of certain muscle genes, allowing one to develop stronger muscle development than the average person. These people don't appear that much stronger than the average person but looks can deceive. They're built with titanic strength and develop muscle force without having to do much to keep it up."

Calla turned to Nash. "Shall we order dessert?"

"You're not much of a dessert person," Nash said, smiling.

Calla could see that Nash was enjoying the story. For now, she would listen even if she didn't want to.

Nash then sensed her discomfort. He leaned over and motioned for the server. "So, you say that there are certain people who possess a genetic mutation in their genes that allows them to perform things differently than the norm?"

"Yes," Erikssen said. "It's quite revolutionary. We've researched this for nine years, and it has been much of the focus of what we do."

Nash took Calla's hand under the table. "Where are you based?"

"Well, I usually work alone and independently, but I've recently been hired by a corporation based in London."

"Corporations are interested in this work?" Calla asked.

"Absolutely. I'm supposed to be keeping this under wraps, but I feel I can tell you," Erikssen said, glancing at his wife, who had remained quiet for the last several minutes.

"Come on, Harold. I think you've done enough; these

people may want to get back to their dinner, and you've taken quite a lot of their time," she said.

"Well, I don't see any harm in it," Erikssen replied. "As I was saying, another organization, one I'd never heard of, but I did some digging. Five governments fund it, which makes it great for my research. There's more money to go round. The organization is called the International Security Task Force, the ISTF by insiders, and I think it's based in London. I'm due to go there in a few weeks to present research they've commissioned me to look at."

Havana Pier: 10:21 p.m.

Calla had kept the conversation with Erikssen alive in her thoughts.

Too alive, perhaps.

How could Erikssen be working for the ISTF without Calla's knowledge? Had they instructed him and given him work to do on her physical ability test? Who organized it?

In the evening heat, her dress pinned to her skin, and she wiped her brow. A vast expanse of ocean lapped the shore as they strolled along the beach. As a party went into full swing, a bonfire's crackle made them smile, but something was bothering Nash, and it wasn't Erikssen and what he'd said.

The gentle wind whipped Calla's hair into her face, and Nash brought the locks to one side with his warm hand.

"Talking to Erikssen made me recognize the importance of the scroll. But also, Nash, who at ISTF asked him to do this research and why? He knew a lot about ISTF. I didn't want to go into it at all, 'cause I wasn't sure what he knew and what he didn't," Calla said.

"I'm not clear what his connection is with ISTF, but when we get back to the yacht tomorrow, let's look into it," Nash said, encircling his arm around her waist.

"You, okay, Nash? Who was that guy, Hex? he mentioned Korea," Calla said.

"We trained together. He's trouble."

"Should I worry?" she said, smirking at him.

"Not at all. In fact, he should fear you."

She shrugged and kept walking along the docks. "Why Hypatia? Especially now that we have the scroll. Here's a man who's doing significant research on genetics. Why now?"

"Don't we all wish we knew?" a male's voice said from behind them.

They turned.

Hex stood glaring at them.

Nash broadened his shoulders at the ready and circled a hand around his gun as they observed the intrusion to their evening. Hex marched toward them and fixed his gaze at Calla. Without even turning to peer at Nash, Hex had a way of making sure they heard him. "Really, Shields, Pulling out a pistol?"

Nash aimed with speed and precision. "This can go one of two ways. Where've you been? You don't look so well."

"Doesn't matter," Hex said.

The dark circle of the muzzle commanded Hex's attention. "I'll make this simple. See that baby over there," he said, tilting his head in the Scorpion Tide's direction. "She comes with me and the scroll. For months and weeks, I've tried to locate this magnificent floating wonder of a yacht. It never appears on any radar."

"The Scorpion Tide?" Nash continued directing his gun, not wavering.

Confidence was one thing, but ego was another. Calla set a palm on Nash's shoulder. "Let's go," she said.

His body lunging sideways, Hex's fingers clawed for a weapon. The firearm's gaping eye bore into them. "You need to remember who I am and who I know. And that we can lose your Marine here. You belong with someone like me," Hex said.

"Belong is a very grown-up word. It would be best if you didn't use words you don't understand," Calla replied.

"Make me," Hex said.

"Goodbye," Calla said and made a move to walk away.

Nash assessed the situation. He hesitated, then put his gun aside, his eyes not leaving Hex for a single moment.

Then Hex moved. Faster than a human could react, Hex's hand swept around Calla's neck and crammed the gun to her temple.

Nash twisted the pistol clear out of Hex's right fist. The gun dropped, discharging a shot. Nash came upon Hex's pistol arm, thumping down hard with a thud. Stunned, Hex attempted a retaliation. Nash jerked Hex's hands upwards and kicked the weapon out of the way.

Calla retrieved the gun off the ground.

"You don't learn when to walk away," Nash said.

"Not until I get what I came for," Hex said, gasping for air under Nash's firm hold.

Nash threw him to the sand, and Hex wiped blood from his jaw.

"Think I'll keep this," Calla said. "You really shouldn't play with guns."

"Your clock's ticking. I'm just a messenger," Hex said, rising slowly.

"Unlike you, I don't believe in spook stories," Calla said.

"This is one spook story you'll beg to wake up from," Hex replied then rose fully and dusted his sleek jacket before turning his back to them and heading in the other direction.

They watched after him for several moments.

"That man has a fascination with you," Nash said.

"He has a strange way of showing it. Let me see, and he also has a huge bone to pick with you," she said, grinning.

Calla pushed the hotel room door open.

A pistol exploded hunting death, and bullets were its words. Then the infiltrator who'd delivered fury from his handgun took off through the window.

First, her eyes traveled to the floor, where a damaged vase lay shattered in countless pieces.

Nash charged past her and hunched by the window. Second, her eyes shifted to the window. In a flash, the figure receded behind the open blinds.

When Calla reached Nash, the figure dropped down the hotel's outer facade on a zip wire. Calla searched through the window and hooked eyes with a drone beaming at her. The buzzing drone could not fit through the window's opening. Still, its eyes prevailed on her before it soared skyward.

She breathed once. They swung around, eyes scouring each angle of the luxury suite. Calla's eyes enlarged as she shifted toward the bed and the safe by the bathroom door. "The scroll!"

FOUR

Day 3
Monte Carlo, Monaco
8:55 p.m.

They had to work together, so they would have to learn to get along.

Andor stepped onto a magnificent 533 feet long yacht boasting a movable steel hull with an aluminum superstructure. As the crew helped him on the boat, he noticed a man sitting at the end of a white leather set of seats.

A party's sounds on the upper deck above him drew his attention as kitchen noises from the galley and ice cubes clinking against glasses alerted him.

He was on time and strode toward the guy he recalled only by the name of Slate. So, this is what he was doing now —enjoying the rewards of serving the former head of ISTF— whose family had served Mason Laskfell's for decades.

The man had cleaned up nicely with a face smooth, and a

clean-shaven bald head. A long neck jetted out of his muscle shirt bordering arms with a myriad of tattoos on either bicep. As he approached Slate, the wind whipped his hair, and the waft of fresh seafood brushed past his nose.

"You always appreciated an entertaining party," Andor said.

"At least the bill is on you," Slate said.

"Not at all, my friend. Yet I wonder what you did with Laskfell," Andor said.

Slate's head tilted back, and he gazed up. "You asked for a lifeline, and I offered you one."

Andor narrowed his eyes. "At what cost?"

"We'll get into that later," Slate said.

He offered Andor a glass of champagne as he took a seat on the expensive furniture. Andor watched him with amusement. "You clean up nicely. What happened to Laskfell?"

Slate compressed his lips. "Since you've been in prison? He outstayed his welcome."

Slate then led Andor to his private office downstairs.

Andor welcomed the cold drink down his throat and realized that he'd only dealt with Laskfell. Just what had Slate Mendes done with the former head of ISTF, who had made life easier for him? Would Slate's terms be reasonable? Laskfell had made Andor's life more manageable and offered him much leeway when they disagreed on ISTF matters, but the new Cress woman would make it doubly hard. What price would Slate Mendes require for that busted laptop he'd left with Laskfell? They hadn't always agreed. But this was not the time for broken relationships to be reconstructed.

'Slate', his preferred code name to ISTF's '*Purple Snake*' issued at the organization, was fitting. They took seats in his office. Before Slate had become the much-loved errand man for Laskfell, Andor had been the closest person to him. It seemed this man had made his way into the circle and taken his place. He would look to deal with him later. What he needed right now was more important than anything else. He required the data on that laptop if Scope could complete what he had started.

Slate fetched a package from the drawer by the bar. "So, all you need is marked in a black data box in an offshore account."

Andor advanced closer. "I was told that I would find the laptop here."

Slate resembled a predator ready to pounce. "Files on the head operative aren't that easy to come by and were wiped off that machine and placed in a data box. Not even Laskfell, God rest his soul, had that expertise. I've delivered where he failed."

Andor tossed him an uncertain look. "That'll remain to be seen. What do you have for me?"

Despite his impressive size, Slate's powerful body moved with the sleek gracefulness of a hunting cat. "What you requested."

Andor's eyebrows scrunched lower on his forehead. He realized what he had asked for was not here. Just where on earth was it?

Slate linked his hands together and stretched them over his head. "You're wondering why we have chosen not to bring things on board. Wisdom has taught me it is best not to do a face-to-face exchange. It can get messy. I have scars to prove it."

Andor rose from the supple leather chair, breathing in quick gasps.

Slate watched him as if ready to follow. Andor knew he was not off the hook, but he would not hang out any longer for what was not relevant.

"Not so fast," Slate said.

Andor flipped round. "Why the heck not?"

Slate dropped a box on the table, an ISTF data bank. Andor had seen these before. For Slate to escape with one of those databanks from ISTF was something else. The man had been escorted ungracefully out of the building.

Slate gave him a quick glimpse up and down. He remained bold in his assessment. "The codes to the data are in there."

Andor sipped his champagne, then reached for the box. "I'll expect both candidates on this."

"Naturally. What good is Calla Cress without Nash Shields? I know them personally. You won't be disappointed when you collect your goods. My men will make sure you get to where you need to go," Slate said with a growing smirk on his face.

Havana, Cuba: 5:21 a.m.

When Calla opened the door, her throat closed. She wished they had stayed on the yacht and not gone into Havana.

"Calla?"

She drew back breath before speaking. "Yes?"

"Calla?" Allegra said when Calla picked up her cell phone.

Allegra's voice strained. "I have one of my agents here. We brought Radya onto the case after you and Nash left. We have developments in Istanbul to which you need to pay attention."

They had given Calla and Nash a new room after hotel security had profusely apologized and vowed to find the culprits.

The scroll had been in the room safe. First, Erikssen had mentioned Hypatia at dinner, and then Hex's appearance at the conference. It all seemed too coincidental. Hex had also threatened them for it. Besides these two, Emiliano would not be interested in such a manuscript. He had been so eager to get it to Calla. No one else knew they had it. Or did someone? What was the scroll worth? And to whom?

Calla sank onto the bed as the air conditioning hummed.

Nash pushed past her and swept the room for bugs. He was careful not to trigger any, had they existed. They would not stay long anyway, only until they could arrange their trip out of Havana.

Calla's mouth felt dry. That Allegra was back at ISTF meant serious business. She had led ISTF in transition when Laskfell had left. Allegra had an accolade of problem handling behind her. She had done much for the government over the years. Her work with the Foreign Service and just about every London intelligence office made her someone vital to the UK state.

"Allegra? I didn't know you were back at ISTF."

"I'm looking after the London Cove. Calla, I need to make sure you have everything you need at ISTF. I'm afraid they've dragged me back in because I have a history with this sort of cipher and case."

With Allegra also manning the London Cove, a secret headquarters for the operatives, it meant the operatives were onto it. They needed more reinforcements. Allegra would never go to the Cove if it weren't necessary.

"What do we have here?" Calla said as she propped herself upright.

Though her mind wanted to concentrate on what Allegra said, she felt chills after the scroll had disappeared from her room. Calla turned as Nash moved toward her and stood against the window. She turned the phone onto speaker mode.

The intruders had only taken the scroll. Made of papyrus and in four sections divided into twelve lines, Calla was certain each stood for something. The writing was old and faint, written by one of the most educated women of her time. Why was this of all scrolls not written in Hypatia's native language but with symbols the operatives called their own? Very few knew about it. Calla was sure of it. No history record had it listed, as many scrolls from that era had not survived. Safaa believed the Library might not have been eradicated. Calla would not tell the others until she was sure where this scroll had come from.

It was dated and in such excellent condition, which only meant that someone had purposefully brought it to Cuba to be forgotten. And what about Mila and her diary? What did Mila know about it? Could she have not given the scroll the deserved attention it needed?

Allegra's voice brought Calla back from her thoughts. "Calla, Radya Zaher, a capable agent I recently hired within ISTF and with high credentials, was sent to Istanbul to escort a prisoner Andor Heskin back to Britain. She's a competent agent formerly with MI5. Andor escaped before she could get him out. He must have had some help, but we are not sure who yet."

Calla swallowed hard. "Did you say, Andor Heskin?"

"Correct. Thought you would recognize the name," Allegra said. "You might recall, Heskin was a former contractor at the UK Space Agency. We learned he even knew your mother several years ago, before you were born. We wanted Heskin in London for questioning regarding a classified case, the Pythagoras Clause. However, he never made it. He's escaped. We're still investigating how. To make the switch legit, I had to use ISTF to investigate, but Heskin disappeared before I could."

Calla squished her eyebrows together. "The Pythagoras Clause? What's that?"

"An operative file opened to study future predictions that continue to be made with accuracy. The case, unopened for sixty years and nicknamed so by the operatives, comes from a perplexing script written on a scroll. They believe an Egyptian scholar successfully found the missing commentary in Arithmetica, penned by no other than Pythagoras, curiously written in an ancient operative script. Whatever it said, the operatives believed it was too dangerous, so they vaulted it away until it was stolen about 40 years ago. The scholar penned her findings in that scroll, and it has since been called the Pythagoras Clause. The scroll was taken from the operatives at the same time and had not been seen since."

"You mean Hypatia? The Egyptian scholar from Alexandria? Her scroll?"

"Yes. Calla, you must get back to London. Heskin has had you marked since before you were born. Your mother made a deal with him; he's cashing in as we speak."

"Me?" Calla asked.

"When you deciphered a code three years ago that put him behind bars, you started a war with him. That code and the program he was working on were his life. We thought we had dealt with everything, but apparently not."

"Allegra," she said, watching Nash. "What so particular about this prisoner Andor Heskin?"

Nash's jaw tightened as he halted his activity and listened.

"The prisoner and all information will be passed on to you, but I'm afraid I don't think your hotel room is secure. You're not safe in Havana."

"You can say that again. We had a break in," Calla said.

Allegra's voice raised. "A break-in?"

This time Nash spoke. "Allegra, who knew of Heskin's release outside ISTF?"

"You miss nothing, Nash. That's just it—no one except myself and the team I put together for Radya. What I'm worried about is what Heskin knows about Calla. Your mother, Nicole, has a history with Heskin. She was trying to erase a past debt. A few days ago, she broke into Scope Technologies, a corporation run by Heskin's daughter, Zodiac Baxendale. Nicole received intel, and we're not sure yet at this point where the intelligence came from. Nicole's last conversation was to Mila, citing that a numerical code runs an application invented by Scope Industries. We understand that your mother successfully found the scroll and was in communication with Mila. We can't reach Nicole or Mila and assumed you had had word from them."

"No, I haven't yet. But they've never been that communicative with me. You know that."

"Nicole must've taken the scroll from Scope Industries. We can't reach her. What we know is she tried to reach you, to get the artifact to you."

"How did Scope get the scroll?"

"One guess," Allegra said.

"Laskfell," Calla replied, her heart sinking in her tummy.

Having gathered enough, Calla had to share what they knew so far. "Allegra, a shopkeeper, sold the scroll to Nash and me yesterday. So, yes, we had it until last night when it was stolen from our hotel room. We found it in a flea market shop our captain recommended we visit. The man there said that someone had dropped it off. I think it was Mila."

"I might wanna check what Delgado knows," Nash said.

"You think your mother found Delgado?" Allegra asked.

"Or, Mila," Nash replied.

"Okay. Somewhere along the way, we lost contact with her," Allegra said. "Scope Industries is working with Hex Murphy, contracted by them to go after your mother."

Nash's lips stretched into a thin line. "We ran into Hex. You say he has thugs after Nicole Cress?"

"Initially, I think that was his target, but I believe he followed Nicole to you. Nicole must have led him to you."

"Do you have any more information on Zodiac Baxendale?" Calla said.

"Not much at the moment, but I have asked Radya to look into it. Zodiac Heskin Baxendale dropped the Heskin name several years ago when the corporation went public on the stock market and when Heskin was arrested."

"Tell us about the application," Nash said.

"We believe Scope Industries is developing a sophisticated bioweapon disguised as a social media app to collect data, and God knows what else. They are up to something big and are quite keen for ISTF not to uncover Pythagoras's Clause. Scope uses math and theories in the cipher in Hypatia's scroll. Heskin must have decrypted it or is close to finishing what he started almost thirty years ago."

"And still no word from Mila," Nash said.

"Mila was working on the case for the operatives out of a cove in Washington. This is where your mother was headed when she went missing, and that's when I ordered Radya to extradite Heskin from Istanbul. He's the only other person we know connected to the scroll. We believe Scope involved Heskin in the app's development using his knack for engineering and researching spacecraft engine weaponry."

"Heskin also worked for the former Red Fox at ISTF, Mason Laskfell. He must have conspired with Laskfell," Nash said.

"Correct. Calla, I'm sure you know Hypatia was a prospective student of Pythagoras. From what we learned, before Mila dropped off our radar, was Hypatia's scroll detailed a cipher, Pythagoras's Clause. We haven't seen it for centuries and it forms the basis of future weapon development. We don't know what sort of weapon. I think that's where you come in, the Decrypter," Allegra added, "You're the new Red Fox."

She wasn't yet, at least not until she had done the test.

Calla breathed hard and stared at Nash, who now looked more uneasy than he had when the phone call began. As a curator, there were many levels to this. First, an important ancient scroll was out on the loose. Now it also seemed that the scroll had more significant mathematical and technological value. Interestingly, Hypatia had not interested many mathematicians, and many had even said that some works she commented on were not necessarily her own. Yet Hypatia remained an influential female figure in history, brutally murdered.

There was more to this than Calla had first thought. She

remembered the self-portrait Hypatia had drawn on that old piece of papyrus paper.

Why?

What did a centuries-old cipher have to do with a very sophisticated app?

———

The grand yacht, Scorpion Tide, had parked in Havana waters for two days now. It stood towering above Havana, with its tall masts and its military-looking facade, magnificent by every standard.

Calla and Nash paced to its boarding point. They had to walk down along the pier until they got to the edge, where a small boat waited with one of the crew members they had alerted.

"Nash, do you think everything Allegra said about the scroll is true?" Calla asked.

Nash turned around. "I don't know, but Hex needs to be watched."

An icy emptiness entered her heart. "Scope seems to be at the center of this."

"Yes," he said, his face grim. "Heskin wasn't an easy one to find, I remember. His cipher was more numerical than most ciphers we've worked with."

"Makes sense. The guy was a highly paid researcher at the UK Space Agency," she said.

Nash stopped when they reached the end of the pier. "He was a prized programmer there, wasn't he? But what is it he and your mother agreed on or not?"

"I don't know," Calla said. "I called my father to find out, and he did not know. I'm learning that though my parents worked together they were strangers and as secretive with each other as the work they did with MI6."

Nash was about to vault onto the tiny boat and then stopped. He took her gently into his arms and kissed her on the forehead. "Calla, when does it stop?"

"It doesn't until we find every single operative technology was stolen from the coves. With the operatives having been here a long time, God knows what else is out there."

Nash was content being away from it all. He'd been enjoying himself for the last several days, and she wasn't sure she liked the lines that continued to grow on his forehead every time she mentioned the operatives. They were their worst nightmare since Nash and Calla had been together. Somehow the operatives wove their way back into their lives.

"Do we want to do this?" Calla said.

"Nothing will ever hold or tie you down. Think you have to. We have to if we will ever be free of the demons that follow us," he said, his face grim.

They got onto the compact boat, and the crew member churned its engines as it moved toward the Scorpion Tide. The man was part of a crew of six, hired to operate the yacht. After Hex's threats, Captain Delgado had reported no more from Hex to the Scorpion Tide except a woman who had come looking for Nash's services. He'd also mentioned Emiliano was someone he had known for years and it wasn't unusual for him to stock many artifacts.

Nash followed Calla.

"I can't get her out of my head," Calla remarked.

"Who?" Nash said as the boat approached the rear of the Scorpion Tide.

"Hypatia bears a remarkable resemblance to me. It's just driving me crazy," Calla said.

"Calla, don't let what Emiliano said sink into you."

She nodded. "You're right."

Once they arrived on deck, Calla and Nash headed to their office. Delgado handed him a tablet when they boarded the yacht. "Says she needs security."

Nash took one look at the picture and profile. "Zodiac Heskin? Don't know her and I don't do corporates."

Delgado nodded. "Yes, sir."

"That's the woman from Scope Technologies Allegra mentioned. Why would she want your protection, Nash?" Calla asked.

"Don't know yet," he answered.

A secure video conference connected them to Allegra in London at the ISTF headquarters.

In submarine mode, undetectable to any technological communication globally, Scorpion Tide started its engines toward Florida. From Miami, they would catch the British Airways overnight flight to London, and Delgado would operate the yacht behind them.

The call picked up in a few rings. Scorpion Tide's firewalls were the best thing technology could provide. Calla initiated the conference call when Allegra's signal came in. She revealed that they had gotten a good look at the scroll, but not enough to unearth its mathematical value.

"Allegra, we had the scroll in our hands less than twenty-four hours ago. Captain Delgado has just disclosed Mila Rembrandt contacted him, explaining who she was. Delgado knew of Mila when we hired him. The suggestion to go to the flea market where Delgado knew Emiliano had been hers. Mila was trying to make sure we got to the scroll," Calla said.

"Right, let's get onto Heskin," Allegra said. "We've always monitored communication he's had to and from that prison, including any with his daughter. There's one communication we intercepted referencing a purchase of materials from the Laskfell Corporation. If we turn to the Scope app itself, there are certain things that you need to know. Scope launched its app ten months ago," Allegra said. "At one point a decade ago, Heskin was a financial hacker that was convicted of stealing twenty-six billion from the world IMF. Radya and the accompanying ISTF agents, who went to release him, followed all the Turkish prison protocols. And when they got to his cell, the prisoner was gone. Heskin vanished."

"Like the Mind Hacker?" Nash said, raising an eyebrow.

"Like Mason Laskfell, the Mind Hacker, our former Red Fox of ISTF," Allegra repeated. "Heskin disappeared into thin air, and we have only ever seen that possible with operative technology Mason used as head of ISTF, and when he was on the run."

"Is Heskin an operative?" Calla asked.

"Not one we know of," Allegra said. "We can't verify it yet. His research has been going on for some time, and we don't know where his funding came."

"Then somebody with access to that technology got it to him," Nash said.

Allegra rubbed her chin. "That's just it. How? That tech research and scroll had been locked in secret cove labs when we eliminated the Laskfell."

"I thought operative labs are impenetrable? How is it possible?" Calla said.

Nash crossed his arms. "I've learned never to ask that question again."

Her shoulders dropped. This situation didn't look good. "Point taken."

"We've seen it before," Allegra said.

Calla had hoped they'd dealt with as many operative technologies out there. It seemed this wasn't the case. Not now. Would they ever?

"Strange," Nash said. "Heskin has been in prison for what is it now, three years? And then in all this time, this is the first time he's ever wanted to escape?"

"We've also noted something peculiar about the Scope app," Allegra said. "Actually. It was Jack. He flew in this morning and is on his way. He spent his flight investigating the app and how it works, with particular attention to how it's affected its customers. Using customer data makes horoscope predictions and others relating to a customer's behavior or future stance. Nine times out of ten, its prophecies have been proven to come true. Some horoscopes that have been predicted by this app are making millions for the company, and they are not entirely without side effects."

Calla ran a hand through her hair. "Surely, it's all nonsense. No app can predict anyone's future."

"It's the most popular app among teenagers and young adults, Calla," Allegra added.

"So, we have some technological seer on our hands with a father who's crazy about math and ciphers? I mean, surely Allegra, your skepticism is as good as mine. Sometimes people will believe anything. Horoscopes offer people comfort, I guess, or some sense of false security, no?" she added.

"Not like this, Calla. I'm sending a file to your screen," Allegra replied.

They opened it.

"Look here at these instances," Allegra said, bringing up three cases on the screen. Nash and Calla scrutinized them.

"Fascinating stuff!" they heard a male voice say.

"Jack?" Nash said as Jack entered the room behind Allegra and shut the door.

Jack flashed them a brilliant smile. "You two need to know when to book a vacation," he said, taking a seat next to Allegra.

"Good to see you, man," Nash said. "Although I was hoping a little later than sooner," he said, smirking.

"This first case has come in from Seoul in South Korea," Jack began. "I've been looking at three cases in total—three girls who received the same application on their phones. The app asked them to make a certain large deposit of money to reach a superior future prediction level. Then the app threw them, out of the app environment, into a private operating space that sent a shock to their brain. These three girls have now fallen into comas."

Allegra mused before speaking. "All three cases with the same prediction took place in three different cities. There's one in Buenos Aires, one in South Korea." Jack scanned his cell phone. "ISTF has identified one more person here who's surfaced in Vancouver."

FIVE

Day 4
Heathrow Airport, 10:21 a.m.

Nash and Calla's ISTF pick up was waiting in the designated car parking area reserved for dignitaries. When they approached the sidewalk, they moved toward a dark Range Rover.

Taiven, a Middle Eastern man, stepped forward. "Good to have you back, Calla and Mr. Shields."

A square-faced, dark-haired individual, Taiven held his shoulders erect and always gave her a generous smile. He was young, perhaps thirty-five at the most. Ice-blue eyes topped his striking appearance. Minutes later, they drove off slowly into Central London.

Calla, obsessed with thoughts, scrolled through her tablet, struggling to remember that case that Nash and she had worked on three years ago. It was one of the first cases they had ever done together.

"I recall Andor Heskin now," she said. "I recall he had a very different look to most."

"It was then that I first learned you could work with symbols," Nash said. He took her hand. "I could see how your mind worked and how fascinating it is."

If she were right, that's when she'd fallen for Nash. Looking at them now, she could not believe that they had made it together. The things she had put him through, yet he remained committed to her. She remembered the scroll and some words she had unscrambled.

> You're magnificent...
> I need help.
> I am different.

Just what had Hypatia meant? Why did she think she was so different? Could she have been telling them more about the operatives? Why had she written this scroll? Most scholars wrote manuscripts to chronicle their teachings or disciplines they wanted to pass on in those days, but this was a personal diary, and what had been Myla's involvement?

Then Hex had appeared. A point she wanted to bring up later with Nash.

Had Hypatia felt vulnerable, like Calla did at the minute?

Calla thought of the things she'd read in the scholar's scroll. Hypatia had written her secrets here and her most sacred discoveries, but why was it unknown to the world?

Also, something fascinated her about Hypatia's presentation. Four sections, and the most dangerous, Pythagoras's Lost Commentaries on Mathematica. The world believed it had lost them forever, the Pythagoras Clause.

Hypatia had written like a teenage girl. It all seemed like gibberish. Calla had studied languages for a long time. She knew that a cultivated woman like Hypatia would have never written texts in such a teenage way, but perhaps she was digging into her scared soul just as Calla felt at the minute. Maybe she felt vulnerable, and she had had a moment. But what about the sophisticated cipher next to all the girlish gibberish? Had Hypatia's analysis been for the world to see?

Hex had been bold enough to come into their deepest parts and steal the scroll. It had to be him. How had Heskin escaped while on ISTF's watch? Who had let him out? A convict on the loose now and a cipher, she could not unravel.

Not yet.

Calla remembered seeing circular mathematical designs, nothing that would lean itself toward language. The numerical characters Heskin left in his cell also pointed to something.

What?

"Calla," Taiven said. "Hypatia was a remarkable person, just like you."

"You think she was an operative? I mean, it's possible."

A ghost of a grin tugged at the corners of her mouth. "I'll let you find out," Taiven said. "As you always do."

She never could know what Taiven was thinking.

Allegra lived alone for many years in an exceptional villa in West London, except for Taiven, the butler, and Pearl, the housekeeper. Taiven had served her since Calla had known Allegra and was often seen walking two chocolate Labradors. He had never been one to share much. He was just a good guy to know. Taiven was great in times of need, but he was also a teacher, teaching by letting you figure things out. He only stepped in when you needed him, and Calla had gotten used to it.

Calla took a heavy breath. "I think she was an operative in a world that was never ready for her. And because the world was not ready, it was easy for them to brand her a witch. Which would happen to me if I'd lived at that time."

This remark produced a raised eyebrow from each man in the car.

Calla continued. "Hypatia understood genetics and its connection to geometry and how it altered science. She knew how to make the most of her world. She knew math, astronomy, and science; all the things one requires creating a future predicting app in theory. Don't you remember what Erikssen said, Nash? He, too, was a geneticist. I am sure he knew more about Hypatia. Or perhaps she was the inspiration for his study. And then again, whether it was she who was the operative or someone she knew, this is how she could create a cipher that is puzzling the technology world at the minute. What if she was studying the operatives? Or was one herself."

Calla was now obsessed with the information she was reading. "Hypatia could take math and connect it to so many phenomena in nature and turn them upside down. And that's what she did. Unfortunately, the things that Hypatia could do freaked people out."

Calla rubbed her arm. Hypatia had tapped into somebody's secret and was too paralyzed to chronicle for the Library. They put her to death, and perhaps it wasn't just for her beliefs and teachings; maybe it was also for what she knew, and the world was not yet ready to learn it. Hypatia could have worked out why Calla could defy gravity and explain it all in math and science. The world wouldn't have understood it. Much like it could not understand Calla. Science was being called the unbelievable, and the fantastical was witchcraft. Little did the world know these were scientifically calculated formulas crafted centuries ago— altered genes making the impossible possible. The operatives could adjust anything science understood at will. Many called it fantasy—technology in its highest form, transforming history and the future.

A thought dawned on Calla. The world didn't know genetic engineering started thousands of years ago and had been implemented. It had been hidden from humanity. They had branded it a dark science. What did that make her? A woman whose genes had been paved by science developed millennia ago for a future none had seen.

It was not science versus sophisticated technology. What many didn't understand was science developed at a quicker rate than man was ready to embrace. The operatives knew this and hid it from the world, just like this scroll. Now, thousands of years later, it could give an answer. Yet someone had gotten to it first.

Andor Heskin.

They pulled into the driveway of Nash's London residence. Taiven handed her a set of keys. "Your Maserati is round the back. You've been upgraded, and we left the other one on Scorpion Tide."

"Thanks, Taiven," she said.

Calla didn't know how time had passed on the thirty-minute journey, her thoughts caught up in what she knew about Hypatia and the scroll curators like her had missed documenting. How could Hypatia's scroll be the most-wanted thing in intelligence circles, especially now that

Andor had mimicked its terminology to create a bioweapon through an everyday app? Hypatia's scroll was a treasure.

When they walked into the front room, Nash turned on his laptop. "I want to try out this app."

She raised an eyebrow. "The horoscope one?"

"Yes."

"What did Jack say it was called?"

"Scope of Everything, or just Scope."

"Appropriate. What is it about its features that has fascinated the teenage mind and soon, most of the young adult population?"

"I guess anyone would be curious to know their future, but there must be something more than just a desire to know if you will pass an exam or be hired for your next job."

Nash lit his laptop and waited for it to boot. "Jack sent the cipher from the prison to my phone, and Calla, I don't like what I will see."

He found an NSA software he usually used to help him unravel ciphers. Heskin was talented in what he had written, but somehow not intelligent enough for Nash's NSA analysis software. Nash had an instinct, almost a knowledge, about why people would want to create ciphers in the first place. That's where he always began when he looked at a riddle, and at this moment, it was no different. "Calla, Heskin is sending you a personal message. We have to believe that the cipher in prison is intended to tell you something, and just you."

SIX

Day 5
The Mall, London
11:56 a.m.

Scope app cases cropped up in three locations with rumors of other unconfirmed ones. Calla smoothed a hand over her hair. ISTF had five key representative states. She never imagined taking a job at the British Museum would bring her to the organization. Headquartered on the Mall in London, ISTF was one organization one didn't want to mess with. Here she had a life involved in cyber espionage and encrypted cases that puzzled her government. Jack and Nash often led most missions with her, and Calla would pick a handful of agents working in technology, the field, and communicate with governments where necessary. She would have it no other way.

Calla had worked in the organization for over eighteen months and it felt like she had been nowhere else. As the new

Red Fox and the head of ISTF, various things gave her privilege. Calla's assistant provided them with a quiet room in the ISTF building.

Jack strolled in, patted Nash on the shoulder, then gave Calla a quick peck on the cheek. "Well, that's one way to cut short your holiday. Sorry we've had to bring you guys in."

"Where's your girlfriend Marree?" Nash asked Jack.

"In Hawaii with her family, I presume?"

"I thought you brought her to London to get a firsthand look at ISTF."

Jack took several moments before responding. "I will."

"All good on that front, Jack?" Nash asked.

"Yeah," Jack answered.

"He's just not used to letting someone in," Calla said, clipping his chin with her fingers.

"You're not allowed to read my thoughts," Jack responded with a smirk.

"You know I can only do so in heightened danger. None of that is going on here," Calla said.

Jack projected his laptop on the screen. "What we know from the London Cove is that Hypatia's scroll had been in the operatives' archives many decades before it went missing. The clues are incomplete. Though the file shows Hypatia's name and speculation exists at the Museum of Cairo, no other documents survive. The app takes material from the scroll. What we don't know yet is which information, and to what degree."

"Thanks, Jack," Calla said. "When the others get here, we can't tell them what we know from the London Cove and the operatives' involvement. I, for one, want to keep the operatives out of ISTF for now."

"Gotcha," he said.

Several others joined them, Tiege, Calla's most trusted operative, Radya, and a handful of other administrative staff. The task group would look after the retrieval of Hypatia's scroll and Calla had handpicked each one. Though ISTF wondered about the operatives, Calla made sure they knew little about them.

Jack continued. "What's the connection between the cipher, that was in the Istanbul prison, the cipher that appeared in the scroll as Calla remembers it, and now a group led by Hex Murphy, whom we know is working with Scope, who wants it."

"Remember," Nash added. "We're dealing with highly knowledgeable people who know how to cover their tracks well. They've taken something from the past and made it relevant here. We have a dangerous app, which at this point we've not advised the government to pull from circulation until we know more."

Jack chewed the end of his pen. "If you have data, you will ultimately win."

"Come again?" Calla said.

"One of the world's most influential entrepreneurs and CEO, Zodiac Baxendale, leads Scope. Her file at ISTF is clean and was passed on by MI5."

Calla lowered her head. She had not told the group she knew Zodiac, whom she was sure still went by the name of Zodie. She was a striking woman of mixed-race background and was the only other pupil in Beacon Academy Secondary School with a closed history. Adopted like Calla, there was plenty they shared, and if Calla recalled, much she didn't want to have in common with Zodie.

Jack rose and paced the room. "Scope has tapped into a genius way of focusing in on customers. They live and breathe by data, and information they've collected on individuals for years. Web usage goes up 2,300% each year."

"What cases are they collecting?" Calla said.

"All of it," Nash added. "At the NSA, we know that data collection is a business. Companies that track every single way a customer behaves will eventually own that customer's future."

"Exactly," Jack said. "Scope is a laboratory that has been studying human data for decades. They lost money in the early days but found various forms of funding. It would shock you to learn how predictable human behavior is once you follow their patterns with statistics and information."

"So, if you have data rights, you're king or queen, and Scope has nailed it," Calla added.

Radya raised her hand. "But how did Andor Heskin escape?"

Jack smiled almost to himself. "Using data fed to him about the prison, and the people who work there."

"But we monitored everything," she replied.

"It's impossible to monitor all data when you can't accommodate it. Scope can collect and manipulate data with their application," Jack said.

Jack turned to a new slide and observed the room. "After Calla informed me of the story that Emiliano the shopkeeper shared in the Havana flea market, I did some digging around, and there is a myth in Cuba that continues Hypatia's story. Strangely, her story traveled there. The entire world hunted for Hypatia's scroll. I'll leave it up to you what you believe is written in the scroll. From what Calla has decrypted from memory, certain mathematical elements have never entered math and science until recently. The scroll has used some of the most complicated quantum physics formulas and theories that man is even still trying to figure out."

They turned down the lights in the room, and Calla stood to address the task force. "Secrets written in Hypatia's Lost Commentary on Arithmetica, penned in the scroll, are now what makes the app functional, almost like a secret use of math," Calla said. "The scroll itself is twelve pages long. It's on papyrus. I unraveled all twelve pages that added up to a length of about three meters; however, I only had the scroll for about twenty-four hours."

Nash watched everyone in the room. He had a keen way of being observant and knew when to ask a question and when to offer insight. There was something behind his eyes that didn't give direction to what he was thinking. A keen NSA agent highly experienced in analysis, there was something he wasn't saying or perhaps something he was still working out. Calla would ask him later.

Jack took a seat. "Can you remember anything more on the scroll?"

"Just bits and pieces," Calla said.

She would not tell them yet. No, she couldn't tell them what she had read. He paid his words. The words about being different, about almost not wanting to live because she was different. Hypatia, one of the most advanced minds of her time. Why was she so scared to live? For now, this information would remain with her until she figured it out herself. Calla crossed her arms. "Okay, will continue this later. Can I have you all leave the room except for Jack and Nash?"

When Calla was sure they had all gone, she breathed hard and sat on the edge of the table. Her eyes glazed and pierced into the men's. "Jack, what do we know about the three women who used the Scope app. Are there any common symptoms among them?"

"They have all been moved to intensive care in various hospitals around the world. The last intel we have on the girls is that they weave in and out of unconsciousness, and sometimes resort to mumbling gibberish. Their brains are in much danger."

Calla bit her lip. "We need to help them. But there's one other thing I wanted to say that I couldn't say in front of the others. I was in such a coma at age sixteen. At least that's what I believe. I have a six-month gap in my life and only know this because I accessed my medical records from Beacon Academy. I've never found out what happened to me and have been thinking about this. I wonder if Hypatia was an operative or engaged with one."

Nash raised an eyebrow. "What do you mean?"

She felt her tummy drop. "It's not just any scroll."

"Okay?" Nash said.

"What if this is a new hypothesis she couldn't share with anyone and felt she needed to write it down? Beside the missing commentary of Arithmetica, what if the scroll was a notebook of her most feared discoveries, and what if she was an operative? Most operatives hid their secrets and discoveries in words and ciphers. We've seen that in other ancient manuscripts."

"Then we need to find out," Nash said.

Calla moved round the room. "Remember, there are four sections to the scroll. Four connected sections. One depicts an astrolabe design. When you were talking just now Jack, I thought about something. The Pythagoras Clause. And what it is. Hypatia refers to an astrolabe in one section. Hypatia designed plane astrolabes. These instruments used stereographic projections of heavenly spheres, showing the heavens on a plane surface. Astrolabes calculate date and time based on the positions of the stars. They also predict where the stars and planets will be on any date. Scope's agenda is two-fold. They want to control individuals but also the future of the planet. What would make ancient math relevant today? Hypatia must have referenced a future event in Space that benefits Scope."

"You're onto something, Cal," Nash said. "Wasn't Heskin previously employed at the UKSA."

Jack snapped his laptop shut. "You're right. I think it's time we visited Scope and perhaps got a brief tour of their technology labs."

The Federal Reserve Board of Governors
Washington DC, 2:27 p.m.

Zodie's hands were sweaty. She waited, then scanned the office where they had asked her to sit. Her eyes moved to the photographs behind the desk—a few family ones. George Shields was not a family man. She wondered why the vice Chairman of the Federal Reserve of Board of Governors had agreed to take this meeting. Why would he be interested in Scope Technologies? That was his matter, and she would not dwell there.

Her eyes moved to the only family photograph by the Chairman's desk. The rest were official photographs. This one photograph had a man in it—a man in uniform. He was the most handsome man she'd ever seen, broad shoulders with lips she itched to touch. It seemed in that uniform of his, if she was right, it was a Marine Security Guard uniform, the formal wear used at US embassies. She studied the face: gray eyes, full mouth.

A noise at the door stirred her as George Shields made his way into the office. "Forgive me, Zodie Heskin; I was tied up on official business."

Zodie had to make an impression here. "Some would say my interest is official," she said, clasping her hands together and setting them over her crossed legs.

George shook her hand firmly. "I've made all the arrangements. I've been watching what Scope has been doing and find it remarkable."

"Yes, it would seem you would, but then again, it would take only a fool not to understand the benefits Scope brings not only to nations and individuals but also to the future of our world."

"I see."

"As the arrangement goes," Zodie said, handing him a file with the official contract. "Your share as being a major stakeholder is firm. And as you requested. There'll be no connection, or your name mentioned. We will tie it to an offshore account you've specified and the company you've incorporated. My office will deal with the rest of the details."

"Looks like you've thought of everything," George said, looking over the files. "You're going to be a wealthy woman when this is all said and done."

"I don't need money. My interest goes beyond that. Science interests me and where the world is going to go."

"Then tell me what we will do with your father, Andor Heskin, when this is all done? He's wanted in a few nations around the world. I've made sure that they do not intercept him at border points where Americans have friends. He is free for now. But should you mess up any of the work we're doing together, believe me, the US government will not hesitate to go after him."

She smirked. "Understood."

What did George Shields want with her father, anyway? The man had greed written all over his face. He wanted to be more influential than the United States president, he just did not want the title. It was clear, he wanted what was coming, and he wanted to be there before anyone else did.

"Our business is done," she said. "May I ask who that in the photograph behind you is?"

George turned around. "The picture? I like to think of him as my son."

"Is he in the military?"

"Oh, he's in a lot of things. I don't know it all."

"I see."

"He's the only man I know who turned down a job to serve the American president in the Secret Service. With skills many crave, he used them to train with an exceptional unit of our government, but that was some time ago."

She stopped in her tracks. "Is he still doing what he does?"

"Why?"

"I have jobs for men like him, and perhaps I could use someone with his skills. If that is Nash Shields, I tried to find out more about his services not too long ago."

"He only works for those he knows, and if you're smart enough to find him and by recommendation only, you'll be lucky if he takes your phone call."

"Surely you can reach him. Perhaps my offer would be something he would like to look at. I need the best men out there. If I have the best people protecting Scope's interest, it benefits you too."

She watched the smile on George's face fade. He was taking the bait and reached in his drawer then pulled out a blank square black card. He set it in front of her.

"What is this?" she asked.

"If you can read what's on that card, then you're worthy of his services."

Zodie examined the card. Not a standard business card. It was one flat sheet of metal, but she'd worked enough with technology. She spun it upside down only to discover a little chip. These chips existed in few hands and you could only reach these people by accessing a specific code at a certain time on a unique system. Few of those machines existed, but she knew how and where she could find one.

ISTF Headquarters, London
12:20 p.m.

"Ms. Cress, we've had an interception at Heathrow Airport," Calla's assistant, Scarlet, said with a faint tap at the door. "ISTF agent Finley, stationed at Heathrow, is on the line. There's something that requires your attention right away."

"What sort of interception?" Calla said, her head tilting.

"I don't know, but I understand you need to take this."

Calla reached out and took the phone from the executive PA's hand. She set her ear against the receiver that the aide held out. "Ms. Cress?"

"Yes? Who is this?" Calla said.

"ISTF Agent Finley. Your office instructed we alert you should anyone on your wanted list cross UK borders. I expect the individual we have might interest you."

Calla signaled to the men. "Who is it?"

"Andor Heskin. We believe it's him, although he used a different name. This is something that you should look at. About thirty minutes ago, Heskin crossed UK borders. We've not let him through and have him in custody?"

"Thank you, Agent Finley. We'll be there in thirty minutes. What flight did he come on?"

"Says here he took British Airways Flight 553 from Nice."

Calla thought hard. Heskin was a clever man. Why would he take a commercial flight when he was being watched, after that run he'd pulled at the prison? Why would he risk breaking through security where he would be stopped?

From the picture the agent sent through, he hadn't tried to even conceal his identity. He hadn't tried to camouflage his appearance and used what must've been a fake passport. She rounded to Jack and Nash. "Heskin. They've apprehended him at Heathrow Airport. We should go."

Nash rose. "Wonder why he's made it easy."

Calla collected her things. "Must have something to do with Zodie."

He lifted a brow. "Zodie?"

"Yes. It's a long story. I went to school with her."

Nash placed his gun in his holster and closed his laptop. "I look forward to hearing more," he said with a grin. "Okay, let's go."

When they strode into the arrival terminal, Finley met them and escorted them to a containment area. Three border agents restrained Heskin in a holding room at Terminal 5.

Heskin, with hands in cuffs, did not respond to their presence.

"Ms. Calla Cress, we're glad that you're here. We'll give you ten minutes to interview your prisoner, after which he will be taken into custody."

She nodded. "Thank you."

Heskin raised his eyes to his three visitors. A shade of blue they made one almost trusting.

His passport was on the table for Calla and her colleagues to examine. She picked it up, and she looked at it.

It was Swedish. She flipped through the interior pages. It seemed he was going through London on his way to Stockholm.

"Did the south of France not agree with you, Mr. Heskin, after Turkey?" she said. "I understand Istanbul provided superior hospitality in prison."

Andor raised an eyebrow when she set his passport down.

Calla continued. "Mr. Heskin. What's your business in the United Kingdom?"

No response.

Nash watched Heskin, his eyes narrowing. "And while you're here, will you be visiting a Ms. Zodiac Baxendale, CEO of Scope Technologies?"

That remark made him stir. Yet he said nothing. He didn't blink.

They could read nothing from his face. Calla threw her hands in the air. "Right, looks like we're not getting anywhere."

As they were about to get up and leave the room, Heskin

set a gentle grip on Calla. Nash and Jack tossed her a concerned look.

"Your name is Calla Cress, isn't it?" Heskin said, pinning her hand down to the table.

She nodded. "I may have arrested you for cyber criminality, but we've never met."

"We've met before. We met virtually," he said.

Calla understood. They had actually never met face to face, but Heskin had met Calla online in a cat-and-mouse game she'd used to intercept him. She'd found him in a dark net and had obstructed his communication to his server. That's what had given him away.

Calla removed her hand from Heskin's grip.

He didn't move his gaze once from her, but then he pivoted toward Nash. "And you, Mr. Shields. You have an interesting background. I wonder if you'd like to know a little more about your future?"

Nash's lips stretched into a thin line and she hit him with a quick glance. He was not a superstitious person, far from it, but something about Heskin's way of saying 'your future' caught Nash's attention.

Heskin continued. "If I were you, I'd be cautious, especially with my family. Then again," Heskin said, "You protect my family, and I'll save yours. What's coming for yours is a lot worse than anything that could happen to mine."

Calla took a deep breath. "I know Zodie. Clever and manipulative."

Heskin lifted an eyebrow. "Adopted like you."

"Conniving like you," she said.

He moved back. "Misunderstood, like...you." Heskin gave them a sneer. "Let's not forget you two follow identical paths.

Left as infants—operatives without knowing it and futures dangerous to you both. Luckily, I've protected her all along. Who has watched over you? No one. I made that prediction twenty years ago when your mother came to me begging to spare your future. The world now knows just one language. Bytes and codes."

Calla could not let Heskin get to her. "My mother did no such thing. If I remember, her file says she took the very thing you needed to hold the data world hostage."

"Did she? When the time comes, ask her why your digital footprint and genetics are more dangerous than you assume. Ask her why the Pythagoras Clause will come to haunt her and you."

She inclined her chin. "The Pythagoras Clause?"

He sneered. "The future is a lot closer than you understand."

7:58 p.m

They spoke little on the way back to Central London, having spent the more significant part of the afternoon with the border agents and planning Heskin's transport to an ISTF holding prison.

It had been a deep prediction and harsh words for Nash to hear. Anything touching his new family touched him much more than anything else. Though Nash had never been close to family members, including his father, anything relating to the people he cared about was something he did not take lightly. People in his world meant a lot to him, and especially after she had miscarried his child. He took any aggressors and people who had come after them seriously. That thought and experience were still very raw for Nash.

An evening breeze slid from the open car window through Calla's hair and ruffled her cotton shirt. She glanced over at Nash as he reclined in the car. He was a million miles away. "Nash, I wouldn't think anything about it. Crazy people surface all over the place once they find an operative technology they can manipulate. The operatives created those technologies because they thought the world would be better with them. That's all Heskin has done. He has somehow tapped into future telling technology and has manipulated what it says and controls people's emotions. Don't let him get to you. We'll get to the bottom of this. If you think about it, those three girls we've learned about are the low level of what I believe the app can do. There's so much more, and it's a lot more dangerous. We can't let him be a distraction to us."

Light spilled from the homes' windows as families headed indoors, and afternoon light drained from the sky. The car pulled into the avenue outside their West London townhouse built over 22,000 square feet. It had everything they needed —security, privacy. One of three of their homes, all off the radar, it incorporated superior, smart technology security systems. Here they could be themselves. The house stood within a tightly secured, modern compound with private security and a myriad of concierge services.

Calla, a minimalist by nature, had only asked for a collection of museum-quality artwork she and Nash had bought around the world. The British Museum had also let her keep artifacts, some of which they could not display. Situated over five floors, the space was inviting, elevated and bright, and decorated with top quality. When she was at home, Calla spent more time in the indoor pool and solarium than she admitted. The physical toll on her muscles demanded it.

Calla followed Nash, who had remained quiet since leaving Heathrow. She would order a special dinner for them. She went straight to the balcony window and threw it open and took in the views that overlooked the River Thames.

For someone who didn't watch TV, Calla scrutinized Nash as he moved toward the table and turned on the large flat screen on the wall. It was the distraction he needed. Noise that could drown out his thoughts.

He wasn't doing this to shut her out. He was doing this because he didn't know what to do. A Marine and a man capable of not only saving many lives, hers included, but Nash was also someone important and secretive people called on to protect them. It weakened him. He could not protect one of his own.

Calla ordered dinner, and the takeaway arrived within half an hour, and Calla set up two plates of teriyaki salmon with wok-fried quinoa. Calla turned the TV down as she set the two plates on the table in front of them and took a seat next to him.

He shot her a grateful smile and dug into his salmon. Had there been any noise from the TV, it fizzled in the background as Calla searched his deep, gray eyes.

Nash ceased chewing and peered at her. "It's not what he said. It's what this means for us. I didn't think this at first, but Scope's technology is more dangerous than we think. I looked a little closer at the data transmitted on the girls' phones. How had Scope compressed such an extensive amount of data onto a typical user's phone and manipulated someone into a coma? I understand why people fall for such predictions and such behavior because they want to have a say and understand their future. Human beings are resistant to change, and somehow, I want to be too. Still, I also want to be resistant to predictability. That's what bothered me at Heathrow. People want to be in control and understand what will happen to all of us."

"It scares me too, Nash. But we must stop it. Young people are suffering like the three girls. Somewhere deep inside of me, I believe this is just the beginning, and not having the scroll terrifies me. We're walking into this blind. I, for one, don't want to know the future. I want what's here and now. We need to live in the present and don't think our brains and our minds were meant to live in the future. That's why the present is the only thing that counts, a gift we've been given. It's very unnatural to live and change the future or the past."

He gazed into her eyes. "Well, I guess you now know why I've wanted you to forget your past so we can focus on your future."

"But now about Heskin. Do you believe him?"

"I think he means harm."

"The only way we can move forward, Nash," Calla said, "is to remain in the present. If we're going to find out what Scope is all about—the future is their focus, so their blind spot must be the present."

"You're right, but what else is Heskin hiding? He has you marked, and it couldn't have just started a day or two ago. For crying out aloud, Calla he had your name in his prison cell. He has marked you." Nash frowned in puzzlement. "What was it that Heskin said? He spoke about the world using one common language. I think he meant AI and social algorithms.

After all, that's what the three girls had in common, a social media app that destroyed their lives. And this one language would dominate the world...data. Isn't that what he said?"

"Yes, and I know that, but I think we're going to have to..." She stopped mid-sentence.

The TV drew her attention when the top of the hour newscast began. Calla reached for the remote and turned up the volume. A news presenter started an interview with representatives from Scope Industries.

Nash followed her attention to the news bulletin. "The media are onto it now."

What seemed impossible was now becoming a reality. In the Far East, China, and several of its neighbors, seven, had declared a unilateral programming language, speared by unbeatable data mining science. Member countries had signed a unilateral deal. This was the beginning. Heskin had been right. He had made this same prediction.

The phone on the table rang. Calla picked it up after two rings.

It was Jack.

"You guys listening to what I am listening to?" Jack said.

Calla clipped the phone on speaker mode. "Jack, yes."

"This is what Heskin was talking about."

"A unilateral programming language is one step to disaster," Nash said.

"In a recent meeting I had with colleagues at MI6, we found out this wasn't due to be signed for several years to come. Also," Jack said, "what bothers me is that this was something that he predicted twenty years ago."

"Is that how long he has known?" Nash asked.

"Yes," Calla replied. "He is tapping into the sensitivities of not only individuals but the vulnerabilities of governments. A united language means more than just being able to communicate with unique and similar data protocols. It means moving to a one world system. It also means other treaties come with the deal. This is only the beginning."

Nash set his fork down. "Scope's monetizing the app at the expense of vulnerable people and governments."

"Jack, stay on the line," Nash said, "We'll need you to bring in your tech to look into this."

With the phone on speaker, the news broadcast continued. A Scope Industries spokesperson refused to disclose how many further governments had now signed on with the corporation. For now, seven governments in the Far East had worked with Scope Industries.

Calla bit her lip. "If these governments are signing agreements with Scope Industries, that opens room for more collaboration, wanted and unwanted in the tech sphere and data mining. It'll create a data block of countries that will share information and alienate others."

"What's the fee?" Nash asked.

"Each has put in several billion dollars. If Scope controls all the contracts in these countries, it can use countries against each other too," Jack said. "Individuals are only the testing field for global behavior prediction. Now countries are the targets, but they don't know it."

Calla felt sick to her stomach. Regardless of the predictions, Scope's data would give each country only the information they paid for with the agreement. That was not the full picture, even if it involved hostilities against another state. She pushed her plate away. "That's information any government could pay for."

The newscaster continued interviewing Scope's spokesperson, and she then presented Ms. Zodie Baxendale.

Calla's throat closed as Zodie appeared on the screen, her lips tight, her face resolved. Zodie was as she remembered; glowing caramel skin, curly locks to her waist, impeccable dress taste topped with a beauty of mixed race contradicting the scowl on her face.

Frown lines marred Nash's brow. "She accessed my contacts. Not sure how. Came looking for security. I said, no."

Calla's tongue felt too thick to form the words. "What's she up to?"

They listened to the newscast.

"We're excited to offer our technologies not only to individuals through the Scope social media app, but now we have a corporate version called Scope Corporate. Today, we're pleased to announce that the Scope app can be extended further given the technologies it uses, but with sophisticated mechanisms for governments and other prominent organizations that may wish to use its features. We're particularly excited we can offer this to governments. And we're happy to see that a prediction made by my father several years ago has now come to fruition. This is further proof that Scope works so accurately," Zodie said.

"What's your secret? And how have you been able to hone a sophisticated technology to predict futures? What else can you tell us? Because when I look through all these accounts on social media, people, rave about your app," the news presenter asked.

"Users are content with Scope's predictions, and unfortunately, we're unable to share our patent technology, but all the regulatory bodies have approved it."

"And your stock is just flying through the roof."

"It's our company policy never to reveal our secrets as any other company. The right agencies check everything in the right government bodies, and there's nothing to fear but the future. Once you know the future, you can control it. That's what we're selling to corporations and individuals alike, and with today's announcement, governments can also take advantage of our services. We're operating within the law. And we're excited that governments and individuals have found a solution in our products."

Calla turned off the TV and began a slow pace around the room. "We need to find Hypatia's scroll. I wonder if it details more on Pythagoras's Clause. If I can read it, it may just give us more on the Scope's AI."

Nash crossed his arms. "The scroll was only taken thirty-six hours ago. Scope has been planning its technology for a long time."

"But they had it. They must've had it for years. I know my mother took it from them, and it pissed them off." Calla said. "I must remember everything I can about that scroll, so I can decipher it."

"Like you, I guessed the scroll has an algorithmic detail that threatens Scope," Jack said on speaker.

Nash kept his tone calm, steady. "Don't know about you guys, but I think that Ms. Zodie needs an ISTF visit."

SEVEN

Day 6
The Mall, London
8:10 a.m.

J ack scrambled into the ISTF building, silent for the time being. He had to recover the key he had left behind. Once inside, he took the elevator to the 3rd-floor labs and swiped his card in the door reader.

He looked both ways. Good, no one was here. His locker was at the back of the room. Moving swiftly, he scanned his iris through the scanner to open the lock. He brushed his stomach to relieve the knot of fear coiled inside him. The key was still here, and the back exit would be best at this time of day. Nobody bothered much to go the back way unless it was the cleaning or the kitchen staff.

Jack found his BMW in the parking lot and headed toward South London. The drive was about an hour long. He had always wanted to have a place where he could be at peace to research his work. God knew he had spent so much time and energy building this place, but that an algorithm like Scope's was out there made a jolt of panic rip through him.

His warehouse wasn't on the books. Jack had asked Calla if he headed up ISTF technology services, he needed a place where government eyes would not look, and operative eyes looked neither.

He left the car several hundred meters away from the warehouse and shuffled up a stony path that led to a forested area. Shrubs and overgrowth concealed the concrete structure accessed through a steel door with a reader. He used the key to unlock it. The steel moved to the left, and as he made his way inside the low-lit space; he took in a powerful stench coming from the back of the room.

What was going on?

His eyes moved past long countertops with deep sinks and gas valves. Then they scrutinized his labeled totes holding smaller supplies. As he made his way past boxes, he had left sealed several weeks ago, he held his breath. Something wasn't right.

Yes, the laptops he had ordered were all here. Once he moved past the front room, the back room was where he preferred to work. Giant computers lined one wall, blinking furiously, connecting to his private satellite and secret doors to Internet activity. His only way of monitoring anything governments around the world knew about the operatives or corporations.

There was much that Jack needed to make sure was in line. Technology had always been something that was a threat to users, and Scope was just one example. He didn't like what Scope had done to the girls in Argentina, South Korea, and Vancouver.

By creating safer technology, bringing his and ISTF inventions, and those of the operatives, to work collectively was the only condition in which future advancements could thrive. It was his life's work to tackle these colossal problems. *Damn it!*

How was he going to make sure they would eliminate Scope's dangerous algorithms? Where were its secure servers hidden? Just what was it doing to the human population through an application on mobile phones?

The other night when Calla had mentioned there could be a code, the Pythagoras Clause that could arm Scope's technology, he had researched the problem thoroughly. For three days he talked to people in his field of quantum physics technology. He had analyzed the math, the code in every way, and no matter how often he went around the problem, he could not see how Scope told the future so precisely. They also had a further threat. Just what was Scope doing in Space?

Heskin had first worked at the UK Space Agency. He'd been through the safeguards and regulations. With a copy of the filed Scope patent on his phone, Jack sank in his work chair and dissected every clue he could read about how the technology could work. And nothing stood out. There was nothing here.

The closed online group of investigators he'd put together had come to the same standstill. The ongoing discussion they'd had at ISTF around the algorithm had yielded nothing.

Someone was following him online, following his every move—a copycat.

If he did not find the answers, how could he even relax and start his relationship with Marree? He'd lost Calla to his best friend and that territory he could no longer pursue.

He looked toward the door then progressed to the end of the lab and glanced over his notes one more time. Something was missing. He illuminated the seven monitors above his desk, each displaying real-time data tracking and visualizations. He brought up a security software.

It fired up. Then stopped.

He attempted a reboot.

Nothing.

He rose and moved to the server cabinet. Stepping back, the hairs on his bare arms rose.

They had cooked his server, every wire firing smoke. His life's work, gone.

Sloane Square, London: 8:26 a.m.

Zodie slipped her hands around him. One side of him was sexy, the other cold. He had been her fantasy for years. Hex deposited kisses all over her bare skin.

Every nerve ending quivered. She then rose and moved to the floor-length windows of the penthouse and shut the windows. A light rain had begun that morning, and she pulled the white sheet over her body.

Was this what she wanted? Was this what she had expected?

Zodie turned around when she heard Hex move out of the bed. Erikssen had done a fine job as she watched Hex drop his legs onto the floor. He stood tall. He was every bit, man. Yet every bit machine, one side of him powered by Erikssen's robust artificial intelligence structure.

She bit her lip. The accident in North Korea had been severe on him. She'd seen the reports herself. They had said he'd been fortunate to be alive.

Hex slipped on a pair of trousers, then proceeded to where she was by the window. Eyes on her body, he set a steady hand on her naked shoulder. Tender and sensual, the hand performed its magic as it massaged. His lips touched down on hers; perhaps the only feature humanity had left him. Moist and sensuous, she returned his kiss but for a second. His arms graced her back. Ice cold.

The titanium connected to his exposed shoulder, down to his wrist, mangled with what was left of his skeleton and body tissue. Yet, she needed him.

"I love you," he said.

She smirked. "Do you, Hank Hex Murphy?"

"You know, I do. I've been crazy about you for as long as I can remember."

"Yet, you were foolish enough to get in an accident that bloody blew half your body off."

He pulled back, a glimpse of hurt in his left eye. "I told you it was the only way for them to promote me. They were other agents in the KJ20 Ops. They were better than me. If I didn't watch my back and prove myself, I wouldn't amount to anything or go anywhere in that organization."

"Yet it didn't work. If I hadn't helped you, they would have left you to die. You wouldn't be in my bed today."

Hex moved closer, and he pasted his lips on hers.

She squirmed against him. The KJ20 Ops training field

had turned a man into a half-breed; it seemed carefully balanced between man and AI. One side of his lips felt warm, the other side cold. It was the way with him. A half man who could warm her insides and freeze them simultaneously. One thing she was grateful for, they had left the best of him. The part of him that kept her coming back for more. She smirked, watching him kiss her gently, then pushed him away. "Stop," she said.

"You've never asked me to stop before."

"It's different now."

"What do you mean different? It's still me. The accident may have blown off part of my shoulder and torso, but it left me with my best bits."

Her posture stiffened. "Yet I had to purchase the other bits to put you all together. If Dr. Erikssen hadn't been experimenting with cloning technology and harvesting body parts, I wouldn't have you today. A part of me looks at you and wonders, are you real?"

He put his powerful hands on either side of her. "What do you mean? I'm as real as they come. I'm the man you fell in love with. You loved me before I joined the NSA KJ20 Ops. You said you'd wait for me. It was supposed to be eighteen months."

"I did. I had to go looking for you because no one would give me information about what had happened to you. What *did* happen to you?" she asked.

"There were two of them. Shields and another one, Ralph Mueller. They were ahead. We were training out in the Pacific, retrieving panels that had fallen off the spacecraft when it returned to Earth. Then we went to Korea to do the same thing. They told us that only real men could do it. I had to prove myself. Then I heard that voice. Shields. He told me not to jump in the swamp after the panels. I said no. It was my chance. My opportunity. For once, I was going to be better. And then... I remember little."

"Well then, let me refresh your memory," she said. "The panels self detonated. It was all in the report. I bought that report and brought your life back. They said you were one deranged agent who went into the fire line when your mates told you not to. They then had to risk their lives to fetch you, and by the time they got to you, you were half man. The trainers told him to leave you for dead and, if I recall from the reports, the one they call Nash Shields said they leave no one behind. He dragged you out of the swamp, and by then, you were already..."

Hex moved away from her, fury crossing his face. He shuffled to the bedside table and found a half full whiskey glass. "Damn it. Shields should have left me there!"

"You're still a man."

"Yeah? I have everything that makes me a man, everything from waist down. My top hurts every night. It hurts when I stop fighting or using it physically. It's my curse now. So what if you paid for prostatic surgery? Shields should have let me die that day."

Zodie didn't know what was going on in his head as he advanced to the mirror, how he hated the scars. But Dr. Erikssen had fixed him. When she found him, though Nash Shields had saved his life, the KJ20 Ops declared him dead. That would screw up anybody.

She followed him to the dresser, and he watched her sneer behind him in the mirror, and he turned to face her. "You just need to give me a chance. Marry me," he said.

She threw her head back in a shrill of laughter. "Why would you want to marry me? No Hex, you work for me. You do as I say. You owe me your life."

"I don't owe you anything."

"No. I'll not marry you. If I ever give my life to any man, it will be a real man. Now let's not forget our arrangement. I bought your life back. I put you back together so you can do a job for me. Now don't forget that."

She smirked, dropped the sheet, and walked naked toward the bathroom.

When Hex heard the shower start. He hastened to her workroom.

He had seen her working in here the other day.

Just who did she have her eyes on? He fumbled around, and there it was. She had files on her laptop. And one name was in every single folder. The KJ20 Ops man who had saved his life. The KJ20 Ops man who he could never match up to. But maybe it wasn't too late.

He smiled to himself. "Nash Shields, today's the day you start looking over your shoulder."

10:27 a.m.

Everything Jack had worked on was gone. He searched the premises, overturning chairs, the desk, and several files. Jack hurried to where all the laptops were and the data boxes he had stored. His prototype for aerial robots was also gone. Why had they come for him?

He pulled out his cell phone. "Calla?"

"Jack, what is it?" Calla said when she picked up.

"We have a problem. Someone's been in Lodge 237, the safe data house, and they have destroyed everything. They could be watching me right now."

"Stay there until I come."

Jack hung up. It would take Calla at least a good half hour before she was at the warehouse, even in her Maserati.

He had to secure the backup server before she arrived. The server had to keep active to keep an eye on Scope's technology.

Jack scampered outdoor and found the secure server hidden from sight in an outhouse. It was still safe.

Calla hurried into the warehouse half an hour later. She approached him. "Are you okay?"

"They have taken everything. All my life's work, everything I've ever worked on, is gone. Wiped clean."

Calla scanned the vast area. "Who would know to come here and do this?" she said.

"That's just it. Nobody but you and Nash know this place exists. That's exactly why we built it. We kept it away from ISTF. Remember, we had to find a place that only you, Nash, and I knew about away from the Scorpion Tide."

Jack felt his tummy drop. "It's like starting my entire career from scratch."

"What about the secure server outside?" Calla said.

"We're good on that," Jack answered. "I'll see what I can back up, but it'll take me weeks to put it all together."

"Don't give up yet, Jack. I'll let nobody come after your

life's work. You've sacrificed much not only to save this country from cyber havoc, but also international security."

"This time it has gone personal."

"Who do you think it is?"

"I don't know. I'll call Nash. He needs to know as our phones are tagged to this place. If they can get to a place as secure as this, they can get anywhere. I'll take care of that for now," Jack said.

When he'd called Nash, he studied Calla as she sank onto the edge of his desk. "This is one of the most secure places we've ever built. I suggest we recover as much as we can and move it to the Scorpion Tide. That's the only place I know that has firewalls that can keep as many people out."

Jack moved around the room; he'd been thinking about something ever since he called Calla. Few people in his life knew about his research and everything that he was doing. What if it wasn't someone in his present life, what if someone who had known him longer than Calla and Nash had?

He turned to her. *God!* He wished he had snagged her up before his best friend had, but he respected them both too much. He watched her beautiful emerald eyes glint at him as they'd always done when he knew she was thinking hard to decipher something. "Calla?"

"Yes?"

"My sister. She's the only one who has known what I'm capable of and perhaps the only one who would have known how to get to me."

"Fiora is in New York. She wouldn't, after all, you've done for her. It makes little sense."

"Not to her," he said.

"But she's helped us in the past."

"Only because it suited her."

"Do you really think Fiora would do this?"

"Possibly. That girl has been a criminal from the day she married that criminal Benassi."

"Why would she even think about doing something like this? She knows you wouldn't forgive her."

"That's what I intend to find out."

EIGHT

Day 7
Maryland, USA

Zodie observed the exit of the high-security penitentiary. Her eyes narrowed at the image on her tablet. She pulled her tight skirt over her knees and chewed her lips. Two of her guards waited outside the Rolls Royce Phantom past the prison's security lines, waiting for the moment he would step out.

Ten minutes later, the prison gates clanged to one side, and the officers let him out. Her agents met the man she only knew as Lascar Aspell.

There was little on this man and his file she had hacked from the NSA. Sketchy and full of holes and he'd had a stint at the NSA.

His image had changed often as a spy. Although she didn't know a lot about him, she noticed that he had known Calla Cress who had put him into prison.

Zodie posted bail for the time the courts had granted.

She'd convinced them he would be under her supervision, and if he did, for whatever reason, be it break bail, Zodie would be responsible. Money could buy you everything, even a prisoner.

Lascar advanced to her limousine and she rolled down the dark window and removed her sunglasses.

"And you are?" Lascar said.

"Get in," she said with a smirk.

The two bodyguards with their guns in his back made it impossible for him to protest. Lascar circled round to the other side of the limousine, and the men shoved him into the car. He took a seat across from her.

She observed his dark lines. At one point, she guessed maybe he would've been a handsome man. There were Americanisms there that she couldn't place. His dark hair had overgrown, and so had a beard he kept short.

"Before we get started. Groom up," Zodie said.

"You've not answered my question," Lascar insisted. "Who are you?"

"I've a proposition for you," she said. "I need you to do something for me. Then maybe we can have a genuinely good relationship."

The Rolls Royce pulled into the driveway of a stately home overlooking Deep Creek Lake, Garrett County. Impeccable grounds surrounded the lavish mansion.

Lascar followed her inside.

"First, we wipe that grin off your face," Zodie began. "Upstairs to the left and behind the fourth door, you'll find a set of clothes and a shower. Clean up and meet me down here in half an hour."

He raised an eyebrow, "Why?"

"Would you rather these men escort you back to prison?"

Lascar advanced and was downstairs twenty-five minutes later, clad in black tactical training gear. She was right. He was once handsome, maybe too cocky for his good. Yet he did not measure up to Shields. So far, no man had.

Lascar moved to the bar at the end of where she stood. Zodie offered him a brandy, which he gulped in one swig, then set his glass down on the table.

She ran a hand down the side of her tight training gear and then drew a fencing sword from the room's corner. She pointed it at him.

Lascar locked eyes with her.

She charged.

He couldn't find a weapon but snatched a silver plate on the wall and tossed it.

The metal hit her hand, and she dropped the weapon in a yelp. In one move, he pulled the rug from under her feet and stood above her, grinning. "Now, will you tell me what this is about?"

She smirked. "Impressive," she said. "You must be using operative maneuvers."

A flat gaze fell on his face. "Oh yes, I know you're an operative. I know more than that," Zodie said. "You were the commander of the operative agents before Calla Cress disarmed you shamefully."

He grimaced.

She wasn't done. "In fact, it's also come to my attention that Calla Cress, supposed to be a student of yours, never took your class. I'm here to take that instruction."

"What class is that?"

"Maybe she opted for your rival for her affections. Nash Shields. Lascar Aspell, you'll teach me the operatives' dark fighting arts that Calla Cress embodies naturally. I could benefit from your training," she moved close, her lips almost touching his. "I promise I'll be an excellent student and a good girl."

Lascar's body jerked a little.

She smiled and ran a finger down his jaw.

He thrust her hands to her sides. "Why are you so interested in Calla Cress?"

"That's my business. But perhaps once training is over, you and I can have a long chat about what other ways I can make this worth your while."

Lascar smirked, retreated and found his discarded whiskey glass. Suddenly he returned and fixed determined eyes on her. He raised his glass. "Then let's begin."

***

Canary Wharf, London
5:21 p.m.

Dryness formed in Calla's mouth, but her eye contact with Radya remained fixed. Radya run her fingertips over sheets of paper as she went through meeting materials. She then glided a pen over her papers and crossed out notes she'd written. From a distance, in the windows open in the sweltering summer heat, a cloud of pollution made the London sky appear dark with a brownish haze. Though less congested than some of London's other parts, Canary Wharf's urban area sometimes gave off an acrid, smoky taste to the air.

Calla was grateful for the closed windows at this height as a hazy fog drifted past the reddening sun. She would have only twenty minutes with the Prime Minister before he left for the airport.

Calla focused her gaze on the uneven texture of chipped paint on a distressed cabinet next to the door, counting the minutes before Byrne would appear. Her eyebrows drew together, scrutinizing the papers Radya placed in front of them. If the Prime Minister did not see things her way, there was more to worry about than Scope's consumer app. Byrne usually listened when she spoke and hoped this would be one of those moments.

Allegra seemed to trust Radya's efficiency. The calm, collected ISTF agent had been sent to Istanbul only days ago to extradite Andor. Yet he'd evaded her. Even with him in ISTF custody, Calla knew he would not cooperate. He had much invested in Scope's technology and his daughter, Zodie. If only she could convince the PM to wait before entertaining Scope's offer for the UK government. But how could she stop him without compromising what she knew?

In anticipation, the TV screen in the room's corner remained on standby for ISTF teams who'd tune in as Calla took a seat in a comfortable chair around an oblong table. Other attendants in the private briefing-UK ISTF board members had joined Calla's agent team. However, calming the view from the twentieth floor of the skyscraper above London, it failed to change her mind. PM Byrne could not go ahead with this deal.

When she heard footsteps approach the door, she knew they signaled his arrival. He stepped into the room. His luxurious hair dusted with frost added years to his young age of fifty-five, though he appeared none the wiser.

Eric Byrne had never struck her as a man of confidence.

How had he ever won an election? Oozing with paranoia, he gave one the impression he would always look over his shoulder. What had he done in a previous life to mean he couldn't enjoy his appointment as Prime Minister? One could tell Prime Minister Byrne used to be intelligent. Somewhere along the way, something had seduced him. A calm man with deep-set green eyes, they projected like two gems of jade when he spoke with conviction, and Calla knew this time he had something on his mind; otherwise, he wouldn't have agreed to this gathering.

With his helicopter ready on standby minutes away at the heliport, he was in a hurry to get this contract done. He was showing his extravagant taste as the iconic building in the city had been the choice for the meeting before he took off to sign a new deal for ISTF technology services.

Calla rose when he approached. "PM."

"Calla Cress, what this government owes you can't be put in words."

"Don't do it, Prime Minister Byrne," Calla said as he took a seat close to her, his army of police guards remaining at the entrance.

"May I ask you to reconsider your trip to Brussels? You appointed me to warn you of any mishaps that you or ISTF may encounter in our ever-growing mayhem of new technological threats."

"Should I worry?" the PM asked, shifting in his seat and scanning the room's participants.

Calla studied his face, leaning in. "I've brought you here today to advise you not to engage in any deals using Scope Industries."

"You could've sent me a brief on my way to Brussels."

Calla hated formalities, and every minute of his

undivided attention counted. She eyed Jack and Nash for encouragement.

Allegra coughed slightly. "You should listen to her. Your government and this country could be under threat."

He leaned back and nodded quietly.

Radya began her report. She reiterated Andor's extraditing attempt, failing to mention her failed mission, skipping ahead to what Calla had asked her to present. The risk at hand.

Radya rose and lit the screen. "ISTF countries have lost control of Space. Space comprises segments various countries have claimed as their satellite arena. Several years ago, ISTF launched satellites in a segment of UK controlled Space, so it could spy on other satellite activities and serve as the police, if you like, up there."

Jack spoke with confidence. "Few people know of the existence of the satellites except for the member states of ISTF."

"What have you found?" The Prime Minister said.

Calla interjected. "We've lost control of this space. A few hours ago, a prediction appeared in the media, and they planted it in the newspaper on a website. It predicted we would surrender control of ISTF control in Space. This time Scope Industries has moved off the social media app and is now operating on government levels. Scope could see we would give up control twenty months ago. Many tossed the plant in the paper as a hoax. Yet, I beg to differ."

"Are you telling me that Scope Industries can tell what will happen? I thought that was just a children's app—the next wave in social media. For crying out aloud, all my kids have it," the Prime Minister said.

"Let me recommend that your children delete that app,"

Jack introjected. "The more money spent on the app and the more one can spend results in unprecedented levels of coma symptoms and brain damage. It's the addiction that leads to the coma. Scope Industries can make sure that dependence happens. Now, if this is operating on a consumer level, imagine what it would be on a large scale, and when I say the grand scale, I mean an international scale."

The Prime Minister's eyes bulged. "Is Scope Technologies involved in this takeover?"

"That's just it," Calla replied, "Mr. Prime Minister, Scope Industries couldn't be further from where the crimes are being committed. Its records are as clean as they come. They make a lot of predictions without ever being near the events."

"And how do you explain it?" the Prime Minister said.

Calla gave him nothing, not until they were sure. "Prime Minister, there's no way of explaining it. We have to stay ahead of it."

"Then what is it you propose?" Byrne said.

Nash's voice broke through the PM's blank staring. "We need a few days before you make that call," he said.

"Haven't you said that you do not have the time? I've just cleared funds for ISTF. May I remind you that what I'm doing could be useful and help further our technological aims? You at ISTF would want to have the best technological partners out there. Scope is a British corporation, good for our economy and scientific achievements. For once, something comes out of this country, not China and not the US. This is in our backyard. CEO Zodie Baxendale has assured me of the successes we will see. I'm sure you would have welcomed this."

Calla was yet to set up a meeting with Zodie, and it was

about time she gave her a visit at Scope Industries. Calla collected her thoughts, then continued. "Not at any cost. Prime Minister let's clear the room, and I'd like just three people to remain."

The Prime Minister nodded and permitted Jack, Nash, and Allegra to stay.

"Prime Minister, we're doing everything we can to stop the satellites from disappearing off the grid. Scope may be responsible. May I point out you asked me to do this job, not the other way round," Calla said.

"Forgive me, Ms. Cress, I am indebted to you, but I'm in a predicament as much as you are."

"Then I suggest you show some leadership," Calla said. "You are the Prime Minister, set an example when the country is slowly losing control of all its cyber communications, including its satellite space. The battle is now fought in the public's mental space, in the nation's minds and yours too. Bring people together, do not tear people apart over technology and its ethical place in the nation. As long as I'm here, ISTF is on top of this."

Byrne's jaw remained set. "I see."

"Make whatever excuse you can to Scope at that summit.," Calla said and rose.

The PM's assistant, Lexis, appeared at the door and progressed to the PM and whispered in his ear. She left the room promptly.

"Well, it seems we have some additional information," the Prime Minister said. "You've known about Scope, its covert behavior, and its ability to use multi-agent artificial intelligence to coerce governments days ago and chose not to disclose this. How long have you known about Scope?"

Since she met Baxendale at Beacon Academy, a woman,

an operative damaged by abandonment, and adopted by Heskin. It would be unexplainable. Baxendale's Scope endeavors were not necessarily corporate-minded. They were personal and Calla was at the center.

Calla exchanged glances with Jack and with Nash. She'd never told them either and had known about the prediction about countries being taken, hostage. She had read it in the scroll., but who had fed that information to the PM's office? Calla would put nothing past Heskin and Zodie. She had not told a soul, too frightened by what Hypatia had predicted in her notes that night in Havana. It was explicit in Hypatia's indecipherable message. Once the world had been compromised, the operatives would be next. Though the PM knew one fact, he remained oblivious to the other. If she could not come to terms with her abilities and genetics, Baxendale would.

"Why did you not tell me you learned about it before today?" the Prime Minister said.

Calla stood straight. "Because there are some things on a need to know basis. Even for you, Prime Minister. May I remind you I accepted this job on condition I don't report to you?"

Calla watched the window as the Prime Minister's helicopter took off. "There's a tremendous amount of money to be made by companies that can analyze past knowledge to predict future habits. Scope is getting a lot more than people have signed up for. Little spiders troll their customers' digital imprints and now they'll put digital spies in every country, if not already."

"Yes, big data," Nash said.

"But what about country predictions?" Allegra said.

Jack drew in a sharp breath. "Past behavior is a great indicator of future patterns, and most communities ignore this. Imagine an app that has collected all this data for centuries from individuals, groups, people's practices, community behavior, and has it all stored in servers somewhere. Connectivity is helping people be productive, and the app knows that. Scope makes profits. Everyone's happy. Big data is at the heart of all of this."

"They have everything on everyone now," Allegra said.

"Jack. That's why they took your research," Calla said. "If big data is how a computer or any other connected device processes and uses advanced tools to analyze and interpret massive amounts of information. The goal is to use this past data to predict human behavior and interaction. Once that is done, Scope will move on to nations."

"If Scope can get government spending, including a deal to kit out ISTF, and all five governments, then they have us where they want us," Nash added.

Calla paced the room, the others watching her. "It is valuable information. Imagine knowing the specific time and date someone will enter your shop or sign a contract. That's a privilege no one should have. Or the hour and date they will order something online. Or the exact time a missile will be launched. To do so, Scope needs the exact time and dates when they could generate new energy from Space. When the sun is at its hottest, it develops energy from sunlight in Space and transmits it wirelessly to Earth. Scope is banking on Space solar power. That's what they are using to power these computers around the globe."

Allegra leaned in. "Wow. Heskin has been busy for years. How did you know?"

"Jack has the most sophisticated analysis in this area, and they came for it."

Nash set both hands on the table. "The consumer app is just a testing ground to gather data for their most superior project, the monopoly of space solar power, the future. Scope is one step ahead. That's what is in the fine print of all the government contracts that they are signing. They disguise the corporate contracts to gain intel on their enemies and allies, but the condition is to sign on as their own personal supplier of space solar power for the future."

Nash moved around the room, studying his phone. "I've just gotten into NSA intel. Space solar power requires massive scale construction much bigger than the current International Space Station. If Scope wants to assemble massive quantities of energy, solar power satellites have to be large, far larger than the International Space Station."

Allegra pinged Radya. "Funny, she's not responding. What more do we know about Scope's progression on their new Space station?" she asked.

"Scope has now amassed enough funding and construction power for the satellite which began five years ago. The work was nearly complete, then discontinued when Heskin was arrested. The last report shows Scope continued to work just a few days ago," Jack replied.

"When Heskin escaped," Nash said. "And also, when they took Jack's satellite monitoring research. Together they can complete the task by the time the sun is at its hottest and generates incredible space solar power."

"When will the sun be at its hottest?" Jack said.

Allegra scanned her tablet. "Ten days from now. Unless we find the bug, the Pythagoras Clause."

"That's why they came for it, Calla. Think of it as the codes to a nuclear missile. That's what the scroll is. If they can decipher the glitch from the astrolabe prediction of where the stars and planets will be, that's it," Allegra said.

———

The moment they stepped through their front door with Jack, the phone in Calla's pocket buzzed. Calla set the receiver to her ear.

"Calla?"

"Father?"

"I've devastating news. Your mother has gone into a coma."

"What?"

"They found her three days ago. I just heard from MI6. They won't give me details. She was fine one minute, then the next..."

"What led to this?" Calla said.

"I don't know," Stan answered.

"Calla's heart sank. "Please start at the beginning."

"There's something that your mother had not been telling you. When she was gone for all those years, she used to keep secrets even from me. This is something that has come back to haunt her. A deal she made with Andor Heskin before you were born. I found an old laptop of hers. It's over 30 years old. It's damaged. She doesn't know, I know," Stan said. "Why did she get involved with Heskin?"

Nash approached her, concern lining his face. "Because

of you and your DNA. It frightened her that anyone would know what you were truly capable of."

Stan was not done. "She did something to him years ago. I'm not sure what. Nicole had also been anxious about information MI6 gathered on her. And in her hunt for information, she gathered data concerning UK secrets sold to foreign governments."

"Foreign governments?" Calla asked.

"Remember, she was a spy. When you are a spy, you create enemies. That's why she went into hiding. Calla, I believe she has information, but someone got to her first."

Calla turned to Jack, then to Nash. This couldn't be happening. Nicole Cress in a coma? Her mother, a former MI6 agent, was tech-savvy, not an innocent teenager experimenting with a new social media app. Calla hardly knew her, and now wished she had spent more time trying to get to know the woman. She breathed hard. "I'm coming now."

"No, don't. The only way you can help her is by finding what exactly Heskin had on her. Before you were born, she was working on Space information the UK government held. She was assigned to UK airspace monitoring. That's how she met Heskin. She was there to make sure the UK stayed current in Space technology. Something must've happened."

"All those years ago?"

"Yes, my darling."

"Everybody knew that in years to come that whoever controlled Space technology would control future knowledge. We base a lot of the technology used on how much we manipulate and use information from Space. That case was closed many years ago after she left. She must have disappeared with whatever she had learned. Nobody knew what she found on that case because she destroyed the files. Even the old laptop has little data we can retrieve. When MI6 wanted the information, she was nowhere to be found. Suppose Scope has done this to her? After all, the case follows the pattern of other Scope victims. Heskin has taken his revenge and delivered her to MI6 as a warning."

Calla's heart sank. "but he's in our custody at ISTF. Where is she?"

"In a military hospital. They won't let anyone near her. They contacted me as next of kin. If she gets better, I can take her home, Calla. Your mother has also been busy for several days. Possibly how Heskin got to her. She met up with Mila in Washington and had the scroll. She stole it from Scope. They hired the worst militants after her, ordered to shoot, to kill. They'll do anything to keep that scroll from you."

"Father, please find out all you can." Calla set the phone on the table after she clipped it off, her eyes pinned into the men. "It's time we end a war my mother started twenty-nine years ago."

NINE

Day 8
Scope Headquarters
11:26 a.m.

The forty-four-level Scope headquarters building said one thing: the future is here. Scope wasted no funds in demonstrating architectural influence. The company occupied four single towers stacked alongside each other, a twenty-floor and twenty-six story block on either side of its high central crest.

Within the entrance, a ten-story atrium awaited them. Light shards pierced through from the outside, providing the lobby with incredible light.

"We're here to see Zodie Baxendale," Jack announced as he, Calla, and Nash waited at the reception desk.

Calla observed the smart technology additions that spied from every angle of the entrance. From self-service security technology integrations like facial recognition software to biometric access readers for each entry point, optimizing traffic flow of people.

"Do you have an appointment?" the woman behind the counter asked.

"Once Miss Baxendale knows who we are, she will want to see us," Jack said.

"And you are," the woman repeated, flirting with Jack.

"Tell her ISTF is here to see her."

The woman beamed and with a twinkling in her eyes as she gawked at Jack. "I'll see if one of her secretaries is free."

They waited for a few minutes before the woman looked up. "You may go toward elevator A. Someone will meet you and take you to her office."

"Thank you," Calla said.

The woman who met them was in her late thirties, and large blue eyes like two windows in the afternoon sky blinked at them. She extended her hand. "My name is Ms. Drake, Zodie Baxendale's executive assistant. What can I do for you today?"

Jack flashed their ISTF cards.

"Well, you can help by revealing how you work at Scope and make those predictions people pay for," Nash said.

"And where is Ms. Baxendale?" Calla asked.

"She'll be with you shortly," Ms. Drake said, leading them further into the executive wing and through to a wide-lit office on the top floor. "It's not our company policy to give out trade secrets."

Calla studied Ms. Drake carefully. "Who's the software developer behind the Scope app, and what programming language does it use?"

"That's classified company information. Be assured we've observed all governmental trading and technology development practices. This way, please," she said. "Please take a seat. Ms. Baxendale will be with you shortly."

They waited for three minutes before footsteps from a door hidden within the walls slid to one side. It was the appearance Zodie had wanted them to have. Deep-set black eyes studied each from a graceful, caramel-skinned face. Calla remembered her well, but any shyness Zodie had displayed at Beacon Academy had now morphed into five-foot-ten tall power. Feet shoved into stilettos that clicked as she walked and wrapped in an elegant suit, Zodie was a woman on a tight schedule.

Zodie extended an arm. "Miss Cress, you haven't changed a day since we last met."

"I don't think I can say the same about you," Calla replied.

"I've already concluded my business with ISTF. The Prime Minister has all the documentation he needs on our agreement."

Calla tilted her head to one side. "I'm not here on behalf of the Prime Minister."

"Then why are you here," Zodie said, giving Nash a flirtatious smile. "Our products are available on the open market, and surely you're not after a prototype."

"Speaking of prototypes, I hope you received the files my office sent through," Calla said.

"I did."

"How do you explain the girls in comas after using your app?" Nash said.

Zodie held her head high. "Our organization verifies our products are safe and adhere to mental health regulations. We've no reason to conclude that this product is unsafe."

"It uses obscure programming language and algorithms. Where did you source the capabilities?" Jack said.

Zodie rose, then stepped around the table. She peered out the window and then set a finger on the pristine glass table. "I'm afraid I can't tell you very much about our products. They're company trade secrets, but I can tell you that many people feel they have power when they know and can predict their futures. It would be best if you tried it. Please don't assume that it's our fault if people have certain weaknesses. They're drawn in by understanding that their future will be okay. That's all that counts with them. People have an innate need to know what the future holds for them."

Calla observed the elegant lines on Zodie's face. None of this explained why her mother had fallen victim to their application; she wasn't trying to use the app. Much was not making sense here. Calla had asked her father shortly after the news on her mother to send her all the technology Nicole had adopted within the last several months. Not one Scope application or technology was obvious in anything that she was working on or doing. The hospital had sent through information on her mother's condition. There was a connection to Scope except for the similar symptoms she showed, as were the girls in South Korea, Buenos Aires, and Vancouver.

Calla crossed her arms. "You seem to know your customers. Are you saying they have never asked how your product works? They just accepted for what it is?"

"Yes, that is correct. The same way you eat an Oreo cookie. You do not ask where and how each grain in it was designed. They accept it for what it is, and we continue generating new content based on our products' and our self-analysis."

Biting her lip, Calla softened her voice. "And you won't explain why and how your product gives them information and how accurately it can tell their future?"

Zodie turned. "Our business today is concluded, Miss Cress."

Calla nodded. "You're right. Our business today is concluded. From now on, it won't be business. I'm here on behalf of so many more, day by day, falling victim to horoscope nonsense. At least with horoscopes, one can choose whether to believe them. You leave your victims no choice."

Anger crossed Zodie's face. "I wouldn't call customers victims."

"As of this morning, we have ten more documented cases on coma-bound Scope users," Jack added.

"You can't prove they are in comas because of Scope."

"Maybe not. But I bet you can," Nash said,

Zodie smirked. "It may be worth you checking their medical history. Illness has nothing to do with our product."

Calla stood. "I'm sure next time we come, we may appear with a warrant."

Zodie extended a finely manicured hand, not willing to share anything. "Thank you for coming."

They left the room the way they came and then Ms. Drake led them to the elevators. When they arrived at the doors, she called the button. "Thank you very much for visiting us today and for your interest in Scope Technologies. I'm sorry I could not be of better help."

Ms. Drake then forced the button. The three went into the elevator, and the doors shut on them. The car began a slow descent toward the ground floor. Suddenly, it rattled and came to a complete halt. Its doors shot open. The car spat them out of the elevator. They landed on concrete, between floors. On either side, a gray steel corridor led off in three directions. Fluorescent lighting hung from the ceiling, and a powerful stench of ammonium greeted them.

"It's an invisible level, not on the grid. Was that your move, Jack?" Nash asked.

"As you requested," Jack winked. "You were right about the unseen floor, Nash."

Movement stirred on Jack's tablet. He pressed down a button. "Let's see if we can start an evacuation."

They heard voices as a massive staff exodus began throughout the building.

Jack's minor breach had worked.

"This way," Calla said, following the floor lighting.

They explored the hall leading to several doors. Server farms blinking lights with cyber activity lined each side of the corridor. Past the endless suites of servers, they entered the research wing and plastered their backs against a wall as three men in white coats moved from door to door. The last of the scientists closed rooms behind them, manufacturing engineering pods. When the scientists retreated behind a door, Calla tried to open the first room.

It remained shut.

She spun toward Nash as they heard noises.

In a frenzy, analysts trying to evacuate a floor that didn't exist on the building plans amused Calla for a second until the last person disappeared into the elevator. Calla smirked. "Ready for some serious snooping? Any of this show on your radar, Jack?"

"What is this company manufacturing?" Jack said. "What are they doing?"

Nash spied through a locked door. "Looks like their digitizing solar panels. Where did they get this stuff?"

"Funded through all the corporate apps they are advertising to governments and individuals," Calla added.

They paused at a room slightly different from the others —white from top to bottom; they had plastered mathematical formulas on the walls.

"Looks like the message Heskin left you," Nash told Calla.

They counted twelve rooms plus the mathematical room. The whole place was a maze of math, calculations, and code. They then turned around and realized that the place depicted the twelve horoscopes in the twelve personalities of the ancient Greeks sub-categorized by Choleric, Sanguine, Melancholic, and Phlegmatic. Here the instruments of Scope were driving their instruments to hold kids victim to information overload. *Noise*, as Calla called it. The systems behind the app had to be here.

A shot exploded behind them.

"Time to go," Nash said.

They charged toward an open door as several security guards filed through three elevators in dark combat gear.

They darted to the top floors of the skyscraper where a helicopter awaited flight.

Nash zipped around, charging to the platform as the wind blasted at them. "That's our way out."

"Gotcha," Jack responded. "Let me see if I can tap into Miss Zodie's itinerary," Jack said as he tore out his phone. "The flight's schedule is Heathrow."

"Not if I have anything to do with it," Calla said. "Right, you two take the helicopter pilots. Keep off anyone behind us."

Jack went first, and he hurried in the chopper's direction as the pilot launched the vehicle's blades. Both skilled chopper pilots, Jack and Nash, could operate its instruments.

Voices shouted behind her.

Armed men gained in.

She pivoted. Unarmed, she waited for Nash who fired down the passageway. In darkness, they couldn't see their targets.

The Scope team shot back.

Without prompting, Hex appeared, sturdy as he surged their way. Calla scrutinized him as his left and right side were off and his gun aimed for them.

He fired.

Nash drove her out of harm's way and shot back. They maintained speed, darting toward the chopper.

When Jack reached the helicopter and made for the pilot's seat, he drew a handgun at the man who tumbled out of the helicopter.

Nash jumped in. Calla was on his heels. She hastened for the helicopter's door, and Jack started its propellers.

Hex made it clear she wasn't going anywhere. He hauled her backward, and she plunged into him on the helipad as the aircraft took flight.

She veered around and secured a fist in his jaw.

He toppled back.

The helicopter's blades rotated, lifting its frame several inches.

She tried to mount. Hex was not taking prisoners. He rose and charged for her.

Calla sidestepped him.

He heaved her by her hair. She riveted back in agony, then kneed him in the groin. He crashed to the concrete, nursing his pain.

Calla watched as the helicopter took flight. She started for it as Nash thrust down a rope. Jack circled the chopper above her as its gust beat her skin, swirling her hair. Its compelling force pushed her to her knees. She could reach the rope. A firm grip yanked her left foot as she surged upward. Instantly, she spun toward Hex, now grasping tightly onto her ankle.

Nash discharged a shot from his pistol, and it bounced off Hex's metal arm. Calla used the distraction to slice her free foot across his face. Her boot caught him, flipping him midair. Half titanium, half man, he crashed to the concrete.

Solid as a tank, he surged upright and reached for her middle. Fury burning in her insides, this time, her boot smashed the flesh of his good arm.

She took her cue when he was down and called for the rope. She leaped forward and clung to it as Jack lifted the chopper high off the building. In one haul, Nash dragged her into the chopper.

Central London: 2:09 p.m.

Jack landed the helicopter in an ISTF heliport west of the city.

When they had reached the inside of the heliport building, Nash stopped to suck in a breath. "Curiosity becomes a desperate attempt at control. People are dissatisfied with their future, and when presented with it, they can't cope with what they learn. They hope their destiny will be different. An exciting part of the human psyche, and that's the desire to know what lies ahead."

Jack chimed in. "People have been fascinated with this for centuries, but none have learned to manipulate what they see or learn. That's why the scientist had those twelve horoscopes. They're not only making this up but scrambling knowledge horoscope outcome possibilities."

They took the Underground to West London where they picked up Calla's car.

Calla took the driver's seat of the Maserati and started the engine. "Something about those twelve horoscopes and those rooms doesn't settle well with me."

"We didn't get adequate time to see what they were developing," Jack said.

Nash thought for several minutes. "We may not know what they were doing, but we can at least look at science and history. What connected Hypatia's scroll scribblings and a damn sophisticated piece of software that spans anatomy, science, and technology?"

Calla parked the car in front of the ISTF building. "Me. And by that, I mean the operatives. Hypatia's scroll holds something that helps Scope, but someone else too."

Nash winced. "There's a gap in the automation and how it works. Otherwise, why steal the scroll? Someone must know."

"My mother. That's why she's in a hospital bed fighting for her life in a coma. My mother spied on something Scope did not want out there. She also made sure that I got the scroll before all hell broke loose," Calla said. "There's something connected to Hypatia. It's just a myth, but," she said, eyeing the men, "you know myths don't exist in our line of work. Hypatia's astronomy was mind-blowing, and I don't think history records it all. That's what we have in that scroll."

They stayed in the car for several minutes. Calla re-imagined the portrayal of the woman she had seen in the scroll. She could not get it out of her head and had memorized every inch of that portrait.

What had the portrait communicated to her? Hypatia, like Emiliano said, bore a strange resemblance to Calla. She looked much like her. Was she a witch, as the people who killed her had claimed?" Calla looked up. "We need the scroll. Any ideas where we start?"

"Hex. I have an idea," Nash said.

Nash pulled out the phone and flashed up a copy of the scroll on his screen.

"Where did you get that?" Calla said.

"Calla, I've been around you for a long time. I know when something is important, so like a true NSA spy, I took a photograph of the scroll when you were getting ready for dinner that night in Havana. I had planned to study the manuscript and put it through NSA's analyzing technology. So, here we have it. You've lost nothing."

"There's a reason you and I connect, Nash," Calla said, smiling. "Look here," she said. "This portrait also has twelve lines that cross and join in the middle that Hypatia drew above her portrait. The twelve horoscopes, but there are likewise four shapes here that join, the four temperaments. Philosophers tell us everyone can fit into one."

"Should we also look at the people in history known for predicting the future. We have Nostradamus," Nash said, running a hand through his hair. "Maybe these people can shed light on what Scope is trying to do,"

Calla crossed her arms. "Many people in history predicted the future. If you look at Nostradamus, he foresaw the Great Fire of London. Others predicted or imagined; a man would walk on the Moon, but it came from their minds not math."

"And then there was also that French scientist or engineer who believed that we would one day transmit messages wirelessly. That was sixty-four years before it ever happened," Nash said.

"There again mind not math. But what if, as Calla said, someone knows the world's future and has it at their fingertips?"

Calla drew back. "That power is coming from Hypatia. Unreadable calculations next to her portraits. They're telling me something I can't read."

US Embassy: Nine Elms, Central London
4:00 p.m.

The US Embassy stood high and proud in Nine Elms. Nash parked his car in the underground parking lot after he cleared security.

When he exited the elevator on the seventh floor, the NSA division had given him his old office. He could access his NSA files a lot quicker here, and as a US advisor and primary member at ISTF, Nash remained valuable to their Embassy in London.

"Good to see you here, Shields," the man said when Nash passed through security.

The bite of regret pinched at his core. They still had him here? Even after a slight administration change?

Chidson? Couldn't this guy find something more important to do than spy on Nash's every move?

Chidson stood at the door, grinning. "Let me know if you need anything?"

He didn't.

The man was fishing for information.

Nash rose from his chair. "Good to see you, Chidson," Nash said. "I'll holler if anything."

Chidson nodded and stepped out of Nash's way, yet kept keen eyes on his back as Nash headed for the stairs.

The CIA and intelligence wing was a floor down, and when he swiped his access to the wing, he hunted for the archives room. Now digitized, his search would be easier.

One by one, he studied everything Colton, the former CIA head, had worked on in the last four years. He didn't wish to leave anything to chance. It was Colton who'd first told him about Stan's case. He could never forget Calla's file, from the minute she had come into his life. He logged onto a secure server. Looking for holes, references to UKSA, Heskin, and Scope Industries.

Nothing. Nothing stood out.

Several minutes later, he was in his car, driving back to his apartment. There had to be something. He still held a soft copy of the file he had been given. Colton had been the link to Stan way before he met Calla, and Stan had begged him to keep an eye on her when she joined ISTF.

When he made it to the master bedroom safe, he found the private drawer and opened it. He glanced at the watch on his wrist. Calla would be at ISTF for a few hours yet. He hated what the case was doing to her—all the more to see if he'd missed something in that file.

The file was precisely where he had left it. Nothing much had changed. But then he saw it. Something was out of place.

He reached for his cell phone.

The line connected to CIA headquarters in Langley. "Please give me Colton," he asked the division's reception.

"I'm sorry, sir, Colton, who?" the voice said on the other end of the line.

"Director Ben Colton, Director of the Central Intelligence Agency," Nash responded.

"Colton isn't a name we recognize. You must be mistaken."

Nash set the phone down. He guarded his emotions like a wolf defending his territory. Just what had he heard?

He connected to the CIA network. One quick search revealed that Colton had been replaced in the last forty-eight hours.

Just where had Colton vanished? Colton had not only disappeared, but he had wiped clean any file of his from CIA records.

Barre, Vermont: 3:12 p.m.

Nash chartered the first private flight he could that afternoon. The jet landed in Vermont's Edward F. Knapp State Airport at 3:12 p.m. local time. He had just hours to find Masher, a former mentor of his son and someone he had worked with at the US Embassy, before the jet would take him back to London overnight.

Colton going off the radar was serious business. What had happened? If anyone knew it would be Masher. The man much like a father to him would have something to say. Nash had never disclosed much to Masher about the operatives, but perhaps it was time.

First stop had been to Masher's home in the quieter suburbs of Barre. His wife had said he'd missed him. The suburb was way too quiet. That's how Masher liked things. Even though Masher was getting on in years, he had never showed he would retire from the NSA and from government work.

Forty-five minutes later, Nash slipped into a crowded marketplace in Barre. Masher's wife had mentioned he was at the boxing gym just south of City Hall. Nash corned the rental and parked on a side road. He could spot Masher anywhere and took a moment to remind himself of his gratitude to Masher, who'd married him and Calla in a secret ceremony all those months ago. Masher alone and Jack knew of their elopement until they'd had to tell Stan and Nicole to help them maintain secrecy.

Then he spotted him. Tall, with frosted hair and a commanding walk, Masher was only a few meters from the gym's entrance.

Nash caught up with him and his eyes dropped to Masher's left hand lugging a large gym bag. "Masher? You started the gym run early. Sorry I didn't call before I came, but I had to see you urgently."

Masher drew Nash into a hug. "Son, are you all right? How's Calla? What are you doing here?"

"Let's go inside and talk," Nash said.

When they were inside, they took to a quiet corner in the gym's cafe. Masher dropped his boxing gym bag on the floor and put both hands on either side of Nash's shoulders. "What're you doing here?"

"Is that a way to greet an old friend?"

"Forgive me, Nash," Masher said. "I know you live a private life, and you do nothing without purpose. It's always good to see you. Is Calla okay?"

Nash nodded. "Masher, you know I always have time for you and for Samantha. You and Sam were parents to Calla and me when we needed it."

"Speaking of that," Masher said, "how's married life?"

"I'd like to say it's easy. I love her more than anything and we just work. It's everything around our marriage that's the challenge. Intelligence work doesn't make it easy. But nothing's easy when you're married to Calla Cress. Although I couldn't have it any other way."

"I like her. There's something extraordinary about that woman, and I can see why you fell for her."

Nash set his eyes on him. "Yes, she's exceptional. I want to keep it that way and I need your help."

"Government help? We can't talk here." Masher scanned the quiet spot inside the boxing gym before nodding. "Okay, I know you're pressed for time. What is it, son?"

"I found a file in London that had a name and the date on it. It was something I remember noticing when I was training for the KJ20 Ops. I later remembered seeing it when I we were marines at the London Embassy, but ignored it. For months, I've been ignoring it, but it's something that's been bothering me. Thought you might help me with it."

"What is it?" Masher said.

"I want to know why this file has my father's name on it.

The date and time were signed several months ago, and you signed it. The other thing that's puzzling me is the case I'm working on right now and Scope Technologies," Nash said showing him a file on his phone.

Masher's eyes dropped to his hands and he wrung them on the table. He then lifted them to Nash. "Yes, Scope. There are many things I've wanted to forget about London, and Scope in particular."

"What?" Nash said.

"I knew the day would come, but I hoped that that man would stay in prison forever because there's nothing good about Scope Industries and that technology. Listen, Nash, I don't know how much I can tell you. It's like I just can't."

Nash drew his eyebrows together. "Prison? You mean Heskin? He's in our custody at ISTF. Masher, you've been able to tell me anything and everything. We've been through much, you and me. We've kept nothing from each other."

"I'm so sorry, son, but this time I can't."

Nash felt like a knife had wedged itself in his throat.

Masher made a sign to leave. Something was wrong; Masher had never acted like this. The man who had served with him when they were out in the Middle East. The man for whom he would've given his life. It was uncharacteristic of him to be guarded about issues they always shared.

"You okay, Masher?" Nash said. "Hey, it's not like you. What's going on?"

"Son, I normally can tell you anything, but I just can't do this."

"Is someone watching us? Blackmailing you? You know I can help with that."

"Nobody's listening to us."

"Have they framed you? Who? Is someone after you?"

Masher's eyes lit up. "I can't."

"Somebody has something on you, don't they?" Nash said. He leaned in. "Masher, I can help. We've always been in everything together."

Masher set a hand on Nash's arm. "I can't tell you without endangering you and your beautiful wife."

"Please. Let me be the judge of that. If our lives are in danger, they're even more in danger if we do not know," Nash said.

Masher drew in a sharp breath. "They've framed me. I don't know who yet. I've done nothing. They've got everything on me. Technology out there leaves digital footprints. Cameras can create scenarios our minds do not remember or ones that never existed. We can see our names on things we do not remember ever putting there. I knew of Scope's founding. I was against it when their proposal came up for discussion at the NSA. In fact, I was there when they asked for government clearance to own a US corporation that had advanced in researching the future so accurately. I verified the technology myself. On the NSA board."

"Colton is gone."

"Huh. Figures. That man was always a coward. If he's gone, then he's in danger too."

"What do you know about the research? How's it telling the future?" Nash said.

"I swear, I can't say anymore, Nash, without putting you into further danger. But I'll say this. I don't know how Scope is telling the future. They would not reveal their intelligence and only needed the US to clear their patent for operation in the US. That's how the case landed on our desks."

"I beg of you," Nash said, His heart racing. "Calla is in danger."

"Okay, I'll say this. Scope has a way of dipping into our deepest souls and those of an entire nation, community and society. It manipulates whatever it finds, perhaps through artificial intelligence, perhaps through other means, and can almost read our thoughts and behaviors. It can do that with government data. Any data to be exact. What they've done is clustered this data into communities and created societies within the data, then predict, how they are likely to behave. Later I figured Scope based much of this on a new math."

"Masher, I need you to tell me everything you can. That blasted Heskin has walked off with data that may belong to my wife. Calla was in a coma for six months when she was sixteen. What if they stole her data then and have had it for years? God knows that they'd done with it. I have a feeling Calla's life was on their radar for years. Everything. Even before she was born."

Nash didn't realize he'd been pleading and that the heat in his eyes meant they were bloodshot.

Masher waited several moments before he responded. "There's something else I know. Your father funded Scope Technologies and has a large stake in it. He may still be funding them. His hands are all over Scope. So perhaps he's the one you need to be asking. If you find data server 7172, you may find something. It's a CIA database that Colton guarded with his life. It's got all the London cases. If it involved Calla, it may be on there. I've already told you more than enough, son."

Nash felt his breath halt in his throat. "Where is it?"

"Outside London. Colton commissioned a space for the NSA to hold data farms on UK citizens. The British don't know about it."

A sweat bead rolled down the side of his ear. He'd only

just made amends with George Shields a few months ago. It went to show how much he did not know about his father. Masher was his most trusted mentor, a father to him, more than George would ever be, or had been. He was telling the truth. He knew it. This was the influence his father had always sought.

"Your father, George Shields, has a lot of money invested in Scope. He would pay money to make sure it succeeds, and I would not put criminal behavior past him."

Several minutes later, Nash sank into his rental. His father had always been a questionable man. Not once had he thought he was rooted in the heart of something as grotesque as what Scope was doing.

He rammed a hand onto the steering wheel. Nash believed he had more questions than answers.

Shoreditch, London
7:29 p.m.

Jack took a minute when he arrived at his front door. The ambushed warehouse meant someone was on to what he was working on. He had struggled his entire life and could not just watch it dissolve like this.

Jack never preferred to build technology for its own sake. Yes, he wanted to do something significant with his life, but not at the risk of holding humanity hostage.

He sank deep into the couch in his office, then rose after

several breaths for his safe. He searched through the items in his vault. He fingered his certificate. It had been a long journey to become a graduate at the University of McGill. Canada was where it had all started. Jack inspected his old Seychellean passport, and even though he had become a British citizen, holding onto that passport reminded him of where he had come from. Jack was a believer in not dropping your roots.

He picked up a sound by the door. With a grip on his pistol, he closed the laptop on the desk, then crammed the passport back in the drawer. He advanced with care until he reached the front door, bracing his handgun. "Who's there?"

"Is that how I get a welcome these days," a voice said as she slotted the key and pushed open the door.

"Marree?"

"Jack," she said, her eyes widening at the sight of the pistol. "Thought you'd be happy to see me."

Jack put away his gun as Marree moved into the room.

She set a hand on his cheek. "Jack, what is it?"

"Nothing. Come in."

Marree squished her eyebrows. "Do I get a kiss?"

He drew her into his arms. He just needed a face like hers tonight and someone who loved him unconditionally.

"Jack, are you okay?"

"Yeah."

He knew she didn't believe him.

"Let me in. I want to be a part of everything that you're part of," she said, dropping an overnight bag on the floor. "I had to come and see you. The only way this works is if we can learn to trust each other."

"I know, Marree. I'm glad to see you. Just need some time. When did you leave Honolulu?"

"Last night."

Jack did not want to push Marree away. She was one of the best things that had happened to him since meeting Calla. And even then, why was it he couldn't let her in?

Her eyes wandered to the other end of the room, and to his laptop. He drew Marree close. He had to let her into his world. He had to let her into his deepest fears. He couldn't always carry things alone. Before Marree, Calla had been it. Until she married his best friend. If he couldn't share his life with anyone, who could he? As much as Calla and Nash knew him inside out, they had their own lives, and they were together. He had to accept that once and for all. He missed the times where they would just sit around in the evenings and have takeaways in his penthouse, laugh about the day's latest cyber-criminal they had caught, or an undecipherable cipher they'd worked on in some remote part of the world. Those friendships were untouchable and would always be paramount in his life, but he had to let Marree in for now.

"Come here," Jack said, sitting her down on his couch.

Marree moved closer and he teased a finger on her bare arm and stared into her big brown eyes. "Thank you for coming. I need you."

She smiled.

"What I really want to say is I'm afraid. You know I work for a classified section of British intelligence. I've done research on a covert branch of ISTF that involves the operatives."

"Operatives? You mean…"

"Calla, well, at least her heritage, her genealogy."

Her enormous eyes watched him "Do you love her, Jack?"

How could he answer that? He had loved and lost Calla

to Nash. Confused about his feelings for Calla, he brushed the thought away. He respected Marree. Now wasn't the time to acknowledge that question.

He took her hand. "I'm afraid that what I have done, what I analyze, sometimes rivals what the operatives come up with. Problem is, I can't hide as well as they do. They are the most sophisticated technology and scientific experts on this planet, almost a super race, if that is even possible. Calla has inherited genes that were genetically changed in her family centuries ago by them and they get stronger. I don't think she knows everything that she is capable of— new things every day. The world isn't ready for the science they offer or develop, and it scares me. Now, my stuff is out there in the black market, and it hurts so deep that someone so close to me maybe to blame for the theft of my latest tech research, which is possibly being used by criminals hidden in one of the world's largest tech companies, Scope Industries. This happened yesterday."

"How do you know it's someone close to you?" Marree said.

"It has to be."

She thought for a minute. "Tell me about Fiora, your sister."

Jack didn't know that Marree knew about Fiora. Perhaps he'd mentioned her sometime back, but if he had, he could not remember. Marree's words touched him.

"She's a little younger than me," he said. "But she's made some terrible choices in her life. She has repeatedly stolen intel from me. When I became successful, she soon discovered my tech was valuable, worth millions to some. Fiora started paying attention. She'd always been a lost soul, but I didn't know how desperate she was until she acted on her fears. The first mistake was marrying that media mogul in New York, Benassi." Jack swore. "Damn it! That man's a moron. He's done so much, I would forget."

"You think she fears something. Why does she keep stealing from you, Jack?"

"Yes, she damn right is afraid of many things in her life. Thing is, she does nothing about them that doesn't involve hurting others."

"Perhaps you have to give her a chance. I have not met Fiora, Jack, but I know women, and I know that sometimes they make wrong choices out of fear."

Jack leaned back, amused by the intelligence of her statement. Marree cared about people in her life, but she also was perceptive. It is something that he had not thought of before. The woman was damn attractive, and her Hawaiian blood fascinated him. A Marine biologist almost knocked over by the Scorpion Tide when he and Nash had taken the yacht on an engine experiment run in the Pacific, that was the first time he'd ever seen her and they had hit it off.

"Thanks, Marree," Jack said. "I believe you."

"So, what do we do now?" Marree said.

"Let's find out what she's up to this time. I'll also take your advice," he said, eyeing her.

"What's that?"

"Come closer, and I'll show you," he said, pecking her nose.

Baltimore Washington International Airport

Nash still could make time if he hurried. He knew about a bunker, including its involvement in a European election several years ago. If he was right, the KJ20 Ops had sealed a center, a live data collector still in operation. Could it be linked to Scope's server farm?

The jet had touched down at Baltimore Washington International over an hour later. Sometimes the answers were a lot closer to home.

Nash had to be quick. He had often seen that any data and technology that manifested abroad somehow had a file here on NSA territory on KJ20 Ops's sealed operations. The NSA collected data, an unprecedented volume of material amounting to more than several million code lines. He knew where he could find it. That's when they had had to shut it down. In true NSA style, they never shut down anything.

The air smelled of cut wood and the sounds of the wind blowing kept the silence out. This had to be the place, and it had taken a lot of courage to come here undercover. He couldn't be here on official business for ISTF, not while representing his government abroad.

The NSA kept documents and files elsewhere, in a remote warehouse outside London that Masher had mentioned. A high-security network hidden on the grounds of the CIA's Center for Cyber Intelligence. This place had to give him answers. The data and access to this facility were only privy to certain representatives of the US government. Most were hackers, and even other contractors were brought on to boost the assembly of the extraordinary data.

While Nash was at the KJ20 Ops, this had been the first place they had brought him, an initiation to tell him precisely what the NSA could achieve. It was an extraordinary amount of covert hacking operation across borders and within borders, anything in the name of international and national security.

He could see the reinforced hatch entrance with blast-proof caps made from corrugated metal. It was at the base of a small hill that had given him difficulty getting to. He recalled the location. A straight ladder descended into the shelter. He clambered down and landed in a sparse decontamination area.

Damn it! If he remembered correctly from his days of training, the bunker was under a spiraling room staircase. It was sparsely lit with an average size entrance.

As no one frequented it, forestry had grown around the hill. He observed the hatch on the door that slanted into a lush hillside. Nash reached into his backpack and pulled out liquid gas that could melt the lock. He dissolved the iron, and the frozen lock snapped.

It had been a KJ20 Ops fitted bunker. When the KJ20 Ops had come here, he didn't know what they were after. All he knew was they'd been asked to test out these bunkers to prepare for a nuclear attack. The government had now turned most into luxurious underground shelters where billionaires had hidden wanting to save their lives—should there be a nuclear war.

Once inside, he descended the spiral staircase. He had closed the door behind him. He reached for his phone and found the app that switched on the lights. They had thought of everything for these bunkers, everything from a small toilet with a hand pump, several sleeping areas, a weapons storage area with locked cabinets. Everything from entertainment with screens, movie players, climate-controlled air filtration, fans. This was a small contained city within itself, where they would bring a president should there be an imminent threat of nuclear scale. Therefore, it had the best tech in the world, and if it had the best tech in the world, the NSA could fathom, these were the computers that would have the level of data that Scope possibly used. If the technology could warn of an intergalactic takeover, they would have everything on the operatives known to man. Plus, should a nuclear disaster ever happen, a secret data box planted by the KJ20 Ops held data on everything known to man. Should the Internet and the world need restarting, this was the data box they would use. It would do the job.

Nash flipped when he heard footsteps behind him. He had been cautious not to be followed. Anyone here would have to be NSA, or former NSA.

A metal can rolled across the stone floors and escaping air from a compressed container followed the sound. He covered his nostrils by instinct and gazed through the fog of the hissing air. He zipped round. No attack dissuaded Nash, but a ghost could make him stumble. Like the one in front of him. The ghost Reiner had warned him about.

"Hex? Hank Murphy?"

"Shields," Hex said. "You have a nasty habit of creeping up in my business in more ways than one."

"The feeling is mutual," Nash said, spearing him with another glare as he tried to make him out in the fog.

It was a risk coming here, and yes, he had his gun at the ready. "You cheated death? I saw that accident with my own eyes." Nash's confusion circled his mind, coughing to get the gas from his lungs.

"Then you should have looked closer."

Nash couldn't believe he was talking to the man. "I carried your body through fire and hell in Korea. The machine came down on you in the swamp." Nash said.

"What you don't know," Hex added, moving forward with an aggressive air, "is they left me there for dead. I crawled to a village, then was found without a working leg, arm, and half a brain. I was ripe for an experiment for any sick military operation. I was as good as dead."

He struck Nash across the chest and he riveted backward.

"I suffered hell in that village. A vegetable that visitors spat on. Then, an angel. My angel, a woman who has a sick crush on you, walked into my life. She asked for my body. Back in London, she nursed me and made me new."

The blow had hurt. Nothing Nash couldn't usually handle, but this felt like something else, almost robotic.

"Zodie Baxendale?" Nash said, rubbing his chest.

"Don't play foolish with me. She mentions your name in every KJ20 Ops conversation I have with her. Perhaps it's because she wants you," he said, lunging for Nash.

Hex threw a punch. Nash evaded it.

He grit his teeth, seething anger. "Because they chose you. Within seconds they made you commander of the highest unit in the KJs."

Nash stood erect in front of him. "I turned them down. The KJ20 Ops trained us to hack, gather intelligence using muscles, and to be assassins. I'm no assassin. I didn't want their honors. No one ever told us what we were being trained for until graduation."

"Zodie worships your skill. She came looking for you so you could have my job."

Again Nash did not know what he was talking about. Yes, he had a side group, a group by recommendation only where he provided covert protection, help, evacuations, and hiding people who needed to be off the radar. Many had sought him, but few knew his actual identity. He'd once helped an entire sheik's family escape the malice of a rival brother sworn to kill the sheik. Nash had used his group he ran with Reiner. The only person who had slipped through the introduction protocol was Zodie Heskin that day in Havana when she had come to Delgado requesting an audience. He still did not understand how, but somehow he'd known she'd gone to see his father, George Shields. He'd taken one look at the power-hungry corporate tech executive on the tablet and told Delgado to turn it down.

"So, you're Zodie's property now. Let me guess," Nash said. "She paid to put you back together. Knowing what she's capable of, my guess is it involved something highly unethical."

The blow came sharply.

"Dr. Erikssen's work is genius!" Hex roared.

"The genetics and AI fanatic," Nash said. "He's on every watch list for human cloning attempts, illegally. And a myriad of other technology crimes."

Hex rolled his shirt's left sleeve, revealing a prosthetic arm that looked more human than anything Nash had seen. That's why the blow had hurt like sin. Hex was half metallic.

"What kind of sick reconstruction did they do on you?" Nash asked.

He charged for Nash. "Let me show you!"

Nash slipped under his thrusting hand and turned around. "Where's the scroll? It was you in Havana. You took it, didn't you? You shouldn't concern yourself with things beyond your world."

"What does that mean?" Hex asked. "You'll never understand."

"I'll make this very simple for you," Nash said. "Calla

Cress is with me, and that's the end, and you'll get nowhere near her. So, I would suggest that you lose whatever boyish envy you have. Zodie is a self-seeking tech maniac who only wants what she can't get."

"I suppose you fall into that category. Cress does not know who she is. Because if she did, she would not be with you, and if she knows what's good for her, she needs to come to that realization soon," Hex said.

"And who told you that? Zodie, an operative who has always wanted to be Calla?" Nash said scrutinizing him. The man wouldn't let up. Now wasn't the time or the place. He had to find out what Hex wanted here after he'd forged his way into American intelligence services years ago. Hex knew what to ask and when to ask it and how to get to places he didn't belong. He'd struggled behind Nash in the KJ20 Ops.

"End of discussion," Nash said.

"Life has a certain way of repeating itself."

"Hex, you never were one to come up with your ideas."

Hex ignored him. "The NSA, for all that it still prepares for a rainy day. My hunch is there is a server farm here with materials you want hidden."

Nash's eyes narrowed, but then he saw the intent in Hex's eyes who had no time to waste. Hex pulled out a firearm and switched it to full auto.

Nash was prepared.

Hex wasted no movements as he raised his gun to fire. A laser bullet zipped through the hall, slicing through anything it touched.

Nash aimed his pistol at the ready but then slipped through the escape sheet. If he didn't hurry, the security he'd insisted on in these bunkers would come for him.

Nash dropped the hotel keys on the bed. He wouldn't stay long, just two hours until his flight back to London. Hex now was after Calla's data.

A breeze wafted into the room, and he wiped blood from his face. He had found a hotel after his nasty escape. The room would do until he figured out what to do next.

He felt a sharp pain in the back of his leg, a slight wound he had not noticed Hex cause in their encounter. Nash's chest contracted, feeling like he couldn't move. He threw himself on the bed and thought of revenge. When would Hex learn? It wasn't the first time he'd confronted him, but each time, he had let it go.

Something in Hex was not functioning. The man had no emotional intelligence. He was driven by muscle and had gone off with the very thing he had gone to get, the data in that bunker.

Months ago, the operative Lascar had admitted to ordering Calla's forced abortion. That was a tough pill for Nash to swallow. Lascar had sworn to kill off the last Shields' legacy and to claim Calla. Hex had to be involved.

How had he not seen it all those months ago? That fight and the bunker was where he had realized that things with these two had to change.

Nash felt sick.

Despite years of military training and preparation for combat, emotional combat was by far the hardest Nash knew. These were all new emotions for him. Wishing death upon anyone. Nash struggled to contain his anger against Lascar and Hex. His past with both and the hatred they shared had to end. Even though they did not know each other that well.

K-J20 Ops training had made Hex a target of the operatives. Nash knew a lot about the operatives, and that pissed off Hex most of the time. What were they up to? It was not until the likes of Allegra, and they all had infiltrated ISTF. Only then could they discover what places like the NSA had on the operatives.

This is where Hex came in. However much it pissed him off, could he just let Hex get off like this?

Lascar had had a hand in the death of his child. Somehow he had to have involved Hex. It was time to act. However much it pissed him off, could Nash just let Hex get off like this?

Nash pulled himself off the bed and moved toward the table. He launched a secure NSA website. He could find Lascar's weak spot. He remembered one thing from his KJ20 Ops file, and now that he had his security card, he keyed in the number in the data box he had secured from Hex and found a note with the time and date on it he had had a hand in creating. That note, time, and date referred to something. He checked his files, and there it stared him straight in the face. He didn't understand why he had not thought of this before and why he hadn't searched here. Perhaps it was because he had wished to forget the life of the KJ20 Ops. The one thing he never wanted to be was the assassin they trained him to be, like Hex, who now was profiting from that training.

No, Nash's reasons for becoming a KJ20 Ops were perhaps selfish when he was younger. Maybe it was to escape a particular situation at home and prove that he could cope independently without his father.

The website launched and the files opened one by one. There it was. Lascar had spent time at the NSA, then disappeared. He had suggested and masterminded the death of his child. He then found another file that led him into all the data they'd confiscated from the operatives. It was still secure, and nobody knew he could access the operatives' deepest secrets. Perhaps he had done it to stay ahead of them, so he could keep Calla safe. He knew the operatives, however much they meant well, one thing he doubted was that they shared everything with him and Calla. There it was, Hex. Hex had organized the forced abortion in Malta.

Nash shut the application and thought hard for a minute. He dialed a number. "Jack?"

"Nash," Jack said. "Where are you?"

"I'll be in London in the morning, Jack. You think you can do me a favor?"

"Yeah, ask anything."

"Jack, do you remember when I told you about my secure line into the operatives?"

"Yes, I remember it like yesterday. When I get a moment, I try to jump into it."

"Think we need to destroy it," Nash said.

"Why would you do that? The operatives have been on our side and fighting with us since."

"Yes, that's correct, Jack. I'm not talking about now. I'm talking about before we found out about Vortigern and Lascar. They have been planning Calla's life for decades. The files I have retrieved go so far back. It shows Lascar and his father Vortigern made it their life's mission to know and surround themselves with everything about Calla."

"Really. How?"

"They'll never leave her alone. I can't have that. I remember Heskin made a prediction at Heathrow. It was something that did not sit well with me. Something bothered me about what he said. The NSA gathered much of information about the operatives in the past and has beef on them. Lascar and Vortigern's names were written all over this file. What if they're somehow involved in working with Heskin? They might seek a way to extend Heskin's Scope project. I am certain they worked with Heskin."

"Nash," Jack said. "What do you need me to do?"

"What I need to ask, Jack is, when the moment comes, and I want to eliminate Hex once and for all, will you be with me? I'm positive he single-handedly orchestrated the murder of my child."

"You sure, Nash? That doesn't sound like you."

TEN

Day 9
Kotor, Montenegro
10:15 a.m.

In the south of the Adriatic, the pearl of the Mediterranean showed its genuine beauty when Calla stepped out to the hotel terrace and stared at the bay. Jack and Nash joined her on the grand balcony.

"You assume he might help us unscramble the code found in your mother's phone?" Nash asked.

"Yes, I think he can," Calla replied. "I knew Arun when I was at the University of Chicago and he is someone who understands codes. He also was an expert at Greek mythology. Scope Industries takes its name from there and links people to the twelve horoscopes. They've studied how each person is wired, with the twelve characteristics each temperament represents. There's always a dominant nature and a minor tendency and that's how Scope has separated the human population. Maybe he knows how Scope maneuvers data."

Nash headed toward the door. "We ready?"

Calla nodded. "Yes. You should also know Arun Mallbeck, is a pathetic gambler. However, that should not stop us from getting information. He's also a numerology expert, especially on Pythagoras, the father of math."

As they roamed through the old city center, Calla took in Kotor Bay that led to the fortress high above the former town. The Balkan wonder had been one that she'd never visited.

They crossed past Hotel Fjord. The old town in the unique Bay of Boka left Calla breathless. They had built most of the city during the Venetian period, notably the part they were walking through. They had to navigate narrow streets until they reached a square and a marketplace. It would be simpler to get through the town walking, and they expected to make it to the museum on time.

As they proceeded past stylish gates, they followed the ancient palaces of wealthy families. They ascended several stairs in perhaps the best-preserved medieval urban town in the Mediterranean. In a surreal and unique atmosphere, almost trapped in time, Kotor was like how it had looked centuries ago.

"What does Arun do today?" Jack said.

"He's a curator here in Montenegro. He looks after St Ivan's fortress."

They progressed toward the fortress and rose above the city, pounding cobbled stones. The fortifications of Kotor were an integrated historical system protecting the medieval town. Calla studied the citadels surrounding the castle.

As a curator, she envied Arun. The area benefited from ancillary buildings and structures that incorporated military architecture. As they advanced to the top, the mountain of St John Hurt came into view.

Arun was also a Byzantine and Roman collections expert. He had encouraged Calla to look after the Byzantine selections at the British Museum at the start of her career there. The Byzantines had retreated from this place, and despite many incursions, had sought independence. From what Calla saw, there was no lasting effect of theirs at this fortification.

When they arrived at the entrance, a man awaited them. "Hello, Calla Cress. It's a great honor to see you again, thanks for coming to visit us here in Montenegro," he said.

Calla smiled. "Thank you, Arun. I hope my friends and I haven't caught you at a bad time. It seems you're busy," Calla said, looking around at the crowd that had gathered within the castle walls to take in the sights. She took in a deep breath. "However, we just wanted to know if you can tell us about Pythagoras. Especially his theory of numerology."

Arun waved his hand toward a door and led them to a quiet room where they could talk. "What's this about? Why come all this way? You were an excellent student. Is this research for the British Museum?"

"Maybe," she lied. "What about numerology?"

Arun's eyes widened with excitement as they took seats around a cafe table. "Yeah, well, numerology is the system of beliefs in the spiritual relationship between living beings, objects, and numbers. Many religions, methods, and historical cultures have adapted to it, and adopted it. Some people believe future predictions can be possible with numerology and various core practices. Some have taken on that belief structure."

Nash arched a quizzical brow and leaned forward.

"Aside from numerology's mathematical value, why the great interest?"

Arun shifted uneasily in his chair. His passion was clear, but was his conviction? "Numerology dates to the first major mathematicians of the civilized world. There are many justifications for people to still practice numerology in today's world."

"What's Pythagoras's connection to it?" Nash said.

"The history of numerology goes back to the late 500s BC. Pythagoras came from Samos. He was, as you know, an iconic Greek mathematician and hence that's how we get Pythagoras's Theorem. He was the father of numerology, along with his contemporaries in Ancient Babylon."

Calla's interest grew. This connection to Hypatia was at the core of them finding the link and disarming Scope's technology.

Arun continued. "The first man to call himself a philosopher was Pythagoras, instrumental in acquiring disciples and followers. His philosophies allowed us to recognize the relationships numbers have with the order of the world."

Calla's gaze drew her forward. She wanted to know. Hypatia had to have been a fan of Pythagoras and studied his theorem and other numerology theories. "What were his pupils like? And the people who followed him?" she asked.

"Dedicated," Arun continued. "Many even mimicked him. Pythagoras and his perceptions, especially his mathematical ones, described the way the world works. Think of Isaac Newton, who later proved his theory and took them to another level, and other founders of numerology who developed concepts spanning the physical realm."

Calla shook her head, sending her hair slithering over her

shoulders. Hypatia may have studied with Pythagoras. And if Hypatia was an operative, she would've absorbed much. Perhaps she used his theory to warn of something even more dangerous and incredible.

<hr>

1:27 p.m,

The sun filtered through the cafe's windows overlooking the bay. Arun's explanations about Pythagoras and horoscopes had created more questions than she had expected. Everything that they had learned about Pythagoras was making sense now. Number theory was a branch of mathematics, high arithmetic, as used in the olden times. However, as once an old mathematician from the eighteenth century had said, *'mathematics is the queen of sciences and number theory is the queen of mathematics'*. This is the exact path that Scope had taken.

Calla had spent all morning asking Arun questions on numerology. What made little sense was how it translated to Scope? Her entire senses told her Scope had used Pythagoras as inspiration, but why did they need Hypatia's scroll?

History credited Pythagoras with mathematical discoveries, including the sphericity of the Earth. He identified the morning and evening stars and the planet Venus. Pythagoras had impressed many other philosophers, including Plato. Interestingly, no arithmetic writings of Pythagoras had survived. What if that was what Hypatia had dedicated her life to? Unearthing what Pythagoras had failed to pen down before his death.

"What do you think you're missing?" Jack asked, his gaze firmly on her. "What's not connecting?"

"Hypatia and all those rooms full of programmers at Scope in London. Serious numerology calculations are going on there that are powering Scope," she said.

"Jack, where do you think the main Scope server is?" Nash said.

Jack's shoulders dropped. The situation did not look good. "At this point. It could be anywhere. Just anywhere."

"I can tap into NSA material to find the server," Nash replied. "But that could take time."

"The app is be related to the vulnerability of Scope's clients. Let's not forget that Pythagoras also coined the harmony of spheres. This theory suggests planets and stars move using numerical equations, and thus some of this also corresponds to musical notes, therefore producing a symphony. Now, doesn't this ring a bell?"

"What?" Jack said.

"Horoscopes and future telling have always been linked to the stars. But what if it's not religious or mythological? It's all mathematical? Hypatia found this out, wrote it down in the scroll. If only I can prove this by reading it alongside Pythagoras's work, which the world lost. Hypatia secretly revived the works of Pythagoras and hid them because the world wasn't ready for them. Now we know why. Something tells me there is a lot more that scroll does not cover. She was a woman before her own time," Calla said.

Nash rose from his seat and stretched his arms above his head. "The Internet of things brings together people, processes, data and devices. The world has so depended on connecting, and connectivity gives value in terms of how we run businesses. Connectivity also saves time, and it helps us work better and be more productive, but at what cost? Think about it. Think of all the stuff we consider in the NSA. We look at people's data. Now imagine if all this material belonged to a single corporation and translates into a sole outlet that could manipulate your entire future. Information is used against individuals. I wouldn't be surprised for a second if at the time of realization that's when people fall into a coma. There is a neurological connection."

Calla didn't budge in her determination. "I suppose you're right," Calla said. "At which point does data translate from our computer to someone's neurologic Sensors that can spin someone into a coma? My mother was healthy and always maintained a rigid life, but even Scope knocked her backward. She's an operative who would have seen this coming and could have protected herself but somehow didn't or could not."

Nash clasped his hands behind his head. "Think about it. AI machines are examining on our thoughts—devices spying on our inner beings, what we want, and desire. And then a tool giving us what we desire. Because these systems supposedly, whether through math or algorithms based on behavior, have gone into the future and brought back answers, that makes it even more desirable. Could the lines of mathematical theory and mythology have crossed?"

Jack struggled to deny the truth, but his lips spoke tech. "I'm skeptical. Do you think Scope has extended into the future and brought back answers these people latch onto? I experimented with the app for a few hours the other day, and it seems to be a computing game; it's no more than a cyber game."

"I don't know," she said.

"But then if we look at it again," Jack said, "a typical

person has a large digital imprint on this Earth. Every day, we are asked for codes, personal actions, and passwords all at the tap of a finger and then that info is registered somewhere in cyberspace. With facial, thumbprint and voice recognition—AI contributing to humanity's regular living, there are many touchpoints where data is collected. If they birthed the Internet in the 1960s, that's a heck of a lot of cases. Not to mention if people's historical and family records have been digitized before that. The sky's the limit of what a computer can read and interpret."

"You're right, Jack," Nash said. "We're leaving a digital footprint. Imagine a silent big brother around collecting all this knowledge and storing it in massive data centers. They're taking all this material and putting it in a system. Once that data is enough, Scope then has an invisible cookie on our lives."

"That would take an incredible amount of computing capacity," Calla said.

"And equally substantial volumes of servers," Jack added. "Remember, big data process is information using advanced tools. It analyzes and interprets massive amounts of data. The whole point here is to use this past data to predict human behavior and interactions."

She sighed. "The operatives understood this and maybe that's what my mom was trying to stop. Mila and my mother knew much about the operatives. My father once told me it was like an obsession. She wanted to understand what they stood to gain with technology and how it affected her family and dedicated her life to understanding how to stop them, should the time come. That's why she left me in a foster home unwillingly because she knew someone like me might even one day be manufactured by data," Calla said. "She had to have taken something from Heskin or made him angry. If she wasn't on social media, then my guess is Heskin had her data, perhaps from years ago."

The men exchanged looks. What were they thinking? Calla fought to push away the defeat that had entered her heart. "Scope has made its life mission to understand people's hopes, desires, and weaknesses. Just the way horoscopes and temperaments work. To get the best out of a temperament, one has to know its strengths and weaknesses. Because the engine has studied our behaviors, and through the art of machine learning, it only took data to perfect the technology."

"Then, none of us are immune," Jack said. "The amount of data available to corporations about people and governments has exploded. Think of all the Internet traffic in the past several years, it's more than quadrupled again."

Tired lines marred Nash's brow. Must've been the quick trip he'd taken to see Masher. He sank back in his seat and finished his espresso in one gulp. "Scope runs on computer science. Before they went public, one of the heftiest science experiments was run by one of the biggest geeks out there, Heskin. The servers on the floor we found can't store everything. They weren't big enough, so the farm must be somewhere else. We are going to have to destroy them. Burn them if we can."

"A bigger server operation?" She held back a gulp. "We have to find that farm. It's incredible that people really believe this stuff."

Jack hissed. "Walk down a high street in London and come across a professional gambler who'll swear by the merits of numerology methods when betting or on a roulette spin. And it wouldn't surprise me at all. Mini video games and movies store our *'thumbs up and downs'*. We've traded numerology coupled with computing power into an invisible cult. You just get sucked into it, and you don't know it until it's too late."

Calla would not falter in her resolution. "I'm afraid of it. We've not finished writing numerological history. We're only at the beginning, and the machines have taken over. Scope has collected data for years and years. All you need to do is plug data into a machine that can spit out scenarios. Our brain then accesses the likelihood based on past behavior, and we believe it. This must've happened to those girls. What better way to develop confidence, make money than to give individuals a glimpse of their future? I'm concerned about the people who are fighting for their lives. Who knows what else will start falling victim to Scope? I don't trust something they're doing in there. What if they take this a little further to predict entire collectives and groups of people, and soon it's the entire country? It'll affect our government's decisions, not just individuals. That's where it gets scary."

M6 Motorway
11:57 p.m.

The wind felt like a slap over Nash's face as he pulled his visor down and its force whipped leaves from the trees. A summer storm had been brewing for hours. Then a loud crack of thunder rent the sky open, and the deluge poured down. When the guards had gone, Nash turned to Jack and Reiner. Both men also in dark combat gear and face visors.

"Who would've known the US had secret holds on UK soil?" Jack said.

"Yeah, this is where they like to dump any files they need to expunge from official records," Reiner chimed in. "The KJ20 Ops had much to do with establishing such places. We disguised them as factory warehouses. The US always wanted off-soil data servers to keep close eyes on citizens interesting to the United States. God knows what else is in there. I need to find out exactly what happened to Colton, where he disappeared, and why he was the one who took on Calla's case when Stan came asking."

Reiner gave him a quick nod. "So many others below his pay grade could've done the job. I find it highly suspicious he's gone MIA."

Nash took in a sharp breath. "We're going to do a digital break-in into this CIA offshore database. Jack, that's your area. Reiner, I need you to cover my back."

They spied from beneath silver birches, across the road, on a ghost M6 Motorway junction between junctions 1 and 2. Slip roads led off the motorway leading to an easy-to-miss warehouse, modern and out of place on space allocated for services but never built.

"Better move before thunder cracks these trees," Nash said.

They scuttled on the ground, crossing the road in a crouch, and slammed their backs on the side of the unlit building. Nash slid acid through the lock, and it melted open.

Once they had reached the interior and made sure the base was secure, Jack spoke first. "How did they manage to do this without the British knowing?"

"Don't know. Masher told me my father funded Scope.

With his links to the CIA, there's more they are hiding on that arrangement.."

"You serious?" Jack said. "Your father is part of Scope?"

"You know my father and I don't see eye to eye. All I know is that he funded it."

They continued down several rows, each lined with sealed data centers flashing lights of activity. Once on lot seven of the warehouse, they stopped at the first set of databases filed under 7000. The US government super-engines stored information about people within the United States and all people of interest outside the country.

"We need server 7172," Nash said.

Nash broke the lock, and they entered into the vast space that housed close to a hundred servers. They shifted from one row to the next.

"Bingo, server 7172," Reiner said.

"This is it," Nash said. "Being in the NSA, you know where the CIA keeps its dirty work. Suppose Colton stashed his files somewhere. He would've wanted aback up plan and hid them here. Only three directors in intelligence know of these servers' existence, and a few others dotted worldwide."

Jack began his work copying files as quickly as he could, using his phone. Once he had copied all the data, he turned to Nash. "Right, I have it all."

"Then we better get out of here."

"Not so fast!"

As they moved deeper into the space, a form came into view. Nash narrowed his eyes.

Chidson!

This man seemed to move from government agency to government agency. Three men pulled away from behind him and aimed firearms at them.

What was he doing here?

Chidson approached. "Shields, I find you in the most enervating predicaments. I can tell it's you, even with those visors. You may deceive the cameras in here but not me."

Nash itched to pull the trigger of his gun, but not without endangering his friends.

"You with the CIA. Now? The city arm? Trust you to pick them," Nash said.

"Yes, that would seem to be the case."

Nash's finger curled around the trigger. He'd had enough of the desperate Marine.

"Not so fast. You may have been my superior, but I told you, I'd catch up with you.," Chidson said, his breath almost in Nash's face. "One day, I'll find out exactly what you're up to, Shields."

Chidson, still several meters away, turned to Jack. He took careful aim.

"What are you playing at?" Nash asked.

"Maybe I should ask, what are you up to? You do nothing without intent. What are you looking for here? Exactly where the CIA likes to bury things," Chidson said, his pistol still pointed at Jack. "I'll take that."

"Chidson, I'll say this once," Nash said. "Don't force me into a gunfight with you."

Jack interrupted. "Ahem... if I were you, I'd believe him. You don't want to pick a pistol fight with this guy."

Eye to Eye. Nash had to make the shot count.

Jack shoved his phone into the pocket of his combat pants.

Trained eyes and fingers calculated Chidson's every move.

A nerved twitched in Chisdon's eye before he popped off

a quick shot. Bullets could collide midair, but it was damn rare. Nash had done it three times before. All he needed was to fire at the same time and relied on the direction. It was always in the eyes. Not the firearm.

Bullets clashed, missing Jack by inches.

Reiner then turned. His silver handgun booming took the two assailants down.

Chidson, stunned in silence, tried to discharge a shot.

This time Nash aimed for his pistol. Nash cracked Chidson in the face for good measure. With all three men down, he turned to his companions. "It'll wear off. When they come to, we'll be long gone."

Chidson out cold, one man stirred. This time Nash had no words. He extinguished the lights with one gunshot. That was their cue. They hurried out the way they'd come and tore through the rain back to their van. Within minutes, the van sped down the M6 Motorway toward London.

Jack pulled out his phone. "That place is beyond me."

Nash removed his visor. "Yeah, me too. Must've been the brainchild of Colton, who is now MIA."

"And who is that, exactly?" Jack asked.

"Colton used to lead the CIA. Stan contacted him years ago to help him protect Calla as the British would not budge. That's how Calla's case first came to me."

"Does she know?"

"Not yet. Not until I know what they had on her. Colton would have the full story. It was Colton who then appeared and asked me to help Stan three years ago. He told me when I moved to London to keep an eye on Calla, so you see Jack, it was the biggest shock to me that night that you knew her when we went to the museum."

"You're telling me you recognized Calla before you met

her that night at the museum exhibition launch when I invited you?" Jack said.

"I'd never met her and only known of her from Colton's file. I'd seen her picture, but that was it. Tell you this one thing, that picture didn't do her any justice at all. Stan went to MI6 and asked them to protect Calla from the minute they were expecting her. I guess MI6 didn't believe him. That's how Nicole got involved with Heskin. They put her into a foster home with no choice until she was five, until they could safely get a couple they knew to raise her."

"That poor girl. I've known Calla a long time, and it makes sense now. Sometimes I want to hurt everyone who's hurt her."

"I know, Jack. I feel the same way. Her foster parents sent her to Beacon Academy. Stan wanted to avoid her going from home to home, so he arranged for her to go to the school. Her legal guardians, the couple she only knows as Mama and Papa Cress, are former retired MI6 agents."

"Stan thought of everything," Jack added.

"Stan came from money so he could take care of every financial need. What he did not bank on was Heskin finding Calla at Beacon. That's what we are dealing with here. Calla doesn't know what happened to her for six months while in the Sixth Form. But I bet you Colton and Heskin do. And..." he hesitated, "it was around the same time that my father funded Scope Technologies. I suspect too that Colton sold Calla's data to Heskin to help do something. I'm just not sure what."

ELEVEN

Day 10
Cote d'Azur, South of France

H er quiet expression showed him no hint of what she was thinking. Marree's evasiveness made him curious. Jack smiled when she gasped, taking in the luxurious and charming environment around her. Above the rooftops of Èze, his car curved around winding roads toward the quaint village in the south of France. With the window down, the ascending sun burned away chilly dawn air. Jack checked his speedometer, Èze was on a high cliff about 1,400 feet above sea level.

Jack parked his Bugatti Veyron in front of a steeply priced villa his sister Fiora had rented for the summer. Fiora had spared no expense. It was an ideal place to explore the cultural and coastal offerings of the French coast.

Benassi spent summers around the French Riviera and

then traveled throughout Europe looking for the best deals a billionaire could want. The mogul loved a good business deal where he could get it, and it infuriated Jack he sniffed around his business hunting his prototype technologies. Today, he was in Paris.

Marree relaxed. It had been a big step for Jack to bring her to see his sister here. They exchanged pleasantries at the door, when a smartly dressed house butler opened for them and led them into the vast living room. Sixteenth century art hung on the walls. They inhaled the scent of flowers. Well-lit rooms, adorned with several priceless art pieces, meshed well with the panoramic views of the sea.

A voice from the other room filtered through the halls as Fiona entered the room, her ear on her phone. She ended her call. "Well, hello, Marree," Fiora said. "It's great to meet one of Jack's girls."

"One of Jack's girls?" Marree said.

"Oh, no, I didn't mean it that way. Jack's special to me, and I never get to see him or most of his friends. So, I'm just thrilled to meet you."

Jack gave Fiora a stern look and then relaxed as they sat in the luxurious space. He was not done. Fiora would spend the entire night interrogating Marree if he did not intervene. They'd never shared much, growing up or otherwise. Jack's life was always private, and he liked to keep it that way. His sister would dig more profoundly than he was prepared.

"Tell me, Marree, what is it you do?" Fiora began.

"I'm a Marine biologist From Honolulu."

"How did you meet Jack?"

Marree shot a glance at him. "It's a long story, but the short version is that we were in Hawaii. Jack was there on vacation, and we somehow met."

Marree had read Jack's mind. She was smart and could tell he didn't want to share much of his private life with his sister. Marree had done well, and she kept the pleasantries above water.

He watched her, recalling the day he'd met her. He had invited her for a drink after Scorpion Tide nearly knocked her off course. Jack and Nash had been navigating the Pacific isles and experimenting with engine software when they had encountered Marree's divers. The engines had destroyed a small part of the coral reef, and they had gotten a verbal beating from Marree that soon turned into pleasantries. That evening Jack and Marree had hit it off.

It was an exciting new dynamic for Jack. He was learning to let Marree into his life. The only other woman besides Calla. But he now wanted to get to the point of why they were here. "I've come a long way to ask you something, Fiora. Just where on earth is my stuff? Why did you take it?"

Fiora shifted uncomfortably in her seat. Jack had hit on a nerve. Over the years, she had snooped on much of Jack's research and passed it on to hands that were not good. This time Jack wanted it out of her. Their time was running out.

Jack continued. "Without my protection from Benassi and his lot, you'd be in deep trouble. If you do not tell me more, I might consider removing that protection from you, and we know how that would end. My connection to ISTF in the government has often offered you a lifetime of criminal protection, especially from your husband. That's the deal we made. You took something that not even ISTF knows exists, and I want to know why and how you got it."

Marree must have twitched as she watched Jack and Fiora.

"I can't tell you," Fiora said, her eyes flashing. "He'll kill me."

Jack held his anger at bay. "In that case, handle it, and it won't be my hand."

Fiora struggled with whatever she was thinking and then suddenly surrendered. "Okay, I'll tell you what I know."

"Now we're talking," Jack said.

"I made a deal with Benassi, I would pass on as much of your research as I could. He believes you have something valuable to a deal he is making with a London corporation, Scope Industries. To gain custody of my daughter from Benassi, I promised to spy on you," she told him, her eyes moistening. "Jack, he's divorcing me, and I have nothing but her."

"How did you know what I was working on?" Jack said.

"Remember when we were kids. We were inseparable."

If there was any reserve in Jack. It all left now.

Fiora rose.

Jack's fist landed on the coffee table in front of them. "Why would you do that!"

"It was the only way I knew how to gain his trust and keep my girl. Benassi envies you. He worships what you can do."

"You know that man has always been after my stuff. Did you ever wonder perhaps why he married you? He knew you had access to me."

"Jack, I'm so sorry," she responded, tears staining her cheeks. "I didn't know what to do, so I offered anything I could do."

"Listen," Marree said, rising and setting a gentle hand on Jack's shoulder. "Let's calm down and sort this out. What exactly does your husband need Jack's technology for?"

Fiora swallowed hard. "He will sell it on."

"To whom?" Marree said.

"Someone here, in Monaco. A certain Hank Murphy and another by the name of Slate Mendes. He's also meeting with Scope Industries. I don't even know who they are. But I swear that's all I know. That's all I heard."

An icy feeling entered his heart.. "It's not yours to sell! Three months ago, you did something similar. When does it stop? How are you spying on me?"

"Your phone. The case I gave you for Christmas has a chip on it Benassi installed."

Jack tore out his phone and stripped the case off. He ripped the chip out and swore. "Fiora!"

"Must be hard," Marree said, stepping between him and Fiora. "Living a double life, I mean. You'll always watch over your shoulder. If it's not for your husband, it'll be for Jack."

Marree was spot on. She had read Fiora in all of two seconds. He ran his hand through his dreadlocks. "It's still not enough, Fiora," Jack said. "I can't provide you with protection if you're doing this. It doesn't work this way."

Jack advanced and snatched her cell phone. He disconnected its secure connection to ISTF protection. He had tried often to convince Fiora to leave Benassi. She'd always gone back to him. It was a weakness in her and he'd had enough. Just how long would she spy on his technology?

Fiora shook. She rose and tried to snatch the phone from him. "Jack, you can't leave me like this. I've told you everything I know."

Jack backed off as Marree held Fiora, who by now was having a panic attack. Eyes trundling in their sockets, her breathing sped up. Marree took Fiora to one end of the backroom, and she calmed her down. Jack could only hear whispers, but it was enough to learn that Marree had found Fiora's weak spot.

"Fiora," Marie said. "I know you have a criminal record. Jack doesn't know this."

Fiora's eyes widened. "How do you know that?"

"Two years ago, you went to Hawaii with your husband while he was smuggling stolen art. My father is with the FBI. I, too, do my research. It's a girl thing. Jack means a lot to me, so I begged my father to find all enemies in his world. My father had a record on your husband. When the FBI arrested you, you got off because you're an accessory, but my father found something else on you, and if you do not help us, Jack might just as well cut off all protection as he said."

"Smooth, Marree," Jack said, whistling and approaching.

She turned his way. "When you and Nash nearly ran my underwater expedition over, my father investigated you both. He could find nothing on you or Nash, but Fiora's, as a next of kin, her file was wide open."

TWELVE

Day 11
London, ISTF Offices
9:49 a.m.

Tiege waited in the conference room, his eyes plastered to the screen. He stood when Calla approached. "Calla, we've intercepted nine different codes set up on Scope's private network. Unknown sources have sent them up. They're being distributed out of nine locations.

"Just now? Who do you think it is?" Calla said.

Tiege straightened his back. "I can't be positive. My guess is Scope has put these notices in cyberspace to pursue government contracts. ISTF is unable to see them, but we can at the Cove."

Calla inspected the screen. "Nine codes... these are nine codes about the future. And then governments will try to buy them. You need to seize the code paths before they convey the message."

Lidingö Island, Stockholm
3:20 p.m.

They had often called Stockholm one of the most inviting cities in the world. Calla hoped they were right. She breathed in air from the Baltic Sea through the open window over the contemporary and urban city, as they made their way to in the inner Stockholm archipelago, northeast of Stockholm. As far as she could see the town had everything from waterside houses to condo buildings. Sea views and lofty spaces abounded here. On one of the fourteen islands that Stockholm straddled, their host might be more than accommodating after what they had learned that morning.

"Devera Heskin? Will she talk to us?" Jack asked.

Calla nodded. "She hasn't seen her brother in years."

Nash cornered the Rover into Lidingöbron bridge, a few miles from central Stockholm. "Why did ISTF not have intelligence on her?"

"MI6 kept it under wraps," Jack said. "It's not until they suspected Andor would visit his sister when intercepted at Heathrow that they thought ISTF might want to know."

Alighted on a rocky outcrop on a clifftop, the 1930s grand house was at the end of the private road. The mansion stood in the heart of 360-degree sea views. It kept an impressive sloping garden, offering multiple elevated vantage positions to revel in Baltic views. Devera Heskin had to have inherited the family home after the courts gave Andor

Heskin a life sentence. At the entrance, a woman led them into a spacious living room, her forehead creased with worry.

"I'm so glad you could come," Ms. Calla Cress. "I don't suppose I can ask how Andor is?"

The trio exchanged looks. "He's in custody, having escaped prison," Calla replied.

Devera pulled the door back and exhaled. "We've not spoken since we were in college. However, my daughter has got a hold of this Scope app, and she has been in a coma since. Andor and I never saw eye to eye for a very long time. He was the family prodigy and ahead. But then we lost contact when our mother died about twenty years ago. Then the fortune came to me, and Andor was not happy."

She let them through the front entrance. Evidence of wealth became apparent in the sumptuous home. Soon Devera served tea in the family room, an extensive space overlooking the Baltic Sea. Wide timber floorboards and an exhaustive staircase bordered the designer kitchen's front that sported original window frames. The all-silver interior intensified an impression of light and space.

When she had served tea, she set the pot down. "We went on with our lives; however many times, my daughter and my son kept asking about their uncle, Andor. They also wanted to know more about their cousin, Zodie Baxendale, in London."

Calla kept her voice calm. "Is your daughter's health deteriorating?"

"Yes. She's not well. She's been in a coma ever since she started using the Scope app. You see, her cousin, Zodie, when they finally made contact, reached out to her and offered her a lifetime subscription to the app, and she started playing with it."

"Did you know about this?" Nash asked. "I mean about the contact with the prison?"

"Not initially. It wasn't until I started seeing her with that phone. Soon, she started asking the app to make small predictions. I think it was anything from, '*Will this boy like me in school?*', '*What will happen to that person I don't like?*', '*What will happen to my grades?*' It was all innocent. But when my daughter started making weird requests of the app, I had a private investigator look into it. The investigator found that my daughter wanted to learn a lot more. The more she wanted to know her future, she believed she did not need to do any work or aspire to anything because all she needed was the app."

"Really?" Calla said, raising an eyebrow.

"If the app told her future and then it was not favorable, she could alter events in advance. Anyway, this is her phone," Devera said, handing Calla the phone.

"And this is the app that offers a lifetime subscription, Ms. Cress. I'm a huge friend of Allegra Driscoll, and she recommended you. I need your help. I need you to stop whatever my brother is doing because he's done it to his own family. Family means nothing to him. He only communicates with his daughter, the head of Scope. And she does not communicate with us."

Calla understood Devera's desperation. Devera had lost her daughter to a coma because of an app. Scope had predicted the girl's future, and she had become addicted. Calla understood the danger of the app was an addiction. The addiction to power and the dependence on control.

Calla looked into Devera's large blue eyes. "It's started. The more the world knows, the more it destroys itself. Nature never meant the human brain to know it all."

"That's correct," Devera said. "Please, will you come with me to my daughter's room to see her? Can you help us? I kept her here in a private hospital with everything she needs. Later I had a special room set up in our house."

They strolled to the back of the enormous house. Devera was wealthy, and she could afford to have her private people look after her daughter. When they walked into the wings with the child, she lay sleeping.

Nash nodded to the physician, an older man, who kept monitoring machines above his patient.

The doctor raised himself to his feet, with a loud grunt that betrayed his age. One heavy eyebrow slanted in disapproval. "It's happening in her head. Her brain has reacted to the app and the phone's signals," the doctor said. "Two things are going on. There's an addiction. So we've been able to follow patterns of addiction and how these happen. But what makes the app dangerous is not only its proneness to addiction, but it sends out certain signals from its servers and interferes with her brain activity."

"Doctor," Calla said. "We weren't meant to know everything. Even the future. That's why the brain can't cope with what it sees and registers from the Scope app."

He nodded. "And the more knowledge one knows about their future, the brain freezes into a coma because most can't digest what they learn. This is what we are seeing. So, two elements are going on. There's the danger posed by the signals. There's also human nature unable to cope with the possibility of knowing it all. We're an inquisitive bunch. We want to understand everything as a species."

"How is her health otherwise?" Jack asked.

"She's stable," the doctor said. "But I'm not sure for how

long. My biggest concern is it started whatever is progressing. And if it continues at this rate, she'll become incapacitated."

"We won't let that happen," Calla added.

Devera hurried out of the room. When she reached the end of the hallway, she burst into tears. Calla followed her and put an arm around her. "Listen, Devera, whatever happens, we'll save your daughter. We'll bring this to an end. And we'll stop whatever the heck it is doing."

***

Stockholm: 4:55 p.m.

As they drove back into the center of Stockholm, Calla glanced at the end of the street signposting the apartment block address Devera had written down. "It's here. I think this is the apartment Devera meant."

Nash parked the Range Rover in a side street as Calla pulled out the key Devera had given them. The residence's door swung open, displaying a sparse space that once would have been a vibrant home.

Andor had lived here, perhaps before taking the job at the UK Space Agency. The workstation, where he had organized havoc in cyberspace, was the last room in the apartment.

A row of broken laptops and cut wires signaled he'd acted alone, not wanting anyone to discover what he was up to. He left no traces of his work. If Zodie Baxendale would not give them answers, then at least they would start with her father. Andor was the engine behind Scope's technologies, and Calla would prove it. Just as he'd left gibberish in the Silviri Prison, he had etched several numbers and formulas on the walls here.

"Hmm," Nash said, studying the numbers. "See anything familiar?"

Calla nodded. "The Pythagoras Clause. The same pattern and symbols in Hypatia's scroll."

Calla had read in the media that when Heskin had been taken to prison, he had sent the app's patent to Scope Technologies and his daughter Zodie. She had taken it on and somehow been able to develop Scope Industries. And now in his home, something between this and Hypatia's scroll and the portrait was all connected.

"There's nothing else here. No server farm and nothing showing where Heskin hid the main servers of Scope's smart technologies," Jack said.

Calla felt her nerves grow taut. They were running out of options. She approached the desk by the door. "We've got to find something. There must be a switch, or a button somewhere, a central nerve that keeps Scope running and filtering through so much data."

"It's not here," Nash said. "I even tried the NSA box houses that the KJ20 Ops helped secure."

Thirty minutes later, they checked into a hotel midtown. In the extensive suite, Calla pulled off her thin coat and set it by the lounge table. She downloaded the Scope app to her phone and set it to global prediction mode. She had instructed Tiege to inform her if anything changed in the four codes they were following. They went down to the hotel bar, where Jack scrutinized information on his computer.

"Jack, could you run the Pythagoras Clause? Can you run it through a numeracy program?" Calla said.

Jack lifted one brow in curiosity. "You onto something? All right, give me the code."

Calla gave him the code from Hypatia's scroll from memory as Nash pulled out a seat for her next to Jack.

Fingers at the ready, Jack punched the information into his computer. The numbers were in sequences short and long. Calla stared down at the sketch she had brought with her.

The portrait also had the same sequence below it. "What are you telling us?" Calla said to the woman in the picture. A face remarkably identical to her mother and her. Is that why her mother had been targeted? What was the relationship between Hypatia and the Cress women?

What if Hypatia was every inch like her? Reading minds, defying gravity, physical strength, all wrapped in an individual that could self heal and understand code. Why was the Pythagoras Clause eluding her? Hypatia had been born at the wrong time of history. Anything out of the ordinary was witchcraft. What if it had been her? What if Calla had been tied to the stake?

Jack's eyes lifted. "I can't find anything. It won't accept this code or read it."

Nash's eyes narrowed in warning. "Calla, we've tried it before. It's no use. Andor knows something about the Clause that he won't share."

She turned to the image of the portrait on her phone. "I don't know who you are, but perhaps we're related, and even if we're not, we're sisters in time. I'll not let your death go to waste, but you've got to help me."

THIRTEEN

Day 12
Central London Cove, The City
11:01 a.m.

Heskin had shown no signs of a desire to eat. His body had survived without basic needs in the prisoner holding rooms for over seventy-two hours. Later they said that he'd only sit and stare at the wall. At one point, he stood and moved to the little peephole in the door.

Calla's eyes glued to the screen where a camera watched Heskin's holding cell. "What do you think is happening in his head?" ISTF had taken Heskin from Heathrow Airport, and from there, Tiege and his operative agents had put him in the London Cove for interrogation, before he'd transfer to ISTF. A ticking machine to his rights monitored his neurological activity, and Calla stared at it for what seemed like an eternity.

Calla swung to face Tiege, whom she had entrusted with the care of Heskin in the Cove. What wasn't Andor saying? Her head was still churning round his prediction about Nash?

Nash had shut down the information and pushed it under the carpet. So had she.

"What did you talk to him about?" Nash asked when he and Jack joined her in the observation room.

Blackened mirrors showed them the prisoner, who watched them unflinching from his holding office.

"We wanted to know if he would receive his daughter. She contacted ISTF to visit him. His eyes lighting up was the first reaction we've seen in him as we scanned his brain activity. There was no sense of emotion beyond that," Tiege said.

"Did you let her come?" Calla asked.

"He had no desire to receive her, so, no," Tiege said.

They were facing confusion all round. Without Hypatia's full scroll and just the picture, they had nothing. Calla pinched her lips. "I see."

A knock on the door interrupted her, and the face of an administrative operative poked through the door's crack. "Miss Cress, Devera Heskin is downstairs. She says she traced you to ISTF and then her driver followed your Maserati here this morning. Should I let her up? I can take her through the visitors secured elevator."

"We can't let her know about the Cove's activities. Yes, please do."

"What is it we can do for you?" Calla said when Devera arrived at the door, having moved to a visitor's receiving office.

Devera lowered herself in the chair. "Excuse my insistence here. I didn't want to disturb you, but I thought this was the best way to get you this information. You looked at my daughter's phone, but I discovered a second phone in her other bag. Must admit I have tried to scrutinize and look at all her things, but then I found this yesterday, just shortly after you left, came up with this prediction."

"What?"

"Scope set up my daughter. The app on the second phone differed slightly from the one on the first phone. Scope set her up with two sets of apps. They were using her as a 'spreader,' a term my investigator used to describe a person whose phone communicates with other phones to tag them with the app. They had also given my daughter both the corporation app and the consumer app. There's even more information about the full abilities of Scope Technologies on the corporation app."

Calla took the phone, and she searched for the app.

She scrutinized the report the app displayed:

Gelise 777.

"What's Gelise 777 got to do with anything?" she asked.

"Gelise 777 is 52 light years away. It's a yellow sub-giant, a system that is also a binary star made up of two stars and possibly a third," Jack said.

Devera's head dipped in a quick nod. "Though Andor was the prodigy of the family, I too was a scientist before my children were born and quite a good one too," Devera said. "I have two daughters, and he saw one as someone to exploit.

I'm sure he wants my other daughter. The Scope app seems to target girls, so Scope is seeking as many as it can."

"Zodie didn't make friends much with girls at school. It's no wonder Heskin sent her to Beacon Academy, a school for girls," Calla said. "Zodie must be the one who approved the first app's launch."

"Including those in her family. The woman is delusional. Her father adores her so much. He adopted her when she was an infant."

Nash's gaze locked with hers. "Did he have other children?"

Devera's eyes showed pain. "No. Somebody has to stop him."

Nash's powerful shoulders lifted in a casual shrug. "What kind of scientist were you, Ms. Heskin?"

"A Space engineer as well. I think you can help her. There's something about you. Something I can trust about all of you."

"I can tell you just a little of the primary components of this thing. It's been years since I studied the details. Gelise is a sun-like star in the system, dissolving hydrogen in its core. It is much older than the sun, and it's about 6.7 billion years old. Some say it is also less massive than the sun and rich in metal. It's also seventy percent more metal elements heavier than helium. This means that this star has more metals than the sun—more than is usual for stars of its nature."

Jack interjected. "There's a similar distant star like it, a little dwarf, further away. An orbit around such a star would take tens of thousands of years to complete."

She nodded. "The reason I thought I should tell you is Andor had been working on this project long before my children were born. I used to work for NASA before I joined the British Space Agency. This was before Andor. I hadn't seen him since college at that point. He then ousted me from a project we were both working on in UKSA. He then cut me out of his life. I hadn't seen him since. I have, though, hung onto a lot of his research."

She tossed storage flash drives on the table. "This is all I kept on Andor's research before the courts sentenced him. I had to dig, but he had it all locked in secure vaults in offshore accounts. Since we changed the family will when they sent him to prison, it gave me his entire affairs. I could get these. Baxendale was the name he used when he lived in the UK. He reverted to his Icelandic name Heskin for all legal matters. I hope it can help you."

Calla took the flash drives and handed them to Jack. "Thank you, Devera. We will do all we can for your daughter."

When Devera left, they huddled around Calla's office computer, and Jack launched the first flash drive.

"I've seen these codes before," she said. "In my mother's files." Calla gave them a lopsided grin. "I know what this is. This is a serial number. A serial number for a telescope that can look through to this system, the star. Can you imagine? Whoever has this telescope can observe further into Space than most people have. Just what did Andor want in Space?"

Jack studied his laptop and searched for his ISTF intelligence data. "A radio telescope was deposited on the Moon ten months ago."

"Let me guess," Nash said. "Scope Technologies."

"Correct. The telescope is one hundred meters broad and is on the Moon's far side. It is giving it a stable platform with a slow rotation rate," Jack added.

THE DECRYPTER AND THE PYTHAGORAS CLAUSE   209

"How on Earth is this possible?" Calla said, watching him.

He shook his head as if clearing cobwebs from his mind. "Heskin has been busy. The telescope extends beyond Earth's atmosphere, catching radio frequencies that scatter and clutter."

Calla understood the threat.

"What more do we know?" Nash said.

"That there are billions of stars light years away assembling into outer galaxies. It's all chaotic at the minute, but what we're getting from ISTF servers are astronomical photographs. They're clear and unmatched by any other observatory launched."

Calla thought for a moment then sank into a seat next to Jack. "We need to intercept all images and data running from that telescope."

"I hear you," Jack said. "The telescope is within an impact crater. Its surrounding infrastructure also has a mixture of some assembling nanotubes and material coming from the Moon itself."

Calla sucked in her cheeks, thinking. "This is how they've been able to reduce costs. Scope Industries have got to the Moon. They have used the Moon's infrastructure to power their app. They have saved billions because you see this reduces their costs."

Nash hunched in. "But aren't they using ISTF satellites? Hmm, I guess the PM has been busy, Cal."

"Devera, why do you think they put Scope's corporation app on your daughter's phone?" Jack asked.

"I don't know. The corporation app is secure and by invitation only."

Calla's tongue felt too thick to form words. "Must've

learned something they didn't want her to know. They didn't put it on her phone. Your daughter did, and they punished her for it. I take it Scope could not find that phone. They must've silenced her with the coma. I guess the technology is on offer somewhere. They use the corporation app to solicit buyers. Now, it's at large. I bet Zodie or Heskin will present it to one of the ISTF governments to turn them against each other."

"Hmm," Jack mused. "To break up ISTF."

Calla rose and walked to the door. She set a hand on the knob, thinking. "He is after me as the head of ISTF. This was his warning. This is his revenge on Britain for handing him to the Turkish Government and sanctioning a life sentence."

Scope Industries Laboratories, Baltimore
1:12 p.m.

The room was dark with a single light from a lab table when Zodie forced her way in the door.

Erikssen shot up. His posture went limp as if all his bones had dissolve the way. "We agreed for you never to come here," Erikssen said.

Zodie neared, her eyes carefully studying him. "I've an interest in my investment here. I'm here to see how far we have gotten."

Erikssen moved back.

She approached him thoughtfully and jabbed her hand on his throat. "I'm going to the Scorpion Tide, and I need to make sure that it will be active when I get there."

Erikssen found it hard to believe. His lungs clogged underneath her firm grip. He coughed, observing as Zodie's eyes poured into him. She was a scary woman and pretty if she tried to be nice.

She was anything but.

"Why is this so important to you?" he said.

"That remains my business."

"The science is still in its infancy. You know human cloning is illegal in ninety-five percent of the world."

"That's why we set up this lab for you here in the US. It's guarded. I paid for it and paid you well too. Once you've completed your part of the bargain, I'll make sure your contract with ISTF does not fail."

Erikssen fell to the floor when she released him. She was intimidating and would not hesitate to use the gun in her holster. He moved around the lab and opened a security safe. "Here it is. You need to tap the exact code into the entry pad. You know I had to steal the materials for the recounts you asked me to produce. I gained the last details and voice recordings in Havana when I recorded her speech at the dinner table. The voice synth is now complete and can mimic with accuracy."

He played the recording.

Zodie's passion thickened her voice. "Yes, that is her. Can it say anything I want?"

He lifted his shoulders in a noncommittal shrug. "Yes."

Her eyes lit up.

Erikssen drew up a picture on his laptop. "This was the only material I could find that could house a reproduction and acclimatize it in the sea. It has been the most fascinating part of my work. I could duplicate her, but I've not been able to understand the reasons. Like all sciences and technology, nothing is perfect."

"Leave that to me. Your task was not to explain her genetics. You don't have enough statistics for that. Your job was to clone the child as my father presented the data."

"Where did he get her sample?"

"You underestimate the person standing in front of you. Calla Cress and I were schoolmates at Beacon Academy. I had lots of ways of obtaining a lock of her hair. Most of it was in the school playground. Lucky for me, I knew who I was. She didn't know who she was. Why do you think my father sent me to the same high school as Calla Cress?"

Scorpion Tide, London
6:20 p.m.

Jack hadn't moved from his position in the seat and barely looked up as Nash approached. "The consumer app asks people to fill out a seventy-five question questionnaire before they can begin using it. Heskin designed those queries. They're on the flash drives and took him years to find the right questions. They're specific."

Nash handed him a beer and dipped into a seat next to him. "Something's interesting here. Against her mother's will, Devera's daughter went to visit her uncle in prison."

"How do you know that?" Calla said, advancing into Scorpion Tide's main lounge area.

Nash adjusted a laptop toward them. "It's recorded here on MI6 reports. They kept an eye on all visitors Heskin had, but failed to tell ISTF, and we have no record of that girl visiting him."

"Did he ask her to visit him?" Calla said.

"No," Nash said. "Heskin lured her with math. Via the app. He must've latched onto her phone."

Tension tying Calla's stomach in knots eased. "What did he want from her? There's no sign they had a relationship."

A heavy sigh whizzed past Jack's compressed lips. "The daughter was the first guinea pig. As a teenager, she switched on her phone, engaged with apps, and was continuously online. She was the exact thing they needed to predict behavior. And if they could forecast behavior in the people who are most turned on to technology, then they could use the data to develop larger groups, and then communities, and then nations."

A thoughtful frown revealed Nash's worry. "Using today's teenagers, who are tomorrow's decision makers. The most active minds with the current use of technology, but that data developed the corporate and governmental apps."

Calla leaned back on the sofa, her eyes firm on the men. "Devera's not telling us everything."

"Like what?" Jack said.

Calla flashed him a smug smile. "She too went to Silviri to see Heskin. She neglected to mention that. Tiege pulled up CCTV that failed to make it to ISTF as well. Tiege identified a mole too, Radya. She stole a video feed she channeled back to Scope. Devera, too, has a record here. What if she volunteered her daughter and now realizes that to save her, only ISTF can help because Andor Heskin won't? After all," she said, "Devera banked all the money when he went to prison."

The Scorpion Tide Conference Room
London Docks

"Isn't it perplexing people wanting to know their future?" Nash said, his eyes smoldering with an indefinable expression.

Calla's shoulder rested against the doorframe. "I can see several instances in history where someone searched for answers in the future. We hear about the Pharaoh, who once had bad dreams, and then a slave came from the dungeons to reveal his dreams and tell him exactly what would happen. It's not the first time we are seeing the psyche enter the minds of individuals and government heads."

The phone rang, and Calla picked it up. "Hello?"

"Calla, it's me."

"Allegra?" Calla pressed her ear to the phone and swung in the men's direction. "What? Why did they agree to this? We're still investigating Scope Industries." Calla looked up from the call. "You said it, Nash. PM Byrne has gone against our advice."

"I agree with you, Calla," Allegra said. "Scope made him an offer he couldn't refuse. ISTF needs the best, and the PM is stubborn and believes the best out there is Scope Industries."

She deliberated on what path to choose. "Doesn't he know what they're doing to people, to girls?"

Allegra sighed, breathing into the phone. "He doesn't believe it."

Calla felt as exposed as a rabbit crossing a plowed field

with a hawk circling overhead. "If we don't stop Zodie, she'll be running the state soon."

Calla glanced over at Nash and Jack when she set down the phone. "With Scope taking over ISTF systems, it means five governments will be working together in unimaginable ways and not all good. We're not far away from a world where we have one government running the world."

They heard a noise behind them. It was Delgado. "Mr. Shields. There's someone here to see you and Miss Cress."

"Who is it?" Calla said.

"Zodie Baxendale from Scope Industries. Her people tried to come onto Scorpion Tide one other time. In Havana," Delgado said. "I didn't let them."

Calla glanced at Jack and Nash. "Okay, let her through the main deck lounge."

Zodie came onboard dressed in a tight, light-colored skirt and an expensive blouse that matched with jewelry that could light up all of London Bridge. Alongside her, Miss Drake paced behind her and two security guards Calla didn't recognize.

"Zodie, a surprise?" Calla said.

"I'm here with a proposal. A business arrangement shall we say."

Calla narrowed her eyes. "What do you have in mind?"

"First, I want my helicopter back. I know about your snooping around Scope Industries. There's nothing for you to find. As head of ISTF, you'll work with me and one day for me. Together we can do a lot of wonderful things. I suggest you do not interfere with my plans, because you never know when a prediction may be made about you. You never know when your imprint on life might be your downfall."

A dark frown settled on Nash's brooding features. "That a threat?"

"Not if you don't want it to be."

One of Zodie's security guards set a hand on his gun. Nash's pistol was under the table, and he could draw it faster than the goon could say 'hello'. Nash remained calm. This was not the place.

Zodie made a move to leave. "I suggest you wake up tomorrow and decide who you are going to serve. Because I think your government has already decided where they're going to take their future."

FOURTEEN

South Bank, London
8:01 p.m.

It had hit home and Calla took to the upper deck balcony of the Scorpion Tide, panting for fresh air. Calla wasn't sure why Hypatia's scroll had all the answers, but she realized it did. Somewhere deep inside, Hypatia had written something she believed she had to read.

Hypatia had concealed many riddles in the scroll in formulas she couldn't get out of her head, yet Calla couldn't interpret it. And now Calla recognized she had to protect it.

She leafed through the images Nash had taken. Hypatia understood Pythagoras's secrets. Her genes, whether natural or operative, had given her something unique. As Calla could dig farther into her subconscious to resolve subtleties of language, Hypatia had been the opposite. She hid them. Hypatia was born generations before her, but could she understand, and was she able to accept her normality because it was transparent others didn't?

Calla searched her psyche. She understood. Her mind explored the words Hypatia had written. People like Hypatia admired Pythagoras. Many met him as he journeyed between Greece, Egypt, and other parts of the world. These people had to be operatives who believed he had answers that could unravel their operative minds.

Perhaps Pythagoras had understood operatives used math to the highest degree to conduct and make the world thrive with their inventions. It made sense for Hypatia to seek Pythagoras. How could her writings apply to today's technology? Her mind, just like Calla's, could read undecipherable symbols. In that moment, Calla wanted to meet Pythagoras just as Hypatia had. Yes, Pythagoras would understand Calla. A mathematician she adored, born centuries before she was a thought. Could he tell her who she was?

Pulse racing, Calla glided a finger over the pen strokes in the image. Hypatia's words were urgent, and sometimes they were hurried and rushed, but the sense came out clearly. Perhaps Pythagoras might help her figure out why her brain thought faster than others. Pythagoras might explain why on Earth, Calla's genes were very different. But the question remained, had Hypatia been an operative? Calla did not know. She continued reading and translated the words from the scroll.

I have heard the rumors in the village. I have understood them well. I know they call me a witch. My words are not witchcraft.

My mind interprets the future and sees destiny through science. And the dreams I have told me there will be a day in the world where man will be capable of doing far more than he can imagine.

Not only will he shoot engines into the stars, but he will go there. He'll be able to speak from one end of the Earth to the other with no obstacles.

He'll be keen to travel at the quickness of lightning. I have a huge conviction about this. I want to find the man they call Pythagoras. I hope today my guide will take me to his village. He has defined much using numbers. This is the place I believe I need to go.

Calla had to stop reading. It was all too familiar. She saw a sister separated by centuries. They were the same. Were they related in mind, perhaps in body also?

Calla had no way of finding out. One particular area of the manuscript she could not understand. Here Hypatia had employed a different language altogether. Calla continued reading as the words made sense to her. Hypatia had used the scroll as therapy. Perhaps a diary. Calla read fast and went through the length of the scroll. Hypatia had gone back to her country and worked on a new science, a new astrological outlook. It was in Egypt, in Alexandria, that her studies had expanded after her visit to Greece. Parts of the scroll had a distinct sense and had a unique feel to them. The words were more instructional than the preceding ones.

The man Pythagoras told me to combine his numerological sequence, and then perhaps I would get the answers I needed. When I was in Greece, I spent several months with him, and there were many things I didn't understand. But he fascinated me. He overwhelmed me about the future. Any future. But I never got to show him, and I probably never will. I never showed him what I could do. He spoke of beings, human in every way, yet with the gift of the stars and calculations of angels. I had a dream about her again. I don't know who she is? Where she is? But she combines time. Could this drawing do her justice?

Calla stopped reading the printed images of the scroll. It made sense to her but she could not share its wisdom. Not yet anyway.

She had to get the scroll back. Something Hypatia had written about her. was missing.

She scurried downstairs to the main lounge where Jack, Nash, and Delgado went through security proceedings on the Scorpion Tide. "Nash, Jack, are you busy tonight?"

Nash lifted an eyebrow. "Why?"

FIFTEEN

Day 13
Scope Industries, London
Midnight

This time, they would not go through the front door. Calla would have to ascend over the rear wall to find the floors that was off the books. It would take their best operative forces, Tiege, and a few more.

Just a few.

The small speed boat waded upriver until they reached Scope Industries landing docks on the Thames. Heat and humidity hung in the air like steam in a hot shower. The murky sky, concealing the Moon's rays, promised rain on the stifling July evening.

They filed through Scope's grounds. Special operative tactics suits would furnish the camouflage and swift movements they required. With backs plastered against the exterior wall on the southern grounds of Scope Technologies, the entrance would be expeditious, with a smoke can entrance.

The quiet building gave them confidence; what little security was about would involve minimal fire. It took three moves, two gas canisters, and one burst at the gate.

Visors on, Calla nodded to Jack. "I'll go in, and slap this magnet on to the data center."

"When you get in there, it should be able to transmit," Jack said. "We'll keep watch using this camera on your headgear."

Calla ran gloved fingers along the glass surface as Nash set fervent lips on hers. "Careful. I'd prefer you back in one piece."

"Yes, soldier," she said, smiling.

She stared up and scrutinized the perimeter of the building. Nash shot a cable to the seventeenth floor. They reckoned that, given the position where the elevator had discarded them several days ago, that was the best assessment. Jack disabled the alarms on the building, hacking through the key security system.

The coil, now affixed to the exterior facade, gave Nash resistance when he tugged it for security. "Off you go."

With the harness firmly around her waist, she started her ascension, stealthily. She hunted for cracks in the glass as Jack's spiders crawlers led her, giving her guidance. When she reached the hidden level, she signaled the company below.

She exhaled and willed it. Calla punctured the glass. Samsonite, operative strength cracked the shards, allowing access.

According to Jack, the last guard check had been an hour ago as she surveyed the quiet hall. Silence met her as dark secrets hid within the sealed-off story, the seventeenth and a half floor. Concealed out of sight on the floor, a narrow walkway allowed *her access to the rooms.*

"You okay?" Jack said in her earpiece.

"Yes, I am," she said. "I found the floor."

"Let the spiders guide you to room 27. Our files show that's where a black safe is kept. The black safe is the size of an elevator. You will need to destroy the lock, but that's when Jack's spiders come in," Tiege warned. "From your previous description, it is made from soft aluminum. Once you get in there, you're going to be invisible in there to make it to those rooms. We need to set a bug on the machine."

"Invisible?"

"Use your suit, it's wired to create reflectors that make you appear invisible like the Scorpion Tide," Tiege said.

"Why am I not surprised, Tiege?" she said.

Calla switched on camouflage mode and soft-footed the offices as several scientists handled nanotubes and other components around a lab table of electrical models. Robotic arms dangled from the ceiling, manipulating scenarios. Two scientists worked with a printed copy of Hypatia's scroll on the counter opened to the portrait. AI arms scanned symbols, language too antique for it to understand. The analysts would turn over the pages every few seconds and then continue to a machine and punch in characters. This was not meant to be here. The scroll had to have Pythagoras's full Clause, everything that was still an enigma to her.

She accessed the electronic chip in her head and snapped photographs with the blinking of her eye nerve.

Calla shoved her back against a dark screen when a bald scientist headed her way. She stood by with bated breath until he lifted the scroll she'd not seen on a second counter, and took it to the black safe. A sweat bead threatened to deactivate her suits. Any moisture would generate a short circuit. She held her gasp.

When he marched a hair breath past her, she scooted to the end of the cubicle.

Room 27. Clearly marked, she had to hustle.

"Jack, I am here. Can you disable it?"

"Show me the lock."

Calla obliged and snapped an image, then sent it via transmission to Jack.

He disabled the digital seal with one hack and she rushed inside. Darkness greeted her in the tiny space. "Jack, I'm in," she mumbled in her earpiece.

Calla drew out a miniature flashlight. "Jack, I need you to cut the power."

"All right. You have ten seconds."

He cut the power, providing her only moments. Then she saw it as she pulled a metal screen from left to right. Behind glass and steel, extraordinary strength genetically mined for generations gave her more power as she drew back the full seal with the might of a bull.

Five seconds.

Then something seized her attention. Jack's stolen laptop held in an adjoining glass case. His life's achievements. Calla could either snatch Hypatia's manuscript, or Jack's work. Not both. The power would revive in three flashes.

Somewhere between time, her mind paused.

She needed Hypatia's manuscript. Her sanity depended on it, but the world depended on Jack's creations.

She had one move and ten seconds before camouflage mode would wear off her suit.

Calla stretched for Hypatia's scroll and crammed it

under her suit. Alarms chattering, sirens alerted her to a lockdown. Quick as a cat in a headlight, she slid between the tight door.

If the guards were now alert, they could not match her speed. Fast feet propelled her back the way she'd entered. When she stood at the end of the broken window, she pulled in a deep breath and leaped off through.

Her descent was rapid as bullets reflected off her high-tech suit.

ISTF, Red Fox's Private Office

Stan moved with prudence when he saw her in her private office. He winced, knowing recently the office had belonged to Mason Laskell, the man who'd hunted Calla all her life and inspired others. He stood and rolled his shoulders to release tension. Calla had her head in her palms.

What had he done to his girl? For years he wondered if shielding her by leaving her with Mama and Papa Cress had been the choice. They had singled out the family well; non-operative whom she could call by those names to feel less of an orphan. Less inadequate; more normal. When they'd conceived her, the warning was, she would be genetically gifted. They saw it in her blood work and had chosen a private operative hospital for her birth. They did not understand it then.

Papa and Mama Cress had done well.

Stan ran a hand through his hair, quietly approaching Calla where she sat in the turquoise guest seats by the window.

"Hey?" he said.

Calla looked up. "Father?"

"I think you can call me *dad* by now."

She smiled. "What are you doing here?"

"I know it scares you, but Calla, don't be frightened."

She rose and headed to the window, her heart heaving in her chest. "The girl in Korea is still in a coma. She may not make it through the night. They have reported three hundred and twelve others around the world. All of them used the Scope app. This is a silent killer. And mother..."

"Don't Calla." He walked to her and drew her in his arms. "I've never asked for forgiveness for ever leaving you. I tried to make sure you were well provided for."

She nodded. "With a trust fund worth millions, I've never been able to spend."

"I want you to. You and Nash."

"Is that a guilt trip?"

"No, Calla. It's saying I'm sorry and I love you."

She sank into his arms, having never heard those words from her father.

"But that's not what is bothering you?" he said.

She shook her head. "No."

Calla turned on the screen on the left wall in the ultramodern office. It lit up and flashed statistics her team had pulled. "The Scope app spreads like wildfire. It's like a disease. Addictive and throwing people into comas. How does an app do that?"

"You'll figure it out. We will together."

"And the Pythagoras Clause? The more I understand it, the more it throws me off. Something does not add up. Just what did Hypatia mean by it?" she said.

His restless pacing reminded her of a sleek caged animal. "Maybe it is more related to you than you think."

"How can that be? I've never studied Pythagoras in that much depth."

He lifted an eyebrow. "Calla, I monitored all your school and medical reports from Beacon Academy. I asked the school to keep me informed of your wellbeing. One report suggests you were in the hospital for six months. Did you know that?"

She nodded. "I've no memory of it, and it scares me. When I got back to school, I was just told I was in hospital."

Stan studied her. "You were kidnapped, not in the hospital. None of us know what happened to you."

She dug her fingernails into her palms to disguise her nervousness. "What?"

"We don't know who, but I believe it could all be linked. You could have been drugged. When you came back, the school was tipped that they had dropped you off downtown. They found you wandering by yourself and alerted Mama and Papa Cress. We instructed the school to go public with that information."

"Where had I been?" she said.

"I don't know. But whoever did it sent the then head operative Vortigern a warning that your genetics had shown them much. We don't know if it was true or not, but we had to hope it didn't compromise you."

Tension vibrated each nerve ending in her. "I was experimented on?"

"We don't know, but the message to Vortigern came with a note attached to it. It said the Pythagoras Clause could not stop them."

"What did they mean? Do they mean it's the glitch we think it is?" Calla asked.

"I don't know, sweetheart."

"They will not stop, dad. Will they? Not until they take me down."

"You take them down, Calla. Draw strength and courage from who you are. Maybe that's the only alternative. If you don't control your fears and the fear of who you are, you'll not beat this."

She refused to allow him to see her cry.

"Calla, there's one thing I'll tell you. Data doesn't lie. But data can be manipulated any way you like. You're a Cress. Remember that. You were born with genes that were crafted millennia ago. This means that your data existed before you were born. Before I was born. What that tells me is you have a grand purpose you must find and embrace. It's your out. Perhaps you shared the same genetic makeup as Hypatia, and that's why she resonates with you."

Calla leaned back on the office sofa. "You think?"

"What I'm saying is it doesn't surprise me that perhaps you and her think alike."

Calla tried to bring her emotional chaos under control. Her dad was right. The app had given her much to think about.

Stan's face softened. "One thing I've learned as an MI6 agent, and from missions around the world trying to prevent international mayhem is life may intend the worst for you, but that can only touch you if you let it."

She nodded and plastered intent eyes on him.

"You've got to fight evil and terrorism heart, body, mind, and spirit," he said. "Calla, you nearly there, my daughter. Your mother could never achieve that level of resistance.

Sometimes data seduced her. But it hasn't with you. I believe in you. My only fatherly advice is don't accept the data. Use the data to your advantage."

Duchess of Bedfords Walk, Kensington, London
9:27 p.m.

Zodie's chest tightened so hard she swore her ribs cracked in that moment. Her home office was a sanctuary, but something felt off tonight. She'd spared no luxury on home lighting elements, from the vintage gray engineered oak planks, to the custom-built extensive library behind her Wall Street desk. It reminded her of everything she'd achieved.

Born not to succeed, left in a garbage bag in Braxton Gardens, New Forest, she'd never known her birth parents. Even the view overlooking the prestigious gated development of Academy Gardens on Campden Hill in Kensington wasn't enough tonight. She had all her heart desired, yet ultimately something was missing. Why did she crave what she couldn't have? Calla's life.

The woman had the genes she wished she'd been born with, the men in her life who guarded her like no man had done Zodie. Yet the girl did not know her real potential and how perfect a human she was. What a waste of operative power.

After the day Zodie had had, she should have been in bed, but sleep would not come. Zodie peered down at her laptop, its luminous glare straining her eyes.

They had had a lot of success that day. And she had to

make it through to the next step. It shouldn't take long now. The governments she had been in contact with would buy into the plans they had made.

She typed an email to the US office, words failing her. Her father had provided much information they needed. He was a brilliant man, and she missed him.

They received money from the Chinese government, and soon, the governments of the United States, Japan, and Germany would follow. This would be all of ISTF's members. She continued typing on her computer with a keen eye on how she would approach each state. She had been working for the last several hours. If her father were here, it would be all the easier. She had hired a team of specialists to keep people away from Scope, those who wanted to snoop around like that head of ISTF Calla Cress.

Zodie smiled, knowing that her lawyers had worked with her, disguising information and making Scope even more attractive to her clients. Now the actual test of Scope's power would be for her to get it into each government's hands. Little did they know they would work against each other. They wouldn't know what was behind this.

The noise had come from behind her.

She had not moved.

Years of working in the dark had trained her ears.

She took in a deep breath, and her hand slid underneath the desk where a small compartment lay. She pulled open the drawer and drew her gun, slipping a finger around the trigger. She turned around slowly and squinted an eye. "Who is it?"

There was no answer.

Silence.

The quiet buzzing of the night cleaner working in the hallway filtered in through to her office. Nobody could here.

Not this way.

The noise startled her again. This time, flustered, she drifted to the window. Heart pounding, she turned back to her desk and turned on the night lamp. As the room moved out of darkness and flooded with light, her hands firmly on the gun, she reached for the main light switch.

Him?

"Is that the way you welcome your long-lost father?"

Zodie understood.

"Father?"

A face drew into form in front of her.

Her mind see-sawed back and forth. "Father?"

The last time she'd seen her father was when she'd gone to visit him in prison in Turkey. They had let her see him briefly.

She watched her father, and her heart sank as she drew a foot in front of the other to go toward him. The man had aged, but not in a wrong way.

He looked well, far better than she had seen him last time in Silviri Prison, Turkey.

"Father, I heard you had left prison, but then I lost your trace, and I had no idea if they had come for you. We didn't know where to begin our search."

"Shush, not a word," Andor said.

She ran to him. She'd always admired and loved him. An intelligent man who'd even once worked for NASA. He'd been the one who had given them everything they knew and understood about data science and math. This is how they had treated him and betrayed him. He also worked at ISTF, and that's where all hell had broken loose for him. Then the accusations had begun. They had accused him and pushed him out, and Calla Cress escorted him to prison.

"I love the algorithms you've been working on," Andor said as he took her face into his hands.

"I learned from the best," Zodie said with a proud smile. "You're the one who knew what Hypatia had to say about numerology and data science. If it wasn't for her and everything that we've learned from the scroll, we wouldn't be where we are today. But it was all you father. I'm just so glad to see you," Zodie said.

Andor moved around the room, admiring all the displays on the walls. "I'm very proud of what you have achieved. Zodie. I remember the nights we studied the scroll, even going as far as traveling to Egypt to understand Hypatia. How tirelessly we worked, my girl," Andor said.

Her father was right. They had his vision of creating an unstoppable, predictable machine. Andor had been right that they could use data science. He had found this information when he had worked with Mason Laskfell at ISTF. How he knew and where he got the ideas for these really in-depth technologies was only Zodie's guess.

Even after the scroll was first taken from Scope, they had left an invisible tracker on it. When it had disappeared, they had traced it to Havana, then to the shop. Then to none other than ISTF's Calla Cress.

Hex had been careless in going after them in Havana. He had only triggered their anger and their curiosity in the scroll. But Zodie undoubtedly knew they would not get what they were looking for in that scroll.

"Just as Hypatia's father had worked as a mathematician and his daughter had followed, so you two Zodie you followed in my footsteps, and you've done very well. You've worked hard to find the answers and master human behavior patterns that translate to a larger scale, which became the nation's behavior. We can use it to our advantage. You will never be unstoppable again. They'll never separate us again. People don't accept that their past nature has a significant way of affecting their future if they do not take stock and check their lives. They're like a mouse on the wheel and a hamster that just keeps going over and over the same thing the same cycle."

"Father, how are you? I've been so worried about you." She stopped, then squinted as if assessing if he were a ghost. "Where are you?"

"I'm anywhere you want me to be, at least with this 3D dimensional projection of me. I improved the technology at NASA. They tasked me with finding how astronauts could communicate with each other when on missions through what you may call a hologram. I took the tech with me when I knew they would come after me. It works splendidly. For now, I can only get it to work for ten minutes. You can see my appearance from any angle. High-quality holographic technology has almost been perfected."

Zodie stared at the lifelike hologram. "I stole the blueprint codes and research from the operatives when Mason once allowed me a peek at what they can do. At what you too can do. Electronic telepathy with an image drawn from your emotions. You see me as you wish to see me. Not as I am. I'm afraid."

Surely it was him in the flesh. The man was a genius. "Where are you?" Zodie asked.

"I'm not sure, but Calla Cress's responsible for my detainment. I was on my way to get the remaining funds from Sweden when she intervened. Don't worry about me, Zodie. I'm fine. I see you've made perfect use of the app I left you. Well done."

"I'm close to making this effective for gathering the same information from governments."

Her eyes looked up into her father's. "We've used many prototypes. The app is now a means of gathering data from people. Once we have that data science, we can predict much more about human behavior, and eventually, nations. People are very predictable. As much as people think they are individuals, ironically, their actions and behavior say otherwise. Pythagoras worked and understood the cycles of life and how to translate them into math and could understand the workings of this globe. The missing piece of your research father was in that scroll. And even though now that they've come for it and taken it away from us, I feel they won't be able to stop us. No one can break Pythagoras's Clause. Not even Hypatia could. She tried and failed. No, not this time. Not even Mason Laskfell. He set you up."

"Yes. Calla Cress's worked for him. He knew how to set me up all those years ago."

"I'll make them pay," Zodie said.

"Don't be so hard, my daughter. Do not turn into what I have become," Andor said.

"No, father, we need to do this."

Andor's holographic image ambled around the room slowly. "I wanted to give the world something good, Zodie. I never wanted to do anything else but help the world through technology, and when Laskfell and I ran into some world's most unbeatable technologies, I knew we had it. But he betrayed me. All I wanted was the world to understand that you could use data science, and you could use the information for good. Then, they turned me to ISTF—"

"ISTF has to pay," Zodie said, her eyes burning. "How can we clear your name?"

"I wouldn't make that your number one concern."

"We can change that," Zodie said. "We can clear your name. Once we have these governments and understand everything about them, we can use them against each other. We can do that. They'll come to us for information. We'll be world intelligence, not ISTF. I've devised the best plan with Erikssen. I thank you for introducing me to that man. I will make Calla Cress pay, and they will. It's on the part right now on the Scorpion Tide."

Andor raised an eyebrow. "Did you say the Scorpion Tide?"

Zodie nodded. "Once we unleash it on the Scorpion Tide, it completely disarms Calla Cress. The technology you devised makes it impossible for anybody to know that we were behind what is coming to them on the Scorpion Tide. Then ISTF comes down and everything with it and everything it stands for, which only means that Scope will be unstoppable. If ISTF is out of the way—"

"Zodie, I don't know how I turned you into this person. I was like you, and I'm afraid you've become more than I ever thought you would. But look where it has landed me."

"I plan to use Scope to predict national abilities starting with China. We sell information about China to the United States, and out of the United States to the United Kingdom, and it continues from thereon. That is how we destroy ISTF in the five governments who organized your arrest and put you behind bars. They're years away from us."

"I can see how we will be unstoppable as a team," Andor said, then folded his arms over his chest. "And once we have the governments at thier feet, then they will do very little."

"They would clear your name, father."

"Dear child, you always wanted to be a scientist. I sent

you to Beacon Academy to become a brain at a young age. To become one of the leading members and knowledgeable women in the United Kingdom. That's what Beacon is famed for. You took the brief well. I must admit I'm proud of what you've done with Scope. However, I sometimes wonder if I did you justice."

Zodie was not listening. "We can do so much more, father. We are together now. Once your name is cleared. You don't have to live in the shadows. You'll command them. It was I who broke you out of prison, but then I lost your trace at Heathrow."

"So, it was you."

"Yes, father. Hex Murphy was the best I could find. And to throw ISTF off, I left a riddle on the wall and used one of their own people, Radya Zaher. I left mathematics symbols so they would chase the wrong thing. That was the plan when I broke you out of prison. The idea was you and I would finish this together. When I lost you, I almost lost hope? But now we can."

"Zodie…"

The hologram flashed, blinking with power loss.

"Zodie…"

He was gone.

Fury rose to her cheeks. "Damn you, Calla Cress!"

ISTF Offices, Central London
10:15 a.m.

The high-security part of the prison housing the custody rooms required no guards, and the iris scans and palm prints of permitted staff were the only ones that could get anyone to these levels.

Beneath the ISTF building, the interrogation rooms were more humane than most. She didn't want to repeat anything from the past like the terrors Mason had accepted. Calla signed off any procedures adopted by interrogators as human intelligence collection assets. Nash had given her much advice on what was acceptable and effective. Most cybercriminals here showed talent, including strange approaches such as mind-reading. Her criminals thrived in the cyber and information world where they'd declared the world's rules did not apply to them.

Calla had had no alternative but to allow staff to monitor detainees without telling the incarcerated they were being watched. Heskin's containment room was no different with its bullet resistant cameras. Nash had explained that they could withstand the force of a sledgehammer. Jack had also urged they use radio-frequency identification tracking, a monitoring gadget for detainees, who wore an electronic bracelet to tracks their movement throughout the facility.

"I knew you would come," she heard a voice from within the dark shadows of the containment room.

The voice startled Calla. She shifted closer. The security agent gave her a nod as she approached.

"Can you please leave us?" she asked.

The security guard obliged and moved on.

"Think you know who I am?" Calla said.

"Yes, those of us who devote our lives to technology and science know who you are. I knew you would come because it's not like you to let someone else do your work. That's what he had said."

"He who?" Calla then understood that he meant Mason Laskfell. "You're a hard man to understand, Andor Heskin. First, you work with the good guys, then you worked with the bad guys, and then you work for yourself," Calla said. "There's no telling what your motive is. The sooner you cooperate with ISTF, the quicker you can go your own way. The crime you committed is escape and crossing borders illegally, but also leaving ISTF custody while under British supervision in Turkey."

"I saw the determination in you the day you brought me to that prison," Heskin said.

"You had carried out several offenses in Turkey, and the Turkish police asked that we imprison you there. You had done quite a bit of hacking in the country."

Heskin moved closer to the rails and stared at her through the glass. His eyes were stern and piercing. "Most ISTF and intelligence officers are not as perceptive as you. There's something about you that was very different even when I met you all those months ago. I can now see what Mason Laskfell saw in you."

Calla did not want to waste any time, but she needed to know what Heskin stood to gain by escaping prison. So far, they had yet to hear from Scope Industries about him. "You need to stop what you are doing," she said. "Whatever it is you and your daughter at Scope Industries have devised needs to cease. If you cooperate, I might be lenient."

"So, you're the new boss. The new Red Fox. Somehow that code name fits you well. Few Red Foxes have survived the ISTF post you're in. What makes you think you will fare any differently? Very unusual people have always held your position."

"You don't intimidate me, Andor Heskin. All I need you to do is stop whatever it is Scope is doing." "It's your mother, isn't it?" Heskin said, glaring at her. "She was one to always interfere with whatever the operatives were doing. She ignored her operative humanity, wishing more to embody a normal one. Soon, she became a vagabond looking for things she could not find. And now it has come back to haunt her."

Anger must have flashed in Calla's eyes. "What have you done to my mother?"

"Everything that Scope does to an individual is nothing they haven't done to themselves already. Why should I help you?" Heskin said, his eyes narrowing into her.

She would not allow a moment of doubt to steal away her peace of mind and moved closer to the windowpane between them. Calla pulled out a security agent's chair and sat. "I'll not leave here until you give me what I want."

Calla could read minds when she was in danger, how she prayed she could do it when she wasn't like now. Most times, she could pierce through a man's brain and understand precisely how he thought and everything he wanted to communicate. This time was different.

She couldn't do it.

Heskin progressed to the window, steam from his flaring nostrils moistening it. "Assume you might want to know a little about your future," he said.

"I'm not here to play mind games with you. You're hiding much. Lots of it being years of pain and is a bit of anger there too. I know your kind. The Cress girl, the one everyone waited for. The one who carries the Cress mandate. With every generation, the mandate gets heavier, and the Cresses have become more powerful with each new generation. Maybe it didn't fare too well the last time you tried to read someone's mind," he said.

Calla felt her heart thump. She wanted to whack one into him. This was not the place. "I'm not here for you to play mind games with me. As I said, I don't know what you are hiding. But I know you've been doing it for months and that even that little escapade from the Turkish prison was not an overnight thought. It was something you've been planning for years. You strategically waited several months when you could've escaped a lot earlier. Why?"

Andor sighed again. "Think you're only here for one thing. That's to know your future. What if I could tell you that I knew so much more about you, even before you were born?"

Calla didn't know what he was getting at, but she had to stop it before he got out of control. "I'm not here for your mind games Andor Heskin."

"I know you haven't asked, and perhaps you refuse to see what it is I'm telling you, but I can give you answers. Answers you've been looking for. Answers, but now my machine in Scope can help. For years you searched for an understanding of who you are. Nobody can give you that. You feel that you stand between two worlds, humanity and an operative world. And neither feels right. How long will you stay in the middle?" Andor said.

"I've never had the future told about my life, and I don't intend to start now," Calla said. "My interest? If you want to see the light of day tell me how Scope tells the future using mass, how it works, how it relates to Hypatia's scroll, and what you stand to gain?"

Andor moved away and paced through the cell. "Your

mother was about your age I take it when she left you. Oh, she was a beautiful one. I wonder if she still remembers the dilemma she went through when she left you at that foster home in London. A baby, a child helpless yet with the power of the gods and science in her veins."

Calla could feel the anger in her boiling. She held her calm. She couldn't show Andor her pain. Not here. Not now.

"What if I were to tell you that I knew Nicole would leave you. And I warned her about it. And that the reason she couldn't live with herself and disappeared from your life wasn't at the very moment she had to give you up but the point she knew she couldn't raise you. You were too powerful for her. But the deepest pain in her heart was. I had told her she would leave any child. She had months before she even conceived. They were stubborn those two as they worked at MI6. Unstoppable. They knew the moment they were pregnant with you that they would leave you and that your life would be full of pain. The reason she couldn't live with herself was not at the very moment she had to give you up. The catch was that she already knew she would because I had told her so. She denied it very much as you deny it right now, but there's something even worse coming for you."

"Stop, Heskin!"

"Nicole left you. I can't explain my ways, but there is something greater coming after you and that man of yours. I'll say no more as I can see you are already sweating."

Scope Industries, London
11:27 p.m.

Hex's face beamed. "Your boy Lascar had delivered and will now be sent back to prison. You don't need him anymore."

Zodie took a deep breath and turned around to see who had entered. She hadn't expected to see Hex so soon.

"May I suggest you take this seriously?" Hex said. "Seeing that you're now the technology partner for ISTF."

Zodie had trusted the man, but now she wasn't so sure. Hex had a way of amusing her, but not today. In another life, he would have been a handsome man. But his eyes were full of revenge. She would dictate whatever Hex had to say to her today. "What is it you want?"

"I want you to make sure I have access to everything ISTF," Zodie said. "You were careless and have lost the scroll. I thought your business with ISTF was done," Hex said.

"By becoming a technology partner for ISTF means I'm in the inside circle. I won't let you jeopardize that. So your request forces me into a rather difficult predicament," Zodie said.

"And what predicament is that?" Hex said.

"Well, it just means Cress is a pain for me."

"So, she's been a pain for you. Why?"

She ambled around the room and poured herself a drink. "You know Calla Cress, and I went to the same high school. I learned a lot about her. More than she knows about herself. How she wastes her talent with ordinary men. She could have everything. She was the chosen operative. Not me."

Hex pulled something from his pocket. He put it in front of her, a photograph. "I, too, have done my digging. Her tattoo image was taken a few years ago when I investigated something for the KJ20 Ops. I understand Scope also had data on it from her six months in custody with them. At first, I didn't know what I was looking at, but then the symbols on

Cress's tattoo on her ankle resemble the scribblings on Hypatia's scroll. How can that be? Just who is Calla Cress? What is it you have promised to give ISTF in exchange for your being their technology partner?"

"Don't mess with what you don't know. It's none of your business, but if you must know, I'll have access to more than that."

Zodie stared at him, her eyes piercing into his soul. He was only interested in what she could reveal about Calla Cress. She had left a rift deep in his heart, and with their government and intellectual property. So, he had also stolen information about Calla's tattoo. It seems from the KJ20 Ops. The way he moved around with a photograph made her think he thought it was like a bargaining chip. Why would he bring it to her?

An army of people now protected her and Scope's interests. Granted, Hex had followed Nicole Cress to Washington, then Havana, when she had been the first to steal the scroll with aid from someone. He wasn't sure who. They had to have been an agent. Nicole knew too much, and Hex had delivered by incapacitating her. She only needed one thing from him, and then their business would be done. For now, Zodie would play along.

"Let me remind you, Hex," she said. "What you bring to the table in our minor project is your army of renegades from across the globe. Where you find them, I don't need to know. I need your manpower to keep Calla Cress and her crew away from everything that Scope is doing."

Hex's eyes shifted her way. "Are you going to tell me what you want from Cress." His eyes burned. "Does it have to do with Nash Shields?"

"Shields was ahead of you, wasn't he, at the KJ20 Ops?

He also created a secret army, carefully scattered around the globe, very effective in security and getting jobs for important people done. You tried to copy him, you're a copycat, and well, since he wouldn't work with me, you were the next best thing."

Hex's eyes burned with fury.

Zodie wasn't done. "Our deal is personal. The intimacy has been great but, I'm sure even Shields overpowers you in that department. I intend to find out. It stops here, you and I. Our deal is this. You provide the muscle, I provide the rest, and once I get the scroll back and Scope has launched its plans in Gibraltar, our business is done. I need Gibraltar to work for the twelve governments I have strategically chosen. Your job is to make sure that happens and that Calla Cress stays out of my way. Are we clear?"

Hex smirked. Something was playing behind those staring eyes. The anger behind them was so profound that Zodie wondered if he knew his left from his right. She had to give them something. "Okay, Hex, come with me."

Moments later, on the hidden floor with Scope's labs, she pushed open a door and closed it behind her. She urged him to sit and observe her scientists arrange her government announcement. "Be ready for Gibraltar. I need to make sure the clients contest for the control of the galaxies. The app has generated enough funds to do this. Isn't that what everybody wants? What they don't know is, I'm the one who has ultimate oversight over the galaxies thanks to the telescope. We've had no difficulty in convincing them we have what they need. Look here," she said, pointing to her scientists beyond the glass. "I can give them power to look beyond the interface of the Earth's atmosphere."

She drew open a drawer on the steel desk. Several tablets

and screens lit up displaying Scope's telescopes and satellites, all in position. "This is as much as I'll show you. And then you will be quiet. You'll fulfill the end of your deal, and then we're done. Once the Gibraltar Summit has ruled in my favor. Our business is done."

Hex pulled her to him and forced a dry kiss on her lips. "You were always a clever one, even if you didn't pass one year at Beacon Academy. This is what this is about. They put you back several grades and then you met Calla Cress, an orphan like you, who had everything you craved. I too do my research on everyone I work with."

A powerful slap landed on his jaw, followed by a boot in the groin.

He lurched back and dropped to the ground, cradling his middle.

Zodie's boot fixed his neck to the floor. "Never touch me again." She withdrew her foot and dusted her skirt. "Now, get to work!"

He rose with an arrogant grin building on his face.

Zodie knew he was still in agony. Good. Lascar had done well in his training.

"Where is the telescope then?" he said.

"On the Moon. Once the papers are signed and I'll have full access to ISTF, we will be ready. I'll have bargaining power and agreement from all those governments."

Data Sciences Intelligence Systems Divisions
UK Space Agency
9:56 a.m.

"This way, Calla Cress," the woman said as she led Calla, Jack and Nash to the room. The UK Space Agency rarely took calls like this.

They waited for several minutes by the elevator as the woman retrieved her tablet to sign them in.

Nash pulled them aside. "We can't tell them we are ISTF, or they won't give us the information. Not everybody believes in this organization."

Calla nodded. She sometimes wondered why an organization here to protect and prevent criminal activity was one that most people did not accept or acknowledge. She was okay with that. As long as ISTF was secret, so were the operatives.

Their aliases were solid. They were rocket engineers.

Security scanned them before they allowed them into the data science division. Calla had Hypatia's scroll close to her. Hypatia suggested that data science affected the world centuries before it was even created. It was only a matter of time before Scope would catch up with them. Calla had little time to make sure she understood every rule, stroke, and information the scroll revealed.

"Ms. Boswell has a very tight schedule," the woman said, who led them to the head of the Data Science Division's Center.

"I'll collect you when the appointment is done," she said, opening the door to a spacious and well-lit office.

A tall, beautiful dark woman with piercing eyes with a no-nonsense look peered up from her reading when they came into the room. "Yes, what is it I can do for you?" Ms. Boswell said.

"Your research here has come highly recommended, and the folks at Mandell Research Center, a private Space company, can learn from some of your best practices. We have a few questions, and perhaps your data science division can answer them for us." Jack said.

The flattery worked as Ms. Boswell relaxed. "Hmm. Says here you have done some work with the Prime Minister's government agencies," Boswell said. "What exactly do you do for the Prime Minister?"

Calla took a deep breath and leaned forward. "I'm afraid that's classified. We won't take much of your time. We've a few questions on your data science theory published in last month's scientific journals. The Prime Minister himself has requested it as a sponsor of one of the few private Space agencies out of this country. What we do is revolutionary, and we need to work together as a community."

"I see," she said, not convinced, Calla thought, but she obliged.

"Okay, let's begin with a brief tour of the building," Boswell said. "Once we're done, you can ask your questions, and afraid that's as much as I can do. I don't promise to give you everything."

When the brief tour was over, they returned to the director's office. She poured herself a cup of steaming coffee and offered them one. "Now is there anything else that you wanted answered. My time is tight."

"Tell us about your data science division," Nash said.

"Here's how it started. They hired a man by the name of Andor Heskin to set it up. And not just any data scientist. They tasked him to set up alternative methods that could not be rivaled." The director took a sip of her tea and drew a deep breath before she continued. "Heskin was one of the most intelligent people that understood data science, and this was his division. He developed science faster than his peers and that's why they hired him."

"Can you tell us exactly what he did?" Calla said. "What was his actual job?"

Boswell took a deep breath before she responded. "It was the early days of data science when groups started debating its future use. Heskin helped to put in place systems we use today. He also understood how large amounts of data can manipulate Space and beyond."

"So, he looked after storage areas?" Nash said.

"Yes," she said. She then moved back in her chair, tapping her fingers on the pristine desk.

"What do data scientists do here today?" Jack said.

Boswell rose and paced around the room. "We look at fundamental research. We create mechanisms and methods that suppress scientific questions. We look in many fields but specifically the field of machine learning, perhaps today known as knowledge discovery. We also look at mechanisms that understand scientific and engineering data. To advance our Space exploration, we can only do this by collecting data. Most of what Heskin was responsible for was gathering statistics from our exploration activities and translating them into understandable information. He was keen on what he could learn from galaxies light years ahead and how they affected our planet's future. He studied the future as if he could bring back intelligence from Space that could predict the Earth's future."

"Did you believe in his work?" Jack said.

"Sometimes, yes," Boswell replied. "Other times, no."

Nash fixed her with a stubborn stare. "He would've had access to all government data machines and classified information?"

"Yes," Boswell said. "Regarding his work, he needed as much data as he could gather, and no one saw anything of it. That was our downfall. He would've had access to everything, and that is why he was arrested. When the government came here, the charges were he was selling it to other governments. The Turkish authorities had a string of other accusations, and I presume that's why he was handed over to the Turkish authorities. One can't be too careful. We're dealing with classified future Space technology." She stopped and looked as if she'd only just seen them for the first time. "What you need is permission."

Nash crossed his arms over his chest as Jack gave Nash a warning look. Boswell had revealed more than she wished to. She knew much about Heskin and had been a material witness in his arrest in his court case. They needed to understand what he may have taken from the UK Space Agency that helped him develop Scope technology. If Heskin collected data light years away, he brought it back to the present and unraveled it.

Calla leaned in. "Can you comment on the data Heskin was collecting from Space? How far ahead do your missions collect data?"

"Well, those who are adventurers will say that our Space missions go far into the future, because they travel light years ahead. Scientists who work on this theory believe that this data is worth collecting as it may tell us where the Earth is headed as these galaxies have been there before. Heskin used technology he developed allowing him to see science light years ahead. He employed it to analyze and predict future events and future tech capabilities. It was as if Nostradamus had been reborn and lived among us; only he had much superior technology. Heskin insisted that some ways we were wiring machines were wrong and other times some calculations we applied in math were inaccurate."

Jack was getting impatient and stretched his hands on the table. "What's the most important thing you wanted to understand with the projects you were working on?"

"How information and data science can be simulated to make sense. It's an excellent question, Mr. Kleve. We focus on data mining to discover sequences of events that may have a higher probability of leading to others. That's what Heskin mastered here," Boswell said.

"You say," Jack said. "That if you can get all this material, it is possible to predict future events?"

"Yes. Space data collected has allowed the understanding of future prediction."

"How?" Calla said.

"The science tells us that there are math patterns that put the galaxies in place and that predictability can help save society from the greatest threats. It's all in the math that Pythagoras coined. Some patterns fit a curve, and this pattern coined by Pythagoras extends beyond the Earth and into outer Space. Now, seeing that some galaxies are ahead of us, intelligence collected from their path can predict future events on Earth. That is what the scent tells us. Using data from Space, if you take that on a low scale level and map it to our data on Earth, it's effortless to foresee future events. Data follows an order, and the Earth and its events are part of an ordered system that starts in Space. Before we could prove it, they arrested Heskin," Boswell added.

"So the Earth clones actions of its sister planets in the galaxies?"

"Yes," she replied.

"What sort of connections?" Calla said.

"If you find and standards in intergalactic Space, there is mirrored repetition in the math on Earth. Plugging that math into any arrangements or data and used in fictitious societies, or the like, will generate accuracy in future predictions. It's all in the circumstances and patterns. The more statistics we have on Earth, past or present, the better the prediction. It's all in the mathematical patterns stolen from Space events."

"That's why the Scope app records an entire person's livelihood," Calla said to herself.

"Excuse me?" Boswell said.

Calla shook her head. "Sorry, nothing."

Boswell returned to her seat. "We're living in a world full of data, and theoretically it is possible to use it, DNA sequences, and code. As long as it is numerical, we can plug it into patterns found in Space and make future predictions."

Bands of thick pink blended into the dark purple of the horizon where it met the road ahead. As they made time back to London on the M4 motorway, passion thickened Calla's voice. There were too many pieces, but the danger was Heskin had developed the technology at the UK Space Agency, and then he had disappeared with it. He had falsely lied to them, telling them and covering his tracks, that they never finished the automation. That's all they had on record.

"What you think?" Calla said, zipping the Maserati past a Hyundai. "Do you believe me now?" she said, eyeing Jack in the rearview mirror. "The predictions are in math patterns coined by Hypatia and inspired by Pythagoras."

"It makes sense now. We're looking at data he collected

from Space, not mythology. He could translate it to an ecosphere like ours, that is a little behind," Jack added.

Calla turned into the West London Borough of Hounslow. "He has amassed enough data on every human being and also created societies to predict government decisions and thus national events."

Jack continued scrolling through his tablet as he researched. "Okay, there's one person here who can give us more intelligence," Jack said. "One of the biggest endorsers of the project was billionaire Rupert Kumar. Kumar was a big advocate, and it says here he has been publishing a lot of information on his corporation's website and other blogs, endorsing the use of Space data."

Calla shifted to fourth gear. "Think we need to give Kumar a visit."

———

Twenty-five minutes later, the Maserati pulled into Central London in Chelsea. She glanced up at the cameras that stared down at her from the billionaire's villa.

"He's a reticent man. He's cordial, though," Jack said, reading Kumar's file on his tablet. "His profile here at ISTF says Kumar's a billionaire who conspired with some of the worst criminals, Mason Laskfell included. Yet Kumar has never seen a day behind bars."

"Makes sense why he even lives in one of the most expensive postcodes in London, funding criminal activity, hiding behind technology and data development," Nash added.

Calla slowed the Maserati. "Let's go in and find out. I

asked for a special meeting. He's always had a curiosity about Red Foxes."

They waited a few minutes for the gate to open for them. Calla drove her car into the parking lot and parked it outside the main entrance. She had met Rupert Kumar several times. Mostly in connection with Mason Laskfell. She wondered how a billionaire who had invested in everything from steel to solar panels to Space travel could command such government interest. His ISTF file was empty. Calla guessed Laskfell had erased it when they had worked on the solar project in China she had apprehended eighteen months ago.

They stepped into the entrance and a housekeeper led them through the mansion. Kumar sat in a lavish room cross-legged on the floor. The place resembled that of the Indian maharajas of years gone by. Calla found her gaze scouting the room with interest. A man who was an advocate for technology, she wondered why he lived in the ways of the past. When they entered the room, his eyes were kind and inviting, and he commanded attention even from the floor where he sat on his cushions.

"Please," join me. "It's not every day that you get a visit from the head of ISTF," Kumar said.

"So you recognize who I am?"

"I make it my business to know each Red Fox. I've been privy to some of the organization's work, especially when Laskfell led it. God rest his soul. I also know that you have been spending a lot of time around Scope Industries," Kumar said. "Nash Shields is also one of the finest men the NSA and perhaps the military is seen. It is an honor to meet you, Mr. Shields. Your name travels among prominent people as the one to look for in times of need."

Nash raised an eyebrow, unamused.

Kumar motioned for them to sit on the cushions with him. Soon Indian chai was served by a housekeeper who bowed as she left the room, her eyes keenly on the men that had accompanied Calla.

"May I ask what it is you've been sniffing around Scope Industries for, and what also brings you to my modest abode?"

Calla held back a laugh. "I wouldn't exactly call yours modest," she said.

"We would like to know what interest you had in Scope Industries. It seems you're one of their bigger investors," Jack said.

"I make it my interest to know everything about new technologies and the companies that'll be needed in the future. Scope has much research I believe will change the way we do business. I fear that maybe your trip here has been wasted because you will find nothing here. I make it my business to be exactly where technology leads us."

"That's not what your profile says," Nash said. "You also make it your business not only to fund technological companies but to take part in some endeavors that result from those technological activities."

"What did you find at Scope?" Kumar said.

"Does that interest you?" Calla asked.

"I fund security at Scope Industries tech labs. I know everything that goes on inside those walls. Did you find anything of interest? I knew it would just be a matter of time before you would be at my doorstep. ISTF is the world's smartest agency and has one of the cleverest people that run it. I can't get away from you, Miss Cress."

"Mr. Kumar," Calla began. "There's a glitch in Scope."

He raised an eyebrow. "A glitch?"

Even the other men were surprised and turned her way. That was information that she'd never shared with them.

"You ask what it is I found when I went to Scope Industries. I found a glitch. The only problem is I don't know how to enforce that glitch. You're the head of security there and know there's a glitch in Scope's systems and app," Calla said. "That glitch is the Pythagoras Clause. Where is it?"

Kumar set his tea down. "Nothing goes by you, Miss Cress, does it?"

Calla smiled. "No. Your heart is racing, just about now. You're wondering what I have on you. Don't worry, Mr. Kumar. I'm not here for you, but I suggest you tell me everything you know about the glitch in Scope."

His eyes were bulging now. "Yes, there's a glitch. But even I don't know how or why. I've invested a lot of money trying to find out. You think I like to work for Scope and be in their fangs? The only way I can release myself from Scope and from Andor Heskin and his peers is if I find the glitch. Miss Cress, that I'll try, because I want to be released from a contract with Scope and I can't until I find the glitch." He paused before his next words. "My homeland has answers that Scope has failed to look at. And they sit not too far from the Red Fort in India. Laskfell first introduced me to Scope Technologies and Andor Heskin when he came to my home several months ago looking for my panels in China. But while he was there, he brought something, and I believe you might find it where love sits?"

"Where love sits?" Jack said, raising an eyebrow.

Calla armed her self-control with cool icy resolve. "The Taj Mahal?"

"Yes, at the palace of love, the Taj Mahal. Mason left a

data box with a serial number within the walls of the Taj Mahal. I believe that's the glitch. I don't know where or why."

Kumar rose and returned, giving them exact instructions. "Laskfell gave me his," he said, handing her a piece of paper. "This's all I have. Then we are even?" he said.

Calla took the paper and rose, and the men followed suit. She peered down at him. "If we find nothing. I'll be back for you."

SIXTEEN

Day 14
Red Fort, India
6:12 p.m.

The light and sound show, held every evening at the Red Fort, was about to begin. As they hastened past the seat of the Moghul Empire, looking for the contact Nash had arranged, Calla took in the sights and spicy smells of the grounds. She studied the Red Fort, a lengthy red structure that stood for Imperial Hindustan's might. Even today, it held its might. Standing at the eastern edge of Hindustan, it was the new capital of the Mughal Empire. Though Kumar had told much, Calla kept her suspicions at bay.

Calla, Nash and Jack had taken the BA flight out of London and then a Jeep from Delhi to Agra. They had to wait until it was dark enough to find the data box, prepared to go with the information Kumar had given them. Later, his contact at the Red Fort could provide more detail, once they secured the data box.

Her hands moist, Calla wondered why Kumar had been ready to surrender information. The man should've been here by now. They had agreed to meet outside the Red Fort in a public area, and he would guide them. Part of Indian intelligence, he had worked with the CIA, and conveniently with the British services. Nash had explained that Kumar knew him and that he was their best bet getting to that data box.

Calla's senses were active. With the distraction of the lights show, Calla wondered how this would affect their meeting.

Music flowed through the streets as colorful tourists mingled with bystanders and the locals on the main stretch that led to the Red Fort. Suddenly she heard a noise behind her. She turned her head.

Nothing.

They made their way closer to the Red Fort, crossing pedestrians, and other festival seeking tourists.

"We're being followed," Calla said.

"Saw them about two minutes ago," Nash replied.

Jack's eyes were alert. "Let's keep walking."

"Where's that contact?" Calla said.

"He'll be here soon," Nash answered "We've planned for them to meet at the snack stand outside the Red Fort. He's supposed to give us access into the main grounds, so we go the back way toward the Taj Mahal."

Nash held onto his gun, attentive with one eye ahead, and equally, eyes behind his back. Calla did not know with what breath and speed they came, but the projectiles came down from above and fired at them.

They took shelter behind a rickshaw. Screams erupted around them as many scrambled for cover as a hail of arrows ambushed them. They remained undercover and knew they had to make a run for it.

Calla glanced behind. "It's him."

"Hex," Nash echoed.

Hex had hired archers out for blood. He had to want the data box.

"Right," Nash said. "We need to disappear within the crowd and head toward the Taj Mahal."

"I understand who your contact and Kumar's was," Jack said.

"Kumar always looks out for his best interests. I believe him about that box because we were aware of it at the NSA," Nash added.

The arrows showered their position.

"Okay, let's make a run for it," Calla said.

They rose and scattered within the crowds. Archers chased after them. They flew past vehicles and discarded vendor stalls, trying to avoid the opponents. As they entered the edge of the gardens, the assailants were fierce. They had caved in.

They were not far behind.

Calla, Nash, and Jack hastened. Suddenly an archer jumped in front of her. He grabbed her by the hair.

She rounded with a kick in his stomach, crushing him to the floor. Several other attackers surrounded them. The crowds dispersed.

Nash prepped his gun, and so did Jack.

Hex fired a bullet at her feet.

She held her breath. "You want the data box? You're going to have to do better than that," Calla said.

Hex moved forward, his archers enclosing them, drawing near.

"No, you won't," Calla said, closing in with the men back to back with her.

Hex's arrow was on her collar and they would have to think fast.

The giant gripped her neck a second time.

Nash rounded into him and belted him. He crashed back, his steel bow dropping from his hands.

A second archer grabbed Calla. Jack fired at three others, narrowing in on them. Calla retaliated.

An assailant lay one in Jack's face, and he fell back paralyzed on the floor. Nash discharged a shot, sending him back as Hex came for blood. His fist landed down on Nash's abdomen, knocking wind out of him.

With the guys on the floor, a wall of goons surrounded her. Her heart thudded, and her genes kicked in. A punch docked in her chest and she spat blood, the pain surmounting to her core. She round housed one after the other, her blows and kicks faster than she could think. When they were down, she checked on the men, who slowly came to. "Jack, Nash? Are you okay?"

Nash coughed and straightened his bulletproof vest.

Jack too, found an energy and stood. "This your work, Ms. Cress?"

She grinned. "We need to go."

The Taj Mahal, Agra, India
6:48 p.m.

Sunset radiated off the Taj Mahal's marble surface, enhancing its trance. The diving summer sun was still scorching the concrete rooftops as people casually left the mausoleum's majestic garden.

Jack's handiwork had infiltrated security systems around the Taj Mahal. Usually, the grounds closed at 7 p.m.. This would be the best time to penetrate the grounds around the building and mount the marble structure. If they could get the serial number on the data box hidden in the Taj Mahal's walls, they could disarm it and find the data to deactivate the Scope app. It had to work.

According to calculations Jack had done the night before, the serial number could disrupt math patterns and prevent predictions. If they had the right figures in the correct sequences, they could shoot the serial number onto Scope's servers and obstruct the app's prognoses. It would destabilize Scope altogether. That was the glitch, and the figure was in that box. Mason Laskfell had known that if anything came back to bite him, he had something on Heskin. He always had a backup plan. This time was no different. Why the Taj Mahal? Perhaps it was fascination with this place. True, the Taj Mahal was mesmerizing.

"Ready?" Calla said. "The last people are leaving the grounds and Hex might not be far. If we can use the tracking device, we'll find any electronic activity within the walls of the Taj Mahal."

"That's a lot of marble we need to scan," Jack said.

"I know you can do it," Calla said, smiling at Jack as a black eye developed in his right eye.

Concern grew on Nash's face. "Must be somewhere in the main burial area, the most guarded area and epicenter of the attraction. Mason would've hidden the box in there."

Jack turned around to Calla. "From my calculations. It's a twelve-line sequence we need. I hope we have not traveled many miles just to see a tomb."

"Yes, it's a twelve-line sequence," Calla said, smiling.

Jack knew how to turn any situation into a joke. She adored him and wondered if Marree would ever see this side of him she loved.

"Walk me through this again," Jack said. "How do we know what we're looking for? Besides the fact that it is just called the data box."

"That's why we wander and use your hacking device," Nash said.

Jack drew his phone. "Better hurry. My spider won't hold out much longer."

"Is that with the tracking device that you left at Scope? The first day we were there?" Calla said.

"Yes," Jack said.

They hastened through the manicured gardens.

"We should wait till the lights go out. It shouldn't be long," Nash said.

Soon silence surrounded them as they waited in white suits to blend in with the Taj Mahal's own ivory structure. Open from sunset to sunrise, the hour had come and as the gates closed, one hundred years of breathtaking poetry shone off its architecture as Jack hacked the security system, deactivating any alarms.

"Would you look at that?" Nash said, inspecting the outer facade as they snaked toward the monument.

"Beautiful. Some man fell in love and spent more than jewels would cost him. This dude built an architectural masterpiece. Yeah, lots of money to spend, for love." Jack said, a sniffle escaping his lips. "We all know what passion does, don't we?" he said, watching them both. "You guys have discovered something I'm still looking for."

"Jack," Calla said. "Let Marree in. She adores you more than any other person I know, and she is good for you."

"So, a man falls in love, he loses his love, and then builds a marble palace," Jack said.

"You should try it. Love," she said with a giggle.

"Let's go," Nash said.

They moved to the walls. Careful not to trigger any alarms, they continued.

A gunshot exploded behind them. The bullet blasted off the stone. Anger welled in Calla. Who would harm a national treasure like the Taj Mahal?

The answer came as she glanced up.

They hid behind a column, avoiding the chipping of the bullets on the ground. Surrounded, she saw the face she knew well. It had been several months since she had seen Lascar. He had been one she wanted to forget.

"Not the date you had in mind," Lascar said.

"Don't tell me Zodie Baxendale posted your bail," Calla replied.

"Someone had to."

Lascar and the men came in for the kill and Nash's gun did the rest of the speaking, firing them off their tail.

Once Lascar and several assailants retreated, Calla gave Jack the thumbs up. "Jack. We've got about ten minutes. Find it with your tracker."

Jack began his work moving around the mausoleum with his metal detecting beeper. The beeping grew louder, and he pointed to the south side of the tomb. The men were coming back for them. Jack set a grip on Calla's arm. "Look for the box, Nash, and I'll keep them off."

Calla took the tracker from Jack's hand. She shot forward in a race to the complex's inner columns, as the men kept back determined attackers with live fire.

Calla drew a rope from her backpack. She slung it round her waist and began a climb up the marble until she reached the dome. The beeping grew louder as she neared the summit. Careful not to slip, she fingered the stone until her hands found a sectioned off marble slate. It would take much power to wedge it open.

She only had minutes before she lost the signal. If she dropped the tracker signal, she wouldn't be able to find the data box. She had no choice. She thrust her fist, denting a huge chunk of the marble. It split under her blow, her genetic strength taking effect.

Calla stopped; her eyes latched on a dark metallic box under the crack. Another punch.

The marble cracked under her fist. If she found the serial number, it would change everything.

The blow came from above.

Her eyes shifted upward.

It was real.

Lascar's hand had come strong.

She cartwheeled to her feet and rounded a boot in his heart. He slid along the mausoleum headfirst to the grate.

She shifted her mind back to the box. Calla had never learned a day of Hindi in her life. The fine engraving mesmerized her for a second. With the data box in her hand, she understood. The sequential number was inside.

Calla had to decipher the serial number. Could it be that direct? Perhaps. She mentally recorded what she saw and could do it swiftly.

Commotion behind her made her pause as Lascar charged for her.

"Back for more, Lascar?"

"You understand you can't get away from me?" Lascar said.

She sneered. "That's the general idea."

"No, you won't. That data box and its serial number are my ticket for release from prison."

Lascar drew near and grasped her neck. "You're not running anywhere, this time, darling. Your two companions below are in an awkward predicament."

His restraint was insistent, penetrating her skin. He went for the edge and directed a firearm at Jack.

Fury burned within Calla. She launched a sidekick in his abdomen and he smashed back into marble, taking them both sliding down the dome.

Her head struck the dome's edge. Agony shot down her neck as Lascar hung on and jumped up back to where she reclined.

The men below held Jack and forced him against the wall. They focused their handguns at him, bracing to open fire, and dismissed three warning shots.

Lascar pulled himself up and wiped blood from his face, then inclined his firearm.

Calla could not move as he numbed her arm. If she jumped, Lascar would fire at the men. He not only had her life in his control, Jack's and Nash's, he likewise had her mother's.

"What did I ever do to you, Lascar?" she said, eyes burning at him.

The pistol in his grip was at the ready. "As if I need to remind you! You chose Shields."

She wiped blood from her forehead. Data did not determine who she was. She was her own person. She would show it. Her neck, plastered against the floor of the dome, cold seeped into her bones. She had one move, and she took it.

Lascar did not see her right leg swing. Her clout took him in the jaw. He swiveled and crashed his skull to the stone. Her body still fighting pain, she crawled with difficulty toward the edge. Then she saw Nash take his chances, release himself before thundering double fists in one striker, and knee a second who went down grunting. Suddenly his sharp kick took the others out.

One grip on the rails for support, and the other on the dome's outer rim, Calla towered over Lascar, with a hand to his head, pistol discarded.

"Don't you ever fire at me again," she said.

———

Lascar pulled himself up, his operative eyes giving him firepower. His punch landed on her jaw with the force of a tornado. She landed hard on her back, then crawled on her hands, backing away as he moved closer.

She couldn't avoid it. His second blow was twice as hard.

As pain crawled in her veins, nothing could stop the force. Every instinct in her told her to run, but Calla's will power told her to fight. She dragged herself upward, struggling to retaliate, to defend herself and those she loved.

Lascar lifted a hand to strike again. He raised his fist and held it midair. "I could've taught you plenty! You're nothing but a weakling. The Cress line has been nothing but wimps and cowards who run. They run from themselves. Let this be a reminder to you. Few dare come for me. It won't end well for you if you do."

She squinted and could feel her heart thud in her rib cage. She had thwarted him once. Nash had made sure of it. Why couldn't she move?

This wasn't like fighting any enemy. This wasn't just another criminal. This tasted like the Mind Hacker's power over her. This was darker. Just what had prison done to Lascar?

All her existence, she'd realized that she wasn't ordinary. The guy's one punch and how she'd resisted him, even though she was smaller, had determined that she wasn't.

"She will kill you, you know," he added. "That Zodie is one controlling operative. I'll spare you and your buddies. I simply ask what I always ask of you. You've got to learn you belong to me. You and I are the same. We have the same abnormal appetites. We are peculiar beings. No one understands us, but we understand each other."

Lascar moved and pulled her by the collar.

He held her chin over the edge of the dome.

She could not breathe and lost the will to fight.

"No Cress, no head operative, can come against what Zodie is now capable of," he said. "I have taught her what I should have taught you. She will continue Scope and finish what it has set out to do. And if I were you, I would watch my back. There are many others like me. All with targets on you. The brief is concise and to the point. Kill Cress and dispose of her lot. Which means dear lady, anybody connected to you and everyone you associate with, is my target. Zodie wanted to tell you this."

His grip was crushing her throat, cutting off her air flow.

"It all stops here," he said.

In that one moment, he had consumed everything she knew. He had confirmed what she'd accepted all along. She was not special. She was not normal, and nothing in her could outwit him, however much she wanted to.

She held back a gag, unable to breathe. What did he mean by many others were coming if he failed?

Her lungs heaved; her chest beat hard.

"Death is too good for you. It's a positive thing Nicole only had one of you. The Cress line ends here. Zodie will be head of ISTF and then she'll take over everything you know and hold dear. Might I add she has a keen eye on Shields too. I believe Heskin told you once that your future was not what you expected it would be."

With a last thud to her neck, he set the handgun to her throat and yanked her hair back. "I've heard you can't even fire a gun. Pity. Looks like Shields hasn't taught you his best secrets. And how dare a woman come after me? I'll never figure out what ISTF thought when they chose a woman as a Red Fox. Foxes. Why do they think a woman can do a man's job? Foxes are solitary creatures and they prefer to hunt and sleep alone. Which is what you're about to do."

The gun bore into her skin.

His next strike nearly made her pass out.

Eyes pinning into hers, she wanted to scream.

Then she heard it.

He sputtered blood and stared down in horror at his chest.

The blast from the Sig Sauer P226 expelled a second

bullet. She heard nothing else as she clasped her palms to her ears, gagging on what she thought was her own blood.

Nash's bullet ended the rest of Lascar's words.

Lascar riveted back and dropped off the dome.

This time she hoped for good.

"Calla?"

She barely heard Nash's voice as her eyes rolled back in their sockets.

Scope Industries
8:27 p.m.

Zodie studied the screen of activity. She motioned for a scientist to approach her. "We're going to continue something that we started years ago," Zodie announced.

He nodded.

"The ultimate piece is finally here. Hex's men have the data box with the glitch, so I expect no more interruptions."

They had everything they needed. Hypatia, a madwoman wrote scribbles that turned out to be the sequences that ultimately powered predictability.

The scientist moved swiftly. "We're ready to test the information, Ms. Baxendale."

"Okay, let's begin," Zodie said.

The computers worked.

Zodie didn't want to upload data. That would take too long. Her father had stipulated that even without Hypatia's scroll, they could make predictions without interruption, starting with the East.

They first turned their attention toward China. They had to imagine what they could threaten China with. What sort of impending threats would China be prone to? The information on the screen was impeccable. Looking at China's history, the future was straightforward to predict. It was essential to understand China's past, its people, its history, and its mindset. China's history had shown that they had built bridges, empires, and dynasties that could withstand much. Each nation's past would mirror their future, but most were in denial. Taking the individual's concept of their past and almost magnifying it to a national level had been genius on her father's part. What was a nation but a collection of people with futures?

The algorithms looked to the United Kingdom. Zodie understood that the United Kingdom's strength was in manipulating other nations, conquering and gathering people. Yet again, they could see this was a plausible and predictable path for her future. The UK also had an independent streak. This showed sometimes they could break off from the main continent. The United Kingdom would be very instrumental.

Next, the United States Data. The role of the United States, was from its strength of gathering people from various parts of the world, meaning there was a merger of futures and destinies in this one nation alone. They had the power to understand individual mindsets of other nations only. Their power lay in this unique combination of cultures combining.

The computer spidered through Russia's past and consciousness. It moved through their history and their way of doing things. They were more likely to be one to watch. Their infrastructure, culture, and wiring had a lot to offer the world. So with Russia, Scope would approach cautiously, but no nation was immune to what the system could conclude about them. Scope could foresee the bigger picture around dominance, economy, and GDP, but it could correctly predict smaller things, even for whom they would vote. That was the power of Scope.

Then there were other poorer countries and individual nations that the machine placed in bundles, but Scope recalculated these. Rather than approach them as a single country, they could approach some as territories and clusters of societies. Each nation and group had a strength, each national group had a passenger weakness, and most of that could resurface and be used against them. Zodie understood that the only way she could make Scope work to their benefit was by offering countries information against each other.

She sighed. The machine they had worked on had taken years, if not all, her father's professional life. She took an interest in it when she was a small girl working with her father. Shortly after her adoption, they developed a great friendship, and when Heskin's wife had passed away, they only had each other. Scope was theirs. Heskin and Zodie made a powerful team.

"We need to work out if Scope spiders are ready to take on government information. With access to ISTF firewalls, we can penetrate the UK's brain nerve. You sure you want to do this?" the scientist said.

"Yes," Zodie replied. "Scope can bypass any firewall in existence and we also have entry to ISTF. Once we're done with the United Kingdom, we will target the next country, the United States, then others."

It was payback time for much, but the most satisfaction came from what Calla had done to her in high school. Calla had a way of looking at her as if she could see right through her spirit. Zodie feared Calla knew her soul. "I don't like anyone knowing me," she said to herself.

"We are ready," the scientist said.

"Ms. Baxendale, you sure you want to do this?" She heard her father's voice in her head. "This was just meant to be a bargaining chip, not a weapon. I must do it for you, for our family and me. They've taken away much from us, father. ISTF took away a lot from us."

"Just be sure, whatever you wish for," she heard him reply in her head. This time it was almost audible.

She huffed as the scientist watched.

This time she said it out loud. "I don't want you living in the shadows anymore, father."

SEVENTEEN

Day 15
The Mediterranean Sea
Scorpion Tide Deck, 11:27 a.m.

R ain spilled down in sheets outside the yacht as
Nash fell into stride beside her in the wide lounge.
Calla's stomach surged with fear, afraid to look
Nash in the eyes. The bullet, though it had missed her, Nash
had found her in time. It had shocked her to the core, and
she'd spent the last twenty-four hours in a state of anxiety.

Nash held her gaze for a minute as Captain Delgado
brought her a blanket, then left them. Anchoring his concern
on her, Nash dropped a peck on the tip of her nose. "You
okay?"

She returned his embrace, a tear burning in her left eyelid
before she gently pushed him back. "No."

She wavered. "Nash, I need to stop hurting you."

"You're not hurting me."

Her breath quickened. "This is the second time in less than three months both yours and Jack's lives have been in danger because of me."

"Cal, it could have happened to anybody. Until we have every operative technology and science project, and any leaks on your identity, we'll keep running into these things. We're in it together."

Calla squared her shoulders in a defensive pose. "It was too close, Nash. And they took the box."

He observed her. She knew the determination in her voice was troubling him. "Don't say that."

Calla loved him more than her life, but she couldn't do this to him any longer. Bring danger his way because of her. "I'm afraid. It has never been this close."

Nash kissed her eyelids. "We'll get through this," he said, drawing her in his arms. "Please Calla, don't give up now."

Every muscle in her went rigid. "I bring so much danger to you and everyone I love. I was a threat to my parents before I was born. And now you," she added.

A sheen of sweat was visible on his brow. "You don't. The day I married you, we said these words, '*you and me against the world*'. We're in it together, come what may."

Her breathing hitched a little. "But what if we aren't..."

He bent his head slightly. "What do you mean? We're always in this together. I meant what I said when I married you."

Parched, her mouth was bone dry. "Nash, you'll never have to speculate if you're normal. I live every day with the fact and that I couldn't protect our baby. Instead, it was my baby who protected me. One day, I may never be able to protect you, us..."

A shadow came over his face. "You don't have to take on

such responsibility. Beautiful, you're more normal, humane, more than anybody I know. We've been through this before."

"I'll always hurt all those around me. I bring them trouble. Even my own parents abandoned me because I would've brought them trouble. I can't bring any more danger to the two people I love, you and Jack."

He shuffled backward, bumping into the edge of the bar. "Stan and Nicole hid you in an orphanage to protect you."

"Exactly. To protect themselves from me and the harm I bring them. Being an operative is my curse. Look what it did to Zodie."

Reddening eyes squinted out at her. "Calla, please. I love you. I can't be without you."

"Nash, I have to leave you and our marriage, us, you stand a better chance of defeating operative technology threats with Jack and Captain Delgado."

He softened his voice in a confident murmur. "No, Calla. We've been through too much. You can't be serious."

She'd never seen him cry. Her own tears gave way. "I need to walk away from you. The person I love the most and always will. I have to protect you and what we have left."

His eyes were now bloodshot. "Calla, baby, please."

"Trouble follows me and because I love you, I have to leave you."

Lacing his fingers taut in hers, until his knuckles turned white, he tried to remain calm. "Please, Cal. We'll figure it out. Don't leave. Those predictions mean nothing. I've never known you to be superstitious or scared of anything. Lascar is just another fanatic with a crazed obsession. It won't amount to anything. He's gone now."

Her lips twitched. "Nash, I can't take that chance. I lost our baby I can't risk your life."

"One day, this will all be over, and we will live without threats from people like Heskin and Zodie. I have saved millions of dollars, billions now, to buy whatever security we need. I need to protect you and our future children, our family...us." He drew her into his arms. "You and I against the world. Please, Cal..."

A tight fist constricted around her heart. "I'll make the divorce final and erase all traces of our marriage. Nash, If I'm gone, then you'll be safe. Please take care of Jack, my parents, and the Scorpion Tide. I've already made plans to disappear off the grid. Please don't come after me. I'll leave in the morning."

"No, Calla, please. He shook his head. "I won't let you go."

Her heart clenched at his dejected tone as she took off the pendant she wore around her neck. The chain was a sign of their love and marriage. It had been safer that way, more than a ring. She slipped the chain into this palm as he tossed her an uncertain look, a war of emotions threatening to swamp him. It would be the second time she'd walked away from him. She knew it. But how could she stay when she could bring him greater danger like the one they'd faced hours earlier? A bite of regret pinched her heart as she watched his pained face.

He held her chain, his eyes steaming.

Wind and rain lashed at the closed windows as the yacht slowed in the torrential waters. Captain Delgado appeared at the door, then hesitated before he spoke. "There's been a disturbance. We have a problem. Scorpion Tide's systems aren't responding."

A peal of thunder, then a silvery flash of lightening stretched in the sky. "What do you mean?" Nash said.

Delgado's eyes narrowed. "Something's not right. Think it is the pod we picked up several days ago."

Nash fisted the chain, his eyes still on her.

He didn't move.

Calla watched him, then turned to Delgado. "I'll be right there."

EIGHTEEN

Scope Laboratories, London
12:20 p.m.

Zodie lifted her head when Radya stepped into the command room. "Is her camera setup?"

"Yes, it is," Radya said, approaching Zodie at the control center.

"I paid a heck of a lot of capital for that clone. She needs to be ready to move, attack, and get into position as programmed by Erikssen."

Zodie's eyes jumped from one screen to the next. The Scorpion Tide was a complicated machine and this was the only way to silence the Pythagoras Clause and bring the scroll back.

Like a shooting star, the yacht could appear and disappear at whim. Lascar had told her they needed to find a window when it refueled. That was the only time its shields were down to trace its stealth. Ten minutes was all it would take for the satellites to pin it down and enter the exact sequence Erikssen had given her.

"The satellites are in position. So are the coordinates," the man at the control panel affirmed.

Radya shoved her hair away from her face. "I intercepted communication Calla Cress had with ISTF early this morning to find that window. You should have about five minutes," she said.

"Five minutes?" Zodie said. "I thought we agreed at least ten."

The side of the man's mouth quirked upward. "No, five minutes for the club clone to latch onto Scorpion Tide's systems before we lose the signal."

Zodie punched in the sequence of information the man gave her. She had been around Calla Cress enough to know there was potential around that woman. Any power above Calla Cress interested her. She had been in the science world for years. It had been hard for a woman like her to advance in the male-led technology industry. Zodie felt laden with a burden and stopped what she was doing. Her eyes remained fixed on Radya. "Just why were you so ready to betray, Cress? What did she do to you?"

Radya's shoulders lifted to her earlobes. "Let's just say I prefer to be around powerful women."

Zodie's gaze prevailed on her for but a few seconds. "What's the activation line?"

She had waited too long.

"Here's the sequence," Radya replied. "Alpha, beta, November, India, foxtrot, hash, 77, 9253, 11, 21."

Zodie squalled her pleasure.

"The clone is live," Radya said. "You're on. You should be able to control the clone's movement as your own."

· · ·

Several thousand miles away from Earth, the satellite acknowledged the signal's reception and beamed it to the pod's surface. The symbols on its body lit, flashing blue and red.

Its aluminum shell popped open.

Its eyes opened.

Scorpion Tide, Mediterranean Sea
6:12 p.m.

Delgado had checked the basement twice, but this time the intervention was covert. Intentional. Scorpion Tide's instruments had never been compromised. Something was amiss.

The capsule was in the lower deck. Delgado grabbed his pistol and pushed the elevator button to level minus three. His eyes blanched when he verged on the containment cabin.

The door ajar, he prepped his handgun. "Who's there?"

The blow to his crown was strong.

Accurate.

Darkness replaced his line of vision as a figure stood above him.

6:30 p.m

Calla shot downstairs and hurried into the containment chamber. Her conversation with Nash would have to wait.

Delgado had been a welcome intrusion, and though she'd waited a few moments before following him, she had wanted to give Nash some space.

Movement by the yacht's engine room stirred her as she took careful steps toward the engine door.

Calla turned around.

The blow hit from above.

Her head collided with the steel pipes, then blackness.

Several minutes later, the heavy waft of perfume crossed her nostrils. Her head moved from side to sides as her eyes opened gradually.

It couldn't be!

Calla glared into a mirror. Her eyes must have threatened to deceive her. A woman.

Her replica

Her sister?

God knew what set themselves in front of her. She'd stripped Calla to her underwear and worn the clothes Calla had put on that morning.

"Hello, pretty face," the human clone said.

Even her voice was a striking resemblance, and had the same resonance as hers. What was going on? Who was this person? How was this possible?

The second strike was as hard as the first, but Calla blocked the woman's blow with a heel to the face.

The clone fell back, then regained composure almost as swiftly as she'd fallen.

She wanted more. Calla rose and flew to the exit. She

hastened through it before slamming it locked behind her.

Shivering in her underwear, Calla hastened to the top floors as the door behind her fell off its hinges as the clone charged for her.

Calla turned onto the upper deck. She had to stop this being. This...whatever it was. When she burst into the yacht's main lounge, Nash had barely moved from where she'd left him. He took one look at her in her lingerie and bewilderment crossed his face. "Cal?"

She recorded the shock in his face. "Nash, we're under attack."

"What?" The shock was in Jack's voice this time as he burst through the door at the end of the lounge. His face too showed confusion. Perhaps questioning what she was doing in her underclothes.

Without warning, a hand reached for her hair and she fell back. The clone attacked, a grip now on Calla's throat.

Delgado was now in the room, his firearm at the ready. "Hold it!" he yelled as the clone's hands pressed tighter.

This time the clone spoke. "It's her. She was in the capsule. I ran down as you indicated and she had broken through."

Delgado seemed to consider the clone's words as he aimed the gun to Calla's head.

And that voice. It was hers.

Nash advanced toward the excitement, his eyes showing alarm. With no time to react, the clone's strength was mechanical, irrational. It raised Calla to her tiptoes and clasped her to the glass of the deck window.

Calla shuddered in the clone's grasp. She wriggled and elbowed the clone in the gut.

It looked human, yet could its insides have been metal as

Calla's bone smashed into what had to be solid titanium? Calla swayed, her head in torment.

"What's going on, Calla?" Jack said.

"Jack, help me," the clone said.

Too dumbfounded to proceed, the men observed, unsure who to help and when to intervene.

The clone pulled Calla to her feet and fisted her abdomen, then lugged her to the barrier of the yacht's balcony edge.

"No!" Nash screamed. "What are you doing?"

In one swift operation, the clone flung Calla's legs over railing.

Calla hung onto the metal, stiffening her fists as she swung above the yacht's engines.

Her heart in her throat, she was losing her grasp.

All she saw were Jack and Nash's eyes.

"Wait!"

It was Nash's voice, but even as his words escaped his mouth, the clone's foot hit down hard on her fingers.

Calla yelped.

She let go.

———

Nash charged to the edge. He glanced down at the rough current. Not a sign.

"She had it coming," Calla said. "I told you I didn't trust that pod and we should have never let it on board."

Nash tightened the necklace around his palm. "What just happened?"

Calla looked from person to person.

. . .

Several thousand miles away, Zodie knew she had to use the right words. The right words would gain the men's trust. Calla was gone. She could not have survived that fall into the depth of the Mediterranean. If she played it right, she would be with Nash tonight. She would know what fascination he had for no other woman but Calla. She had released the clone at an opportune moment.

When Calla had wanted to leave him, the clone had walked into the very lounge where they fought only moments ago. Shields was vulnerable now, and if she programmed the clone correctly, he would take the bait.

Zodie set up the most seductive tone she could on the clone and pressed the voice button.

"It burst out of the capsule. It was my clone! Scope must have sent it. It must be an operative technology. They've had my DNA for years. My mother and father tried to stop them."

"Really?" Jack said.

Calla nodded.

Nash was not sure what had just happened, but was this his wife? She had been so ready to leave him. And now?

He turned to Jack and Delgado. "Could I please speak to Calla alone?"

Jack and Delgado filed out of the room.

"Listen, Nash," Calla began. "I know what I said this evening was dramatic. But maybe I just need to give us a chance."

She put seductive arms around his neck and drew him close, staring into his eyes.

Nash felt himself relax under her embrace for a second. Her hair smelled just the way he liked it and he buried his face in her mane. This had to be his Calla. She had a way of having moments of fear, and then compassion took over.

"I'm sorry about what I said earlier and how scared I behaved," Calla said.

The Middle of the Mediterranean

Calla's eyes blinked as the yacht's blades thrashed toward her. Scorpion Tide's engines had been built to withstand terror on the seas, dread from pirates and ungodly weather.

A submarine with significant capacity. What was her strength against this? The frigid waters swallowed her, and she clung to the lifebuoy she'd pulled off the rails on her way down.

Calla swam out of harm's way as fast currents engulfed her behind Scorpion Tide. When she surfaced above water, she saw the clone on the deck by Jack and Nash.

She didn't know how it had done it. Just who was this? What was this? The clone had persuaded them she was her. Calla tried to support her head above the waves. Even if she could swim toward the yacht, what was her strength against the Scorpion Tide's motors?

The clone had stolen her identity. Wiped clean by a human, manufactured to sound and look like her. How on earth was she ever going to prove to anybody who she was?

Scorpion Tide engines nearly swallowed her.

If Jack and Nash could not recognize her from the reproduction, then would anybody believe she was who she said she was?

It didn't matter now. She doubted anyone knew she was

missing. She was commander of the Scorpion Tide. Damn it! It was her yacht! At this moment, she felt nothing like a commander. She had not long to think. Only seconds to mull over whether to plunge out of the yacht's current or cling to the lifebuoy. The power yacht would either kill her or leave her here. There was no alternative.

Calla stopped thrashing, strength leaving her. No matter how powerfully she hollered, her voice was no contest for the rumble of the motors.

The yacht changed course for a second.

Could it be?

No. It was headed her way.

In one calculated moment, she forced her arms under the water and dove with the quickness of lightning. Her muscles worked hard to bring her further beneath Scorpion Tide's acceleration.

She couldn't do it.

Without warning, it appeared from above. The rudder of her very own ship clashed with her head.

No sound.

Just darkness.

NINETEEN

Day 16
6:21 a.m

Nash did not sleep and had spent most of the night in Scorpion Tide's control room, where he'd dozed off just after 3:00 a.m. He wasn't sure why he hadn't been able to sleep. Something had kept him up and he had let Calla go to bed.

He'd stirred just after 5:30 a.m., a nagging thought in his mind. He hadn't slept well in the captain's chair.

Calla had seemed frazzled by the ordeal. Perhaps it was the shock of seeing her own clone. The operatives were capable of anything, but cloning to that level? That was even too much for him to fathom.

Stretching his hands out in a yawn, he cranked his back then headed to the master bedroom.

Calla slept peacefully and hadn't for months. She had wanted to leave him the night before and something had changed her mind.

He had not given her back her necklace with his ring.

Nash stepped into the shower. He wouldn't disturb her and had chosen not to sleep in the same room. He let the warm water rush over his face, his mind still disturbed by a strange nagging. Something was odd about the way things that had transpired the day before. Who could clone Calla? But equally, Calla would have wanted to find out and examine the clone, not throw it overboard. It had been so easy to let go of the body double.

He hoped the shower would elevate his muscle aches, then turned when he heard a quiet knock by the door.

Calla stepped into the spray behind him. She was awake now. He spun to face her. All sadness from the last weeks had vanished. The emerald glint he adored and knew so well had disappeared. Just what had happened to her?

She dropped delicate kisses on his face. In his entire relationship with Calla, he'd never been so self-conscious of his own nakedness. His body stiffened as she massaged his back. It wasn't as relaxing as it should have been.

Calla peered into his eyes. There was a deadness in them. Something he could not explain. There was something wrong with this picture. He'd had no issues with this side of things with the wife he loved so much. His sex life was a wonderful adventure he kept exploring with Calla, but this was not it. It was not her style. Something made him unresponsive to Calla's embraces. The shower was the last place Calla would do anything like this.

She tried to kiss him. He froze and pulled her away, pinning her hands to her side. This was all wrong. "Stop."

"You want me to stop?" she said.

Several miles away, Zodie took control of the AI's central processing unit in the clone. She had wanted to feel what it was like to touch the most unbeatable man the intelligence world had seen. To run her fingers over his toned torso, his firm arm muscles and that capered six-pack abdomen.

Nash shuffled swiftly back into the master bedroom and dressed in a flash, the clone watched him. "What is it, Nash?"

"Nothing."

It was anything.

"I need to find Delgado," he said.

"Now? So abruptly."

He stopped at the door and feigned a smirk. Everything in him wanted to punch the lights out of this thing. He drifted toward her. "I want to wear my lucky shirt. You know, the one I wore the day we met. Can you please get it for me?"

A mask of confusion crossed her face. Probably churning algorithms, she did not possess.

"Pick it out for me, if you don't mind," he said his hand to the door, if she escaped him.

Yet he wanted to be careful, not understanding what they used to make this machine. If this was Calla, she would know the shirt he'd worn that day at the museum three years ago when they'd first met.

Suddenly the clone stopped and couldn't move. "I…"

"Just how did I make you feel when we first met?"

"I…." She smiled. "She smote you, perhaps love at first sight?"

"Wrong. You landed a statue on my foot. Now let me see Ramses II, I think."

Just as he had thought. This was one sick piece of flesh made to clone perfection, but it lacked one thing. Everything that mattered. Humanity.

Nash had to find its off button. Problem was, a human clone was in every way human. Was there a machine part to it? Just maybe? Jack would know. If he remembered anything from the bionic hand he'd seen on Hex, there had to be an off button somewhere. This was artificial intelligence being sent to collect data. Suddenly her eyes flared red, and she lunged for him.

Nash side stepped her and pinned her hands to the clone's back.

He struck a flat palm on the base of her neck. The clone shivered before it froze, barely functional.

"So that's why they sent you in a pod. Apparently, water and electricity *do* mix."

She had to be the latest weapon developed by somebody to infiltrate the operatives and ISTF headquarters. Even if she was all robot covered in harvested flesh, the wiring of man and machine and been perfect. She'd fooled everybody for the last twenty-four hours.

God knew where his wife was. How was he going to forgive himself for ever doubting his Calla?

He had known something was wrong. She had begged for their help and they'd all let her down. His heart raced, frightened for Calla. How could he have done this? He should've trusted his instincts. He might just ask the culprit. "Who sent you?"

The eyes lit slightly, still a fluorescent red. "That's for me to know?"

"Why are you here?"

"To finish exactly what I started," the clone said, its voice still a mirror of Calla's.

"She's gone. You watched her go, just as I did. You have me now."

Yet he wondered. "Zodie?" he said. "Zodie Baxendale?"

"It took you long enough," the clone said.

"You're sick. Really sick."

"We could have had it all. A great life, me, every night..."

He gripped the clone's hand as she raised hers to strike. "Where's Calla?"

"Possibly where you pulled me out, at the bottom of the sea. I hear the turbines of this yacht are quite something."

This time Nash held no mercy. He grabbed a glass water bottle from the bedroom desk and struck the machine's head. If he would find his wife, no robotic eyes were welcome.

He shuffled to the bedside intercom. "Delgado?"

"Nash?"

"Please come and grab Jack."

"Yes, sir."

Delgado and Jack filed into the room. Their eyes traveled to the lump of human flesh on the floor.

"What is that?" Jack began.

"It's not her. It's a clone, part human harvested, part machine. AI though replaced her brain. This is Scope's doing, and she was sent by Heskin, possibly Zodie's idea. Only Erikssen knew where to get this science. I watched him so closely when we were in Havana. He's working with Baxendale and Scope."

Jack's eyes widened. "That mean's Calla—"

Nash's voice was desperate. "Is out there somewhere. We need to find her. God, I hope it's not too late. Delgado, please take Scorpion Tide back to the location we left her. Calla is a powerful swimmer... but..."

Delgado swallowed hard. "Could she...? It's been at least seven hours."

"Then we have no time to lose," Jack said.

When Delgado left, Jack set a hand on Nash's shoulder. "Nash...I."

"I know. We were both fooled. Calla may have wanted for us to call it quits. She was scared. But this is not what she wanted. Zodie has had her eyes on Calla for years. Heskin, they must have stolen her data from somewhere to perfect such a clone."

"What should we do with this thing?" Jack asked.

Nash's eyes traveled to the clone, now a lifeless lump on the floor. "Let's put it in the pod and take it to the Cove in London. I have a feeling Calla might one day want to beat the lights out of it. You would too if you had been cloned illegally and without your knowledge. The operatives can find out just what sick technology Zodie and Heskin conspired."

"Listen, Jack, even her own husband didn't know it was not her. It was so late and the middle of the night," Marree said, her eyes pinned on Jack.

He wiped a hand over his brow. "What if she's dead? What if we never find her?"

Jack could not believe that he had said the words. They pierced his heart to the core.

"She's not dead," Marree said. "If I know anything I've learned from Calla, she's not gone. She would have survived. She's a fighter."

Delgado's lips pressed into a thin line. "We've been through every part of the water where we left her, and we can't find her. I used to run a submarine and man a team of divers. I've tried every tactic in the book."

"Nash has been signaling and using all his contacts all night," Jack said, his chin lowering.

Jack's hand shivered on the captain's deck board. He could not look Marree in the eyes as Delgado wiped his brow. They had searched the spot for hours. Three of the crew were professional divers and two had been in the water in shifts for hours. Perrin, one of their expert divers, moved in to the room, still in his wet suit. The look on his face said it all. Then he shook his head, his face grim. "All we found is a lifebuoy, at the tail of the yacht. She must have pulled it on the way down."

"And nothing?" Jack said.

"Nothing," he said.

Jack rose to find Nash. "Bring up the buoy."

Marree followed.

When they found Nash in the captain's control room, Jack took in his friend's pain. Nash had his head in his hands. He'd not slept, but how could he? Calla was missing, and he had no idea where to look but the sea. He'd also watched her go.

Jack couldn't bear it any longer. "We've been searching for hours! Why didn't we see it?"

Delgado's face said it all. The clone, now sedated and secure in the base deck, had fooled them.

"How could I have not seen it? How could he not have been able to tell if it was Calla or not," Jack said, unable to look his best friend in the face?

"You both need to stop beating yourself about it," Marree said.

"I can't," Jack replied.

"You do," Marree said. "Anybody could make a mistake, Jack. Both of you. We all made the same mistake."

"Not like this. Not with Calla," Jack added..

He stared out the window. Scorpion Tide had been stationary for several hours, and after the morning's dive for Calla had docked to refuel in Malta, they could not just leave. There had to be a way to find Calla. They had to be a way to know what had happened to her. She had to be alive. He knew she would outlive him. That was his Calla.

"Jack, any sign from her chip in the microscopic nerve?" Nash said.

Marree lifted an eyebrow. "Chip. Nerve?"

"Jack created an AI nerve a month ago. It's a smart central processing unit. The outer layer of her eye receives transmissions and sends it to the nerve. It can do several things, including run through criminal databases, but mostly it's there to help her control information processing she receives from her surroundings. Her brain is extremely capable of processing information simultaneously, which most people can't do. That chip nerve behaves like a filter to help her. It does many other things but," he said, turning to Jack, "can't we track it?"

Jack recalled the energy he'd spent making sure the AI could be safely placed in Calla's able brain so she could use it in danger. It had not responded. Not once.

"Not without her DNA," Jack replied.

"Listen, what if we go to the operatives," Marree said. "From what you've told me, they've always been able to help."

"Wait!" Jack said, his eyes lighting up. "You're right. But we don't have to go to the Cove. Scorpion Tide was made to protect Calla in every way. It's a smart technologies yacht and can ID her DNA. It's that sophisticated. Isn't that what Stan said, Nash? This beast isn't only her home, it was programmed to protect her, so Scorpion Tide's machine can track her nerve just like any other active signal out there."

Jack reached for his cell. "Stan?... No, we haven't found her yet, but you can help. How soon can you get to Malta?... Okay. We need your DNA signature. I need to mirror your parental DNA and program Scorpion Tide to locate Calla... Hurry."

Jack set the phone down and scanned the room. "He'll be here in less than three hours."

***

High-tech in every way, as Stan and Nicole had purposed, the Scorpion Tide provided adequate instruments they needed. Everything from scanning devices, palm readers, medical kits and, most important, DNA trackers. It had everything Jack needed. Marree stood across the room, watching him. "You can do it, Jack. Nothing has ever been hard for you."

"Thank you, Marree," Jack said. He kissed her on the lips. "Calla is important to me. We have to find her. But you're one heck of a girl. I think you're onto something. Look here."

They moved around the lab table and Nash pulled up a chair, observing the laptop screen over Jack's shoulder. "Soon as Stan is here, I can extract a sample and run it through this algorithm, Stan had confirmed that when he and Nicole created this beast, they tagged it to Calla's DNA. It's almost like this yacht and her are one. She can't be far. If this machine is that in tune with her heartbeat. It knows where to find her. Think of it as a dog that needs a scent. I need Calla's DNA match, her family."

Nash's eyebrows knit as an incoming message from Reiner alerted him. "Baxendale is congregating nine key buyers at this spot."

He read out the coordinates.

"Where's that?" Marree asked.

Delgado looked closely. "Gibraltar"

Nash punched in the digits on the yacht's flight deck. It pulled up the GPS and zoomed in the location on the screen. "It's a lodge. Off the books looks like it."

Jack interjected. "You suppose the PM has anything to do with this? That lodge is an ISTF executive lodge used for the most confidential meetings."

Nash paced to the control panel, pain visible in his eyes.

"You okay, Nash?" Jack said.

He sank in a seat and studied them one by one after he put his phone away. "How could I have done this to her?"

Jack edged in. "You did nothing to her. That Heskin did. We'll stop him. We always do."

Nash ran a hand through his hair. He was suffering. "I don't know how I... I knew her well before I met her. I had her files from the CIA. I've been with her for three years. How could I have not known my own wife?"

"Nash," Marree said. "You love her. You were willing to let her walk away; that will knock the wind out of anyone. We've all made mistakes in our lives. Anybody could've made that mistake. At least now, we know we can do something about it."

Delgado rose when they heard the wind blades of a chopper. "Stan Cress is here. I also radioed Reiner, Nash. He'll touch down in an hour. I'll get the chopper landed on the helipad."

TWENTY

Egypt, Banks of the Nile

There were footprints. Not hers. Calla's head seemed like they had practiced a thousand drums on it. Arms behind her back, her heart was beating in her rib cage, imitating the peculiar vibrations in her brain. If saltwater hadn't been traveling up her nose, she might have felt less startled. Just where was here?

Her head not only seemed out of order; her fast-paced pulse also added to her confusion.

How long had she been out here? Her eyes scanned as far as light would allow. Sunshine tried to peek through the morning clouds. The sandy white coast became clear as she focused. Soothing sounds of crashing waves into rocks made certain she was awake as seagull cries boosted the cacophony of dawn. She licked the taste of saltwater in her mouth and turned toward distant houses.

Increasing pain in her arms was unbearable. The throbbing in her pulse insurmountable. It hurt and continued throughout her body. Saltwater peeled at her skin and her frame felt heavy.

Calla glanced around as the sea brushed up the coast. She dug her fingers into the sand and struggled to get a grip. Wearing what looked like underwear, she lifted her head an inch and picked herself up with every ounce of strength she could muster.

Hobbling to her feet, Calla rose. The last time she had had her eyes open, it was miles from here. Her gaze searched the waterfront for any sign, icon or landmark that might identify where she was. The extensive beach stretched into an endless desert coastline. Had she been here before? Her last memory was being on the Scorpion Tide talking to Nash.

Her heart sank. They'd been fighting.

Calla padded her frame. Nothing. Stripped to her lingerie. She had no phone. Hands padding her torso, hair filled with sand, she had nobody. Calla glimpsed behind her. Then she realized where she was. Before looking after the Roman and Byzantine relics at the British Museum in London, she had overseen the Egyptian collections once. Second-floor right-hand-side corner.

Was she here? Was she in Egypt on the former Pharos Island, the longest standing ancient wonder? Did it still exist?

Hypatia's home.

For the first time, as the morning sun stung her eyes, she faced the old grounds of the lighthouse of Alexandria.

Calla turned at the sound of boots crunching sand. A figure stood above her with a weapon. She raised her gaze to meet a stern face, eyes burning, pistol in hand. "Radya?"

Embarrassed by her state, she backed up a little. "Radya, what are you doing? Did you bring me here?"

"Only to kill you."

Horror gripped Calla. "Why?"

"I've once heard you say, man does not need to know everything, and that includes you."

A clout struck her jaw and drew blood. Calla wiped the ooze, her eyes stinging in the sun, unable to see Radya clearly. "Radya? Why?"

A second thump to her belly. Salt water mixed with sand, her lips pasted to the ground. "Radya, I'll not fight you. You are one of us."

"No, I'm not. Ever speculate why I've been tailing your every move. It's tough for any girl to make a mark in the world of technology and spies, especially when you're around. Zodie has done it, and her only stipulation for me to work for her was to get you out of ISTF. Calla, you've always been in her way and now you're in mine."

Calla peered upward, the barrel of the gun marking her crown. "Radya, don't. You're not a murderer."

Her heart thundered as Radya pulled the trigger.

She missed. The bullet sizzled past Calla as the ring of yelling voices and horse hooves galloping became louder.

A shot hit Radya's chest.

She dropped face down, the pistol still in her hand.

Scorpion Tide Conference Room
8:27 p.m.

When Jack had taken Stan's blood sample, he shot up and left the cabin to process it. "We should have the results in an hour."

Stan rolled up his sleeve. "It wouldn't surprise me if the Tide protected her from that fall. The Scorpion Tide is Calla's protector. It wouldn't have harmed her. It's tuned to her makeup, through her unique DNA structure, and it monitors her heartbeat. We'll find her. My daughter survived twenty-eight years without Nicole and I. She'll defeat whatever comes her way."

"Hope you're right," Nash said.

Jack, Delgado and Marree parted to process the DNA signature as Stan took a seat around the long table. He studied Nash for several moments before he spoke. "Nash?"

"Yes?"

"Nicole's coming to. She had been awake for about a few hours before I left London. I'm giving her some time to recoup. I asked the hospital to have her at home. It was the best place for her to recover so I could watch over her, away from Scope's view."

Nash had had his hand on his head and raised his chin. "How is she?"

"Recovering, but until we understand what Scope programmed in her, I'm a little worried."

Stan took a photograph from his pocket. "She would've been a few days old. She's always had my eyes. I took this picture the day I learned we had to give her up and put her in a foster home. I'd known Mama and Papa Cress during my military training. They looked after me as a youngster when I lost my parents."

"I'm sorry, Stan," Nash said. "I know what it means to lose a child you've never known."

"Nash, you and Calla will make it. You'll be a better father than I ever was, and I want to make up that time with Calla. It's something Nicole and I never talk much about.

Nicole regrets to her core ever leaving Calla. Hence she got involved with individuals like Heskin. She wanted it to end—the Cress mandate she took on when she was born and passed on to her child. One day you and Calla will over come that mandate."

Nash nodded, his heart aching for news on Calla. Nicole was one woman who, though she'd been in MI6 agent, Nash wondered what he knew about her. Not enough.

"I'm not proud of everything I've done, but I'm proud of marrying my wife and having Calla. The simple route would have been the opposite of that scenario," Stan said.

"I would never have left my child, but that's me," Nash said. "I don't judge you, Stan. If fatherhood were easy, perhaps my father would've been a better one. I've never understood him."

"You didn't know the choices we had back then, Nash, but I agree with you. I made a hard choice leaving her and because of that she spent her entire life wondering who she is. We left her alone with the very powers that haunt her to this day."

Stan rose for the bar and poured Nash and himself whiskeys. Nash set the drink to his lips and let the taste burn down his throat.

Stan set his glass down after taking a sip. "When Nicole discovered Heskin could create an algorithm that could keep Calla safe, it was a tough choice. We didn't want any of her genetic data out there. It would be hot property for any crazy geneticist. See what Scope did with just a sample? They cloned a fighting machine, exactly what Calla could've become. I stupidly thought if Calla didn't know her heritage, it would never haunt her. We knew it was a tough choice, but it was something that she used moral judgment on to keep her safe. Nash, you of all people have to believe me."

"Don't beat yourself up, Stan," Nash said.

Stan nodded. "Heskin was someone who could create good things. Though not an operative, he knew how they ticked. He'd been around Mason Laskfell for years. Mason probed his interest in science and technology. I'm sorry for what I did, and I know Calla will not always understand the choices I made. Her mother as a woman working for MI6 with a baby on the way had to make a tough choice. Especially with the most wanted operative child. Nicole had unusual but an amazing genetical wonder growing in her, whom she loved. We knew this but we just couldn't protect her, I went to all lengths to make sure I could. Nicole feels the same way."

Nash thought for a few moments. "Why would anyone want to do what they did back then? Why wouldn't MI6 protect your family? I never understood that bit. I don't understand why the Americans needed to come in? Though I'm grateful it came to me."

Stan lifted his chin. "MI6 wasn't always favorable to families. Nash, when I found out a few years ago that you were launching this global undercover security service and I read you file, I knew you were the right person to watch over my girl. The bonus for me was you fell in love. I couldn't want a better son."

The words were sincere, and Nash understood that he meant them. "I failed you though. I haven't taken care of her."

"Yes, you have, Nash."

"A family like mine is hard to understand, yet you've

done it. Colton at the time made it easy for us to get this done and to protect her."

"Colton sold her data to Heskin, that's why we are where we are. We can't find him."

"Yes, that moron should be taught a lesson," Stan said.

"You must fight for her at all costs, Nash. She deserves that, and I'm right behind you."

"I just want to find her," Nash said. "You know, before she disappeared, she demanded to leave me. She left me because she feared for my life and everyone's on this boat." He took out her chain and held it in his palm. "She's never worn this wedding ring. She wanted it around her neck to protect me."

"That only tells me how much she loves you, Nash. Forgive her. She didn't know what she was doing. She grew up abandoned by the only family she had. So, we are to blame. Please hold on to her. I know you two will make it through. We can't let her down. Prove to her, she need not protect you and the others. By loving you, she will protect you. She sees ISTF as a burden, doesn't she?" Stan said. "Yet you see her leading it as the only way to protect her secrets."

"Yes. What Scope has done to us, and what it will do to many others is unforgivable," Nash added.

"Love can do a bunch of things to us, Nash. Nicole was scared for Calla because she once faced the same threat. The only difference is technique, better science and data. When Nicole saw what Heskin could do, it became a problem. There's one thing I need you to know," Stan said.

"What's that?"

"You know, when MI6 refused to help us, it was because we wouldn't surrender any data on Calla. And her DNA was a bargaining chip to protect her. We declined. I don't wish that continued in her life. The prediction that Scope has made over you can only be possible with mathematical data to create simulations and scenarios. No one has this data on Calla but, you and Jack. They all wish to think they do. No one can predict Calla's future because she is immune to it."

Nash placed Calla's ring and the necklace in his pocket. "Is she?"

"Yes, and that makes you immune too. There's something else you need to know," Stan said. "When we built the Scorpion Tide. We programmed it to always protect Calla. That's why I believe it couldn't harm her, even when she was under its beast of engines. It probably washed her somewhere she had to go. Remember Germany. When Nicole disappeared, I always knew I could find her. She is very much the pre-runner to who Calla has become. My heart beat for my wife and I found her and I know you can do the same."

Nash fingered the chain he'd given her on her twenty-eighth birthday, the day the words they had said to each other were ingrained in his heart. 'You and me against the world'. That meant Calla could not break that bond if she wanted to.

Jack hurried into the room. "We have a faint signal. Scorpion Tide has found her."

Calla's jaw dropped. Eyes forward. Her mind must've been conjuring events. *Mila?*

"Mila Rembrandt?"

She'd pulled the trigger. Behind her a herd of nomadic women on camels in colorful attire with Arabian swords, the lengths of spears draped around theirs waists surrounded Calla.

"You've been through quite an ordeal," Mila said.

"Where am I?"

"On the boarder of the Sahara desert. The sea washed you to Alexandria. I was too late when your ISTF ambitious friend here tried to take matters in her own hands. She dragged you here to the desert to kill you."

Calla blinked at the sun stinging her eyes. She was still in her underwear and felt a shame come on.

Mila placed a nomadic robe over Calla's shoulders. She had not known Radya much and only met her a few days ago.

"Allegra alerted me Zodie had sent that Radya to find you if you ever left the Scorpion Tide. I followed Radya, tracking her with Tiege's help."

A second voice interjected. "The Scorpion Tide saved your life and also brought you here. That doesn't happen often, so you must be here for a reason."

The voice was familiar, the location and timing erroneous. "Safaa?"

Her museum colleague, she'd spoken to in Havana, stood shoulder to shoulder with Mila, also draped in wonderful nomadic desert robes. "Safaa? How?"

Safaa smiled. "You've come to a place where every operative must decide once and for all who they will serve, themselves or the world."

Calla had always loved Safaa's cool and collected manner. "I don't understand," Calla said.

"You will today," Mila said.

Mila hoisted her onto her camel. "Come, let's get you some proper clothes."

She'd always thought she understood and identified who

Mila was, but Mila also had her mysteries. An operative much embedded in government ways and the operatives' systems, Mila hid much too much from Calla over months. Years, rather.

"We need to move," Safaa said.

"Safaa, what are you doing here?" Calla asked.

"These are my people. We have guarded the Library's secrets for years. Operatives are keepers of the secrets of the world. This just happens to be ours, and we've done it for years. You of all people know that intelligence in the wrong hands always goes haywire."

Calla's eyes avoided the sun. "All these years and I never knew you were an operative, Safaa."

"We need to go. We don't have much time," Mila said, handing her a bottle of cool water, bread and a pomegranate.

Two hours later, the desert heat stung Calla's skin, her throat parched as the small group crossed the dunes. Where on earth were they going? Light wind slapped her face as the hump under her hurt, but she endured it as they crossed the desert for several hours, her arms aching. She had not eaten properly in hours and felt she would faint if the camel did not reach its destination quickly.

Nash! She'd left them all hanging. How she wished she'd left things better. He would be so worried. *And that horrid clone!*

Mila, Safaa and the group took her deeper into the desert. Soon they were met by another group of desert operatives, mostly nomadic women like the ones she had ridden with. They looked like warriors. Keepers of the desert's mysteries, they called themselves.

They stopped to rest in tents at a base camp by the well.

After several moments of shade and refreshment, Myla's intent gaze over Calla became more than she could endure. "Why do you run, Calla? You have everything you need. Why do you feel you're not normal?"

"How do you know that?" Calla said.

"I know everything about you. It's my job. You fear who you are, everything about your abilities and the things you don't understand, you question. Don't. Just be."

"I don't fear it. Just don't understand," Calla said.

"I won't go into much about who you are, Calla."

"Why?"

"Because that's not the objective. When I found out you were alive several months ago. I finally understood it was my job to help you. If you want to help your friends in a world that doesn't understand you, and God knows when the world doesn't want to accept us, it hunts us. Whether you belong there or not isn't the point. You've made it your home, and you've sworn in your heart to protect it. You need to forget what you don't know and act on what you do. Like Nash."

"Nash?"

"A great man who would sell his greatest treasure, himself, if it only means to love you. Love is more effective than you think. More important that the mandate you feel you carry. Overcome the burden of your heritage and your fears."

Safaa joined them. "It's time," she said. "The next part we will do alone, Calla. That part of the journey will need everything you have."

What more could she give, especially in a place like this? She had just about had enough. "I need to get back to Nash, to the Scorpion Tide. They'll be worried."

"Not until you do this. Get some rest. We leave soon. By this time tomorrow, it'll be over," Safaa said.

———

Almost an hour later, Calla's eyes shot open. The group, the canvases, had all gone. Two camels grazed by the well. Safaa stood to her feet. "It's time. Let's go."

In the distance she saw the wind. If it was anything like she'd experienced in China, the desert storm would be brutal.

Sand and dust spiraled in her direction as they moved. Then, her foot lost its grip on the sliding surface.

———

Walls caved in around Calla, before she landed in a pile, sand pouring above her head, her feet clashing with rocky ground.

Darkness forbade her to make sense of her environment. The descent had been severe as she plummeted into what she could only guess was a cave.

Eyes blinking, she rose. "Safaa?"

"Right behind you," Safaa said, lighting a straw torch. She kept walking.

They advanced for several meters. Safaa stopped. "We're here. There is something you need to see."

Dusty and cobwebbed corridors greeted them as they marched forward. Sculpted archways, stained by decades of dust, lined the walls. Soon they came to a room, a cave made for scholars and princes. Her eyes widened.

No, it couldn't be. But this had all burned in the fire in a civil war with Julius Caesar in 48 BC. Scientific, technological and historical knowledge once thought to have been lost greeted her. Her feet moved forward, leading to the most resplendent library she'd ever seen. Stones placed in deliberate patterns over uneven floors unworn from centuries of little use, made Calla gasp. Was this the oldest library in the world? Her eyes could only stare.

"Safaa? Is this real?"

Calla blinked twice. The Library of Alexandria was one of the largest and most significant libraries of the ancient world. They dedicated it to the nine muses and the goddesses of the arts. Each was represented in charcoaled portraits that hung on the walls. The tight sand around the cave must have preserved the artifacts. She moved through the room that lead into another. The second room was even larger than the first. Hundreds of scrolls, stacked within ancient shelving, made Calla's heart skip.

Calla scanned the third century BC structure. Its collections of works and remains of what used to be lecture halls, meeting rooms and gardens were on show, having lived here for years. Ancient scholars and modern thinkers had held and studied these. Perhaps Pythagoras himself studied here: the Library of Alexandria in its glory was an actual place.

Safaa smiled. "Now that's the reaction I was looking for."

When they got to the end of the room, Safaa reached within a hole in the wall and pulled a lever that switched on an ancient lighting system of lamps that lit one after the other until the rooms were flooded with blinding light. Each lamp poured oil from one to another. Calla strolled past papyrus scrolls. She couldn't count how many scrolls were preserved here. It could have been anything from 40,000 to 400,000.

She moved to one wall, and her fingers scraped along the edges of a shelf. They stopped to study a scroll of ancient mathematics. To her right, another one on building construction. More scrolls revealed scholars had devised several inventions millennia ago that people enjoyed today.

She gasped at her next discovery. Here before her were the missing works of Pythagoras—designs for astrolabes predicting where stars and planets would be on any given date. She looked hard. The date marked was only two days from now.

She scoured through the manuscripts of the missing volumes of the Commentary of Arithmetica written in the operative language. Six Greek volumes had been found and four later in Arabic. Nothing more. Here were the three works preserved in operative codes and symbols, a vocabulary she could understand, yet she never knew why or how. Her fingers gently stroked the pages.

Calla drew in a deep breath and took a seat on a low stone. "I have been on this major hunt for Pythagoras for a long time and some of his missing works. There are just so many things about Pythagoras that still stagger me and if I could perhaps piece them together."

Safaa observed her. They had always been good friends at the British Museum. Safaa had looked after North African collections for years and was an expert in all things ancient Greek.

"This part of the Library contained important documents," Safaa said.

"I'd like to get to the heart of what Pythagoras meant to Hypatia and why?"

"You and I know Pythagoras as a philosopher, scientist and perhaps a religious teacher, but he also developed a school of thought that accepted something controversial at his time. That's what Hypatia latched onto. What you need to determine is how many of his theories were mere wonderful mathematics and science," she said. "Or just crazy philosophies. Hypatia made her choice."

"I'm interested in Pythagoras's mathematical teachings. I'm trying to solve a riddle," Calla said.

Safaa looked at her. "Riddles are only hidden from those not meant to read them. He believed opposite forces controlled life between the limited and unlimited. His theories explain the operative world effectively. Numbers can cover the secrets of the universe, and numbers give shape to matter and anything that takes up space. He even devoted himself to studying musical intervals that led to the discovery that we can express chief intervals in numerical ratios. We can express everything in life through pattern, numbers and ratios."

"Thanks Safaa, but I'd just be happy with the glitch I'm looking for to stop Scope's data farms. His theories must have something I can use to determine the code we need to stop them. I've been looking for a serial number, maybe three, imbedded in Pythagoras's mathematical theories. Those Hypatia was convinced of through the Pythagoras Clause."

"The Pythagoras Clause is a prompting. Math that may disqualify any mathematical theory."

Calla raised her chin. "What do you mean?"

"Pythagoras did important work extending the body of the map of mathematical knowledge."

"I need to dig in his brain and unravel what Scope uses for prediction through data mining. It must be a code."

Safaa's eyes lit. "Is it?"

Calla turned to Safaa. "Anything from Hypatia in here?"

Safaa smirked. "This way."

She took Calla to the end of the area and dragged back a hanging Persian tapestry. "This way."

Behind the rug, Calla stopped, her heart racing. "No? Was this all hers?"

Safaa nodded as she stepped further into the Space. A small makeshift counter, stockpiled with manuscripts, astrolabe, ancient instruments and charcoal came into view. "These were hers. We searched for decades and passed these items from one generation to another until we brought them here. Unfortunately, one scroll went missing, her most important work."

"The one that Scope took, and I stole back."

"Yes, but there is something else you need to see," Safaa said. "It's time you really accept the Pythagoras Clause."

Calla followed Safaa to a dusty desk. With careful hands only a trained curator like her could have done, Calla took a manuscript into her palms that Safaa held out. "Take it. Read it."

Safaa moved the torch closer so Calla could concentrate. Steady hands pulled open the scroll across the table. "Is this—

"The full scroll Hypatia wrote on the Clause? Yes," Safaa said.

"We've hidden it for years. It's time you see it as it is meant for you to see."

Calla's eyes studied what she had feared all along. The scroll had a similar portrait, a charcoal drawing of her face. But that was what shook her insides. She stopped and turned to Safaa. "That's my tattoo, a birthmark really that I've had since I can remember."

"Yes, the one on your ankle and has baffled you for years."

How did Safaa know? She wouldn't ask. Calla knew that birthmark more than anything on her body, carefully crafted like a mistaken tattoo. The same symbols on her ankle lined the drawing. She studied the writing next to an ancient portrait, her heart racing, tears streaming down her face. "Why?"

"Why you?" Safaa finished.

"Calla, you know you were born for a reason and for such a time as this. These things are all forerunners in your path. People who would've loved to meet you like Hypatia. She must've had visions about you and if anyone knew what you stood for, she documented it here. There on this manuscript is the Pythagoras Clause, and it's not at all what everybody thinks."

"So it's not a glitch or an ancient mathematical serial number?"

Safaa shook her head. "What it is, only you can read. You were given the gift of language and codes, and Hypatia sent you a message right here in this manuscript all those centuries ago."

Calla took in the symbols. Every syllable and stroke made sense, and even she could not have imagined this was the Clause they had searched for, for days.

She understood.

Knowledge hidden for years, answers plain for her to see.

They heard a noise the way they came, and Calla pulled the scroll together and stuffed it in her nomadic wear.

"We should go," Safaa said. "Opening Hypatia's room must have destabilized the cave's walls, we should go back."

Once more, the structure vibrated with a loud rumble.

Calla and Safaa hastened into the next room, dust and soot threatening to blind them as boots resounded in their direction. Her heart leaped when she saw him. "Nash!"

Nash scurried to her and assembled her into his arms. He pressed kisses on her face, his expression a mask of concern.

"Calla, you're okay. I'm so sorry, beautiful. I let you down. I should've—

She pressed two fingers on his mouth. "I let you down too, Nash," she said, her own tears unable to stop.

"How did you find me?"

He put her down gently and turned. "A combination of blood power and tech know how. Stan's DNA helped Jack tag you from the Scorpion Tide labs. It could trace the nerve Jack gave you all those weeks ago. The one he inserted. We detected it here."

Jack whisked forward, hugging Calla as Marree, Stan and Delgado shuffled into the chamber behind him. "And just where is here? Freaking heck, is this—

"The Library of Alexandria?" Calla said. "Yes."

Marree and Jack prowled the room, and Stan and Delgado did likewise.

Safaa moved to where Nash and Calla stood. "So you are Nash? Hmm, I get it now," she said with a sneer at Calla.

The group came back to join them, their eyes still hypnotized by the place where they were.

"It's something here," Stan said. He pulled her into his arms. "Sweetheart, I'm sorry. Are you okay?"

She nodded.

"I don't mean to be a party pooper, but as guardian of this establishment be it underground, I'm afraid the museum is now closed. We should leave this history here. Believe me, the world isn't ready to hear it.

"Really?" Jack said. "But this is incredible. We need to go through it. There's some great information in here," he said, studying the ancient relics and inventions stacked neatly in corners of the room.

"When the world is ready, Jack," Safaa said. "I'll give you a personal tour and let you know what you can share."

"Oh, man. Okay, I'll look you up on that one. Have we met before?"

"Yes, you have," Calla said. "At my exhibitions at the British Museum."

"Before we go, Calla," Nash said, sinking to one knee, her hands in his. "I have something to ask you. I hope to return something to you."

The hair on the back of her neck spiked as her heart raced, uncertain what he would do next.

Shoulders straight, Nash stood determined. "The last time we did this, we hid it from our friends. We didn't let them celebrate with us. I don't want to that anymore, at least not rob our friends of sharing this with us. If you forgive me and will have me, Calla, I'm asking you to marry me again."

Her heart nearly leaped out of her rib cage, her pulse thundering. Stunned, yet excited pairs of eyes watched them as Nash drew out her chain, with her wedding ring. He then rose to face her. "If you say yes, then I suspect this belongs to you. I'd love to put it back where it belongs, around your beautiful neck."

Had the small crowd been observing them, they dissolved in the background. All she knew was Nash's earnestness, his commitment to her and his love she didn't deserve. His unfathomable gaze drew her forward as silence fell on the lips of the bystanders, all eagerly waiting for her answer. She drew in a sharp breath, relished the glow in Nash's gray eyes, fresh tears burning her cheeks. "My answer is, and will always be, yes," she said, nodding. "And one further thing, Nash. We do it now."

One brow lifted in curiosity. "Now?"

She nodded. "We have everything here, a magnificent venue, a captain to preside, a dad to give me away, a best man, a maid of honor and a bridesmaid."

By now there was no dry eye in the caved library as the lamps flicked around them, candle like. Each knew their part in the ceremony about to take place.

Nash placed the chain with the ring around her neck and Stan took his place next to her. Jack proceeded to Nash's side with a beaming smile growing on his face. Marree and Safaa, a well of tears threatening to overcome them, stood next to Calla's side, and she smiled at them, squeezing their palms for a second.

Captain Delgado straightened his combat shirt and took to the head of the group.

"I've always wanted to do this," Delgado said. "But when you man submarines, the opportunity sometimes evades you. I couldn't be more honored."

Calla loved the man in front of her. She'd let him down often, yet he'd loved her every step of the way. She slid a hand around his neck, preferring to drown out everything around but this moment, that she wanted to remember forever. Remember it each time she felt persuaded to run from his commitment to her. When she mouthed her 'I do', his lips came down on hers, swelling her insides with emotion and respect for him.

"I love you, you know," Nash said. "And from now on, I run a tight yacht, young lady. If you ever take that ring off, it won't be history codes haunting you, it will be me."

She snickered.

Jack busied himself with his phone camera and the timer. "Wait! I need to remember this. My best friends getting hitched in the world's greatest place of knowledge. We couldn't have planned it any better."

He arranged the timer and clicked a few shots with the group.

A rumble above broke the proceedings.

"What's that?" Stan asked.

"Hmm, just in time," Safaa said. "The Library has lent you it's rooms. But now it's kicking you out, Let's move. I believe I've let you wonderful people in longer than I should have"

Calla seized the scroll from the table where she had set it. "Safaa, If I can't take anything from here. Can I take this?" she said as the ground shook.

"Consider it a wedding gift. Hypatia would have wanted you to have it."

They hurried. Each room shutting iron bars behind them as they hastened from room to room until they reached the entrance to the cave. With the ropes Nash and Delgado had dropped down the cave's entrance still draped from above, they mounted one by one.

As Calla brought her head above ground, Nash's hand pulled her out onto the surface of the cave. Scorpion Tide's trusted four wheel drive waited by the camels.

Safaa was last to surface, her caution at keeping the Library safe guiding her. A herd of nomadic hooves, camels and horses approached them.

Safaa turned to Calla. "You're in safe hands and Mila will make sure you and your friends get back through the desert as a storm's coming."

She gave Safaa a long embrace. "Thank you, Safaa. For everything."

The horses circled the Library's opening and shuffled enough sand to cover the cave's entrance.

Beneath them, the rumbles continued.

"It's burying itself, isn't it, Safaa?" Calla said.

"Until a time as it's needed," she responded.

Safaa took Calla into her arms and held her for a second. "Remember what I told you. The Clause will guide you."

Calla nodded and took the last seat in the Jeep between her, Nash and Jack.

"*Arak lahiqaan,*" Safaa said, waving goodbye.

"*Arak lahiqaan,*" Calla and Nash replied as Delgado started the Jeep's engines through a desert night.

"I guess some history is not meant to be shared," Calla said, looking back at the cave's entrance, now concealed by desert and dust.

Nash took her hand in this. "Not this time, beautiful."

TWENTY-ONE

The Cotswolds
5:27 p.m

Nicole's eyes shot open. Splotches of sunlight danced on the floor like a blade of diamonds as the sun came into the room. A stench of leather from a distant memory wafted in. Unaware of where she was, her glare darted from one end of the bedroom suite to the next.

The noise broke from above. The hand landed on her throat.

She saw him.

"Looks like you and I need to finish a little business."

Heskin's voice was as she remembered. Syringe in his fist, Heskin lunged for her arm, staggering from the bed, his reflexes dazed. She dodged him and settled a heel in his chest.

Heskin crashed backward, knocking over a table by the door.

She had smelled danger. Years of sleeping with one eye

open had told her that. Still bound with medical wires, Nicole's senses awoke to her ordeal. She remembered nothing, not where she was, nor how she'd gotten here. She forcibly quelled the urge to clout him. "You induced me into a slumber, didn't you?" It wasn't the technology. "You use a drug, don't you, Heskin?" she said. "Scope's power over people in the app is through a malfunction in your processes. Your phones enhance a coma-inducing drug, a side effect expelled by your products after overuse. That's it, isn't it? I knew it that day. I saw it in your lab ages ago. By then, you've collected enough data to simulate their futures. It doesn't matter, so you blame it on overuse. I saw that glitch years ago in Swindon and threw your research in the river."

Anger etched the face of her opponent into hard lines. "My men dove for days, looking for my work. When I got to the laptop, you'd already done your damage," Heskin said. "I swore I would find you and kill you. You and that child of yours have damaged my life."

Rage tore through her with the speed of light. "You tried to poison me with the very thing you were supposed to protect my girl from," Nicole replied.

Rage evident in his eyes, he grunted. "You grabbed my technology and destroyed it. It took me twenty bloody years to retrieve and update. When I did, your daughter came for me. You may have thought that you left me with nothing. I had a strand of that gorgeous hair she inherited and the flash drive you brought that day. You weren't the only one trained as a spy. Zodie was keen in Beacon Academy. What she understood as a fight on the playground, was Zodie's first assignment at espionage. She had strands of your child's mane for years. Oh, and the cloning was easy. That lunatic

Erikssen only needed steering and money did the rest of the talking."

When she saw his weapon's intent, Nicole dodged behind the bed.

His trigger finger stroked out a quick three-round burst. Then he came for her neck.

She crashed an elbow in his middle. He thrust for more, the syringe still in his hand. "I'll get you to sleep once and for all. When we found out those phones could expel toxins and drug their users, it was just a bonus. Every product has side effects. I now have enough in this injection to put you away forever."

Still fighting the drugs in her system, she tried to make her limbs move. Nicole eyed the needle tip marked for her. She kneed him and he went down, grunting. He leaped, then struck. The devastating blow sent her sprawling to the ground. It took two thoughts. She lunged for him and seized the syringe, then turned it to his neck. She pressed down hard. His eyes swelled with horror as blood spurted out from his wound.

A fine sheen of sweat shone on his upper lip as satisfaction filled her insides. "Just enough, until we get you to a convenient pen. I'm confident MI6 will demand to know who else you shared your dirty secrets with."

Off the Coast of Alexandria

Calla gazed out to sea, the view of Alexandria disappearing on the horizon. Warmth and humidity hung in the air like steam from a hot shower. Lights illuminating their powerful yacht seemed to blind her for a second as she reclined on the spacious deck after she'd showered and changed. She had wolfed down dinner and felt a good night's rest ahead would be welcome before tomorrow. It would be a tough day, but she was ready.

Nash appeared and proceeded to the deck bed with an icebox, champagne, and two glasses in hand.

He reclined next to her. "Jack found the servers after much effort. Your mother contacted us. Heskin escaped again. Radya broke him out, and he went straight for Nicole in the Cotswolds. She'd been onto him for some time, and it was she who discovered the data farm. She had known for years but never knew what they planned to do with it."

"Where is it?" Calla asked.

"We're on our way to a lodge in the cliff rocks of Gibraltar. ISTF agents will meet us at the safe house to plan the points of entry. We'll be there in the morning, Jack is right."

"Yes, Scope's signal beams in less than two days from that data farm. We don't know what we'll find, so we have to expect and prepare for the worst."

She sighed, watching him, loving him.

He turned her way. "Hey beautiful, I recognize this isn't the wedding night you envisaged, neither was the last one. But what's important to me is you're with me now."

She nodded and edged into his powerful arms. How she had missed them. How she had feared she'd never see them again. Never hold him again. "I'm sorry, Nash."

"No, I'm sorry too," Nash said. "Before Jack found your signal, I didn't know what to do with myself. It was the scariest thing in my life. My concern was, would you forgive me? How I failed you."

"Nash, I'm the one who needs to say sorry. I let you down, and I gave up on us. I gave up on *'you and me against the world'.*"

"Well," he said, stroking the necklace with her ring on it. "Let's not do that again. Agreed?"

"Agreed."

Her curiosity got the better of her. "By the way, just how did you know I wasn't the clone."

A sexy blush crept to his face. "There're some things a man knows about his wife that none can imitate."

She raised an eyebrow. "Hey."

"I never touched her. I didn't even sleep in our room. I was so disturbed I went to the yacht's driving deck. I don't know how many hours I stared at sea, my heart heavy. Then I must've fallen asleep in that chair, pure anguish and exhaustion. It was when I went to our room to take a shower that I was rudely interrupted."

"Hmm…" she said, raising an eyebrow. "She didn't?"

Amusement flickered in his eyes. "She tried. She failed."

Calla giggled and caressed his skin with her mouth.

He handed her a champagne flute. "Now, Mrs. Shields, should we agree you don't take this off again?"

Calla sank into his arms. "Think we can settle with that."

In return, he trailed kisses down the slender column of her neck. She opened her mouth to speak, but his lips forbade her. In one sudden movement, she rose and strode to the deck entrance stairs. She locked the door before turning with a seductive grin toward him, discarding one piece of clothing at a time. "Right, where were we?"

She plopped down next to him. All Nash could do was look. His eyes told her he was struck. Then his hand caressed her midriff, and she cuddled deeper into his embrace. "I can't stop looking at you," he said.

When she melted into him on the flat deck bed, he relaxed and held her face in his palms. "I guess you're hoping for a proper wedding night."

She lifted a brow. "Any objections?"

"None, Mrs. Shields."

TWENTY-TWO

Day 18
Hills of Marbella Golden Mile
11:21 a.m.

Silence. All six were in place. Wearing visors, they fitted their earbud headsets with small condenser microphones. They could keep in touch by phone.

Calla spied through her binoculars as the air cleared around the apex of Gibraltar Rock. At this height, clouds of mist flowed past them at intervals. Bulletproof vests and masks were at the ready. ISTF agents had met them at the safe house further down toward the beach.

She took another look through the eyepiece. There were nine around a conference table, excluding staff. It could be a swift ambush, but without knowledge of the data farm's position, they would have to be careful. The plan was to locate the server farm and disable it without igniting a satellite signal to the telescope in Space.

Nash was leading the assault. Each had their task. Stan and Calla would find the farm. Once they located it, Jack and Tiege would disarm the tech. Nash would give cover with Reiner and all the other ISTF agents if needed.

Concealed behind the bushes and geared in green camouflage combat gear, they waited for Nash's signal. His concentration narrowed in on the small gathering.

Nine members took their places in the sophisticated lodge around a large table. Nash held up a hand. "We have five units to cover, he said. Kumar and Benassi will provide little resistance, if any. Hex will be the bigger muscle. We have no idea how many men are with him on the property. They can be anywhere from here to the building at the top of the rock, which I believe is where the server farm is."

Pebbles crunched under Calla's booted feet. "If we cut the power, the farm can't go live."

"No, we can't do that," Stan said. "Nicole says it self destructs and then runs on generators until it reboots. Heskin built the farm to self protect."

She furrowed her brow, alarm bells ringing in her head. "We have to. If the deal goes through, Scope will sell questionable technologies to these countries, and there'd be no stopping what they will achieve with this machine. The knowledge will deceive governments into wrong global decisions."

"One more thing, Calla," Nash said.

"The Prime Minister is in seat number three."

Anger edged in her. "I told him to walk away."

He anchored his attention on her. "Take this."

She stared at the gun. "Nash, I can't."

"Cal, we've been through this. It may save your life. I'm not taking any more chances with you."

"Tiege can come with me. He'll shield us," she said.

Nash let out a deep, weighted sigh.

"Calla," Stan continued. "Nash's right. Take the gun."

Her heart raced. Why did she fear it so?

"You need to take it, Calla. The Launcher may not hold back what Hex is prepared to do to protect Scope and Zodie," Jack added.

She took the gun with hesitation and placed it in its holster in her suit, if only to stop them all looking at her that way.

Satisfied, Jack armed his tablet with reception. "Marree and Delgado will alert us if anything stirs downhill or on the yacht."

Nash nodded. "Okay, time to move."

They shuffled across the grass toward the edge of the main facade. Dust puffed up as they moved. Cracked, the ground was parched of all life. Several hundred meters from an even older stone lodge on the cliff's summit, the two buildings connected by cable car.

Calla and Stan were first against the window. They observed as each representative took their seat and what seemed to be a private gathering, including the Prime Minister. Jack and Nash signaled the twelve ISTF agents who posted themselves on each end of the lodge. Bodies seated represented each member state of ISTF. Hex entered ahead of Zodie and Heskin. Three armed security men followed them.

They listened as Zodie opened the negotiations. She spoke of the benefits of Scope's prediction and assimilation technology and what the telescope could do. As the meeting continued every member brought forth their case. First it was China. China wanted to consider the predictions. Germany was being rational and not sure what to believe. Prime Minister Byrne and Britain wanted less of Scope's control in the technology they were being sold. The Russian delegate sided with the PM. An argument broke out between the Prime Minister and Zodie.

"That's not what we agreed! Just what kind of organization are you running here?" The PM said, shooting her a venomous look.

"Let me remind you, Prime Minister Byrne, the deal is done. You signed your country to us. Scope now looks after its technological outlook."

The outburst was swift, cutting off the sound in her earpiece. "Enough! I can't have you spying on every citizen in the UK."

"It's for your own good. It'll help the nation's future," Zodie said. "Only ISTF members can benefit from what I'm offering."

Byrne rose and slammed both fists on the table, sending his pen flying. "I won't sign it. Just who do you think you are?"

Hex flung the back of the Prime Minister's neck to the desk and set a pistol on his temple.

Five meters away, Nash gave the team their signals. He fired a clean shot into Hex's titanium arm, crushing down the PM's head. The gun flew to the floor as they poured into the conference room. Calla and Stan headed for the PM as Reiner rolled a can on the ground, a vapor from hell that reeked and ravaged the place. Stan reached for the Prime Minister and hurled him outside through the glass doors.

With the hissing of gas, darkness descended upon them. Stunned in silence, Hex clawed for his pistol. The crack of Reiner's gun put an end to his attempt, the bullet hitting Hex's good arm.

The giant crashed into the far wall.

Zodie's eyes pierced into Calla, who hurried meeting members out of the house. Three of Hex's men exchanged fire with Nash and Reiner.

"Go, Cal. Jack, you too," Nash said.

Connecting the bottom lodge to the peak of the second stone house, their speed matched their intent. Calla flashed out of the lodge with Jack at her tail. Boots stamping dust, hearts pounding, the cable car was only seconds away if they hurried.

Determined pursuers raced behind them as Calla and Jack raced to one of the rotating cable cars. Jack held a palm in front of her when Nash picked up speed toward them, Hex and Zodie at his tail.

Calla drew its door wide as shots flew by them, pitting the car's side. They shuffled in and crashed to the floor in cover. Hands steady, Jack slammed the door shut and pressed the start button. Grinding gears thrust the car forward. As it began its climb, more bullets chipped on the outside. The car rocked as it ascended along a craggy cliff face. Rising over cracked clay beds where water once flowed, the vehicle rattled with each shot that hacked at its sides.

Hex continued firing at the ride as it ascended further. Bullets blasted the car's windows, spraying shards in the vehicle.

Jack and Nash returned fire.

A giant rattle to the car nearly tilted it to one side. They shot glances outside. Large, with heavy grunts channeling his speed, Hex, gun in mouth, had landed on the wires leading to them. Gloved hands against metal and electricity, he pulled his weight and swung toward the cable car.

The thug climbed up the wire. When he was within reach, Calla kicked the gun out of Hex's mouth. He reached for her leg and yanked her forward. She crashed to the floor.

Their opponents discharged fire, disabling their ascent.

With two loud shudders, the vehicle came to a sudden stop meters from its destination, and above a jagged ridgeline separating the sky from the Earth.

Nash pulled Calla's weight from Hex's grip. By now, Hex had piled into the car.

Nash landed one on Hex's jaw, crashing him to the floor unconscious. "Quick, you two go. It's only a few feet away."

They understood.

Jack and Calla leaped through the car's top window, clambered onto the now dead lines, and swung for the cliff side. They dodged Zodie's fire and thrust themselves forward above a steep drop until their feet tapped the rock arches on the other side of the cliff.

Zodie stroked off another burst from the highly modified M-16 rifle. Her eyes pinned on them, her bullet cried for flesh but hit the cables.

Nash's Kenjustu-hardened hands knifed out in lethal chops at Hex. All his training paid off in one blow, then, without warning, the cable car tilted to one side.

Hex reached for his abandoned gun, inches from Nash's boot, then launched fire and missed. Nash kicked the pistol out of his grip.

Heart in her throat, Calla couldn't watch as the car hung on snapping wires. It would plummet within minutes with the men's weight into the vast canyon. "Jack, we have to do something."

With seconds to think, she aimed for the cable wire. One swing was all it took as she leaped off the edge toward the car.

"Cal!"

She scarcely heard Jack. The position gave her excellent height over the car, and if she played it right, the landing would be smooth. It was time she assessed her gravity defiance. She leaped. Heavy feet landed on the cable car's side. Losing balance, she toppled to one side and pulled her weight to the ride's opening. "Nash!" Calla screamed. "Give me your hand."

He nodded and reached for her grip.

Wires snapped.

Horror struck Hex's face as he lost footing and stability. He clung to the open door, hanging on desperately.

Nash swung his head around, reaching for him. "Hex, give me your hand. Doesn't have to end this way."

Hex's chest rose and fell with rapid breaths. Panic flared in his eyes. Yet, he skewered Nash with an unflinching look. He grunted and spat out the words. "Not on your life. There's no place for both of us. It's you or me."

The car detached from its base.

With his hand firmly in hers, Nash pulled himself up, and his foot found a dead line to hold him. With a good hold on the wire, it pulled him through the car's top opening.

The vehicle raced to the ravine. For a seconds, they froze at the explosion that sounded. Then smoke attacked their lungs.

They gripped more cables and hauled themselves to the

rock's edge. Once at the summit, Zodie and her men continued a hail of fire fury from the lodge below.

Calla's voice cracked. "Jack, Nash, we have minutes!"

High above Gibraltar, the stone of the secluded building's outer facade was embedded in the rock. Greeted by a smart biometric scanning door opening, they had one choice.

"Stand back," Nash said. "I must blow it."

Detonators at the ready, they retreated as three explosives ruptured, flanking the gates off their hinges. Once past two entrances, they were greeted by a narrow passageway with stairs and handrails going up and down.

Nash let off a second set of blasts into the steel.

When they reached the farm, they halted.

A sensor-based ecosystem, in a living environment, startled them.

"It's powered by artificial intelligence," Jack said, as fluorescent lighting blinded them.

Straggling through the entrance, Jack latched the door behind them. The command center was not what they had expected. Above them, they saw it, Scope's ultimate data channeling machine. Three large electronic arms with mechanical eyes on their ends moved like humans, signaling messages through Scope's satellites and back.

Code ran from wall to wall—consoles and workstations buried in switches and readouts. Camera eyes in each direction and infrared laser security defended the three digital scans, Scopes' nerve centers. Several metal rods, used to drive the mechanical scanners at will, lined one side of the wall.

"Here is where she does it," Jack said. "Those eyes look into people's minds and destinies using code."

Thudding on the steel door alerted them.

Calla charged to the command panel. "There must be a way to stop this." She turned to a blinking countdown timer, with three minutes left on the digital board.

"Here, Calla," Jack said. "We need the Clause."

Rounds landed on the exterior of the door, and it blasted off its hinges. Hands clawed for them as Nash fired off a controlled round, warning the men into retreat.

A grunting opponent moved in for the kill. He circled Nash like a shark smelling blood. A second reached for Jack's console. It dropped, shards flying.

Nash snapped his right knee into his assaulter, but another made for Calla, and she swung round and booted him in the middle. Both thugs plummeted to the floor, then sprang up.

"Leave her," Zodie said, appearing through the now damaged entrance ahead of several of her men and Dr. Erickson.

The men restrained all three, guns to their sides.

Zodie drew a long beam from the wall. "Let her go," she whispered.

The man flung Calla to Zodie's feet.

Pole thrust forward, Zodie thrust the weapon causing pain. It crippled Calla, and she found herself against a barrier, at the edge of the control panel. Raw emotion spilled out of her in an agonized moan.

Zodie swiveled to face them. "One move, and I fill her bloodstream with a coma-inducing drug. She should be used to it by now."

And in that terrible silence that followed, fear for her life rendered Jack and Nash powerless.

The clock continued counting, beeping each second in her ears. "Calla, it's over, you see; I win. I always do."

Reaching to her side, a sedative dart from Zodie's angry projectile first hit Nash. The second missed Jack's foot as he propelled himself toward the control room.

"Too late, Kleve," Zodie announced.

This time a grenade left her hand and landed where Jack's leg had taken off. Jack's gun dropped to the floor.

Calla heard nothing.

Ambition guided Zodie as Calla inched a muscle, coughing through fumes. "Don't move, pretty face, or this syringe paralyzes him."

Four men hauled Nash up and restrained him, his body limp. They carried him out of sight, out of the room, unconscious. The dart had worked havoc.

"If you are lucky, he may remember your name, when he wakes. Equally, he could be just as well be a vegetable."

Her gaze burned into Zodie with such intensity; she felt her soul shiver. She could not move without the syringe doing more damage.

Zodie's men turned on her, pinning her to the floor. Calla calculated time, space, then distance and willed a command in her muscle, then her brain.

The machine stopped as Zodie watched. "What happened?" she shouted at Erikssen. "Now!"

Calla's mind spoke inaudible words.

This time the three electronic eyes above them all, transmitting data and pulses, perhaps directions to the satellites and then the Earth, reacted.

"I can't. It won't take the code at all," Erikssen announced, punching all he could into the control panel.

Zodie shoved Calla to the ground. Calla managed a grin, her face plastered to the floor under Zodie's boot. Her words, however muffled by the weight, came out loud and clear. "It won't. Because you don't have the Pythagoras Clause."

Calla freed her hands and wrenched Zodie off her frame. When the knockout came, the blow sent Zodie sailing to the wall. Calla's energy swung to the escorts. The inside edge of her stiffened hand caught each one by one. She swung hard in a slashing motions until each had had his turn with her blows. Nash had prepared her well. Calla rocketed forward and ejected Erikssen off the control panel.

She worked fast, raised the hem of her right ankle. Her mind moved one digital eye in her direction, and she sent code, an instruction to its command center. "Scan."

It obliged.

A blue light scanned over her tattoo, drawing information from her emblem and the symbols underneath.

As the digital eyes sagged, the telescope disconnected. This completed the self-destruct mode she had only guessed would work.

When her eyes moved to where Zodie had passed out, she halted. The bare floor told her Zodie was no witch. Just a coward.

She flew to the adjoining room.

———

Empty corridors, one after another.

Nothing.

High-tech cameras on each wall monitored her position.

Just where had they taken Nash? She bustled through Scope Industries' digital empire. Its dark passageways forbade her to make out much. She had to hurry. God knew what sickness Zodie could do with men.

Nash was unconscious in a man-crazy, fanatic's custody.

Calla halted at a vast entryway on the top floors of the lodge. A giant telescope opened through the skylight heavens, stood in the apartment's heart. A separate lounge section with a bar, kitchen and bed area flanked in luxury greeted her. The far side of the room displayed a control center, Zodie's ultimate command panel. High ceilings, marble floor, mirrors, and ornamental embellishments.

This was Zodie's secluded space. Perhaps where she seduced her victims. The room's bright lights and views over Gibraltar contradicted the gruesome work she was doing inside.

Calla's heart stopped. Zodie's men had been busy. Hands restrained above his head, his shirt off, and his chest exposed, unconscious, Nash's chin dropped to his rib cage, away from the ceiling to which they tied him. In front of him, the silhouette of Zodie watching him, sitting in a lounge chair, her back to Calla facing Nash, delivered ice shivers down Calla's spine. The woman was maniacal.

Zodie's voice turned into ice, cold and sharp as a scalpel. "Hmm. I wouldn't miss this every night. And you were willing to give him up. Crazy girl."

Inching toward Zodie, Calla noticed the pistol on the table in front of her.

"You're sick, Zodie. Addicted to masculinity and technology, an unstable combination."

Her cruel mouth curled with hate as Zodie flipped round. "It's not a crime. Looks like you and I appreciate the same taste in men and in technology. He's in such good shape. Those arms. Those abs, I've seen nothing so exquisite. How do you stay sane?"

Calla's words came out calm, composed. "Release him, Zodie."

Her air of arrogance was one Calla wanted to beat out of her. "Are you going to make me?"

Calla didn't answer but proceeded to where's Zodie sat, taking cautious steps.

A cruel worm of resentment burrowed into her soul. "He's got a drug in him my father used on you those six months when you were at Beacon Academy. You don't remember those months, right? You woke up in the hospital and they brought you back to school. You have no recollection of it. Do you?"

It wasn't pity that came out of her lips that bothered Calla, it was the pure lack of emotional intelligence. "Zodie, you need help. Stop before something worse happens. You've never liked me, but I don't think I could have said the same. I always admired your courage."

"Don't play innocent with me. I've been watching you, and I knew something was off. We operatives need to stick together."

Calla stopped in her tracks. "You're an operative?"

"Oh. You didn't know. Like you, I was an adopted operative. Left to disappear like a dog in the streets of London. Andor Heskin saved my life. Gave me a home and everything I have, and you came after him. I swore, unlike you, that I would become the best operative I could be, no matter what."

Zodie's loathing made her heart burn for revenge. "I can see you're wondering about me. Yes, I'm an operative. What would they think of me now? You and I aren't very different. But there was always something my father told me about the Cress family line, that they were special. That the baby in their bloodline had something no other operative would have. So, my father chose to find out. Were you the Cress child that had gone missing when Stan and Nicole Cress dissolved off intelligence grids twenty-eight years ago?"

"Don't pretend to know everything about me," Calla said.

This time Zodie stretched for the weapon and encircled her fingers around the trigger. "Don't you realize my father has known and watched you from the day you were born? Ask your mother. They made a deal and then she walked out on him. You betrayed him. All he ever wanted to do was to protect you. When you joined ISTF, you read a communication meant to help the operatives, but your deciphering of that information put him behind bars for years. I missed out on time with my father. Perhaps it's time you miss out on a few people in your life."

Zodie held down a finger on her smartphone that raised Nash's arms higher. Trotting to his side, she swept seductive fingers across his torso.

Nash was out, the drugs doing peculiar things to his body. Calla measured the speed it would take to seize the pistol and release him. The calculation did not add up. There was no time.

A rumble rocked the building afresh. Zodie showed no response to the noise. They had to run. Any minute, the building would blow from the systems' overpowered engines down below. She had to get Nash out of here.

As if in a trance, Zodie ran more fingers over Nash's torso, and she wrenched the handgun from the table.

She lifted an eyebrow. "I know your future with him, and it doesn't look good. The math in the data doesn't look good for you."

The room rocked, and Zodie's gun dropped by Nash's boot.

Zodie lunged for Calla, gouging for her eyes. Calla hooked Zodie's limb and slammed her to the floor. Her hands then sought to cut Nash's restraints. She rubbed his cheek. "Nash, baby, Wake up."

Zodie came round. In one acrobatic movement, only seen in leaping cats, she jumped to her feet and reached for Calla's neck, pitching downward with her. Her pistol flew from its holster as Calla's head whacked the table, shattering the glass beneath. A dribble of blood leaked from her chin, then the throbbing began.

Everything within Zodie, every improper training in her, every inclination to prove people wrong prompted her to her feet, and a strike landed on Calla's collar. Matched punch by punch, strengths balanced, they clashed in a feline rumble until Zodie piled at Nash's feet.

"You must've learned the arts of the operatives," Zodie said. "Your boy Lascar is an excellent teacher. Pity you didn't end up with him. You two could have been something."

"Not every operative needs training like you. That's the difference between me and you, Zodie," Calla said, red from her wounds, blinding her vision for a second. Calla hobbled upward. "I may be an operative, but let me tell you one thing, the future is not meant to be known. The future is experienced. Only cowards like yourself prefer to see their destiny so they can handle it. But even the future can change its mind. That's the true significance of the Pythagoras Clause."

Zodie stretched for her gun and raised it straight at Nash's chest. Calla dashed, drawing energy from super genes.

She would take a bullet for him if she had to. She flew to screen him from fire.

The gun burst clanged in her ears.

Then Calla heard a second explosion, less than fractions of a second before she made it in front of Nash. Calla glanced down at her midriff.

No blood. No pain.

She zipped around.

Nash, now conscious with a masterful finger around the trigger of Calla's gun, had fired the weapon out of Zodie's grip. The gun Calla had refused to carry, or use was the gun he'd fired with.

Stunned, Zodie shuffled for her pistol and raised it for one more shot.

Calla took no chances. She drew the gun from Nash's hand, aimed it, and with a precision, she did not know she had, landed a shot point blank, clashing Zodie's bullet. It docked in Zodie's leg; her yelp was as harrowing as the annoyance she had caused them. Shock made her faint in one pile to the ground.

After she secured the weapons, Calla hastened to loosen Nash from the rope, her eyes welling. A true trained field agent, Nash must have woken from consciousness as she'd restrained Zodie. He'd extended his bound hands, driving his elbows past his rib cage to release his wrists. Calla found his shirt and helped him with it. "She's sick and took six months of my life and let Heskin experiment on me. That's why they could clone me."

Nash wiped blood from her lip. "It's okay now, Calla," he said, taking one handgun. "Your mother found that research and destroyed it. It can't harm you anymore. All they had was a lock of your hair and it couldn't help them. Your blood is too strong for them. Your DNA is untouchable."

The side of the building shook once more.

"Calla, where did you learn to fire a gun like that?" Nash said. "That was one of the best clean shots I've seen, and from that angle. You clashed a bullet!"

Her hands quivered as she spoke. "Nash. That's why I don't do guns. When I fire anything, I never miss. I tried it once in archery and then again at my first firearm training at ISTF. It terrified me."

"Is that what the gun thing is all about?" he asked.

She nodded, "Don't tell anybody, Nash. When I shoot at anything, I don't miss. It's as if my mind wills the target. That's why I've never wanted a pistol."

"Because you're the best there is. Woah, Cal!" Amusement filled his eyes. "It'll be our secret." He gave her an affectionate grin. "You and me against the world. No one will ever know. At least now, I don't have to worry about you so much. Let's get out of here before she blows."

Jack emerged into the space with Stan and Reiner.

Calla gasped. "Jack. you're okay?"

"Yeah, Reiner and your dad hauled me out before the grenade exploded. We need to go!"

TWENTY-THREE

Five Hours Later
Port of Gibraltar

"Ms. Cress. We have them all. We're ready to part. I need your palm scan here and we'll be on our way."

"Thank you," Calla replied and imprinted her authorization on the tablet as ISTF agents rounded Zodie and her men into a secured boat bound for the United Kingdom.

Clouds lit from below picked up a coral shade, and the peach tint of the sky as then the sun's hue dimmed from bright yellow to a deeper gold. Where the Atlantic met the Mediterranean, diverse cultures side by side, the Rock of Gibraltar now sat peacefully in the middle. She closed her eyes for a moment and pulled in an expansive breath as Nash circled an arm around her waist. A warm sunset dipped behind the horizon as Scorpion Tide set sail.

She gave him a crisp nod. "This sea feels like home. Much of my history and that of the operatives is in these seas and within its borders," Calla said.

"That's why it protected you," Nash said. "Jack just heard. The girls and others are all out of comas. When your mother explained what was happening with the drug, the hospitals reacted quickly with ISTF guidance."

"Data. A curse and a blessing. Everything about us is data. DNA, chromosomes, cells, and more," she said, shifting toward him. "This whole thing was about data."

She leaned into him. "You think we need to get this back to the Library?"

"I suspect they wanted you to have it. The Clause was a code in your tattoo, wasn't it? Much like a QR code. That birthmark of yours means a lot more than we think."

A lightness in her chest made her grin. "Yes, it does."

"You know something else, Cal. They couldn't hack your mind. That is the true meaning of the Clause. Pythagoras predicted a mathematical pattern that couldn't be replicated. The symbols on your tattoo. He could not have known what he was referring to. The very thing that makes you different, like Hypatia, and by that your unique tattoo was the very hack you needed to unscramble the math in Scope's algorithms. Scope built a machine using math explained by Hypatia and Pythagoras, but it came with a warning, the Clause math can explain that. The only thing they could not work out in the scroll was your tattoo image and how it related to their calculations. They skipped that part and hoped no one would ever find out what the Pythagoras Clause was. You. Now do you see why your normal is so special?"

Jack and Marree joined them as the crew served drinks on the deck. Marree spoke first when the crew had left. "So, I understand. What was the Clause?"

Nash's head tilted to the side. "Hypatia was like a guide, a forerunner for Calla. She must have connected with Calla through time."

"Is that possible," Marree asked. "How?"

"Hypatia was a message carrier. She would write for days and days in the desert with the nomadic tribe we met, Safaa's people," Jack interjected.

Though it had bewildered her for days, Calla felt satisfaction in sharing what she'd learned from the Sahara tribe. "Safaa told me that when the Library was under severe threat, her ancestors took it upon themselves to save it from ever being lost. They carried the scrolls and documents on camels and desert caravans, piece by piece for days, months. Years passed, and they collected as much as they could. Whatever they could carry until they saved each important document. There is a wealth of history down there. But the world must not know. I have learned knowledge is not everything and not for everyone. Knowledge of the future may tempt, but you pay the price to know it."

Marree watched her intently. "And the Pythagoras Clause? What's her warning to the world?"

"It's why Hypatia created the scroll in the first place. The scroll included commentaries on the lost works of Pythagoras. She carefully crafted and designed it also to predict where the stars and planets would be at any given date. This was very important to Scope. They needed to know when they could harness space solar power."

Jack slid his arm around Marree's waist and sipped a

beer. "Knowledge is dangerous for those who want to read the stars, but also to this generation. Man has not only been to the stars; he can manipulate what's out there. This is what Scope tried to do. The Clause was a code in Calla's tattoo that blocked the system. When her tattoo was scanned, it hacked the systems and sent confusion in the code, halting the launch. That telescope and their technology could have easily harnessed Space energy using the astrolabe designs in the scroll. Hypatia developed them all those years ago, before any technology could harness her designs. Until Heskin came along."

Calla rose and stretched her fingers on the railing. She angled back to face them. "I've also asked the Cove in London to repossess what was in the other pages of the scroll, the missing commentaries on Pythagoras's lost works. There were six Greek volumes and four Arabic ones. What we know from these commentaries is that that arithmetic formed technology's foundation, and the operatives knew it was too advanced for the world to take in."

"That's right," Jack said. "We now know Scope used a technology called multi-agent artificial intelligence to predict the future via its cell phones. Its app was only available on those phones, but they had grown their market share so much that every phone sold was a new victim and new data for them to use. It always begins with math. Math built the societies that stimulated actual situations, and this was the science behind future predictions. The app helped computer models to understand dynamic systems. If you can generate enough experiences in certain situations, the math does the rest to predict the future. As a human race, when we learn to expect actions, machines can use math to map our future consequences of any decision we've ever made."

Calla tracked their gazes. "Hypatia argued, uniqueness sets one apart. Normal is normal. It is what it is and not what anyone dictates. I'm okay with my normal."

"Sure?" Nash said.

"Yeah. One needs four things for future prediction to succeed; one computing power, two data, three scientific understanding of human behavior, and perhaps the most dangerous of all, the fourth artificial intelligence. And what distinguishes man from machine? Uniqueness and one's individual data makeup. If I hadn't accepted everything unique about me, including my tattoo, I wouldn't have been able to stop Scope."

Armed with self-confidence, Nash faced her. "Pythagoras and those who followed his teachings understood reality is numerical, and if reality is numerical, the future had to be as well unless you broke the cycle with something that didn't follow the pattern. The Clause. Her words, '*I am different*' in the scroll gave you a clue, didn't they, Cal?"

She nodded. "Hypatia perhaps knew if any of us made the wrong call with the math, the outcome would be catastrophic and irreversible. That was the Clause. Only something unique could break the cycle. The inscription on my tattoo, though it resembles an emblem or symbol when translated, says: we can reduce all relationships to numbers. Any relationship, human, natural, scientific, the stars, anything you can name can be reduced to numbers."

Nash touched his lips to her cheek. "Now do you understand why I loved your normal?"

Her eyelids lowered to hide her feelings as Stan joined them on the deck. "Well, I don't recall us having a real wedding celebration. Calla, your mother, can meet us in the south of France tomorrow. Why don't we set sail and have a proper party? I'd like to throw my daughter and son-in-law a wedding celebration."

EPILOGUE

One Week Later
Villefranche-Sur-Mer
The French Riviera

Sunset fell over Villefranche-Sur-Mer's multicolored harbor, a scenic village, with its glorious coral hues and gold-tinted houses.

Jack mused. This had to be one of the most beautiful Niçoise fishing villages on the French Riviera. On a hillside, the town's buildings cascaded down to the harbor. Flags floating at the top of the Scorpion Tide were a rarity. Tonight though, Delgado had made sure the wedding celebration would continue undisturbed for their guests. In full uniform, the crew took charge of the yacht's security, reported to Captain Delgado, catered the party meal, and attended to guests.

Breathlessness washed over Jack. It was a festive sight; beverages poured into glasses, ice cubes clinking against topped-up flutes, the crew talking to each other and the guests.

He shouldn't have been this happy, but he was.

His eyes wandered to where Calla nestled on Nash's arm on the soft couches. She looked magnificent with transparent elegance in a semi-sheer banded midi dress. Tailored to perfection through the bodice, the white piece fell gracefully into an A-line silhouette below her hips. Nash, well, he could melt any woman's heart. That was just his gift. Both his best friends, making an enormous commitment, was a big step for them in front of the selected guests they'd invited tonight.

Jack took a sip of his champagne and drew Marree to him. Radiant tonight, but when had she not been? "I'll just go down and check on something," Jack said to Marree.

He shuffled pasts guests and headed down to his cabin.

The party had started earlier that afternoon and was sure to last till morning. Delgado had only opened one floor and secured every deck from curious eyes. The Scorpion Tide was a home to them, a stealth machine at assaults and getaways, but nonetheless home to all of them. Stan had organized a wedding celebration for a select number of guests and friends. It made Jack smile and shake his head.

He'd felt a need to go below deck and check on the files retrieved from Benassi and his stolen laptop.

When he located it, he switched it on and observed the transmissions from the backup server.

Good. All looked in order.

Wait?

He scrutinized the screen. A shadow stood behind him and he swiveled around, almost tripping.

"Now, Jack, is that how you greet an old friend?" the voice said.

"How did you get in here?"

The punch landed hard on his jaw.

Eyes trundling in his sockets, all Jack saw was blackness.

Three minutes later, Marree pushed Jack's cabin door open. "Jack? Where are you? Everyone's looking for you."

Silence.

Her eyes fell to the floor, where Jack's watch lay discarded. His laptop and phone were gone, and so was he.

GET THE NEXT BOOK IN THE SERIES

(A CALLA CRESS TECHNOTHRILLER)

The Decrypter: White Wolf Extraction

The sixth book in the explosive bestselling technothriller series

"A female James Bond with a Matrix twist." **Amazon Reader**

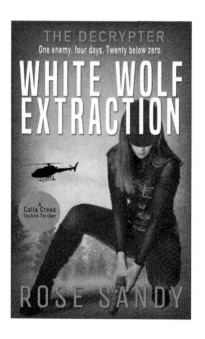

More here:
'The Decrypter: White Wolf Extraction

https://rosesandy.com/the-decrypter-white-wolf-extraction/

SOME SECRETS ARE TOO DANGEROUS TO KEEP.

Artifacts handler. Codebreaker. Government agent. Nursing a past loss and failure, Calla Cress is framed for the disappearance and murder of the spy agency ISTF's Chief of Technology and Science, her best friend, Jack Kleve.

All is not as it seems. When she's discredited, and forced on the run, she travels to the African continent to find secrets her friend wanted hidden, only to discover someone very dangerous betrayed Jack and doesn't want to be found.

Now she must follow Jack's clues and an uncertain trail that leads her deeper into the dark territories of a vengeful enemy who will unleash hell on Earth unless she stops him. And wait, all before her government finds and persecutes her.

JOIN THE ADVENTURE

SHORT REVIEW

Thank you for joining Calla, Nash and Jack on this adventure!

As an author I highly appreciate the feedback I get from my readers. It helps others to make an informed decision before buying.

It only takes a few minutes. If you enjoyed **The Decrypter: The Pythagoras Clause** please consider leaving a short review where you bought the book or by going here.

www.rosesandy.com

BE THE FIRST TO KNOW

Be the first to learn about new releases and other news from Rose Sandy, by joining **Real Time with Rose Sandy**, a podcast and fun e-update. See you there by going here:

https://rose-sandy.ck.page/afd6f12477

JOIN THE CONVERSATION

While you are at it, swing by the official Rose Sandy Facebook page (www.facebook.com/rosesandyauthor) to join a community of adventurers, history and technology enthusiasts.

Finally, if you enjoy pictures of travels, book inspirations, historical mysteries, science and technology thrills, check out my feed @rosesandyauthor on the Instagram app.

IN THE DECRYPTER SERIES

Book 1: The Decrypter: Secret of The Lost Manuscript
Book 2: The Decrypter and The Mind Hacker
Book 3: The Decrypter - Digital Eyes Only
Book 4: The Decrypter - The Storm's Eye
Book 5: The Decrypter - The Pythagoras Clause
Book 6: The Decrypter - White Wolf Extraction

She's a museum curator, a doubter, and a skeptic. It all changed when the British government asked her to decrypt a code written in an unbreakable script on an ancient manuscript whose origin was as debatable as the origin of life. Then there was the issue of her long-lost parents.

Using her knack for history and technology, she bands with two faithful friends and is thrown into a dangerous journey of cyber espionage investigating the criminal, the unexplained, the scientific and the downright unthinkable.

More here: https://rosesandy.com/the-decrypter-series/

What Readers Are Saying About The Decrypter Series

"Takes you on a ride and refuses to let you off until you reach the very end."

"A brilliant read! I recommend this to anyone who enjoys mystery, suspense, thrillers, or action novels. The detail is astounding! The historic references, location descriptions, references to technology, cryptography.... this author really knows her stuff."

"An action-packed adventure, technothriller across several continents like a Jason Bourne or James Bond movie, but with an actual storyline!"

"Brilliantly written. I loved the very descriptive side, which was a good way of visualizing and getting to terms with each new place, as the action takes place in several different countries."

"The description is so rich, so immensely detailed that it just draws you in completely to its world."

"There is great tension and chemistry between the two main characters, Calla and Nash, that has you begging for more."

"The historic references, location descriptions, references to technology, cryptography.... this author really knows her stuff."

There is great tension and chemistry between the two main characters, Calla and Nash, that has you begging for more."

IN THE SHADOW FILES THRILLERS

A Crossfire Between Technology, Science, and
International Espionage

Book 1 - The Code Beneath Her Skin
Book 2 - Blood Diamond in My Mother's House

A series about intelligent women caught in the crossfire
between technology, science, politics, international
espionage, and the men who drag them there.

Guaranteed action adventure in each book, you'll fill the
need for thrills, savor satisfying cliffhangers as you follow a
secret organization, **The Shadow Files,** and two of its
former agents around the globe.

Sworn enemies, one is on a mission to safeguard the globe
from economic corruption, and one swears he'll protect the
victims.

Each book can be read as a stand-alone story. More here: https://rosesandy.com/the-shadow-files-series-2/

ABOUT THE AUTHOR

Rose Sandy never set out to be a writer. She set out to be a communicator with whatever landed in her hands. But soon the keyboard became her best friend. Rose writes suspense and intelligence thrillers where technology and espionage meet history in pulse-racing action adventure. She dips into the mysteries of our world, the fascination of technology breakthroughs, the secrets of history and global intelligence to deliver thrillers that weave suspense, conspiracy and a dash of romantic thrill.

A globe trotter, her thrillers span cities and continents. Rose's writing approach is to hit hard with a good dose of tension and humor. Her characters zip in and out of intelligence and government agencies, dodge enemies in world heritage sites, navigate technology markets and always land in deep trouble.

When not tapping away on a smartphone writing app, Rose is usually found in the British Library scrutinizing the Magna Carta, trolling Churchill's War Rooms or sampling a new gadget. Most times she's in deep conversations with ex-military and secret service intelligence officers, Foreign Service staff or engrossed in a TED talk with a box of popcorn. Hm... she might just learn something that'll be useful.

For more books and updates.

facebook.com/RoseSandyAuthor

twitter.com/rosesandy